YEARS
of pure reading pleasure

100 Reasons to Celebrate

We invite you to join us in celebrating
Mills & Boon's centenary. Gerald Mills and
Charles Boon founded Mills & Boon Limited
in 1908 and opened offices in London's Covent
Garden. Since then, Mills & Boon has become
a hallmark for romantic fiction, recognised
around the world.

We're proud of our 100 years of publishing
excellence, which wouldn't have been achieved
without the loyalty and enthusiasm of our
authors and readers.

Thank you!

Each month throughout the year there will
be something new and exciting to mark the
centenary, so watch for your favourite authors,
captivating new stories, special limited
edition collections…and more!

Two handsome, wealthy, gorgeous brothers.
Can any woman tame them?

THE BRAVOS:
AARON & CADE

An exceptional author, Christine
Rimmer delivers two irresistible stories
of pure emotion and passion.

We're proud to present

MILLS & BOON

Spotlight

*a chance to buy collections of bestselling novels
by favourite authors every month – they're
back by popular demand!*

January 2008
Crown & Glory
Featuring

The Princess Has Amnesia! by Patricia Thayer
Searching for Her Prince by Karen Rose Smith
The Royal Treatment by Maureen Child

The Bravos: Aaron & Cade
by Christine Rimmer
Featuring

His Executive Sweetheart
Mercury Rising

February 2008
Seduced by a Prince
Featuring

Taming the Prince by Elizabeth Bevarly
Royally Pregnant by Barbara McCauley
Mail-Order Prince in Her Bed by Kathryn Jensen

Tall, Dark and Male
Featuring

Tall, Dark and Irresistible by Joan Elliott Pickart
Tall, Dark and Difficult by Patricia Coughlin

THE BRAVOS:
AARON & CADE

by
CHRISTINE RIMMER

His Executive Sweetheart

&

Mercury Rising

MILLS & BOON®
Pure reading pleasure

*This collection is first published in Great Britain 2008
Harlequin Mills & Boon Limited,
Eton House, 18-24 Paradise Road, Richmond, Surrey TW9 1SR*

THE BRAVOS: AARON & CADE © Harlequin Books S.A. 2008

The publisher acknowledges the copyright holders of the
individual works, which have already been published in the UK
in single, separate volumes, as follows:

His Executive Sweetheart © Christine Rimmer 2002
Mercury Rising © Christine Rimmer 2002

ISBN: 978 0 263 86093 1

064-0108

*Printed and bound in Spain
by Litografia Rosés S.A., Barcelona*

His Executive Sweetheart

CHRISTINE RIMMER

CHRISTINE RIMMER

came to her profession the long way around. Before settling down to write about the magic of romance, she'd been an actress, a sales clerk, a janitor, a model, a phone sales representative, a teacher, a waitress, a playwright and an office manager. She insists she never had a problem keeping a job – she was merely gaining "life experience" for her future as a novelist. Christine is grateful not only for the joy she finds in writing, but for what waits when the day's work is through: a man she loves, who loves her right back, and the privilege of watching their children grow and change day to day. She lives with her family in Oklahoma, USA.

For my own sons,
Matt and Jess,
with all my love.

Chapter One

It happened on Valentine's Day.

Which was just a coincidence, really. An irony. An accident of timing that made the whole thing all the more pitiful, somehow.

It was Valentine's Day and it was a Wednesday, at 9:15 a.m. in the Executive Tower of High Sierra Resort and Casino. Celia Tuttle was taking a memo—well, getting e-mail instructions, really. Her boss, Aaron Bravo, never actually composed the in-office e-mails he sent out to the managers and senior vice presidents who labored under him. He told Celia what he wanted to get across. As his executive secretary/personal assistant it was her job to put appropriate wording to his commands.

Her boss said, "We've got to do something about the line for that damn raft ride...."

Celia smiled to herself as she scribbled on her note-pad. High Sierra contained its own river, complete with rushing rapids and a whitewater raft ride. The ride was incredibly popular—so much so that the long lines of customers waiting their turn sometimes got in the way of casino traffic. At High Sierra, as in any gaming establishment worthy of its name, *nothing* was allowed to get in the way of casino traffic. They called it a resort and casino, but everyone knew it was really the other way around.

"Send an e-mail to Hickock Drake." Hickock was a senior vice president. "Tell him to sit on Carter Biles." Carter Biles was Director of Rides and At-tractions. "It's too many people standing around in a line when they ought to be at the tables or playing the slots. Carter should know that. Up the price on the ride till no one will pay it. Shut the damn thing down. Whatever. The line is in the way and I want it out of there."

It happened right then. Celia looked up from her legal pad, still smiling a little at the whole idea of an amusement park ride upstaging the mighty gaming tables. Aaron said, "And before the meeting with the planning commission, I need you to check with..."

She didn't really catch the rest of it because every-thing seemed to spin to a stop. It was something out of a sci-fi movie, the kind where the world freezes in place and one woman is left walking and talking in the usual way while trying to deal with the fact that everyone she knows is suddenly a statue.

Yes. The world went still. All of it.

Including Aaron. He was sitting in his glove-soft

black leather chair at the huge glass-topped chrome-legged table that served as his desk, in front of a wall that was also a window. Behind him and below him lay the Las Vegas Strip, a modern-day Mecca, a land of turrets and towers, sphinxes and circus tents. Beyond the strip stretched the glittering sprawl of the magical, impossible city in the desert.

But it wasn't the city of Las Vegas Celia Tuttle was staring at.

It was Aaron.

And all of him, every last physical detail, was suddenly achingly clear.

Tall, she thought, as if that was news. Broad-shouldered. Lean. A face that wasn't quite handsome. Long and angular, that face, with a cleft in the strong chin. And a nose that would have been bladelike, had it not been broken at some point in his checkered past.

He wore a gorgeous lightweight designer suit. Navy, chalk stripe. A lustrous silk shirt. A paisley tie in plum and indigo. The suit had been handmade by his ultra-exclusive Manhattan tailor, everything in the best fabrics.

He had his computer in front of him, a little to the side. He'd been clicking the mouse as he spoke, his blue gaze mostly on the screen, but now and then flicking her way. What did he see on the screen? Probably his e-mail—to which Celia would end up composing the replies.

Or could be he was looking over some marketing or design prospectus. Aaron rarely did just one thing at a time. He was a driven man. Only thirty-four and part owner and CEO of one of Las Vegas's top super-casinos. Multi-tasking was not a concept to him. It was the way he lived his life.

In that frozen moment, as his image seared itself into her brain, it hit her.

She loved him.

Somehow, the thought of that, the *admission* of that, brought the world to life again.

She heard a siren, out there somewhere in the vast city beyond the window wall. And far out over the desert, just above the rim of the mountains, a silver jet streaked by, leaving a white trail in its wake.

And in the huge office room, Aaron was clicking his mouse again, frowning at the computer screen, giving her instructions at the same time.

Not that she was capable, right at that second, of making sense of anything he said to her. But it was okay—at least the part about not really hearing him. She had her mini-recorder going, as she always did for their morning meetings, providing a backup in case her own notes fell short. She would need it big-time later, since right now, incoming information was not getting through in any rational form. She felt...so strange. Disordered. Confused. Embarrassed. In complete emotional disarray.

All she could think was, *How can this be?*

She and Aaron Bravo enjoyed a strictly professional relationship. The only time he really noticed her was when she wasn't getting her job done— which, at least in the past two and a half years or so, was pretty much never.

It had always been just fine with Celia that her boss didn't notice her. He was a fair boss. Yes, he worked her very hard; she rarely got a weekend off. But he also paid her well. She had a great benefits package and points in the company.

And she loved her job.

But she didn't love her boss. Or at least, she hadn't until about forty seconds ago.

Then again, maybe she just hadn't realized it until now. Maybe it had been happening for a long time, coming on slowly, like a nagging cold that never quite catches hold for weeks and weeks and then—bang—in a flash it hits you. You've got pneumonia and you've got it bad.

Oh—she held back a small, anguished groan—this was ridiculous.

Over time, it was true, she'd grown…rather fond of Aaron Bravo. He was really a much nicer person than a lot of people thought. And all those rumors about junk bonds and Wise Guy connections? Patently untrue.

Celia was certain of that now, after three years of working for him. He wasn't a shady character at all, but an honest businessman with lady luck in his corner. He'd made a few very risky investments—in computer games and real estate. He'd seen those investments pay off in a major way and put the profits into carving out a niche for himself in the gaming industry.

Frankly, Celia had been a little nervous when she first took the job with him. After all, they'd grown up just blocks from each other, up north in New Venice—yes, named after that famous city in Italy, though New Venice, Nevada, was pronounced *Noo-*

vuneece, with the accent over the "neece." It was nowhere near the sea and it didn't have a single canal. Instead, it lay tucked against the eastern slopes of the Sierras in the beautiful Comstock Valley not far from Lake Tahoe.

Celia was eight years younger than Aaron, but she'd grown up on the stories of the notorious Caitlin Bravo and her three wild boys—each of whom, by the way, was now doing nothing short of spectacularly in his chosen field.

And yes, all right. Maybe there *was* an air of danger, of risk, of something not quite safe, about Aaron Bravo. But that, Celia had decided, was part of his charm. He was the kind of man you didn't challenge unless you were willing to fight to the brutal end.

He was tough. And uncompromising. He had to be. But at the core, she knew him as a fair man, and essentially kind.

And she was proud—yes, she was—to work for him. She had, at least in the past couple of years, felt *warmly* toward him.

But love?

How could this be happening?

"Celia? Are you all right?"

Celia blinked. Aaron was staring at her—*noticing* her—because she was very obviously *not* doing her job.

She checked her recorder—working fine, thank God—and straightened her shoulders. "Uh. Yes. Okay. Really. I am."

"You're certain? You look a little—"

"Honestly Aaron, there's nothing. I'm okay." Yes, it was an outright lie. But what else could she say?

Right then, the phone in his pocket rang.

Saved by the bell, she thought with an inward sigh of relief.

Aaron pulled out the ringing phone, flipped it open, spoke a few sentences into it, swung it shut and put it away.

Celia cleared her throat and poised her pen. "Now. Where were we?"

They got back to work.

But from that frozen moment on, for Celia Tuttle, nothing was the same.

The hours that followed were pure misery. Insanely, now that she'd acknowledged its existence, the longing she felt seemed to grow stronger minute by minute. It hurt, just being near him, going over the rest of the calendar with him—and having him not once look up and make eye contact.

Now, really, why should that bother her? It certainly never had before.

But all of a sudden she was...so hungry for any kind of contact.

And yet, when she got contact, it hurt almost as much as having none at all.

Take, for instance, his hand brushing hers....

It happened all the time, though she'd hardly noticed it before. He would ask for something—an update, a file, a letter, a cup of coffee, black—and she would see he got it. And if she had to come near him to deliver it, he would touch the back of her hand or maybe her wrist or her forearm. It would be just a breath of a touch, a little thank-you, without words. Something that was so small, so unremarkable, that she hardly recalled it once it had happened.

Well, until *now* she'd hardly recalled it.

"Did the estimates come in on the South Tower remodel?" At High Sierra, the hotel rooms and the rides, the casino and the showrooms, were in a constant cycle of remodeling. Things had to stay fresh to lure in the crowds.

She told him where to look for it.

"It's not coming up."

She put down her legal pad and went around behind him where she had a view of the screen.

Oh, Lord. He did smell good. So clean and fresh and…male. She'd always liked the aftershave he used. She liked his hair, short but kind of wavy, a dark brown that sometimes, in the right light, still managed to show glints of gold. And the shape of his ears…

He glanced back at her, one eyebrow lifted.

Her heart lurched in her chest and she ordered her face not to flush beet-red. "Hmm," she said. "Let's see…" She reached for the mouse. Two clicks and the information he wanted appeared.

"Good. Thanks."

As she withdrew her hand, he touched the back of it—just that quick brush of warm acknowledgement. She almost gasped, but somehow held back the sound. Her skin flamed where his fingers had grazed it—so lightly, so fleetingly. For Aaron, she knew, the touch was the next thing to a subconscious act. He did it and forgot it.

Not for Celia. Not anymore. Suddenly, his slightest touch seared her to her very soul.

She made herself cross back around the desk and return to her chair. She picked up her legal pad again and waited for him to go on.

For the next ten minutes, the situation was almost bearable. They got through his calendar for the day, the rest of the memos and letters he would be wanting, the reports he needed her to get in hard copy and bind for the next managers' meeting.

They were winding things up when he added off-handedly, "And would you get something nice for Jennifer? Since it *is* Valentine's Day…"

It felt like a knife straight through the heart, when he said that. *Get something nice for Jennifer….*

Jennifer Tartaglia had a featured role in the hit review, *Gold Dust Follies,* playing nightly in High Sierra's Excelsior Theatre. Jennifer was Cuban and Italian, drop-them-in-their-tracks gorgeous—and a very nice person, as well. The first time the showgirl had visited the office tower, she'd made it a point to say hi to Aaron's secretary.

"Hello, so nice to meet you." Jennifer had stuck out her hand and beamed a radiant smile. "I hear you take fine care of Aaron."

They shook hands. "I do my best."

"You *are* the best. He tells me so." Still smiling that wide, friendly, breathtaking smile, Jennifer tossed her honey-blond mane of hair and turned to walk away. Celia had found herself staring. The rear view of Jennifer Tartaglia—especially in motion—was something to see.

But so what if no woman had a right to look that good? Celia *liked* Jennifer. She considered Jennifer a good person who was, no doubt, very good to Aaron—not that the relationship was anything truly serious. It never was, with Aaron.

Aaron Bravo…enjoyed women, and a man in his position had his pick of some of the most beautiful, talented and seductive women in the world. But none of them, at least in the years Celia had worked for him, had lasted. Aaron always gave them diamonds— a bracelet or a necklace—at the end. Eventually, Celia knew, she'd be buying diamonds for Jennifer.

He really was married to his work. And so busy he thought nothing of asking his assistant to buy his girl-friend thoughtful gifts and expensive trinkets when-ever the occasion arose—like for Valentine's Day.

"Something nice for Jennifer," Celia parroted in the voice of a dazed windup doll.

He was frowning again. "Are you *certain* there's nothing wrong?"

"I am. Positive. No problem. Sincerely."

An hour later, Celia left High Sierra to get Jennifer that gift. She found a heart-shaped ruby-encrusted pin in one of the elite little boutiques at Caesar's Forum Shops. High Sierra had its own series of exclusive shops, the Gold Exchange, in the central court be-tween the casino and the 3,000-room hotel. But Celia never shopped in-house for gifts "from" the boss. To her, it seemed more appropriate, more *personal,* if she went outside Aaron's realm of influence to get little treasures for his lady friends.

And hey, wasn't that great reasoning? she found herself thinking, now unrequited love was souring her attitude. He wasn't even choosing the gifts. How personal could they be?

She bought the pin, brought it back to High Sierra and showed it to him, so that he'd know what lovely little trinket Jennifer was getting from him.

"Great, Celia. She'll love it."

Tears tightened her throat as she wrapped up that ruby heart. But she didn't cry. She swallowed those tears down.

By then, it had been a mere six hours since she'd realized she was in love with him. She couldn't afford to start blubbering like a baby from day one, now could she? And maybe, she couldn't help thinking as she expertly tied the red satin ribbon, this sudden, overwhelming and inconvenient passion would just…burn itself out. Soon.

Oh, yes. Please God. Let it be over soon….

But her prayer was not answered, at least not in the next week. The days went by and the longing didn't fade.

She managed, somehow, never to cry over it, in spite of how close she'd come that first day. And he never guessed. She was sure of it. She took a kind of bleak pride in that, in the fact that he didn't know she was hopelessly, utterly gone on him.

Yes, sometimes he gave her a faintly puzzled look. As if he knew something wasn't quite right with her. But she did her job and she did it well and after that first day, he never asked again what might be wrong with her.

Fresh torments abounded.

Simple things. Everyday things. Like his brushing touch, they were things that had meant next to nothing before. Things like following him around the executive suite taking last-minute instructions before he met his managers for lunch—as he stripped to the waist and changed into a fresh shirt.

She tried not to stare at his muscled back and lean, hard arms, not to let herself imagine what it would be like if he held out those arms to her, if he gathered her close against that broad chest, if he lowered that wonderful mouth to cover hers....

It was awful. She had seen him change his shirt fifty times, at least. She'd never thought of a fresh shirt as a new form of torture. Until now.

Really, their lives were so...intertwined. They both lived where they worked. Aaron had a penthouse suite. Celia's rooms were smaller, of course, and several floors below his.

She'd always loved that, living on-site. She loved the glamour and excitement of her life at High Sierra. In many ways, the resort was its own city. A person could eat, sleep, shop, work and play there and never have to leave. The party went on 24/7, as the tired saying went.

Celia was far from a party animal. But working for Aaron, she felt as if some of the gold dust and glitter rubbed off on her. Growing up, she'd been just a little bit shy, and not all that popular—not unattractive, really, but a long way from gorgeous. She came from a big family, the fourth child of six. Her parents were good parents, but a little distracted. There were so many vying for their attention. She felt closer to her two best friends, Jane Elliott and Jillian Diamond, than she did to her own brothers and sisters.

She'd earned an accounting degree from Cal State Sacramento and worked for a Sacramento CPA firm before she stumbled on a job as secretary/assistant to one of the firm's clients, a local morning talk-show host.

Celia adored that job. It suited her perfectly. She needed to be organized and businesslike—and she also needed to be ready for anything. She handled correspondence and personal bookkeeping, as well as shopping and spur-of-the-moment dinner parties. Her duties were rarely the same from one day to the next.

The talk-show host had done a segment on High Sierra. Aaron had agreed to a brief interview. And then he'd been there, behind the scenes, for the rest of the shoot. And he'd remembered the girl from his hometown.

Two months later, the talk-show host got another show—in Philadelphia. Celia could have gone, too. But she decided against the move.

Aaron's human resources people had contacted her. She flew to Vegas to see him and he hired her on the spot.

"You're just what I'm looking for, Celia," he had said. "Efficient. Cool-headed. Low-key. Smart. And someone from home, too. I like that. I really do."

It had been a successful working relationship pretty much from the first—impersonally intimate, was how Celia always thought of it. She was a true "office wife" and that was fine with her. She was good at

what she did, she enjoyed the work and her boss knew
her value. She'd had a number of raises since she'd
started at High Sierra. Now, she was making twice
what she'd made in the beginning. She'd been happy
with the talk-show host, but she'd really come into
her own since she became Aaron's assistant. Now,
instead of shy, she saw herself as reserved. Serene.
Unruffled.

She was that calm place in the eye of any storm
that brewed up at High Sierra. Aaron counted on her
to keep his calendar in order, his letters typed and his
personal affairs running smoothly. And she did just
that, with skill and panache. She was a happy, successful career woman—until she had to go and fall
for the boss and ruin everything.

Now, it was all changed. Now, it was the agony
and the ecstasy and Celia Tuttle was living it. Everything about being near him excited her—and
wounded her to the core.

By the fourth day, she felt just desperate enough to
consider telling him of her feelings.

But what for? To make it all the worse? Make her
humiliation complete? After all, if he *were* interested,
even minimally, wouldn't he have given her some
hint, some *clue,* by now?

She told him nothing.

By the sixth day, she found herself contemplating
the impossible: giving notice. Less than a week since
she'd fallen for the boss. And she'd almost forgotten
how much she used to love her job.

Now, work seemed more like torture. A place
where she suffered constantly in the company of her

heart's desire—and he was totally oblivious to her as anything but his very efficient gal Friday.

Maybe she *should* quit.

But she didn't. She did nothing, just tried to get through each day. Just reminded herself that it really hadn't been all that long since V-day—yes, that was how she had started to think of it. As V-day, the day her whole world went haywire.

She hoped, fervently, that things would get better, somehow.

The seventh day passed.

Then, on the eighth day, Celia got a call from her friend Jane in New Venice.

It was after midnight. Celia had just let herself into her rooms. A group of Japanese businessmen had arrived that afternoon. High rollers, important ones. The kind who thought nothing of dropping a million a night at High Sierra's gaming tables. The kind known affectionately in the industry as *whales*.

Aaron had joined these particular whales for their comped gourmet dinner in the Placer Room. He'd asked Celia to be there, too. She'd been in what she thought of as "fetch-and-carry mode." If there was anything he needed that, for some reason, the wait staff or immediately available hotel personnel couldn't handle, Celia was right there, to see he got it and got it fast.

The phone was ringing when she entered her rooms. She rushed to answer it.

And she heard her dear friend's voice complaining, "Don't you ever return your calls?"

Celia scrunched the phone between her shoulder and her ear and slid her thumb under the back strap of her black evening sandal. "Sorry." She slipped the shoe off with a sigh of relief, then got rid of the other one and dropped to the couch. "It's been a zoo."

"That's what you always say."

"Well, it's always a zoo."

"But you love it."

In her mind's eye, she saw Aaron. "That's right," she said bleakly. "I do."

"Okay, what's wrong?"

"Not a thing."

"You said that too fast."

"Jane. I love my job. It's not news." *Too bad I also love my boss—who does not love me.* "What's up?"

"You're sure you're all right?"

"Uh-huh. What's up?"

Jane hesitated. Celia could just see her, sitting up in her four-poster bed in the wonderful Queen Anne Victorian she'd inherited from her beloved Aunt Sophie. She'd be braced against the headboard, pillows propped at her back, her wildly curling almost-black hair tamed, more or less, into a single braid. And she'd have a frown between her dark brows as she considered whether to get to why she'd called—or pursue Celia's sudden strange attitude toward her job.

Finally, she said, "Come home. This weekend."

Celia leaned back against the couch cushions and stared up at the recessed ceiling lights. "I can't. You know I can't."

Jane made a humphing sound. "I don't know any

such thing. You work too hard. You never take a break.''

''It's Thursday. Home is five hundred miles away.''

''That's why they invented airplanes. I'll pick you up in Reno tomorrow, just name the time.''

''Oh, Jane…''

''There will be wine. And a crackling fire in the fireplace. The valley is beautiful. We had snow, just enough to give us that picture-postcard effect. But there's none in the forecast, so getting here will be no problem. And Jilly's coming.''

Jillian Diamond, Celia's other best friend, lived in Sacramento now and got home almost as rarely as Celia did.

''Also, I'm cooking.'' Jane was an excellent cook. ''Come on, Ceil. It's been way too long. You know it has. At some point, you just have to put work aside for a day or two and come and see your old friends.''

Celia gathered her legs up to the side and switched the phone to her other ear. Why not? She thought. She hadn't had a weekend to herself in months. And she could certainly use a break right about now. Yes. A change of scenery, a little time away from the object of her hopeless desire—and everything connected with him.

''Celia Louise?''

''I'm here—and I'm coming.''

Jane let out short whoop of glee. ''You are? You're serious?''

''I'll get a flight right now, then e-mail you my

flight schedule. But don't worry about picking me up.''

''I don't mind.''

''Forget about it. I'll rent a car, no problem.''

''I'm holding you to this,'' Jane said in a scolding tone. ''You won't be allowed to back out this time.''

''Don't worry. I'll be there. Tomorrow afternoon. Expect me.''

''I will.''

Celia hung up and ran upstairs to her loft office nook, where she scheduled a flight online—quickly, before she could start thinking of all the ways her unexpected absence might be inconvenient for Aaron. She sent Jane a copy of her itinerary.

Jane e-mailed her right back: *Since you're driving yourself, I'll go ahead and stay at the store until six.*

Jane owned and operated a bookstore, the Silver Unicorn, in the heart of New Venice, right on Main Street. It was next door to the Highgrade, the café/saloon/gift shop that Caitlin Bravo, Aaron's mother, had owned and run for over thirty years.

Celia stared at the computer screen, remembering....

Aaron and his brothers used to hang around on Main Street. They all three worked on and off at the Highgrade—in the gift shop or in the café, where they bussed tables or even flipped burgers on the grill. But they were a volatile family. People in town said those boys needed the influence of a steady father figure and that was something they would never get with Caitlin Bravo for a mother.

They were always getting into trouble, or just plain

not showing up when it was time to go to work. Caitlin would pitch a fit and fire them. Then they'd end up hanging out on the street with the other wild kids in town—until they got into some mischief or other. Then Caitlin would yell at them and put them to work again.

Once, when she was eight, Celia had borrowed her big sister's bike and ridden it over to Main Street. It was twenty-six inches of bike, with thin racing wheels, and she'd borrowed it without getting Annie's permission. But she figured she wouldn't get in trouble. Annie was over at the high school, at cheerleading practice. By the time Annie got home, the bike would be back on the side porch where she'd left it.

It was a stretch for Celia's eight-year-old legs to reach the pedals and she kind of wobbled when she rode it. She had wobbled onto Main Street—and lost control right in front of the Highgrade. The bike went down, Celia with it, scraping her knees and palms on the asphalt of the street as she tried to block the fall.

Her legs were all tangled up in the pedals. She grunted and struggled and tried to get free. But it wasn't working and she was getting more and more frustrated. She was on the verge of forgetting all about her eight-year-old dignity, just about to start bawling like a baby in sheer misery.

But then a pair of dusty boots appeared on the street about three feet from where she lay in a clumsy tangle. She looked up two long, strong legs encased in faded jeans, past a black T-shirt, into the face of the oldest of those bad Bravo boys, Aaron.

He knelt at her side. "Hey. You okay?"

She didn't know what to say to him. She pressed her lips together and glared to show him that she wasn't scared of him and she wasn't going to cry.

He said, "Here. I'll help you." He gently took her beneath the arms and slid her out from under the bike. She was on her feet before she had time to shout at him to let go of her.

He stood her up and then he knelt again, just long enough to right the bike. "There you go."

Her tongue felt like a slab of wood in her mouth. She knew if she tried to answer, some strange, ugly sound would be all that came out. She managed a nod.

He frowned at her. "You sure you're all right?"

She nodded again.

"Maybe you should get a smaller bike...."

The cursor on her computer screen blinked at her. Celia ordered her mind back to the present and read the rest of Jane's note. *Key where it always is. Jane.*

She typed, *Can't wait. See you.* And sent it off.

Then she shut down the computer and went to bed. She didn't sleep all that well. She kept obsessing over what Aaron might say when she told him she had to be at the airport at four.

He did depend on her. He could be angry that she was leaving for two days on such short notice. He often needed her on the weekends.

Well, if he said he needed her, she'd just have to cancel, she'd have to call Jane and—

Celia sat up in bed. "Oh, what is the matter with me?"

She flopped back down.

Of course, she wouldn't cancel. She'd promised her dear friend she'd be there, and she would not break her word.

And what right did Aaron have to be angry? She'd worked weekend after weekend and never complained.

She was going. And that was it. No matter what Aaron said.

Chapter Two

As it turned out, she needn't have stayed awake stewing all night.

Aaron was staring at his computer screen when she mentioned her plans. "Hmm," he said. "You'll be here until four?"

"Well, I'd have to leave by three or so."

"Three..." He frowned at the screen, punched a few keys, then added, "No problem. God knows you deserve a little time to yourself. Your parents all right?"

"I'm not going to visit them. They don't live there anymore. None of my family lives there anymore. Remember I told you my folks moved to Phoenix last year?"

"Yeah, that's right. You did." He typed in a few

more commands. She knew that he hadn't really heard her. The next time she went home, he'd be telling her to enjoy her visit with her parents.

"I'll be staying with my friend, Jane Elliott," she volunteered brightly—as if he really cared or needed to know.

"Jane. The mayor's daughter, right?"

The Elliotts were the closest thing New Venice had to an aristocracy. Jane's father was a judge, like his father before him.

"No," Celia said. "It's Jane's uncle, J.T., who's the mayor."

A half smile lifted one side of that wonderful, sculpted mouth of his—though he never took his eyes off his computer screen. "J. T. Elliott. Her *uncle*. Got it."

J. T. Elliott had once been the county sheriff. If Celia remembered right, he'd locked Aaron up in his jail more than once in the distant past. Or if not Aaron, then surely his baby brother, Cade, who was the wildest of the three bad Bravo boys.

"So it's all right, then, if I go?"

"Of course. Have a good time."

Somehow, it felt worse that he didn't seem to care she was leaving than if he'd been a jerk and demanded she cancel her plans and remain at his beck and call the whole weekend through.

Celia told herself to snap out of it. She was getting what she'd asked for and she would take it and be happy about it.

She worked until two-thirty and she was on that plane, flying to Reno, by a little after five that evening.

It was the second bottle of Chianti that did it. Celia probably could have kept her mouth shut if they'd stuck with just one.

But it was such a perfect evening. The three of them—friends since the first day of kindergarten, bosom buddies all through high school—together again, like in the old days.

Jane had cooked. Italian. Something with angel-hair pasta and lots of garlic and sun-dried tomatoes. After the meal, the three of them kicked off their shoes and gathered around the big fireplace in the front parlor. Jane had the stereo on low, set to Random, playing a mix of everything from Tony Bennett to Natalie Imbruglia.

Jillian raised her glass. "Triple Threat." That was the three of them, the Triple Threat. Though, of course, they really hadn't been much of a threat to anyone.

They were three nice girls from a small town, girls who studied hard in school and got good grades and didn't get breasts as early as they would have liked—well, not Celia and Jillian, anyway. At the age of twelve, Jane had suddenly sprouted a pair of breasts that instantly became the envy of even the most popular girls at Mark Twain Middle School, eighth-graders included.

They were all well behaved. Yep. Jane and Jillian and Celia were good girls to the core, their transgressions so minor they generally went unremarked. They only dreamed of rebellions—at least until their senior year, when Jane ran off to Reno and married Rusty Jenkins.

That had been a real mess, Jane's marriage to Rusty. He was trouble, capital T, that Rusty. He'd ended up getting himself killed three years later. Jane had scrupulously avoided all forms of rebellion ever since.

Jillian had tried marriage, too, when she was twenty-two. Her husband had a problem with monogamy—a problem he never bothered to reveal before the wedding. But it turned out that Benny Simmerson found being faithful way too limiting. That marriage had lasted a little over a year.

"Triple Threat," echoed Jane. Celia said it, too. The three of them clinked glasses and drank.

Jillian grabbed a sapphire-blue chenille pillow from the end of the couch, propped it against the front of an easy chair and used it for a backrest. "So, how's construction going next door?"

About six months ago, Cade Bravo had bought the house next to Jane's. Since then, he'd been remodeling it.

Jane sipped more wine. "Who knows? He'll probably never move in."

"Why do you say that?" prodded Jillian. "What? He's never there?"

"He's there. Now and then. You can see he's got the new roof on and the exterior painted. And I do hear hammering inside every once in a while. I'd say construction is moving along."

"The question," said Jillian, "is *why?* Why buy a

house here? I heard he's got a huge place in Vegas. And one in Tahoe, too, right? What's New Venice got to offer that he can't get in Vegas or Tahoe? And why an old house? Cade Bravo is not the fixer-upper type."

"A hungering for the home he never really had?" Jane suggested. "A yearning for a simpler, gentler kind of life?"

Jillian pretended to choke on her wine. "Oh, right. Cade Bravo. Not."

Jane shrugged. "It's only a guess."

"And speaking of Bravos…" Jillian wiggled her eyebrows. "Rumor has it Caitlin's got a new boyfriend."

"Could be," said Jane.

Jillian giggled, a very naughty sound. "Janey. Come on. Who is he? What's he like?"

"Hans is his name. I've seen him tooling around town in that black Trans Am of Caitlin's." Caitlin had owned the Trans Am for as long as Celia could remember. She kept it in perfect condition. It looked just like the one Burt Reynolds drove in that old seventies classic, *Smokey and the Bandit*. Jane added, "Hans has come in the bookstore once or twice."

"And…?"

"Sounds like Arnold Schwarzenegger. Looks like him, too. At least from the neck down. Arnold meets Fabio. Remember Fabio? Long blond hair, major muscles. That's Hans. Buys books on body culture and vitamin therapy."

"A health nut."

"Could be."

"How old?"

Jane tried to look disapproving. "Honestly, Jilly. You're practically salivating."

Jillian let out a long, crowing laugh. "Boytoy! Admit it. I've got it right."

Jane shrugged. "She always did like them young."

"And vigorous." Jillian giggled some more.

Jane gathered her legs up under her and stood. "I'll get that other bottle."

Celia looked down into her almost-empty glass, thinking of Aaron again, feeling disgustingly sorry for herself. There was no escape, really, from thinking of Aaron. Reminders were everywhere. She worked for him, they came from the same hometown where everybody loved nothing so much as to gossip about his mother. And now his brother was moving in next door to her best friend....

Jillian said, "What's with you, Celia Louise?"

Celia looked up from her wine glass. "Huh?"

"I said, what's with you?"

She made an effort to sit straighter and tried to sound perky. "Oh, nothing much. Working, as always."

Jillian looked at her sideways. "No. I mean right this minute. Tonight. You've been too quiet."

"A person can't be quiet?"

"Depends on the *kind* of quiet. Tonight you are...suspiciously quiet. Something's up with you."

"You think so?"

"I do."

Celia put on a frown, as if she were giving the whole idea of something being "up" with her serious thought. Then she shrugged and shook her head. "No. Honestly. Just…enjoying being here."

"Oh, you liar," said Jillian.

Jane came back with the fat, raffia-wrapped bottle. "She said there's nothing bothering her, am I right?"

"You are," said Jillian.

There's something," Jane said. "But she isn't telling."

Both Jane and Jillian looked at Celia, their faces expectant, waiting for her to come clean and tell them what was on her mind. She kept her mouth shut.

Finally, Jane shrugged. "More of this nice, rustic Chianti, anyone?"

Celia and Jillian held out their glasses and Jane filled them. They all sat back and stared at the fire for a minute or two while Tony Bennett sang about leaving his heart in San Francisco.

"Good a place as any," Jane said softly.

Jillian sighed.

Celia drank more wine. She grabbed a couple of pillows of her own, propped them against the wall between the fireplace and the side door that led out to Jane's wraparound porch and leaned back, getting comfortable.

"So, how's the book biz?" Jillian tipped her glass at Jane.

"The book biz is not bad. Not bad at all." Jane's dark eyes shone with satisfaction as she talked about her store. "Events," she said. "They really bring in the customers. Events. Activities." Not a week went by that she didn't have some author or other in to answer questions and sign books. "I still have my

Children's Story Hour, Saturdays at ten and Thursday nights at seven.'' And then there were the reading groups. She offered the store as a place to hold them. "So far, I've got four different groups meeting at the Silver Unicorn at various times during the week. Now and then I've been doing a kind of café evening on a weekend night, with a harpist or a guitar player, that sort of thing. They can have coffee and tea and scones and biscotti. They can read the books while they enjoy the music. Folks love it. I'm building my customer base just fine. I get the tourists in the summer months and during the winter, the locals have started thinking of the store as a gathering place.''

Jillian said, ''Speaking of speakers, how 'bout me? I am an author now, after all—more or less, anyway.''

Jane grinned. ''I thought you'd never ask. Maybe we could set something up for next month. You could talk about the column. Give a few helpful hints on wardrobe basics, tell them what items they just can't be without this year.''

Jillian had her own business, Image by Jillian. She showed executives and minor celebrities how to spruce up their wardrobes; she gave makeovers and seminars on dressing Business Casual. She also wrote an advice column, ''Ask Jillian,'' for the *Sacramento Press-Telegram.*

Celia sipped her wine, growing dangerously mushy and sentimental as she listened to her two oldest and dearest friends talking shop. Really, she *was* glad she had come. It was just what she'd needed, to be sitting here by the fire at Jane's, getting plotzed on Chianti.

And also, I need *truth,* she thought, with a sudden

burst of semi-inebriated insight. *Truth.* Oh, yes. I need it. I do. I need to *share* the truth with someone—and who better than my two best friends in all the world?

So she said, "Well, the truth is, I'm in love with Aaron Bravo."

Chapter Three

Jillian, who'd been making a point about flirty reversible bias-cut skirts in light, floaty fabrics, shut her mouth right in the middle of a sentence. Jane turned to Celia and stared.

Celia took another large sip of wine.

"Get *out*," said Jillian, after several seconds of stunned silence. A wild laugh escaped her, but she cut it off by clapping her hand over her mouth. Finally, she whispered, "You're serious."

"I am. I love him." Celia looked into her glass again and wrinkled her nose. "Maybe I'll become a drunk. Drown my sorrows…"

Jane reached out and snared the glass.

"Hey," Celia protested, but without much heat.

Jane scooted over and set the glass on the coffee

table, then scooted back to the nest of pillows she'd made for herself on the pretty lapis-blue hand-woven rug in front of the fire.

Jillian asked, "Does he know?"

Oh, no, Celia thought. *Here come those pesky tears again....*

Well, she wasn't having any of them. She jumped to her feet and looked down at her friends. She swallowed. Twice. Finally, her throat loosened up enough that she could tell them, "He hasn't got a clue."

"Oh, honey," cried Jillian. She reached up her arms. So did Jane.

With a tiny sob, Celia toppled toward her friends. They embraced. It felt really good, really comforting.

So much so that she didn't end up bawling like a baby after all.

Once they'd shared a good, long hug, Jane gave Celia back her wineglass. "But don't get too crazy with that."

"I won't. I promise. This is all I'll have. I was only joking about becoming a drunk."

"Good." Jane folded her legs lotus-style and adjusted her long, soft skirt over them. "So. All right. Talk to us. Tell us everything."

Celia explained about V-day.

"Wait a minute," Jillian said. "So you're saying, all this time you've been working for him and you were—what—*fond* of him and nothing more?"

"Oh, I don't know. *Fond?* Is that the word that comes to mind when I think of Aaron Bravo?"

Jillian made a low, impatient sound. "What I'm getting at is, this is way too sudden, don't you think?

Out of nowhere, you're in love with him? On Valentine's Day?''

Celia nodded. ''Yes.'' Then she shook her head. ''No.'' And then she looked at the ceiling. ''Oh, I don't know.''

''Well, that clarifies it for me.''

''Jilly, I can't be sure if it *started* on Valentine's Day. Maybe…I've loved him for months. Maybe years. But if I did, I didn't know it until a week ago.''

Jillian started to say something. But Jane shot her a look. Jillian blew out a breath.

Jane said, ''Go on.''

Celia poured out her woes. ''He doesn't notice me. Not as a whole person. And certainly not as a woman. I'm…a function to him. And it hurts. Bad. Which I know is totally unreasonable. My falling for him wasn't in the job description. He hired a secretary/assistant. Not a girlfriend. He doesn't *need* a girlfriend. He's got his pick of those.''

Jane was nodding grimly. ''Showgirls?''

''That's right. *Nice* showgirls, too. I hate that. It makes it even worse, somehow. I can't even despise the competition—not that there *is* any competition.''

''Does he seem—'' Jillian sought the right words ''—as if he *could* be interested, if you told him?''

Slowly, pressing her lips together and swallowing down more tears, Celia shook her head.

''You're *sure* of that?''

Jane jumped in. ''Oh, how can she know for sure? She's not objective about this. Look at her. She's gone around the bend over the guy.''

''That's right,'' Jillian said. ''Of course, she can't be objective.''

''I *can* be objective.'' Celia protested. ''I *am* objective. I'm sure he's not interested in me as a woman.''

Jane scooted over and took her by the shoulders. ''Look at me, Ceil.''

''Fine. Okay.'' Celia met her friend's eyes.

''Are you sure this is the real thing? Are you sure it's really love? Are you sure it's not—''

''Stop,'' said Celia. ''Yes. I'm sure. It's *all* I'm sure of lately. This is love, I know it. I've known it since V-day. I can't explain it. I can't convince you if you won't believe. But it is the truth. I'm in love with Aaron Bravo.''

Jane stared at her for a several long seconds more, her eyes narrowed, probing. Then she whispered, softly, ''I see.'' She let go of Celia's shoulders and went back to her pillows.

Jillian grabbed the bottle and refilled her own glass. ''I'm going to ask you again, because I don't think you really gave this question a chance before. Could he *be* interested, if he only knew how you felt?''

''No.'' Celia sank back against the wall again. ''I don't think so. I really don't.''

''But you don't *know,* not for certain. You'll never know for certain, not if *he* never knows how you feel.''

''I'm certain enough.'' Celia traced the rim of her glass with her index finger. ''I just have to decide whether I can stand this anymore. Or whether I should just…spruce up my résumé and find another place to work.''

Jane and Jillian exchanged looks. Then Jillian said, ''But you love that job. You're making *lots* of money. You have points in the company. And it's only going to get better. Aaron Bravo hasn't gotten where he's going yet. And until now, you've been looking forward to being there when he does.''

''You think I don't know that?''

''And it's only been—what—a week since you realized how you feel about him? You don't need to go rushing into anything too drastic.''

''Jilly, you're not telling me anything I haven't told myself at least a hundred times.''

Jane said, ''Well, here's my opinion. Honesty is the best policy.''

Jillian groaned.

Jane looked vaguely injured. ''All right, so it's a cliché. That doesn't make it any less true.'' She pointed a finger at Celia. ''Tell him how you feel.''

Jillian slapped the edge of coffee table to get their attention. ''No. Hold it. Bad idea.''

''Why?'' demanded Jane. ''Why is telling the truth a bad idea?''

''Because when it comes to love, you should…never ask a question you don't know the answer to.''

Jane winced. ''And *you* get paid to give people advice?''

''Well,'' Celia reminded Jane, ''she mostly gives advice on things like which fork to use and how to get peach-juice stains out of silk blouses.''

"I beg your pardon," Jillian huffed. "I give advice to the lovelorn, if they write in. I'll advise on any subject. That's my job."

"Scary, very scary," muttered Jane.

"I heard that," snapped Jillian.

"Sorry." Jane adjusted her skirt over her knees.

Jillian said, "I mean it. There's another way. A *better* way."

Celia sat forward eagerly. "All right. *What* way?"

Jillian cleared her throat. "Absolutely first of all, you have to make him notice you as a woman."

"Oh," said Celia, sinking back, disappointed and letting it show. "And how do you expect me to do that?"

Jane stopped fiddling with her skirt. "Oh, my God. I think she's talking makeover."

It was an old joke between them. Jillian gave her first makeover when the three of them were twelve years old. Jane was her subject. She cut Jane's hair and dyed it—green. Jane wore a hat for months.

Jillian sniffed. "Oh, come on. In case you've forgotten, I now get paid and paid well to do what you're groaning about. And I act as an *adviser* now—an extremely *knowledgeable* adviser. I let the experts do the actual cutting and coloring. I've come a long way from that first haircut I gave you."

"And a good thing, too," Jane said.

Jillian pulled a face at Jane, then turned to Celia. "Brighter colors," she instructed. "Softer, more touchable fabrics. We aren't talking beating him over the head with you. We are talking subtle, sexy little changes—and I think you ought to bring out the red in your hair. With that gorgeous pale skin, you'd be a knockout. And you've got those darling rosebud lips—what are those called, those cute, fat old-time dolls with those darling rosebud mouths?''

''Kewpie dolls,'' Jane supplied. ''And you're right—about her lips, anyway. She's got Kewpie-doll lips.''

''Lips that she never makes anything of.'' Jillian sent Celia an I-mean-business scowl. ''A deeper, riper shade of lipstick. Are you with me?''

''She's right,'' Jane conceded. ''You'd look great in brighter colors. Red hair would be good on you— so would darker lipstick. Go there if you want to. But as far as Aaron Bravo goes, *tell him*. Three little words. *I love you*. There is no substitute for honesty. It's the place where every relationship should start. If you let him know how you feel, you give him a chance to—'' The ringing of the telephone cut her off. ''Don't you move.''

Celia slumped among her pillows. ''Where would I go?''

Jane uncrossed her legs and stood. She went to the phone on the table at the other end of the couch. ''Hi, this is Jane… Yes…'' A smug little smile curved her lips. ''Of course. Can you hold on? Thanks.'' She punched a button in the headset and turned to Celia, one dark brow lifted.

Celia frowned at her. ''For me?''

Now Jane was grinning. ''Speak of the devil, as they say.''

Celia's heart started pounding so hard, it felt as though it slammed against the wall of her chest with every beat. It was a very disconcerting sensation. "Aaron?" She more mouthed the word than said it.

Jane nodded.

Jillian let out a short, loud bark of laughter.

"Shh!" Celia reached over and bopped her on the knee. She hissed in whisper, "He'll hear you...."

"No he won't," said Jane. "I've got him on Mute—and did you want to speak with him or not?"

Celia shot to her feet and raced to grab the phone. She put it to her ear. "Hello?"

No one answered.

"Here," said Jane. Celia held out the phone and Jane punched the right button. Celia put it to her ear again, opened her mouth—and shut it. Jane was still standing there, watching expectantly.

Celia made frantic shooing motions. With a sigh, Jane returned to her pillows.

Celia turned away, toward the wide double doors that led to the entrance hall, seeking just a tiny bit of privacy. "Hello. Aaron?"

"Celia. There you are. Good." He sounded pre-occupied, as always. Preoccupied and wonderful. His deep, rich voice seemed to pour into her ear and all through her body, melting her midsection, turning her knees to water.

She asked, quite calmly, she thought, "Is something wrong?"

"Wrong? No." She heard the telltale clicking sounds that meant he was sitting at a computer. "I was typing a note to Tony Jarvis...." Anthony Jarvis was Senior Vice-President of Project Development. For Aaron, High Sierra was just one step in the road—a big step, but not the only one. Silver Standard Resorts, High Sierra's parent company, had to keep growing. Tony Jarvis was the main man responsible for scouting future venues. "The note has vanished. Can't seem to bring it back up."

She couldn't help grinning. Since he never typed his own e-mails, he'd forgotten the finer points of the program they used for them.

"Celia. Find my memo."

She told him what to click on.

"Ah," he said after a moment. "There it is. Thank you."

"No problem—Aaron?"

"Hmm?"

"How did you get this number?"

A pause, then, "You're irritated, that I called you there?"

"Not at all." Never. Ever. Call me anytime. Anywhere. For any reason… "I just wondered."

"You said you were going to Jane Elliott's. I called information. It's a listed number."

He'd remembered that she was going to Jane's! She could hardly believe it. He so rarely remembered anything personal she told him. Her heart pounded even harder, with pure joy. "Oh. Of course. You called information. I should have known…."

"Celia?" He sounded puzzled. "Are you all right?"

"Oh. Yes. Fine. Just fine."

"Have a good weekend."

"I will…."

The line went dead. She pulled the phone away

from her ear and stared at it, wild joy fading down to something kind of hollow and dejected.

Really, the call had meant less than nothing to him. She had to face that, had to *accept* it.

Jillian said, "See? He can't live without you."

Celia put down the phone. "That is so not the case." She returned to her spot against the wall, dropped to the floor and flopped back on her pillows.

Jillian was adamant. "He can't live without you. He just doesn't know it yet."

"Tell him," Jane commanded for the third time that night.

"Give *up*," Celia cried. "I'm not telling him. And I'm not changing my hair color, either."

"Then what *will* you do?" asked Jane.

"I haven't decided yet."

Her friends groaned in unison.

They worked on her all weekend, advising, cajoling, prodding and instructing. They wore her down, little by little.

Jane kept pushing honesty. Jillian talked hair and wardrobe and subliminal seduction. Celia moaned and protested and begged them to let it go. They would, for a while—and then they'd start in again.

She couldn't hold firm against them forever. And she loved that they listened to her, that they *cared*. They really were the best friends any woman could have.

By noon Sunday, when she got in her rental car to drive to the Reno airport, she had made a decision.

She would take Jane's advice and tell Aaron of her love.

Chapter Four

Celia's course of action seemed perfectly clear to her when she was waving goodbye on that crisp, snowy Sunday in front of Jane's wonderful old house.

First she would tell Aaron of her feelings. And depending on how he reacted, *maybe* she'd consider some of Jillian's suggestions—if she wasn't too busy nursing a broken heart while pounding the pavement looking for another job.

It was the ''if'' part that ruined her resolve.

Because how could she help fearing that the ''if'' part was reality? She would tell him she loved him. And he would tell *her,* very gently, because he was a kind man at heart, that he was sure she'd be happier working for someone else.

She'd lose him *and* her job.

All right, she was miserable now. But she was miserable and *employed*. She just couldn't see the trade-off. If she told him, she'd still be miserable. And she'd be out of work, as well.

"Oh, that's negative." She'd lie in bed at night, staring up at the dark ceiling, giving herself advice. "I am so negative." She would tell herself, "Celia Louise Tuttle, you've got to snap out this. You've got to give it up, get over him—or tell him how you feel."

Jillian called on Tuesday. "Well? Did you do it? What did he say? How did it go?"

Celia let too long a pause elapse before answering.

Jillian figured it out. "You didn't do it."

"I'm *trying*."

"Celia. If you're going to do it, do it."

"I will, I will…."

"Tomorrow morning. The minute he comes in the door. Look up from your desk and say, 'I have to speak with you privately about a personal matter.' Get him to set a time. Have him come to your suite."

"Oh, God."

"Better if it's on your turf."

Right, Celia thought. Easier for him to get up and walk out.

"You can do it, Celia."

"Yes. I can. I know…."

The next morning, when he called her in to go over the calendar, she was ready. She truly was. She stood from her desk and she straightened her fawn-colored skirt—brighter colors, hah! Like wearing fire-engine red and Jolly Rancher green could make him love her.

She tucked her yellow legal pad under her arm, grabbed her pencil and her miniature tape recorder and crossed to the high, wide door that led to his private office.

She paused there to smooth her hair and tug on the hem of the jacket that matched the fawn-colored skirt. I'm okay, she thought. Pulled-together. Calm. Collected. Ready to do it.

She pushed open the door and there he was, right where she expected him to be, at his big glass desk in front of the wall of windows, engrossed in something on his computer screen.

She quietly turned and made sure the door was shut. Then she marched across the room and stepped between the two black leather visitors' chairs that faced his desk, planting herself in front of him.

It took him a moment to stop punching keys and look up. His bronze-kissed dark brows drew together. "Celia?"

That was it. All he said. It was way too much. It was, *Is there a problem and do we really need to address it right now?*

No. They didn't.

She sidled to the right, dropped into one of the two chairs, indicated her legal pad and chirped brightly, "Ready when you are."

Jane called next. On Thursday, after midnight. "Did you do it?"

"Oh, Janie."

"You didn't."

"I *almost* did."

"But you didn't."

"It's really...hard for me."

Jane let out a long breath. "Look. I've been thinking...."

Celia clutched the phone as if it were a lifeline. "Yeah?"

"Maybe you're not up for reality right now. Maybe you're not ready to face him with the truth." That was sounding pretty reasonable—until Jane went on. "Maybe you're enjoying this a little, kind of reveling in your misery."

"Jane!" That hurt. It really did. And partly because it had the sharp sting of truth.

She was getting kind of...used to being miserable. Yesterday was two weeks since V-day. Two weeks of suffering. She'd kind of gotten into a groove with it now, hadn't she?

"Celia Louise, you are the classic middle child, you know that you are."

"Is this a lecture coming on?"

"You are a middle child and you know how to be...ignored. Passed over. You don't get out and make things happen like a first child. You don't expect all good to come to you, as the baby in the family always does. You...accept being in the middle. You can easily become stuck."

"And I'm stuck right now, is that what you're saying?"

"Yes. You're stuck in the middle, sitting at the trestle table, clutching your sad little bowl of gruel, knowing when you finish it, you'll still be very, very hungry—and yet unwilling to get up and ask the headmaster for more.''

''My bowl of *gruel?*''

''Come on. You remember. Dickens. *Oliver Twist.* In the orphanage. We read it in Mrs. Oakley's freshman English class.''

She remembered. ''Shall we go into what happened when Oliver actually got up and asked for more?''

Jane was silent for a count of two. ''Okay,'' she conceded. ''Bad analogy.''

''No kidding.''

''But in the end, Oliver succeeded in *life.* Because he was someone who could get up when he had to and ask for more.''

''Hooray for Oliver.''

Jane made a small sound in her throat—one that spoke of fading patience. ''I'm merely saying, if you don't want to tell him, fine. Maybe you should quit working for him. It wouldn't be the end of the world for you to have to get another job. And at least that would be taking *action,* which I sincerely think it's time for you to do.''

There was no getting around it. Jane had it right. ''I'll tell him. I will.''

''Good. When, exactly?''

''Tomorrow…''

Tomorrow came.

Celia went to the office tower a determined woman.

And when she got there, she learned her boss had taken off for New Jersey on a site-scouting trip with

Tony Jarvis. He wasn't due back until Sunday. He'd left her an e-mail.

> TO: Celia Tuttle, clerical/PA
> FROM: Aaron Bravo, CEO
> SUBJECT: Trip to New Jersey
> Back Sunday. Take a three-day weekend. Aaron.

And that meant, unless something came up and he really needed her, she wouldn't see him face-to-face until Monday.

Reprieved, she thought. And felt mingled relief and despair—tinged faintly with worry. As his assistant, it was part of her job to be at his side when he traveled. Why hadn't he wanted her presence on this trip?

She told herself not to make something of nothing. Now and then, he traveled without her. This was probably just one of those times.

She considered going home for another weekend. But she didn't think she could bear facing Jane again until she had done what she'd sworn to do. And there were plenty of projects for her to dig into. She worked all day Friday and half a day on Saturday.

Every time she returned to her rooms, she expected to see the message light blinking on her phone—a call from Jane or Jillian to find out if she'd finally done what she'd vowed to do.

But her friends didn't call. Maybe they'd given up on her. She could hardly blame them if they had.

Sunday, she woke early, thinking, *He's due back today....*

But she didn't know what time.

And what did it matter what time? She wasn't going to ask him for a private meeting until tomorrow, anyway.

She lasted until noon and then she called his rooms. His machine picked up. Quietly, stealthily—without leaving a message—she returned the phone to its cradle. Then she went to her computer, logged onto the company system, and used her employee code to look up his itinerary. It was unethical, really. Celia Tuttle, secretary/personal assistant didn't need to know exactly when her boss would arrive back in town. But Celia Tuttle, woman hopelessly in love, did.

He was due in at eight that night. Which meant he wouldn't get to his own rooms till nine or ten at the earliest.

It helped to know that. Made it marginally easier not to keep dialing his number and hanging up when his machine answered.

The day dragged by on lead feet. She read the Sunday paper, watched a movie on cable, her mind hardly registering what her eyes were seeing. In the afternoon, she called down to Touch of Gold, High Sierra's full-service luxury spa, and booked the works—mud bath, massage and two-hour facial. Maybe it would help her relax.

It did, while she was down there. And it took up four hours she would have spent stewing. She didn't return to her own rooms until after six.

The rest of the evening was downright unbearable. As eight and nine came and went, she wondered.

Where was he now?

Had he reached the hotel yet?

Was he already in his tower suite—or was he down in the casino somewhere, or in one of High Sierra's luxurious bars or fine restaurants, maybe having a last drink with Tony Jarvis, or possibly courting some recently arrived high rollers?

There was no way to know.

And it didn't even matter. Wherever he was, whatever he was doing, she had no intention of tracking him down tonight, anyway.

She put on her pajamas and she got into bed.

But sleeping fell under the heading, *as if.*

She reached for the phone more than once. But she never picked it up. She knew that if he answered, the sound of his voice would send her into a mindless state of pure panic. She'd hang up without identifying herself—and he would know who it was, anyway. After all, there was such a thing as caller ID.

Which she should have considered earlier, before she'd made that first call.

Jane was so right, she thought, as the night wore on and sleep never came. Here I am, at the bare trestle table, clutching my sad, half-empty bowl of gruel, afraid to stand up and ask for more....

Not sleeping and worrying all night long did nothing for her appearance the next day. She troweled on the concealer to cover the dark pouches beneath her eyes and she put on her nicest suit, which was pale blue, of a particularly fine-gauge gabardine and usually looked very nice on her.

Today, well, nothing she could have worn would have made her look anything better than tired and washed out. Her hair, which was a color somewhere between blond and auburn, seemed flat and lusterless as a brown-paper bag. Her skin looked pasty.

Really, she couldn't help thinking that maybe today just wasn't the day. Maybe she should get to bed early tonight, get a good night's sleep for a change. And then, *tomorrow,* when she felt fresh and didn't look like the walking dead, she could—

"No!" She glared at her own pasty, pale face in the bathroom mirror. "No more excuses. So you look like hell. You're telling him. Today."

She was at her desk when he entered the office suite.

"Good morning, Celia."

Her heart felt as it if had surged straight up into her throat. She swallowed it down and attempted a smile—one that never quite happened.

He was already past her, approaching the door to his private office. "Give me twenty minutes and we'll go over the calendar."

By then, her heart had dropped heavily into her chest again and begun beating so hard and loud she was certain any second she'd go into cardiac arrest. She stood.

"Aaron."

He paused with his hand on the door and turned back to her. He looked puzzled.

Really, now she thought about it, he'd been looking puzzled way too much lately. Probably because she'd been acting so strangely, he couldn't help but notice, even oblivious as he was to her as anything but a function most of the time.

He was waiting—waiting for her to tell him whatever it was she had stopped him to say.

"I...uh..." Her voice sounded awful. Tight. Squeaky.

"Yes?"

She coughed into her hand, to loosen her throat. And then, somehow, she was saying the words she'd been vowing she'd say. "I need to talk with you. Alone. It's a personal matter. I wonder if you would mind stopping by my rooms this evening?" *Suggest a time,* the part of her mind still capable of rational thought instructed frantically. "Uh. About seven?"

He didn't answer for a count of five, at least. He just stood there, looking at her through those blue eyes that really didn't give away much of anything. Finally, he said, rather gently, "Celia. What's this about?"

"I'd rather...wait. To speak with you alone."

He gestured at the outer office, which was decorated in cool grays and midnight blues and was empty except for the two of them. "No one here but you and me. It's as good a time as any to talk. Come on into my office now and we can—"

She put up a hand. "No. Really. I'm sorry, to be so vague about this. But I'd much rather we just kept it to business here in the office. I would honestly appreciate it if you'd just come to my rooms this evening. We'll discuss it there."

He looked at her for a long time. It was absolutely awful. What could he be thinking? Undoubtedly that she was inconveniencing him. Just possibly that he was going to have call down to human resources and get them to find him another PA.

Finally, he said in what seemed a half-hearted attempt at humor, "Well. Am I busy?"

She managed a pained smile. "Uh. No. Not at seven. Not as of now, anyway."

"All right then," he said. "Your rooms. At seven." He turned from her and went through the door to his office, closing it quietly behind him.

Chapter Five

Once in his office, Aaron Bravo stood at the door for a moment, his hand on the doorknob, thinking, *What the hell is up with Celia?*

Then he smelled coffee.

She had it ready for him, as always, waiting on the credenza. He went over, poured himself a cup and drank it right there, staring out the glare-treated glass beyond his desk, not really seeing the city sprawled across the desert landscape below.

He still had Celia on his mind. She didn't look well. Hadn't for a week or two now.

So could she be ill? And if so, was it serious? Was she planning to tell him she needed some time off—or worse, that she'd have to give up her job?

Damn. She was young, too young to be dangerously ill. And he'd sure as hell hate to lose her. She was the next thing to a genius at what she did. Always there when he needed her—and yet never in the way.

Pregnant.

The word popped into his head. He frowned. No. Not Celia. Celia didn't have *time* to get pregnant, not with the kind of demands he made on her. He kept her working hard—too hard, really. He knew that. He also paid her damn well. And he tried to remember to cut her a little slack now and then. Like this last weekend, when he'd let her off the hook for the trip back east, leaving instructions for her to take three days off.

He poured another cup of coffee.

Re the pregnancy angle—on the other hand, why not? How much opportunity did it take, anyway? One encounter could do it. If she hadn't been careful.

Not careful? *Celia?*

Hard to believe. She was such a model of efficiency. He couldn't see her *not* being careful, couldn't imagine her slipping up on something so basic as birth control.

But then, he could hardly imagine Celia *having* sex, let alone dealing with what method of contraception to use. He just didn't think sex when he thought of Celia.

Well, and why the hell should he? She was his *secretary*. And her sex life was her business.

However, accidents did happen. And if she now had a baby on the way…

Well, if she did, okay. It should be manageable.

He'd be willing to deal with a kid in the picture.

They could work around it, if she wanted to stay with him. It might be tough. There'd be some serious inconveniences for both of them. But his mother had done it; raising three sons and running the Highgrade all on her own after his father, the notorious Blake Bravo, had supposedly died.

Yeah. They could work it out if she was going to be a single mom.

But what if there was a man in the picture, too? What if, as busy as he kept her, she'd somehow managed to find herself a guy, a nice stable nine-to-five type who'd want her home every night when he got off work?

Strange. The idea of some stable, ordinary guy stealing Celia away rankled more than a little. He scowled.

The woman would not be easy to replace. Aaron's work was demanding and often chaotic. Celia made sure the chaos was kept to a minimum, and she did it so well that most of the time he was able to take her completely for granted—or he had been, until the last couple of weeks.

And damn it, he wanted things back as they had been. He wanted her problem—whatever it was— solved, so that he could go back to enjoying the benefits of taking her for granted.

He carried his half-full coffee cup to his desk.

Maybe it was something to do with her parents....

He turned on his computer and sat back as it booted.

Hadn't she said that they'd retired and lived in

Phoenix now? How old were they, anyway? Maybe they were failing and needed more of her time.

Time...

He glanced at his Rolex. Ten minutes had passed since he'd entered his office.

And he'd spent most of it staring into space, worrying about his assistant.

It was counterproductive in the extreme. An assistant was supposed to decrease the worry quotient, not herself be a source of concern.

He wasn't going to know for certain what was bothering her until that night. Why stew about it now when there really wasn't a damn thing he could do?

Good question—and one to which he had no answer.

As a rule, Aaron Bravo was not a man who borrowed trouble. He effectively compartmentalized his thinking, gathering facts first and foremost, avoiding what-ifs, never getting hung up on things he could do nothing about. After what he supposed could be called a troubled and turbulent early youth—no way of escaping turbulence with Caitlin Bravo for a mother—he'd realized at the age of seventeen that he wanted money and he wanted to run things. Big time. Neither was going to happen unless he changed his ways.

He had.

And look at him now.

He hadn't gotten where he was by wasting mental energy.

Therefore, he would forget the problem of Celia for now. No sense in trying to come up with answers when he didn't even know what the questions were. She'd tell him what was up tonight and then he could decide what to do about it.

His copy of the *Wall Street Journal* was waiting at his elbow. He picked it up. While he read, he paused now and then to check his various stocks online.

Ten minutes later, Celia tapped on his door armed with that little tape recorder of hers and her trusty notepad. They went over the calendar for the day. She didn't mention her mysterious problem again, kept things strictly on business, which was great with him.

He left the office at ten for a meeting with his vice-presidents.

After the meeting, he met Jennifer for lunch at one.

Jennifer was charming and funny, as always. And so easy on the eyes. She wore the ruby heart he'd given her for Valentine's Day.

She touched it, lightly, and beamed her beautiful smile at him. "Aaron, I love it. You always know just what to get for a woman…"

He looked at the heart, riding just above Jennifer's spectacular left breast and a vague irritation moved through him, a…dissatisfaction, a sense of unease.

Celia. Her name came into his mind in spite of the fact that he'd decided not to have it there.

Celia had picked out that heart. She had an unerring sense of what to choose when he asked her to go out and find a gift.

If Celia quit, he'd have to find another assistant. A stranger. Someone…not from home. Some other woman—or man—would compose his e-mails, tell him where to look for files he couldn't find, buy trinkets for his girlfriends....

"Aaron? What is it, *caro?*"

"Hm?"

"You are thousands of miles away." She stuck out her full lower lip in a playful pout.

"I'm right here." He reached across the table and took her hand. "And I'm glad you like the pin."

"I do." She squeezed his hand. She must have slid off her shoe, because under the table, she was lifting his pants leg with her bare toe. "Allow me to prove my gratitude...."

That afternoon, he met with his managers. Celia was there, at his right hand, as always. After the meeting, they both returned to the office. He closeted himself with Tony Jarvis for a couple of hours. They discussed the failing casino they'd looked at in Atlantic City. A grind joint, as they said in the gaming business. A grind joint catered to low rollers, everyday Joes who bet small. Aaron had got his start in Vegas in a grind joint downtown in Glitter Gulch, right on Fremont Street not far from the big neon cowboy known as Vegas Vic. There was good money to be made catering to the grind trade, though buying and sprucing up small casinos was not the focus of Silver Standard Resorts. Still, Tony thought they should take the place, give it a general face-lift and rake in the profits. His numbers were solid. Aaron agreed they would bring it before the board.

It was six-forty when Tony left. Celia was long gone by then. Unless he needed her to stay late for something, she always left the office tower at around five-thirty—with the understanding that he could reach her just about any time should the necessity arise.

He often had her with him at dinner, when he entertained high rollers or board members or potential investors. Celia was attractive, but, unlike Jennifer and the other breathtaking women he had dated, she was not the kind of attractive that distracted anyone from the business at hand. And it often came in handy to have his secretary right there beside him. She remembered what was on his calendar. She would immediately take steps to solve any minor problem that came up. And sometimes, she picked up on things he didn't—what his people were up to, what they might be dissatisfied over. Or what minor insurrections might be brewing among his managers.

But she wouldn't be sitting beside him at dinner tonight.

No, tonight he would be meeting her alone.

In her rooms.

Celia stood in her bedroom, wearing only a sky-blue bra and matching panties. Most of the contents of her walk-in closet lay strewn across the queen-sized bed. She'd been trying on clothes and discarding them in disgust for over an hour now. She'd planned to decide what to wear, take a soothing half-hour bath, then put on fresh makeup and fix her hair.

So much for that soothing bath. Too bad about the makeup and the hair.

It was 6:57. Aaron would be at her door some time

in the next four or five minutes, and she hadn't even gotten past choosing what to wear.

Nothing looked right. She tugged an eggplant-colored ankle-length knit skirt from the pile and shook it out, thinking, well, at least it's not gray.

She had discovered, in her extended search through her closet the past hour, that she owned way too many outfits in varying shades of gray.

Brighter colors, Jillian had advised. Celia hated to admit it, but she was beginning to think that Jilly was right—and she fervently wished she had seen the light sooner.

Now, it was too late. No time for a last-minute shopping spree. She *had* to make a choice from the mostly gray pile in front of her.

She stepped into the skirt, settled the elastic waist-band in place, smoothed it with both hands and then dug the matching boat-neck tunic top out of the tangle on the bed. She shook it out and glared at it. It, like the skirt, was one of those packable knits, the kind that never wrinkled. There was nothing *wrong* with it. In fact, like the skirt, it had something major going for it, in that it was not gray.

Too bad it was just so…not what she had in mind. Everything in her closet was utterly and completely *not* what she had in mind. Not for this. Not for the moment when she told her boss that somehow she'd managed to fall madly and hopelessly in love with him.

She groaned at the tunic.

And right then she heard the buzzer that meant there was someone at her door.

Celia muttered a very bad swear word. She tossed the tunic back on the bed and wriggled out of the skirt.

Now what? She had to choose something. And she had to choose fast.

A swatch of lustrous silk caught her eye—okay, it was gray. But the fabric was beautiful, nubby with a gorgeous sheen. She grabbed for it—a pair of pants, flat front, tapered legs. That, and her nicest white silk blouse.

Best she could do, given what was available.

She yanked on the pants and grabbed for the blouse, sticking her arms in the sleeves, tugging it onto her shoulders. Zipping and buttoning, she raced for the closet, where she stuck her feet in a pair of plain black-suede ballet flats.

The buzzer sounded again. "Coming, coming," she whispered under her breath as she paused to look at herself in the full-length closet mirror.

It was…okay. Not great. But okay.

She smoothed her not-quite blond and not-quite auburn hair and tugged on the hem of the blouse. She needed lipstick, at least.

But there was no time.

With a tiny, frustrated cry, she turned and rushed from the room, pausing only to pull the door shut behind her so that, if for some unknown reason he ended up in her hallway, he would not be able to see the disaster she'd made of her bed.

The buzzer sounded for the third time just as she got to the front door.

"Sorry," she said breathlessly, when she pulled it

back and found him standing there, frowning. "I was just—" She cut herself off. Jeez. Like he needed to know what she'd put herself through in order to end up in a white blouse, gray pants and a pair of flat-heeled black shoes. She waved a hand—airily, she hoped. "Well. Come on in." She stepped back and he stepped forward. She closed the door behind him.

"Can I take your jacket?" He was still wearing the gorgeous gray silk suit he'd been wearing earlier, when he disappeared into his office with Anthony Jarvis—and why was it, she wanted to know, that he had to look so splendid in gray? *She* ought to look that good in gray. She certainly had enough of it.

"Great." He slid the jacket off and handed it to her. She hung it in the small closet next to her front door, breathing a tiny sigh of relief once she got it on the hanger and in the closet. She wasn't visibly shaking, thank God. But inside, every atom seemed to be quivering. It would have been all too easy to fumble and drop it.

"This way." She led him out of her small entrance hall and into the living room of her suite—which was a full apartment, complete with kitchen, loft office above the living area, and a bath for each of the two bedrooms.

He looked around him, at her wine-red sofa and buff-colored easy chairs strewn with a number of big pillows in bold prints.

At first, her apartment had been pretty much hotel-issue. It was furnished when she moved in and she lived in it as it was—no hardship, as accommodations at High Sierra were of the best quality. But over time, she'd made her own choices and substituted things she found herself for what the resort had originally provided. Just last year she'd done the living area walls over in sponge-mottled mustard and olive. And she'd bought an old low plank-topped table, had it refinished, and now used it for a coffee table. Her rooms, she realized at that moment, had a lot more variety and visual interest than her wardrobe.

"Nice," he said.

Her smitten heart soared at that monosyllable of a compliment. "Thank you. Uh. Drink?"

"I'll pass." He stood a few feet from one of the easy chairs, waiting for her to tell him why she'd insisted he come here.

"Okay. Well. Have a seat, why don't you?"

He moved in front of the chair and sat down. She perched across from him, on the edge of the red sofa, behind her attractively refinished plank coffee table.

"Well," she said, and smoothed the knees of the gray silk pants it had taken her over an hour to choose. "Okay..."

He waited.

She found she was gnawing the inside of her lip and made herself stop. "I..." she began. But that was all that would come out.

Her whole body felt numb. Numb and too hot and yet shivery at the same time. There was a ringing in her ears, her heart was beating so hard.

She could not do this.

She did not know how to do this.

Aaron leaned forward, his brow furrowed, that

wonderful angular face a portrait of honest concern. "Celia. Please."

She tried again. And the same thing happened. She managed, "I…" and that was all.

"Look," he said carefully. "Whatever's bothering you, whatever's…come up in your life, I'm sure we can work through it. That we can find a way to deal with it. We've been together for long enough now. You should know that you can trust me, can…come to me, if there's a problem."

"I…well, I…"

"You do know that, don't you? That you can come to me?"

"I…yes, well, um…" She swallowed.

"Damn it, Celia." He stood, stuck his hands in his pockets, turned and paced the width of the room, then spun on his heel and paced back again. He stopped in front of her. "What the hell is the matter? Are you sick, is that it? Or…well, just tell me. Are you pregnant?"

She stared up at him, stunned. "Uh. Pregnant?"

"Well. Are you? And I'll tell you right now, if you are, it's okay with me. If you want to keep your job with me, you've got it. I'm not going to get rid of you just because there's a baby on the way. If you think you can handle a child and your job, I'll take your word for it. Because I know your word is good."

"Aaron."

"If that's what you want, I mean. You know what your job entails, the kind of demands that I put on you. You know what you can handle, don't you?"

"Aaron."

"Don't you?"

"Yes, but—"

"But what?"

"Aaron, I'm not."

"Not?"

"Right. Not—"

"Sick?"

"Right."

"Pregnant?"

"Yes...I mean, no. I'm not pregnant, either."

"Well." He stepped back. "All right." He looked at her sideways. "Your parents, then? Is that it?"

"It?"

"Are your parents the problem?"

"No."

"Not your parents..."

"No, they're fine. Retired. Taking it easy."

"In Phoenix."

Her heart lifted. "You remembered."

"What I mean is, they're getting older, right? You have to start spending more time with them. They need to feel they can count on you...."

"No. I told you. They're fine. Both healthy. So far..."

"Fine? Healthy?"

"Yes."

He threw up both hands. "Then, Celia, what?"

"Aaron..."

"Yeah?"

"Aaron, I..."

"Damn it, *what?*"

"Aaron, I love you. I'm sorry, I can't help myself. I love you. I do."

Chapter Six

Aaron backed up until he reached his chair again. Very carefully, he lowered himself into it.

Right then, he stiffened. Celia recognized the expression. He had his cell phone on Silent Page and it had just vibrated.

"It's all right," she said. "Go ahead and answer it."

He pulled the phone from his pocket, glanced at the display, then answered, "What?" He listened, nodded. "Okay... No... Great. Do it now...." He spoke into the phone, but those blue eyes were focused on her.

What she saw in those eyes wasn't good. Her declaration had come as a very big surprise. And not a welcome one.

"All right," he said to whoever was on the other end of the line. "Fine." Then he flipped the phone shut and stuck it back in the pocket of his shirt. He shook his head. "Sorry."

"No problem," she said, because it wasn't—not the phone call anyway.

The rest of it, her asking him to come here to her private rooms, her confession of love, the look on his face right then—well, for all that, *problem* was way too small a word.

And what now?

She stared at him and he stared at her and neither of them seemed to know what to do or say next.

Correction.

She did know one thing.

She knew she would go around the bend if she continued just sitting there. She shot from the couch like a sprung rubber band—then hovered at the edge of the coffee table, stuck on the verge of taking a step.

"Oh, God," she whispered miserably. She looked down at herself, wondered what she was doing standing up. She wasn't going anywhere. She sank to the cushions again.

Aaron said, oh-so-cautiously, "Celia. What can I tell you? I...didn't have a clue."

She could barely contain her own nervous energy, had to fold her hands tightly to keep them from fiddling with the hem of her boring white shirt. "Yes. I can see that."

"I honestly don't know what to say."

"Right. That's pretty obvious, too."

Another bleak and yawning silence followed.

She was the one who broke it, her voice, out of nowhere surprisingly calm. "You know, I've never seen you look terrified before."

He made a low sound in his throat. "That's ridiculous. I'm not terrified."

A small, dry laugh escaped her. "Oh, yes you are."

"No." He shifted in the chair. "No, that's not true."

She opened her mouth to argue some more, then shut it without letting anything get out. He looked pretty scared to her, but if he didn't want to admit it, that was certainly his right.

And maybe she was reading him all wrong, anyway. After all, he'd yet to actually *say* he wasn't interested.

"Aaron. Please. I just want to know if, well, I mean, if there's any possibility that you might—"

He put up a hand, a warding-off kind of gesture. "Celia," he said. It was enough, just her name. The way he said it, so carefully, so…uncomfortably, told her everything she needed to know, though he still had yet to actually put it in words. "I'm flattered, I am. But I'm not what someone like you should be looking for."

"Someone like me?"

"Yes. Someone like you. And that's a compliment."

"A compliment."

"Yes. You are stable and smart, with both feet on the ground. Someone like you deserves the very best in a man."

Oh, why wouldn't he just say it? "Aaron."

"What?"

"In other words, you're not interested."

"Celia—"

"Just say it. Please. Just say it right now."

"Celia..."

"No, listen."

"All right. What?"

"You are not doing me any favor by not saying it."

He let out a long breath. "Okay. I'm not interested."

She'd thought things had gotten as bad as they could get. But somehow, hearing him say it out loud managed to make it all even worse.

And why was she just sitting there? She couldn't bear that, to just sit there.

She shot to a standing position again—which didn't help anything. Oh, she was the biggest fool in all of Las Vegas. And that was saying something, because Las Vegas, everyone knew, was chock full of fools who gambled everything they had—and ended up busted.

As Celia Tuttle was right now.

She started to sit—again—and then stopped herself. It was too ridiculous, to keep popping up and down like that. She was not going to do that anymore. She remained standing, head high, shoulders back.

She really could not fault him, she realized through her own misery, for the way he was handling this. She could see the concern in his eyes, mingled with something else...what was it?

Ah, yes. Embarrassment.

He hated being put in this position, he'd rather be anywhere but here. Still, he hadn't gotten up and walked out. He didn't want to hurt her any more than she was already hurting.

To her tender heart, that was just one more proof of his basic loveableness—that he could be so very, very *sweet* about this, in of spite how agonizingly awful it all was.

"Aaron, I am so sorry." She took a step toward him, but he stiffened, a tiny movement that nonetheless spoke of pure dread. She put out both hands in a placating gesture. "Don't worry. I won't…come near you." He opened his mouth to say something, but she couldn't let him. Not until she'd made some kind of attempt to explain herself. "Oh, I do hate that I did this, that I put you on the spot like this. I just…well, I didn't know what else to do. I've been so miserable, since I realized that I…" She didn't finish. How could she, with him staring at her as though the only thing he wanted was out of that room?

She closed her eyes, sucked in a breath and let it out in a rush. "Oh, why am I telling you this?" She hung her head. "You poor man. You obviously don't need to hear it."

"Celia." His concern for her must have overcome his dread that she might physically throw herself on him. He rose again and took a step toward her. "It's okay. Honestly."

How could he say that? "No." She looked up and glared at him. "It is not, in any way, okay."

He froze where he was.

She felt about an inch high. "Oh, look at me. This is terrible. Now I'm snapping at you. Please. Forgive me."

"Of course."

She managed a grim smile. "I may be acting like an insane person. But I promise, I honestly do realize that this is not your fault."

"Well," he said gently. "That's something."

She didn't know what to say next.

Apparently, neither did he.

The silence stretched out, a great, gaping hole of it. They stared at each other, both of them just standing there, about four feet apart in the middle of her living room.

At last, she said, "All right. I'll tell you what. Tomorrow morning, you'll have my formal resignation."

He frowned. "Why?"

She was certain she hadn't heard him right. "Huh?"

"I said, why? Do you want to quit working for me?"

"Well. That's hardly the question."

"Sure it is. Do you?"

"Well, come on. I mean, this changes everything, don't you think?"

"Not necessarily."

What was it about men? They could be so thick-headed sometimes. "Aaron. Come on. Do you honestly think it's going to be possible for us to go on working together now, after this?"

"It's certainly possible for me." He looked at her levelly. "How about you? Do you *want* to turn in your resignation now, is that it?"

"Well, wouldn't that be for the best?"

"From my point of view, no, not at all. I'd rather you didn't."

"You would?"

"That's right. We have a hell of a fine working relationship. I don't want to lose that if I don't have to. You can always hand in a letter of resignation later. But give it a while, why don't you? See how you feel, now your big secret is out?"

How she felt, right that moment, was vaguely insulted. "'My big secret'? You make it sound like a joke."

"Celia. Honestly. That's not my intention. I'm just saying, give it a chance. Maybe it won't work. Maybe you'll be unhappy and I'll be uncomfortable and we'll both end up admitting we'd be better off if you went elsewhere. But for right now, you like your job, right?" She didn't answer immediately, so he prodded, "Well, do you?"

"Yes. I do. Very much."

"Good. You like your job and I like the way you do your job. Why turn our backs on that unless we absolutely have to?"

Was he right? Could it work? "You're saying we'll more or less pretend this conversation never happened? We'll try to go on as we were before?"

"Exactly."

"Do you really believe that's possible?"

"I wouldn't suggest it if I didn't."

She tipped her head to the side and studied him through narrowed eyes. "I just don't know...."

"Sure you do. You give it a try. If after a few weeks, you find you're unhappy, you give your notice. Simple as that."

Chapter Seven

Five minutes later, Aaron stood in the hall outside Celia's rooms shaking his head.

She thought she was in love with him.

He couldn't believe it. Smart, cool-headed Celia Tuttle had more sense than that. He was sure she'd get over it—and soon, he hoped. Pulling his phone from his pocket, he headed for the elevators.

By the time he reached the ground floor, he'd made two calls, one to Tony Jarvis concerning a small point that had been nagging him about that New Jersey casino, the other to the manager who had called him while he was in Celia's rooms. Tony answered Aaron's question, and the manager reported that his problem had been solved.

The mirrored elevator doors parted. Aaron stuck

the phone back in his pocket and stepped out into the greedy heart of High Sierra, her 110,000-square-foot casino.

Aaron liked to walk the floor. He found it soothing. He liked the sounds he heard there—the electronic ringing of slot machines, the clink of coins cascading into chrome trays, even the occasional triumphant cry of some lucky sucker who had managed, for once, to buck the odds and beat the house. He liked to see things running smoothly. And he knew that the dealers and pit bosses, the stickmen and floor managers, the cocktail waitresses and change girls all worked a little harder and played things just a little straighter because the chairman of the board and CEO of Silver Standard Resorts lived on-site. They knew that there was no telling when he might decide to come down from his tower office or his penthouse suite and wander among them—and they modified their behavior accordingly.

Silver Standard had a reputation as a company that promoted for talent and performance, that *juice*—the old Wise-Guy word for influence—didn't mean near as much when you worked at High Sierra as it did at a lot of the other casino/hotels along the strip. It was still Las Vegas and who you knew mattered. But in Aaron's book, *what* you knew and how good you were at what you did counted, too.

He'd grown up around gaming. There was always a card game going on in the back room of the High-grade. His mother ran her own small-time version of keno, and slots lined the walls. Aaron and his brothers had never had much of what most people thought of as a family life. But all three of them could spot a con a mile away. And they knew most of the thousands of ways to cheat.

That night, Aaron stood near one of the roulette tables and watched a couple of idiots try one of the oldest scams in the book. The first guy—the decoy— placed a late bet, distracting the dealer, so his buddy could lay down his cash *after* the roulette ball had fallen onto the winning number. The cheat was so common, it even had a name: past-posting—and the cash itself was another dead giveaway, since most gamblers bet with casino checks.

The dealer had blown it, allowing herself to be taken in by the decoy, giving him her attention as she explained that it was too late for him to bet. But the eye in the sky—the security cameras located all over the casino—recorded everything. And the "mucker," who helped the dealer clear the table of losing bets, was on the job. He saw the second man past-post his bet. The pit boss appeared with a couple of security guards. The two would-be scam artists were escorted from the table with a minimum of fuss.

Aaron moved on, spent some time watching the blackjack tables, and then observing the action at craps, which everyone knew was the true gamblers' game, fast and exciting, not for the shy or faint of heart.

He spotted his cousin, Jonas Bravo, the famous Bravo Billionaire, rolling dice, his sexy blond wife, Emma, at his side. The Bravo Billionaire gambled for relaxation. He kept five hundred thousand on deposit in High Sierra's cage. And Aaron knew for a fact that he kept similar deposits at most of the other major resort/casinos on the strip.

Aaron knew a lot about his wealthy, powerful cousin. And he had no doubt that his cousin knew about him. But they never spoke. Aaron's father, after all, had been Blake Bravo, the blacker-than-black sheep of the Los Angeles Bravos, a man who had done murder and worse. The connection between the two branches of the family had been severed before either Aaron or Jonas was born.

Aaron watched, keeping well back, as the cousin he'd never met placed bets and won more than he lost. His pretty wife laughed and clapped her hands every time Jonas added to the stacks of checks in front of him, occasionally blowing an errant platinum curl out of her shining eyes.

Aaron should have moved on long before he did. But he found the sight intriguing. His cousin and his cousin's wife. Married for—what? About six months now, according to the scandal sheets. And happy together. Now and then, they'd glance at each other. Heat would arc. And more than heat. Affection, too. Yeah. A blind man could see there was a real bond between the Bravo Billionaire and his blond bombshell of a wife.

Celia came to mind—which was logical, given what had transpired in her rooms less than an hour ago. Clearly Celia wanted a Jonas-and-Emma-Bravo kind of bond in her life. She was a good woman, one who certainly deserved to get what she wanted. He probably should have let her quit, let her find another job—and another man to pin her hopes on. Too bad a good secretary was so damned hard to find.

Also too bad that the Bravo Billionaire's wife had spotted him. He'd spaced off for a second or two there, on the subject of Celia. And now Emma Bravo was staring right at him, those shining eyes wide, her lush mouth a round *O*. She grabbed her husband by the arm and whispered something in his ear.

Aaron faded backward, turning and striding off, disappearing into the crowd, eliminating the possibility that he and his long-lost cousin might actually make eye contact. Aaron didn't need contact of any kind with Jonas, or any other estranged Bravo relatives. He had enough trouble with the Bravos he already knew—his two brothers and his wild-hearted, short-tempered, heavy-handed mother.

The phone in his pocket started vibrating as he entered the Forty-Niner, the smallest of High Sierra's six bars. He sat down at the end of the bar, signaling the bartender for his usual. Then he pulled the phone out and answered it without pausing to check the caller ID display.

Big mistake.

"Hello, my darlin' boy." Speak of the devil, as they say. "How come you never call your poor old mother?" Caitlin Bravo had a voice like no other. Rough and low, a voice that spoke of smoky rooms and strong whiskey and the risky temptations of bold games of chance.

"Did I give you this number?"

"Aaron. Don't get smart with me."

"What do you want, Ma?"

"I told you. A phone call. A visit. I miss your bad attitude and your sweet, handsome face."

The bartender set his drink in front of him. Aaron laid down a generous tip. "Is there some kind of problem?"

"Yeah. I never see my boys. Cade hasn't been around for a couple of weeks now. He's supposed to be moving back to town—did you hear?"

Aaron sipped his whiskey. "He bought that place next to the old Elliott house, right?"

"That's right. He's been fixin' it up, or so I've heard. But I haven't seen him. And you know Will. Off in Sacramento all the time, doing whatever lawyers do in their fancy suits. And then there's you, Mr. Las Vegas, Mr. Chairman of the Board. Damn it, I miss you. I truly do."

Aaron had a pretty good idea of what had inspired this excess of motherly feeling. He'd bet and bet large that Caitlin's latest boyfriend, a Nordic type, younger than Aaron, with muscles on his muscles and shoulder-length blond hair, had moved on. "What happened to Hans?"

"Nothing lasts forever, my darlin', and you know it, too. Come home. I'll wish you a happy birthday in person." She'd remembered. His birthday was that Friday. "I'll bake you a cake."

"When did you ever bake a cake?"

"So I've been known to exaggerate." He could hear the shrug in her voice. "There's a new bakery around the corner. I'll give them a call. Have them send one over, with your name on it and thirty-five birthday candles." Her tone turned wheedling.

"Come on. Come home. Blow out your candles, do my taxes...."

Aaron said nothing. He didn't like what he'd just heard.

"Yoo-hoo, you still there, birthday boy?"

"Ma. What happened to the accountant I found for you?"

"A stranger from California—and Modesto, at that? You know very well that I couldn't trust him."

"He was a damn good man."

"Look. When it comes to my money, I don't want a hired gun. I want my own flesh and blood on it, you know that."

"Caitlin, I have a corporation to run. I don't have time anymore to personally fill out your Schedule C."

"Come home. This weekend. It's two days. You can spare it."

"I'll see what I can do."

"I know what that means. Something will come up, you just haven't decided what yet."

So okay, she did know him better than he often gave her credit for. "Maybe. In a week or two."

"No maybes. You come here this weekend, or I come there."

That did it. Every time she showed up at High Sierra, she drove him absolutely nuts. She couldn't just yank the one-armed bandit and get in a little shopping the way any normal fifty-four-year old woman on a visit to Vegas would do. She had to walk the floor, hang over the shoulders of his dealers and his boxmen, barge into his office every few hours with endless criticisms of the way things were run and detailed advice as to how he could make it all better.

"Aaron? You still there?"

"I'm here."

"Well?"

He could hear it in that whiskey voice of hers. She knew she had him.

"All right, all right. I'll fly up Friday night. And you said it—only for a day or two."

"Thank you, my darlin'," she replied, oh-so-sweetly. "See you then."

Aaron put his phone in his pocket, finished his drink and signaled for one more. He was halfway through that second whiskey when he decided he'd ask Celia to go with him on Friday. After all, New Venice was her hometown, too. She could see her friend, Jane.

Also, Celia *was* a CPA. When Caitlin started in on him again about doing her taxes, he could put Celia on it. He could point out that he trusted Celia implicitly—which he did—and that she was, after all, a hometown girl. Not Caitlin's flesh and blood, admittedly, but almost as good.

Yeah, okay. His mother wasn't all that easy to deal with. She'd probably drive Celia as nuts as she drove him. Celia would find herself wondering how she ever could have thought herself in love with someone who had a mother like that.

And what was wrong with that?

Not a damn thing.

Celia needed to get over him and if his overbearing, loudmouthed mother helped her do that, well, great.

Everybody wins.

He brought up the weekend the next morning, when she came in his office to go over the calendar.

"Celia, about this weekend…"

"What about it?" Her tone was pleasant and professional. He watched her settle into one of the chairs opposite his desk and fiddle with her little tape recorder.

She definitely looked better. More relaxed. Not so stressed out as she had in the past couple of weeks. The dark circles he'd noticed under her eyes last night had faded to faint smudges this morning. Her pale cheeks looked pinker. There was a bloom on her skin.

Apparently, he thought wryly, getting her grand passion for him off her chest had been good for her. "You know, you look great today."

"Thank you."

Aaron was right.

Celia *was* feeling better.

She'd laid her deep secret on him. He'd turned her down. It had hurt. She'd been terribly embarrassed.

But the world hadn't ended.

Yes, she still loved him. However, he didn't love her and he'd told her straight out that there was no chance he ever would. She could accept that. Now, she'd decided over the light meal of broiled chicken and Caesar salad she'd fixed for herself after he'd left her rooms, she could start getting over him.

She'd cleared off her bed and hung her clothes back in her closet and turned in around ten. And for the first time in several days, she had slept through the night.

Celia set the tape recorder on the edge of the wide glass desk, then sat back in her chair, resting her elbows on the arms and folding her hands lightly over the legal pad that waited in her lap. She gave her boss a bright, attentive smile to show him she was listening to whatever it was he had to say to her. "Okay, now. About the weekend?"

"Ah," he said. "Yes. I have to fly home Friday. I'll return Sunday. I'd like you to come with me, if that will work for you."

An absurd little thrill shivered through her. He wanted her with him for the weekend! Now, wasn't that wonderful?

But almost as fast as it went zinging through her, the thrill faded.

She reminded herself of what he'd said last night. He wasn't interested in her romantically—and there was no chance he would *get* interested.

So why, all of a sudden, did he want to take her home with him?

"Is Silver Standard scouting properties in New Venice now?"

"Scouting properties?" he repeated, sounding way too vague for her peace of mind. "No. This will be a personal visit."

She pondered that information. "A personal visit…"

He leaned back in his chair and regarded her through hooded eyes. "Is there a problem? I thought you'd be pleased at the idea of a trip home."

She almost smiled. Men. You told them you loved them and they suddenly thought you had *sucker* scrawled across your forehead. "Your mother called, right?"

That deep blue gaze slid away. All of a sudden, something really interesting was happening on his computer screen.

She waited while he typed a series of commands and did the point-and-click shuffle with the mouse. And then he decided he had a call to make, one that just couldn't wait.

"Give me a moment?"

"Of course."

He picked up the phone on his desk and punched up a number from auto-dial. When the other party answered, he fired off a series of quick questions and brief commands. "Fine," he said in conclusion. "All right. See to it." He dropped the receiver back into its cradle and resumed pointing and clicking with the computer mouse. "Hm," he said. "Ah." Finally, he faced her. "Celia."

She lifted an eyebrow to show him that he had her full attention.

He grunted. "There's no doubt about it."

"Yes?"

"You know too much."

She grinned. "I do, don't I? What did she want?"

"To see me."

"Any special reason?"

"My birthday's coming."

She already knew that, of course. She'd bought him a silver money clip engraved with his initials back in

January when she'd made the rounds of the after-holiday sales. Since she'd started working for him, she'd always bought him small, thoughtful gifts for birthdays and at Christmas—a pair of cufflinks, a tie that matched his eyes. She knew he liked the things she chose because he wore them—or used them, as the case might be. In return, he gave her bonuses on her birthday and at Christmas. Big ones, which she very much appreciated.

He added, grudgingly, "She's ordering a cake, evidently. With thirty-five candles and Happy Birthday, Aaron, in fancy lettering across the top."

Celia tipped her head to the side. "Hm," she said, nodding, giving him her most patient smile.

"Damn it. All right. Tax time's coming up again."

Ah, thought Celia, we approach the truth at last. "How could I have forgotten?" Every year, getting Caitlin's taxes done was a problem. She wanted them done by someone she trusted. She trusted three people: Aaron, Will and Cade Bravo. Since Aaron was the one with the degree in finance, she inevitably hounded him to do the honors. "But I thought you finally found someone for her."

"Apparently, she fired him."

"So she's after you again?"

"Right."

"But what has that got to do with…" In mid-sentence, the light dawned. "Oh. Aaron," she groaned. "No."

"Help me out here, Celia. Please?"

She should have refused. Right then. Her job description had a lot of leeway in it, but even a personal assistant who had to be ready for just about anything couldn't be expected to do her boss's mother's taxes.

But her ''no'' got stuck in her throat. He just looked so pitiful. ''Listen,'' she said, reasoning with him when she knew that she ought to be holding her ground with an unequivocal no. ''If she wasn't satisfied with the CPA you hired last year, she's not going to be satisfied with me.''

''She might. You *are* an accountant.''

''I was. But I hated it. That's why I'm not an accountant anymore.''

''But you can do the work.''

''I was in audit, you know that. Never the tax department.''

''You're as qualified to do it as I am—hell. More so.''

''No, I'm not. Let's face facts here. Only *you* are qualified because *you* are her son.''

''Will you just come with me? Let's just give it a try.''

The problem was, when he looked at her like that, so hopefully, so...vulnerable, it was way too easy to forget how she intended to get over him. Way too easy to imagine what a trip home with him might be like, hanging with him at the Highgrade, getting to know his crazy mother, who, whatever anyone said about her, was always very entertaining.

And worst of all, when he looked at her like that, she couldn't help but start imagining that there might be hope for the two of them, in spite of what he'd said last night. That maybe, subconsciously, he was interested in her, after all.

And he knew it, damn him. He was using her own heart against her, the rat.

She spoke in a pleasant tone, but she said what she was thinking. "This is really low of you, Aaron, you know that?"

He met her eyes straight on then, didn't hide behind his computer or his telephone. And he had the grace to look faintly—and also oh-so-attractively—ashamed of himself. "What can I say? I'm a desperate man."

"I should refuse to do this."

He gave her a thoroughly heart-stopping hopeful grin. "Was that a yes I just heard?"

She glared at him.

"Please, Celia. Just give this a try. If anyone can handle my mother, I have a feeling you're the one."

"Wonderful. And if I *can't* handle her?"

"If it doesn't work out and you find she drives you as insane as she makes me, just say so. Believe me, I'll understand."

"You'll pull me off it if I say I want off?"

He winced. "I'm hoping that won't happen, but if it does, just speak up and you're off it. You have my word."

The problem was, she'd started thinking, *Why not?* She had no desire to go back to accounting work full-time, but she did have the skills and she might as well use them.

And, okay, she had to admit, it was lovely to have him look at her so *hopefully*. If she said yes, he'd be grateful.

Now, *that* would be pleasing....

He was waiting for an answer. She said, "I shouldn't…"

"That *is* a yes. Admit it."

"There are conditions."

"Name them."

"I'll prepare your mother's taxes. But I won't take payment—and don't give me that look. If I take payment, I have to sign as the preparer and that makes me liable. I don't want that, Aaron."

He nodded. "Yes. Of course. I understand."

"You'll have to go over my work and approve it, so maybe you'd be better off to just find another CPA with a tax background to do the job—or give in and do it yourself."

"No—to both suggestions. Just give my way a try. You deal with her, getting everything together. Frankly, that's where the real headaches come in for me. Then you do the math and fill out the forms. I'll check your figures—which should make Caitlin happy, that I'm on the case. And then she can sign the damn thing herself."

It sounded reasonable enough. "All right, then."

"Terrific." He was beaming.

She felt warm all over, to have that smile focused on her. Still, she made the effort to keep her tone all business. "What time are we leaving?"

"Barring some unforeseen crisis here, we'll leave High Sierra around five. I'll be flying the Cessna." Aaron owned his own small plane and the Comstock Valley had a tiny, two-runway airstrip. "We should be there by seven, easy, if the weather cooperates. I like that place you found for me last time. See if you can book us in there.''

''The New Venice Inn?''

''Was that it? Fine. Get me the same room as before, if you can. It had a nice big desk in it, and extra phone lines.''

Caitlin had a large, rambling apartment over the Highgrade. But Aaron never stayed with her when he visited. He'd told Celia once that he'd lived with his mother for eighteen full years and that was more than enough for any man.

''And I promise,'' Aaron said, ''that you'll have time to yourself, to be with your friends. So give them a call. Let them know you're coming.''

''Yes, I'll call Jane.'' And Jane would keep after her until she told her all about last night….

Aaron was still giving instructions. ''We'll talk to Caitlin Friday night. Saturday you can get her going on collecting her records for you. Sunday will be all yours. I'll fly out Sunday morning. You can stay over till Monday or Tuesday to finish up with Caitlin, then take a commercial flight home.''

''All right.''

''Celia,'' he said. ''I won't forget you did this for me.''

Her heart started fluttering. *Down girl,* she thought. She warned, ''Just because you've talked me into this doesn't mean your mother is going to go along with it.''

He frowned. ''Shall we get to work, then?''

She got the message: the subject of Caitlin and her taxes was, at least for the time being, closed.

* * *

Celia called Jane that night to say she'd be in New Venice that weekend. "I'll be in Friday. Aaron will need me that evening, and at least some of Saturday. It looks pretty likely that I'll get Saturday evening off. And Sunday should be all mine."

There was a significant silence from the other end of the line.

"Jane? Hull-o."

"I'm here."

"Well. Are you free Sunday?"

"Sure. Are you going to tell me what's going on?"

"About…?"

"I really hate it when you make me bully you to get you to tell me what you know you really *want* to tell me in the first place."

Celia blew out a breath. "Oh, all right."

"So?"

"I told him I love him."

"Omigod. You're serious?"

"You think I would joke about such a thing?"

"No. No, of course not." Jane cleared her throat. "So. You did it. Great. And?"

"He's not interested."

Jane was silent again—but not for long. She let out a small groan. "Oh, Ceil… He said that?"

"Yeah. He tried to be kind. Truly. He was very sweet and very considerate. But in the end, he told me he's not interested and there's no hope he *will* be interested."

"Well," said Jane. Celia thoroughly understood. What else *was* there to say? "And you're still working for him?"

"I volunteered to resign. He convinced me not to—for a while, anyway. We'll see how it goes. And Janey, I'm okay with it. I am. I feel a lot better, having it out there, you know? You were right. Honesty is the best policy."

"Well, of course it is. It's good. A good thing, for you, that you told him. No matter what his response was. And I just have to tell you I am so proud of you."

"Thanks."

"I mean it, Ceil. Congratulations."

"Janey?"

"Yeah?"

"Let's not carry this *too* far. I said I'm okay and I meant it. Congratulations, however, are not in order."

"You're right. Of course you are. So. You'll be home this weekend and I get you Sunday, at least."

"That's right."

"We'll talk more about this then."

"Whatever."

"Celia, are you sure you're okay?"

"Yes, I am. I'm not jumping up and down for joy. But I'm dealing with it. I honestly am."

About ten minutes after she said goodbye to Jane, Jillian called.

Jillian was talking almost before Celia could get the phone to her ear. "Jane just called me."

"What a surprise."

"I am so pleased with this."

"You're pleased."

"You bet."

"And why is that?"

"Because the cards are on the table. Now let him stare at them for a while."

"Jilly, it was a no he gave me. A very clear no. You've heard that word, haven't you? It's the opposite of yes."

"Right, sure. And then he asked you not to quit working for him. If he wasn't interested, that never would have happened. He would have fallen all over himself waving goodbye the minute you offered to resign."

The problem was, that sounded kind of good. Way too good, really. "Jillian. He said no."

"You're not listening. Yes, he said no. And then he begged you not to quit—*and* asked you to fly home with him for the weekend. He—"

"Jilly."

"What?"

"The reason he doesn't want me to quit is that I'm about the best there is at what I do. He knows replacing me won't be easy. I perform all the services of a corporate wife, with none of the messy complications that come with intimacy and sex. I buy great gifts for his girlfriends, I'm a whiz in Word, Excel, Quicken—you name it. I type eighty words a minute and when I take a meeting, I've got my ears open and my mouth firmly shut."

"Well, at least you know your own value in a professional sense."

"I certainly do. As for the other—his taking me home with him—it's nothing romantic."

"How do you know that?"

"I know because he had a bona fide non-romantic reason for asking me to go with him."

"And that is?"

"He needs me to do his mother's taxes."

"Oh, come on."

"It's true. I swear to you. Caitlin drives him crazy every year at tax time."

"But—"

"Jilly, don't make me go into detail about this. There's nothing about it that you really need to know, except I'll be helping out with Caitlin Bravo's taxes and I'm flying home with Aaron this weekend to get started on them."

"All right, all right. You win. It's not romantic."

"Thank you."

"Janey says you're spending Sunday with her."

"That's right."

"I'll be there, too."

"I'd love to see you—and I know that tone of voice. What are you planning?"

"Planning?" Jillian faked guilelessness for all she was worth. "I'm not planning anything. I'll be in New Venice, at Jane's, this weekend. I'm speaking at her bookstore Friday night. 'The New Romantics and the New Millennium.' I'll do hot clothing looks for spring—and relationships, too. Clothes and men. I figure that about covers it."

"I like it—but you *are* planning something. I can hear it in your voice."

"I'll tell you Sunday."

"Jilly—"

"Sunday. I promise. Gotta go now, see you soon."

Chapter Eight

Aaron landed his single engine Turbo Stationair at the Comstock Valley airstrip at a little before seven on Friday night. Celia had booked a rental car. It was waiting for them when they got there. They tossed their suitcases in the trunk and Aaron slid behind the wheel.

His phone rang as he was starting up the car. He looked at the display before he answered it. "It's Caitlin," he said to Celia. "Checking up on me." He spoke into the phone. "What?" He listened, then answered, "Yeah. I'm here. At the airstrip… Yeah, fifteen minutes, tops."

He hung up and they headed for New Venice, a short ride across the valley floor, with the gorgeous, white-capped mountains looming proud above them.

He drove straight to Main Street, which Celia thought looked as homey and welcoming as ever, with its old-fashioned Victorian-style streetlamps and flat-topped two-story buildings, some of brick and some of weathered clapboard. The locust and maple trees that lined the street were still winter-bare, but even in the darkness, Celia could see the bumps along the naked branches that signified spring leaves on the way.

The beauty shop and the post office, the grocery and hardware stores were all closed for the night. But the lights were on at Silver Unicorn Books. Celia smiled to herself. This was Jilly's night: "The New Romantics and the New Millennium."

Aaron turned into the alley between the bookstore and the large white clapboard building that housed the Highgrade Saloon and Café. The parking lot in back was packed, except for a couple of spaces near the door, which were marked, very clearly, Reserved.

Aaron pulled into one of those. The car to the left of them was a handsome, sporty-looking Mercedes, and to the right a dusty celadon-green Porsche. "Looks like Will and Cade are here," he said.

"To wish you a happy birthday?"

"It's a distinct possibility." He scowled. "I smell surprise party. What about you?"

She gave him a nod. "I'm afraid so."

He reached across her and opened her door, his arm brushing the front of her in the process. "There you go."

Celia suppressed a gasp. She could not move. Frantically, she told herself that it had been nothing, the briefest of touches. He didn't even seem to realize he'd done it. Yet, for her, it set off a chain reaction of sensation. Her pulse rocketed into high gear, her stomach went all fluttery and a flush of embarrassment burned on her cheeks. And not only that, her nipples reacted, drawing up instantly into hard little peaks.

"There you go." He seemed totally oblivious to her distress.

"Thank you." Her voice surprised her, it was so level and calm. She pulled her coat closer around her and got out of that car before he had a chance to notice what his slightest touch could do to her.

He was already out, shutting his door and striding toward the back entrance to the Highgrade. She hesitated for a moment, absently tucking her purse under her arm, hugging her coat around her against the cold northern Nevada night, feeling lost and strange and thoroughly out of her depth.

He paused, turned and glanced back at her, lifting an eyebrow.

He wore one of his beautiful silk suits, a black coat of softest cashmere thrown over it, black calfskin shoes and black leather gloves. He should have looked out of place at the back door of his mother's clapboard saloon. But he didn't. He stood tall and exuded confidence. He was every bit as much at home here as he was striding beneath the glittering lights of High Sierra's mammoth casino.

Her heart ached anew, just to look at him.

I'll get over it, she thought. I'll get over *him*.

"Celia?"

She shoved her own door shut and hustled to catch up with him. When she reached his side, he grabbed the big door handle and pulled the heavy door open, ushering her in ahead of him, letting the door swing shut behind him, which it did automatically with a slow, hydraulic sigh.

A long hallway paneled in knotty pine and lit by two widely spaced, bare ceiling bulbs confronted them, with shut doors at intervals along each side. Celia could hear the ping and clatter of pinball and slots, the whiz and whine of video games. And voices, down that hallway—faint, unrecognizable words, sudden bursts of laughter. She could also smell the smoky, greasy, savory scent of grilling burgers, mingled with the yeasty smell of beer. She hesitated, right there beyond the door.

"My guess is they're all lurking in the bar," Aaron said quietly from behind her. "Go to your right at the end of the hall."

He was quite close—closer than he needed to be, really. She could almost feel the warmth of him at her back.

She should have started walking down that hall.

Instead, she stayed where she was and sent him a glance over her shoulder. "I know where the bar is, Aaron. I grew up here, too, you know."

He didn't seem in any more of a hurry to move on than she was. One corner of his mouth curled lazily in a half-smile. "Oh, that's right. You did, didn't you?"

Was he teasing her? It almost seemed that way.

But why? Why would he do that?

They had an understanding, didn't they? They were going to continue their strictly professional relationship. They would go on as if that conversation in her rooms four nights ago had never taken place.

But it did *take place,* a wiser voice in the back of her mind whispered knowingly. *And we're kidding ourselves if we really think we can go back.*

"Then again," he added, still in that teasing tone, but with a slight edge creeping in, "you didn't really grow up *here,* the way I did. You lived a nice, stable *normal* life—in a real house, with brothers and sisters, a mom *and* a dad."

She turned and faced him fully. "Aaron. Is something the matter?"

He *was* looking at her strangely, his eyes very dark and deep—and shining. "Do you remember," he asked softly, the faint edge that might have been anger fading away again, "oh, you must have been about six or seven? You rode a bike onto Main. It was too big for you. You were struggling along, managing to stay upright. But then you lost it, went over sideways right out in front."

"Eight. I was eight…"

His mouth curled again, in that wonderful lazy half-smile. "You do remember."

"You came to my rescue."

"Let's put it this way, I gave you a hand." He chuckled, a lovely, deep, warm sound. "You didn't say a word. Your eyes were big as saucers. I was one of those crazy Bravo boys and you were terrified of me."

"Oh, I was not." Somehow, she'd sort of backed

up against the wall and he had moved in close. They were only inches apart. She could smell the exciting male scent of him, feel his body heat.

And it was…different…than a minute ago, different than when he'd brushed his arm across her breasts in the car. It was no longer nerve-racking or strange. Now, it seemed very natural to be standing here in the back hall of the Highgrade, flirting with Aaron Bravo.

Flirting? The word repeated itself in her head.

Was that what they were doing?

It sure did feel like it.

"Celia." He clucked his tongue. "Come on. Don't lie to me. You were scared of me."

"Well, all right," she heard herself admitting. "Maybe I was, just a little. But I—"

She didn't get to finish, because Caitlin Bravo's rich and husky contralto interrupted from the other end of the hall. "Aaron, what the hell are you up to back there?"

Aaron's grin changed, grew rueful. But he didn't stop looking right in Celia's eyes. "Go away, Ma. I'm busy."

"Who's that with you?"

Aaron let out a weary breath. "She's not going away," he told Celia in a whisper.

She nodded and whispered back, "You're right. She's not."

"Get on out here, the both of you," Caitlin commanded. She stood dead center at the end of the hall, hands fisted on her hips, the lights of the room behind her outlining her tall, stately figure, a figure that even now, in her fifties, remained shapely enough to turn heads. She wore black jeans so tight it was a wonder she could breathe in them, red cowboy boots and a red Western-style shirt splashed with black sequins that glittered and winked with each breath she took. A red bandana was tied around her neck.

Aaron gestured Celia on with a wave of a black-gloved hand. "After you."

"Gee, thanks."

He made no reply to that, but she could have sworn she heard him chuckle. Celia kept her shoulders back and her head up as she marched toward the raven-haired woman at the end of the hall.

"Ah," said Caitlin, as Celia moved beneath one of the overhead lights. "It's little Celia Tuttle. How are you, sweetie?"

"Just fine, thanks, Mrs.—"

"No." Caitlin put a red-tipped finger to her even redder lips. "You call me Caitlin. Mrs. Bravo sounds like somebody's wife." Caitlin's dark eyes narrowed. "I haven't been any man's wife for over thirty years now—at least not that I realized."

Folks said that the mysterious and long-gone Blake Bravo, the only man Caitlin had ever married, had been the great love of her life. Until recently, they'd all believed he had died years and years ago, leaving Caitlin a widow. But lately, it had come out in the national newspapers that Blake Bravo had lived a lot longer than anyone in New Venice had thought he did, that he had committed the kinds of crimes for which he should have got the gas chamber—or at the very least, been locked up for life. And that after he'd left Caitlin behind forever, he'd married another woman and given *her* a son.

So it didn't surprise Celia that Caitlin seemed pretty ambivalent about being called Mrs. Bravo.

The hall opened out into a big knotty-pine game room: slots, pinball machines and video games on every wall. Aaron and Celia paused there with Caitlin. The whole room was alive with the sounds of the games. On the left wall, by a wide doorway that led to the café and gift shop, stood a long cashier's desk and a big old-fashioned cash register.

A tall, skinny man in a pair of paint-spattered overalls glanced over from one of the pinball machines. "Hey."

"Hey." Aaron nodded in greeting.

The man went back to working his machine, which pinged and bonged with each punch of the buttons.

Caitlin turned for the bar. "Come on, birthday boy. Everyone's waiting to jump out and surprise you." She led them through a wide arch into the bar, which was darker than the game room. Beer signs and a couple of hooded lamps over the twin pool tables provided most of the light.

When Aaron walked beneath the arch, the dark room suddenly erupted with shouts and whistles and raucous catcalls.

Celia scooted to the side and out of the way. Aaron stood where he was, wearing his lazy half-smile, casually removing those black driving gloves. Caitlin headed straight to the battered piano on the far wall, where she slid onto the stool and started beating out

a lively rendition of the birthday song. Everyone—
and there were lots of people there—joined in.

The crowd parted as they reached the last line of
the song and a big freckle-faced woman with carrot-
colored hair worn in two thick braids tied with green
satin ribbons came marching toward Aaron. She carried a white sheet cake ablaze with candles. Celia
knew who she was: Bertha Slider. She'd been
Caitlin's right hand for as long as Celia could remember—some said since before Blake Bravo had faked
his own death in an apartment fire and disappeared
forever from the lives of Caitlin and his three sons.

They sang the last line extra loud. "Happy birthday, dear Aaron, Happy birthday to you." Everybody
shouted and stomped and clapped their hands.

Bertha stopped in front of Aaron. The candles
shone upward, lighting her face to a moon-white
glow. She smiled broadly, revealing small, wide-
spaced teeth. "Make a wish, now, then blow 'em
out."

He tipped his head to the side, frowned—and then
grinned again.

"Blow!" Bertha shouted.

It took him two breaths, but he blew them all out.

After that, he made the first cut. Then he held out
the knife. "Bertha. I think you'd better take over."

"Well, okay, I'll do that, honeybunch." She went
to work cutting up the cake and passing out slices to
all the guests.

Aaron's brothers approached, both tall and handsome: Will dressed in khakis and a cable-knit sweater,
Cade in worn denim with a jacket of soft suede. They

pounded him on the back and called him an old man. He said he wasn't so old he couldn't take on both of them if he had to.

Caitlin left the piano and joined her three sons. "Darlin'," she said to Aaron. "Aren't you hot in that coat?"

"Sure, Ma. A little."

"Hand it over."

He shrugged out of it and she turned for the coat rack in the corner—which was where Celia just happened to be standing.

"Come on, sweetie," said Caitlin. "You take off your coat, too. Stay a while...."

So Celia hung her coat on a hook already layered with other coats. As she turned from the rack, Caitlin reached out and draped an arm across her shoulders. "You have a drink, why don't you, baby doll?" Heady perfume teased Celia's nose—a little strong, yes, but also enticing. Something spicy, with more than a hint of musk.

Celia looked right into Caitlin's black eyes, felt the raw energy of the woman, the will and the strength.

Those dark fingernails squeezed Celia's shoulder. "Sweetie, you with me here?"

"Yes, Caitlin. I'm with you. And I'd love a beer."

"Well, good, then." Caitlin gave her shoulder another squeeze and turned her toward the crowd around the bar.

The party went on until two in the morning, when Caitlin ran everyone out and closed the bar for the night. By two forty-five, there were just the three of them: Caitlin, Aaron and Celia. Cade and Will, like Aaron, had found lodging elsewhere and had already retired to it.

But Aaron hung around, intent on broaching the subject of who would be doing Caitlin's taxes. Since Celia had her own part to play in this scheme, she stayed, too.

Caitlin perched on a barstool and leaned her elbow on the bar, resting her cheek on her fist. "Okay. I guess you're not sleepin' here, right?"

Aaron took the stool next to her. "Right." Just the slightest lift of a brow and Celia got the signal. She slid onto the stool on Caitlin's other side. "Celia booked us at the…" He leaned around his mother and gave Celia a questioning look.

She supplied the name. "The New Venice Inn."

Caitlin turned and looked at her. "Celia sweetie, you are a jewel." Those dark eyes were sparkling.

It occurred to Celia that Caitlin knew exactly what was happening here. She decided a modest smile was all that was required of her at that moment.

Caitlin turned back to her son again. "All right. No cons here, okay? Just lay it right on me."

Aaron said, "Celia's a CPA, did you know that, Ma?"

"Hmm," said Caitlin. She looked at Celia again. "That so?"

Celia nodded.

And Caitlin said, "Well, fine. You convinced me."

Aaron was the one who blinked. "I have?"

"Yep. She's a good girl and she's from town and I like the look of her."

"You do?"

"Yeah. And plus, I get the feeling she'll be a lot easier to get along with than you ever were."

"Well thanks, Ma."

"It's my taxes we're talkin' about here, right?"

"Er, right."

"Well, okay. Celia Tuttle can do my taxes. That's fine with me."

"She's up to something," Aaron said about fifteen minutes later, when they were back in the rental car and on the way to the New Venice Inn.

Celia refrained from rolling her eyes. "She's agreed to do things the way you want them done. What are you worried about?"

"It was too easy. I don't like it. You'll have to keep your eyes and ears open. Watch your back. Understand?"

"Sure. No problem." Celia stared out the windshield at the dark road ahead, thinking that there were times when he really did sound like some Mafia guy.

They reached the inn a few minutes later. It was a charming old Victorian house with lots of cute gables and gingerbread trim. Inside, it had been thoroughly renovated, with marble floors in the bathrooms and big, comfortable queen- and king-sized beds boasting lovely, firm pillow-top mattresses. Aaron had the Rose Suite, which was the largest guest room in the house, on the ground floor. Celia had booked herself a cozy attic room upstairs.

Aaron got their suitcases from the trunk and Celia went to the mailbox in back, where the innkeeper had told her he'd leave the keys. She let them in the back door.

Aaron's room was the first one to the right, near the back entrance. As Celia turned to secure the back door, he set his suitcase on the floor and draped his garment bag over it.

Celia handed him his key. "Here you go." She spoke softly, in order not to disturb any sleeping guests. She already had her little overnighter in one hand. All she needed was the suitcase he had carried in for her. "Thanks for bringing that in. I'll take it now." She reached for it.

He moved it slightly out of her range and whispered, "You're upstairs, you said?"

"That's right."

"I'll carry this up for you."

"Aaron, it's not necessary."

"I don't mind." He turned for the staircase at the front of the long hall that ran through the center of the house.

She watched him walk away from her, wondering what in the world was going on with him—the way he'd flirted with her at the back door of the High-grade. And now, carrying her bag to her room when it wasn't that heavy and there was absolutely no reason she couldn't carry it herself.

He *was* acting strangely.

Tonight, more than once, she'd felt distinctly *not* like his girl Friday and very much like an attractive woman who had caught his interest—his *romantic* interest.

Could it be that Jilly was on to something—that he

really *was* interested, though at first he hadn't let himself admit it?

Aaron must have realized she was still hovering by the door to his room, staring dazedly after him. He paused and glanced back at her. "Are you coming?"

She hurried to catch up.

Chapter Nine

Aaron could hear her soft steps on the stairs behind him.

The past few days, he'd been doing a little... reevaluating.

He'd started to think that maybe he'd been a little hasty in turning Celia down flat.

Though he'd hardly realized what was happening at first, he couldn't help being more and more aware of her as a woman. He supposed it was natural—now she'd told him she cared for him—that he'd take a second look, that he'd see her in a different light.

Not that seeing her in a different light was particularly wise.

She was a damn good secretary and an even better personal assistant, and he was probably a complete idiot to so much as consider messing with that.

But he *was* considering messing with that. He was doing more than considering. He was taking steps.

Now. Tonight. He'd made his decision hours ago, when they were standing in the back hall at the High-grade and he was teasing her about the incident with the bicycle all those years and years ago. He had found himself looking at her soft, plump rosebud of a mouth and accepting the fact that it was a very kissable mouth, a mouth he himself *wanted* to kiss.

He *would* have kissed her, right there, if Caitlin hadn't butted in and ruined the mood.

He reached the second-floor landing. From behind him, Celia whispered, "It's right up there, the attic room."

He stepped aside so she could go ahead, up the final short flight of stairs, to the small third-floor landing with its single door. He mounted the stairs behind her and when he reached her, he waited, so close she brushed against him more than once while she put her key in the lock and pushed the door inward.

She turned to him. "Thanks. Let me—"

"I want to come in, Celia."

She looked eight years old again, staring at him through wide, scared eyes. "Come in?"

"That's right." He started forward. She backed into the room ahead of him and then stood there, between the foot of the bed and door, looking adorably unsure of what she should do next.

She said, cautiously, looking around her, "This is lovely. So cozy, don't you think?"

"Yeah. It's great." And it was, he supposed. If you

went for slanted ceilings and lots of nooks and crannies.

There was a skylight over the bed, a carved armoire for a closet on the wall to the left, next to the bathroom, and a desk against the other wall. He went to the desk, set her suitcase beside it, and flipped on the lamp there. When he turned back to her, she hadn't budged from her position in the middle of the room. She looked very sweet and more than a little bit lost.

He went to her. "Let me take that other bag."

She gave it to him. He carried it over and set it by her suitcase. She still had her coat on, with her black notebook-size purse tucked under her arm.

He returned to her again and teased softly, "You can put your purse down now. I don't think you'll be needing it any time soon."

She took the purse out from under her arm, but instead of setting it aside, she clutched it, hard, against her chest, as if it could protect her from whatever dangerous things he might be planning to do to her.

"Uh. Aaron?"

"Yes?"

"I've got to ask…"

"Go ahead."

"Well, what is this? What are you doing?"

He stepped up even closer. Her eyes got wider. "I'd like you to put the purse down and take off your coat."

"Why?"

He shook his head. "Come on, Celia. The purse. The coat…"

She shut her eyes, dragged in a ragged breath, then let it out hard. "Oh, all right." She tossed the purse on the easy chair, swiftly shrugged out of the coat and threw it on top of the purse. "There. Happy? Now, what's going on?"

He took off his own coat, pitched it over on top of hers.

"Aaron?"

He shrugged. "I wanted to kiss you—earlier, in the back of the Highgrade."

Her face flushed a warm, sweet, tempting pink. "Oh."

He pulled off his gloves, one and then the other. "My mother got in the way. She likes to do that. So I waited for another opportunity to present itself."

"Another opportunity…like now?"

He nodded.

"Oh." She was nodding along with him, looking terrified and excited and very, very kissable.

He tossed the gloves on top of the coat and moved in close to her again. He took her soft chin in his hands, breathed in the sweet, clean scent of her and lowered his mouth to hers.

"We should talk," she said, before his lips actually made contact with hers.

He pulled back enough to meet her eyes. "About what?"

She looked at him, probingly, seeking answers he really didn't have. "About…this. Why you suddenly want to kiss me? Why you told me you weren't interested and you wouldn't *be* interested and then, out of nowhere, tonight…you're interested."

"Can't we just do what comes naturally?" He stroked her hair. It was sleek and smooth and felt good against his palm.

Her breath caught. "Do what comes naturally?"

"Those were my words."

"Well, that depends."

"On?"

"Well, how far, exactly, do you think what comes naturally might go?"

"Celia."

"Hmm?"

"How about if we just start with the kiss?"

"Oh," she said. "Oh, well…"

"And that means?"

"Okay."

"'Okay.' That's a yes?"

She nodded.

Finally.

He lowered his mouth and tasted hers. It was every bit as soft and moist and yielding as he had hoped it might be. He teased at the seam where those soft lips met. She sighed and let his tongue inside. He explored the sweet, slick surfaces in there, wanting her closer, his body already aching and hard with arousal.

He stroked both hands down the sides of her throat, clasped her shoulders and then gathered her to him, wrapping one arm around her and sliding the other one down the smooth curve of her back.

She let out a tiny, lost cry and rubbed herself against him. *Yes,* he thought. *Happy birthday to me….*

He started walking her backward, toward the waiting bed.

She took one step. And then another.

And then she planted her feet and made a protesting noise in her throat. She also started pushing at his shoulders.

He lifted his head. "What?"

That kissable, slightly swollen mouth of hers started moving. "I don't want to do this, Aaron. Not now. Not tonight."

That grated. Seriously. "Wait a minute. Four days ago, you told me—"

"That I'm in love with you. That's right. I did. I am. And you told me no. Never. Forget about it. So I've been working on that. On forgetting about it. And all of a sudden, you're ready to jump into bed with me. I'm not comfortable with that. I'm really not."

He knew he should just turn around and walk out.

Unfortunately, he'd learned something when he kissed her.

He really did want her. He wanted her naked, under him, in a bed.

It was unexpected and inconvenient. But he didn't think turning around and walking out was going to make it go away.

He stepped back. "Celia. What do you want from me? Declarations of love? I'm sorry. As it turns out, I've got some sort of *thing* for you. But love? No. I can't give you that."

She stepped back, too. "A *thing?* You've got a *thing* for me?"

"A yen. An attraction. You get to me. I want you. Am I making myself clear?"

She backed another step and dropped to the end of the bed. She was frowning, considering. Finally, she said, "So you're saying, you don't think you could love me. But you do want to sleep with me."

"I thought I just said that."

"An affair, right, that's what you're after?"

Truth was, he hadn't thought that far.

She took note of his hesitation. "So. You don't know yet, whether you want an affair or not. You just know you want to sleep with me at least once, to-night?"

"Celia..."

She blew out a breath. "And what about our professional relationship?"

He shrugged. "Business is business. I can keep the two separate. Can you?"

She frowned. "I'm not sure."

"So? Give it a try. Play it by ear."

She looked down at her sensible black pumps, then back up at him. "I just, well, I keep thinking about Jennifer."

Jennifer? What did Jennifer have to do with this? "Why should you think about Jennifer?" *He* certainly hadn't, not since the last time he'd seen her, Tuesday, at lunch.

"Well, I just think, if I'm going to have an affair with you, I would like to be the only one—at least for as long as it lasts."

He got the message loud and clear. "You want me to break it off with Jennifer."

"Oh, don't look at me like that. I *like* Jennifer. You know I do. But it wouldn't seem right, sneaking around behind her back."

"Who said a damn thing about sneaking around? Jennifer knows the score. She and I aren't married and she knows we never will be. We have a clear understanding that we don't own each other, that we're both free to do as we please."

"Oh, Aaron…" She was shaking her head, looking at her shoes again. "I wouldn't like that, you sleeping with both of us. It would just seem icky to me."

"Icky."

"Yes. Icky. Sorry, but that's the way I feel. I can live without your loving me—obviously. You don't, and here I am, still breathing. But if you think you want to get something going with me, then you'll have to say goodbye to Jennifer first."

Chapter Ten

Jilly threw back her head and let out a loud bray of laughter. "You *said* that?"

Fierce approval shone in Jane's eyes. "Well, I think it's terrific. She laid it on the line with him. As in, 'Say goodbye to Jennifer or it's not going to be happening between the two of us.' More women ought to do that. They'd lead much happier lives."

It was Sunday night and they were sitting on the blue rug at Jane's in front of a cozy fire, all comfy in lush piles of pillows, drinking green tea with honey and eating biscotti left over from the refreshments at Jillian's bookstore appearance Friday night.

Jillian was suddenly thoughtful. "I should have said something like that to Benny, way back when. But then again, Benny was such a hound. It probably wouldn't have done any good. What's that old saying? 'You knew I was a snake when you brought me into the house'?"

"Well." Jane paused for a sip of her tea. "We live and learn, don't we?" Her gaze shifted away just the tiniest bit. Celia knew she was probably thinking of her own disastrous marriage.

Jillian leaned toward Celia. "So? What happened next?"

"He said goodnight and left."

"That's *all?*"

"Pretty much. He flew his plane back to Las Vegas yesterday afternoon. I drove him to the airstrip."

"And?"

"And nothing. He was polite and professional. Neither of us said a thing about what had happened the night before. I gave him his birthday present. He opened it on the way to the airstrip."

"It was?"

"An antique silver money clip. He said, 'Thank you, Celia. Very much.'"

Jillian groaned. "Girl, you amaze me. Nerves of steel."

Celia pondered the tea leaves at the bottom of her china cup. "The hardest thing for me was telling him in the first place. There's just nothing that can be as tough as that." She looked from one true friend to the other. "It's funny, when you work with someone as closely as I've worked with Aaron. You learn things about them. You learn…what they are. Deep down. He doesn't have the faintest idea how to make a lasting relationship with a woman. Men and women, together, forming permanent bonds, well, that's strange and scary to him. But then again, he's always honest with women about where he stands, about what they can expect from him.''

Jillian gestured broadly, both palms up. ''Which is?''

Celia looked in her cup again, then back up at Jillian. ''Lots of glamour and good times. If you're with Aaron, you'll eat at the best tables in the finest restaurants and he'll shower you with fabulous gifts. It's not a bad deal, really, as long as you're not in the market for anything permanent.''

''Which you *are*,'' Jane reminded her softly.

Celia set her cup carefully on the fireplace bricks. ''That's true. I am.'' She settled back into her pile of pillows. ''And it's very likely I won't get what I'm after. I can accept that. And I know *he* accepts what I told him Friday night. Aaron Bravo may not be the marrying kind. But he has true integrity, deep down, where it counts. Maybe he'll break it off with Jennifer, and maybe he won't. But he won't make another move on me until—and unless—he has.''

Aaron shifted the bouquet of flowers to his left hand and rang the doorbell with his right.

A minute later, Jennifer opened the door. ''Ah,'' she said, granting him her gorgeous smile. ''Flowers. I like flowers…'' Then she looked closer, into his eyes, and a frown drew down the corners of her full mouth. ''But that serious face of yours, I'm not so sure about that.'' She reached out, wrapped her slim hand around his sleeve. ''What else you got, *caro?*''

Gently, he shook off her grip and reached in his pocket. He pulled out an oblong blue velvet box.

She took the box, opened it, sighed, and closed the lid. "It's beautiful."

"I thought you'd like it."

"And you'd better come in, I think." She took his arm again and pulled him into her apartment.

They'd moved into the kitchen to microwave a bag of popcorn when Jane asked, "So how's it going with Caitlin?"

"You won't believe this. It's going great."

Jillian made a scoffing sound. "You're kidding, right?"

"No, honestly, she's been completely cooperative, gave me everything I needed. I'm meeting with her once more tomorrow, to get a few more figures she didn't have for me yesterday. Then I'm on my way back to Vegas. I'll fill out all the forms and pass it on to Aaron and that's it. I'm done."

Jillian leaned against the counter and crossed her arms over the breasts that had been the envy of all the girls at New Venice High. "I thought you said she drove Aaron crazy every year at tax time."

"She does. She has. And up till now, every accountant he's found for her, she's fired. But not me. I've got no problem with her. As I said, for me, she's cooperative. She gets me what I need when I ask for it. She's actually very well organized. And if you think about it, she'd have to be. The woman *has* been running her own business for over three decades and doing a darn good job of it, too. My theory is, Aaron expects her to drive him crazy—and she obliges him. It's part of the way they relate to each other. I, on the other hand, don't have any family relationship stuff going on with her.''

''*And* you're a woman,'' Jillian added. ''I'll bet all the other accountants he found for her were men.''

''Now you mention it, that's right. At least in the past three years, since I've been working for him.''

''Hmph,'' said Jillian, ''I thought so.''

''Plus, she likes me. She pretty much said so Friday night.''

''Said what,'' Jane demanded, ''specifically?''

''She said, and I quote, 'She's a good girl and she's from home and I like the look of her.'''

Jillian let out a gleeful little squeal. ''Oh, I love it.''

''She calls me baby doll and sweetie.''

Even Jane chuckled at that. By then, the popcorn was popping like mad. The three fell silent and stared into the window of the microwave. The bag turned in a stately circle, inflating as the kernels within exploded.

Finally, Celia said, ''Aaron thinks Caitlin's up to something, since she was so agreeable about my taking over on the tax front.''

''And what do *you* think?'' asked Jane.

''I don't know. Could be. It's hard to tell with someone like Caitlin. On the one hand, she's so volatile. Always the center of attention, never afraid to say what's on her mind. On the other hand, well, who *really* knows what goes on inside that woman's head?''

Jillian wiggled her eyebrows. "I heard Hans is no more."

Jane turned and got a bowl down from the cupboard. "Well, he hasn't been in the bookstore lately, I can tell you that." The popping sounds had slowed. Jane set the bowl on the counter. She punched a button at the base of the microwave. The popcorn stopped turning and the door swung wide. Jane grabbed the bag, held it over the bowl and tore it open. "Ouch!" she cried as the fat, buttery kernels tumbled out. "That is *hot*."

They returned to the front room and their piles of pillows. Celia stuck a big handful of popcorn in her mouth and chomped away. "Umm. So good..." She was reaching into the bowl again when she realized her friends were staring at her. She pulled her hand back. "What?"

Slowly and knowingly, Jillian smiled.

Celia understood. "All right. I know that smile. It's about what you're planning, right? What you just couldn't talk about on the phone the other day?"

Jillian said, "Even Jane agrees with me now."

Celia glanced Jane's way and got a quick nod of confirmation.

Jillian continued, "You've told him how you feel about him. Jane is very proud of you."

"Oh, yes," said Jane. "I am. So proud."

"And now it's time you took some of *my* advice."

Celia got the picture. "Hair, lipstick and wardrobe. Right?"

"Exactly. We are flying down to Vegas next weekend."

"We?"

"Jane and me. You will save Saturday for us. All day Saturday. Is that clear? I'm pulling a few strings, and I expect you to make yourself completely available. Because I'm putting the best in the business to work on you. Hair. Makeup. Nails. And then shopping..."

Celia thought of all those gray clothes she'd dug out of her closet last Monday night. If Aaron did say goodbye to Jennifer, Celia wouldn't mind having something that wasn't gray to wear when he next attempted to seduce her. "Will I be a redhead?"

"You want to be a redhead?"

"You know, Jilly, I do. I really do."

"Good answer. Is that a commitment? You'll give us all day Saturday, and no backing out?"

"Yes. All day Saturday. I promise. I do."

"Triple Threat," said Jane, raising her teacup.

"Triple threat," Celia and Jillian responded in unison. They raised their cups and drank.

"Well, baby doll," said Caitlin. "You got everything you need?"

"I think so." Celia gathered up the pile of papers Caitlin had given her that day. She tapped them on the edge of Caitlin's big green metal desk and slipped them into the briefcase she'd brought with her from her room at the New Venice Inn. "I'll fill out all the forms, pass everything on to Aaron to check over, and then he'll get it back to you. Should be ready in a week or so."

"Thanks, sweetie, I—" The phone rang. Caitlin put up a red-tipped index finger. "One minute?"

"Sure."

Caitlin picked up the phone. "Highgrade." She listened and then she sighed and sat back in her swivel chair. "Umm." She listened some more, lightly touching one corner of her red mouth and then the other, wiping nonexistent smudges away. "Hans," she said at last, her smoky voice infinitely tired and wise. "Hans. No…I can't…I mean it. And I've gotta go now. Goodbye, my darlin'." She hung up the phone, the purple spangles on her black shirt shimmering and winking as she heaved a second sigh. "Young men. They have way too much energy…"

Not sure what she ought to say, Celia nodded too hard. "Oh, well. I'd imagine so."

Caitlin sat forward and folded her hands on the desktop. "Now. Let's talk about what really matters."

Celia had a sinking feeling. Was Caitlin getting to it then, to the thing Aaron had warned her about, the reason she needed to be watching her back? "Uh. Sure. Go ahead. Talk."

Caitlin's black eyes shone now with a probing light. "I am with you here, you get me?"

"Uh…?"

"I'm sayin' I saw you with Aaron the other night, back there in the shadows at the end of my hallway. I know what's going on. And I like it. I like it a lot." She picked up a pencil, tapped it on the desk once, then tossed it down. "And I'm not sayin' a word to him, either, about what I know. I'm stayin' out of it, one hundred percent. I'm lettin' you play this hand, just play it out your own way. 'Cause I got a good feelin' 'bout you, baby doll. I truly do. I'd put my money on you in this game. And I'd come out a winner, too.''

"Well," said Celia, for lack of anything better, "thanks."

Caitlin smiled. ''You need anything, you can come to me. Anytime.''

"Well. Okay. I'll remember that.''

"Anything. I mean that. Anything. Anytime.''

Celia was at her desk Tuesday morning when Aaron entered the office suite.

She looked up, their gazes locked for perhaps two seconds, and then he smiled. An all-business smile. "I'm surprised. You're back so soon.''

She produced a smile as professional as his, though her blood raced in her veins and her heart pounded madly. "I had everything I needed from your mother. I decided I might as well get back to work.''

He slanted her a doubtful look. "You're telling me that she didn't give you any trouble?''

"That's right. No problems. I'll crunch the numbers and fill out the forms. In a few days, I'll have it all ready for you.''

"You're serious? And you got no indications from her of anything else going on, anything...suspicious she might be up to?''

She decided to finesse that one. "It all went smoothly. I have nothing to report. Except...mission accomplished.''

"Well. I don't know what to say. Thank you, Celia."

"You're welcome, Aaron."

"And I'm glad you're back early. Managers' meeting this morning at ten-thirty. I'd like you there with me."

"Will do."

"Great. Give me ten minutes, we'll go over the calendar."

"Fine. Ten minutes it is."

Strictly professional.

That was how they kept things. Tuesday went by, and Wednesday and Thursday.

Aaron never said a word about what had happened between them the night of his birthday party. All physical contact had stopped, too. He no longer brushed her hand or her arm in casual acknowledgement when she brought him coffee or handed him a file.

And that was just fine with her. She didn't want any more of those little heartbreaking, meaningless touches from him.

He could touch her for real. Or he could keep his hands to himself.

He never mentioned Jennifer.

And Celia didn't ask.

The next move, the way she saw it, had to be his.

It wasn't easy, waiting. Wondering. Hoping. Jillian was wrong. She didn't really have nerves of steel.

More than once, she caught herself hanging on the verge of inquiring out of nowhere, "So, tell me.

How's Jennifer? Did you happen to break it off with her?''

But she managed *not* to say that, somehow. Whenever she got close, she'd think of Caitlin, leaning toward her across that big green desk, spangles glittering, all that impossibly black, black hair gleaming in the hard light from the ceiling fixture above. ''I got a good feelin' 'bout you, baby doll. I truly do. I'd put my money on you in this game. And I'd come out a winner, too....''

And after Caitlin, she remembered her friends, who were coming that weekend to give her the full treatment, to enhance her makeup, change her hair, help her get into some brighter clothes. If she was going to end up throwing herself at him, she wanted to be wearing something stunning when she did it.

And speaking of stunning, what was it with her underwear? It was all in pale blues and pinks—and yes, all right, gray. It was good quality, and a lot of it was satin, some of it even trimmed with lace.

But when Aaron Bravo saw her panties, she was determined that those panties would be red. Or purple. Or black. Some strong, assertive color, something naughty and bold.

Friday, she kept waiting for him to say he would need her on Saturday. She was all prepared for that, to tell him she was sorry, but she had *plans* for Saturday, plans that she simply was not willing to change.

But he never asked. So she never to got to tell him how she wasn't available. He left the office at four-thirty.

"Have a good weekend, Celia," he said on his way out.

She did not look up from her computer screen. "I will, thank you, Aaron. See you Monday."

And he was gone.

Celia listened to the door closing behind him and stared blindly at her computer screen, imagining him rushing to Jennifer's place. Oh, yes. She could just see it: the gorgeous, kind-hearted showgirl greeting him at the door wearing nothing but a red sequined thong, a see-through chiffon robe and that unforgettable smile.

Celia blinked. "Enough of that silliness," she told herself firmly and forced her mind back to the columns of figures in front of her.

Jane and Jillian got into McCarran at seven that night. Celia was waiting for them. Jane said she wanted to cook at least a couple of meals during their visit. So they stopped off at the supermarket and picked up the things she'd need. Then Celia took them back to her rooms at High Sierra so they could drop off their bags and freshen up a little.

For dinner that night, Celia took them to Casa D'Oro, right there in High Sierra, where the fare was a nice blend of Mexican and California cuisines. Once they'd eaten, they returned to Celia's apartment. By eleven, they were saying goodnight. And at seven, they were up and dressed. Jane served them French toast as only Jane knew how to make it—with whole wheat bread, heavy on the cinnamon, fresh blueberries on top.

Jillian had the day all planned. Celia was due for hair at nine, and a makeup consultation at eleven. At one, they all took a break for lunch.

And then they spent the afternoon at the best and most exclusive shops Las Vegas had to offer. They put some serious stress on Celia's gold card.

"You can afford it," said Jillian with a shrug. "Aaron Bravo may not be husband material, but I know he pays you well. Might as well get some mileage out of those hefty paychecks."

Celia didn't argue. What was to argue about? Jilly spoke the truth. And no matter what happened with Aaron, well, at least now Celia knew what it felt like to be a redhead. That alone, was worth all the money she'd spent.

That night, they went over to Bellagio to catch one of the shows there. Sunday morning, Jane made her famous huevos Californios, which, besides eggs, included salsa, sour cream, avocado and hot, soft flour tortillas.

"With food like this, who needs sex?" Jillian wondered aloud.

"Jilly," said Jane. "It is balance in all things for which we strive."

Celia drove her friends back to the airport at eleven so they could catch separate flights. Then she returned to High Sierra, went straight to her rooms and finished preparing Caitlin's taxes.

She wore her new red satin teddy to bed.

"A redhead," Aaron said Monday morning when he entered the office suite and found the "new" Celia sitting at her desk.

He watched her straighten her shoulders and smile—a smile that was half nervous and half naughty. "That's right. Do you like it?"

"I do. It suits you." And it did. Not carrot-colored, not auburn. A truer kind of red, rich and spicy—like cinnamon. Or maybe paprika....

"Aaron?" she prompted.

He realized he'd been standing there staring at her. He shook himself, demanded gruffly, "Ten minutes?"

"Of course."

He went into his office, where he found his mother's completed tax return waiting on his desk. He picked up the forms. And then he set them down.

He punched a button on the phone in front of him. "Celia."

"Yes?"

"I wonder if you could come in here right now?"

Twenty seconds later, she stood in front of his desk, with her notebook in one hand and her miniature recorder in the other.

He said, "That's a new suit, too, isn't it?"

She looked down at the snug-fitting suit—a warm, spicy red, like her hair, like her soft, oh-so-kissable lips—and back up at him. "Yes, Aaron. It is."

A glass desktop did have its advantages. He let his gaze travel down, all the way down. The pencil-thin skirt ended right above her pretty knees. Her shoes, which matched the suit, had skinny high heels and very pointed toes—not her usual practical pumps, no not at all.

"Celia, what have you been up to?"

She didn't answer—at first. Not until he raised his gaze and met those hazel eyes. They shone bright with challenge—and apprehension, too. "That sounds like a personal question."

"Probably because it *is* a personal question."

"I don't think we should get into that—not now, not in the office."

"Would you care to suggest a different time, then?"

"Uh. Yes. I would. How about tonight, seven o'clock, my rooms?"

"I have a better idea."

She gulped. "You do?"

"Let's take a couple of hours off and go to *my* rooms. Right now."

She almost dropped her tape recorder. "Oh!" She caught it just before it hit the edge of the desk.

He hid a smile. "Nervous?"

"Yes. I am." She turned and set both the notebook and the recorder on the chair behind her, then made herself face him once more. He saw the small shiver that traveled through her. And it pleased him. "Very nervous," she whispered, more to herself, it seemed, than to him.

He asked again, careful to be gentle this time, "Will you come to my rooms with me?"

"Er, right now?"

"Yes, Celia. Right now."

"But is that advisable? I mean, during working hours?"

"Celia—" His cell phone started bleating. He took it out of his pocket, glanced at the display, then switched it off and dropped it to his desk.

A frown formed between her smooth brows. "Shouldn't you answer that?"

"It's nothing important."

"But—"

"Celia. I am the boss. I set the hours."

"Well, um, that's right. I suppose you do."

Her face was almost as red as her hair. He found her enchanting. He'd been waiting for a week for some kind of sign from her, some indication that she would welcome another move, if he made it.

He said, "Look. I thought…the hair, that new suit, those sexy shoes…" He waved a hand. "I'm reading them as an invitation. Have I got it all wrong?"

"Uh, no. No, you haven't. You have got it very right." A sweet, high laugh burst from her. She clapped her hand to her mouth to stop it—and blushed all the harder.

He let his own smile show. "So? What do you say?"

"Yes," she said, adorable and firm. "I say, yes. Let's take two hours off and spend them in your rooms."

Chapter Eleven

Aaron's suite was in a different tower than the one that housed the office complex. They rode down in one elevator and walked through the casino, ablaze as always with glittering light, alive with bells and whistles and electronic buzzing, with the clattering of coins, and the clicking whirr of roulette wheels.

People recognized Aaron, of course. Those people nodded and muttered respectful greetings. Aaron always nodded back.

To Celia, it felt…strange, unreal. Like a dream. They walked close together, but not touching. Surely to any casual observer, they were just what they'd always been: the boss and his assistant, en route from the office tower to meet a manager or a vice president or one of the board members—or maybe some major high roller. A whale—like Dennis Rodman, or the oil-rich sultan of a certain Middle Eastern country. But whatever their destination, whoever they might be meeting, surely all assumed them to be intent on business as usual.

Could anyone tell, by looking at them, that they were headed for his private suite to spend a couple of hours crawling all over each other, naked in his bed?

No way, Celia decided.

No one would guess.

Oh, eventually, she knew, if they did this more than once or twice, word would get around that the boss and his assistant shared more than a professional relationship. One of the maids or some other employee would spot them going into or out of his or her rooms. There would be whispering. The story would spread.

But not yet. No one had a clue yet.

She kept half-expecting someone to stop them, to pull Aaron aside with some question or other, some issue that simply could not wait. She kept thinking, *this isn't really happening, this is just a daydream, just a crazy, impossible fantasy. I'm really sitting at my desk, staring blindly at my computer screen. Any minute now, I'm going to snap out of it.*

But she didn't snap out of it. And no one stopped them. They left the casino and proceeded down two intersecting hallways where the floors were marble, crystal chandeliers hung from the high ceilings and the walls were papered in gilded leaf patterns on a ground of antique gold. They approached another set of elevators. One of them was open, a uniformed operator perched on a stool inside.

"Mr. Bravo," said the operator.

"Miles." Aaron nodded, as he'd nodded at all the others on their way here.

And right then, for the first time since the night that he'd kissed her, Aaron touched her. He laid his hand, so lightly, at the small of her back, the way a man will do. He was ushering her onto the car—and also, in a subtle way, laying claim to her. A shiver of pure arousal coursed through her. And the feeling of unreality shattered.

This *was* happening. Not a daydream. *True.*

She stepped into the car, sparing a quick, polite smile for Miles. The door—which was mirrored in gold-veined glass—slid shut. And there she was, looking at herself, red-haired in a red suit, a red clutch tucked neatly under her arm, standing next to Aaron Bravo. So very disorienting, to see how calm she looked on the outside, while inside she was all tangled up in yearning, in a strange and wonderful admixture of heat and jitters and fear and glorious, giddy, light-headed joy.

They went up, slowly at first, then kicking into high speed. In less than a minute, there they were. On the top floor. The door slid wide. She looked beyond and saw that the elevator opened directly into the foyer of an apartment.

Aaron took her elbow. Heat sizzled where he touched her, radiating outward, setting her whole body on fire.

"Thank you, Miles."

The operator nodded. Aaron and Celia stepped out into the entrance hall, a large, high-ceilinged room where morning sunlight poured down on them through a huge round skylight. Celia looked up, saw twining flowers and leaves etched into the dome-shaped glass. The desert sky, seen between the frosty patterns of leaf and petal, was pastel blue and cloudless.

Behind them, the door to the elevator whispered shut.

Celia noted the iron-framed glass entry hall table, the simple, white-shaded lamps, the walls that were a color between green and khaki and beige, the blood-red freesias in a tall glass vase. Twin Ionic pillars and a single, pulled-back silk portiere of a lustrous brown framed the entrance to the living room.

It was all so like him. Understated. And yet somehow theatrical to the core.

"You're quiet," he said.

She turned to him. "I...one minute I feel certain this can't be happening. And then the next, I realize, my God, it *is*."

He touched her again—a miracle, each time he did that—his lean hand brushing a caress along the line of her hair at her temple. "Is that a backing-out remark?"

She captured his hand. He let her do that. It felt so good, his palm touching hers. "No. I promise. It's not."

He twined his fingers with hers, then pulled her into him, placing their joined hands at the small of her back, cupping her chin with the warm fingers of his other hand.

Slowly those fingers moved, sliding downward, caressing her throat. He lowered his mouth so it hovered no more than an inch from hers. Her eyelids felt heavy. She longed to just let them drift shut.

But some part of her couldn't quite do that. She couldn't help feeling that certain things had to be said first.

He pulled back a fraction. "What?"

She made a small noise of protest, of avoidance.

His arm tightened around her. "Go ahead. Say it."

She struggled to find the right words. There didn't seem to be any.

He touched her nose, so lightly, traced her cheekbone, and the line of her brow. "This is about Jennifer. Right?"

She closed her eyes then, not terribly proud of herself that she just had to ask him, she just *had* to know. "Right."

She felt the brush of his lips across her own—once, and then again. With a hungry sigh, she pressed herself closer to him. She could feel how he wanted her. That thrilled and excited her—and made her pretty nervous, too. "Oh, Aaron…"

He released her and pulled back. "Okay, let's get it over with. What about Jennifer?"

She dragged in a ragged breath and opened her eyes. He was watching her, studying her. It took a real effort to make herself meet that probing gaze directly. "Well, I know that you must have ended it with her…."

He was smiling, but his eyes were dark as midnight. "How do you know that?"

She gave a small, embarrassed cry. "Oh, don't tease me. Please."

He studied her face some more. Then he shrugged. "You're right. I ended it with her. A week ago Sunday. I went to her apartment, gave her flowers and a diamond bracelet. She invited me in. I stayed for about ten minutes. Just long enough to tell her goodbye. I haven't seen her since then."

He must have read what she was thinking in her eyes, because he added, ruefully, "Yes. It's true. I went out and bought the damn bracelet myself."

That did make her smile. "Good for you." She felt her smile fading as she couldn't help but wonder when she would be the one getting the diamonds.

He said, as if, again, he saw into her mind, "It always ends in diamonds, Celia."

That made her so sad. She looked down. But he wouldn't allow that. He put a finger under her chin, guiding her face up so she was looking at him again. "I'm the son of a murdering bigamist and a woman who, to this day, has never settled on one man. I don't *do* marriage. I have sense enough to know the things I'll never get right. You know that, you *understand* that?"

Her throat closed up so words wouldn't come. But she did make herself nod.

"Then we're clear about this? You don't expect me to be someone I'm not?"

She swallowed, shook her head.

He chuckled. "No, you're not clear, or no, you don't expect me to be someone I'm not?"

She wrinkled her nose at him. "Yes. I'm clear. I don't expect you to be a person you're not."

"Okay then." He wrapped his arm around her again and pulled her body into his. "Anything else?"

She came up against his chest. It felt warm and hard and absolutely lovely. "Uh. No. I'd say that's pretty much it."

"Then, will you let me kiss you now?"

"Oh, yes." She lifted her mouth and closed her eyes. "Please do."

She sighed as his lips met hers, her foolish heart lifting, her body going soft and needful, her pulse pounding out his name.

The kiss was long and wet and very thorough. Celia gave herself up to it, gladly, with joy.

When he lifted his head, his mouth looked swollen. One corner of it kicked up in that characteristic lazy half-smile of his. "You can put your purse down now, Celia." He gestured with a flick of his head. "There. On the glass table, by the vase of flowers…"

She had her arms around his neck by then, and clutched the purse in her left hand. "Uh, no. I'll just…take it to the bedroom with us, if that's okay with you."

Now he lifted a dark brow. "Some reason you need it?"

"Um, yes, there is."

"And that is?"

"Well…." She cleared her throat, suddenly embarrassed and wishing she wasn't, wanting to be more…sophisticated about this.

"What's in the bag, Celia?"

She told him. "Contraception."

"Ah." Those eyes of his gleamed at her, blue as Lake Tahoe at its deepest point. "Contraception. In your purse?"

"That's right."

He laughed then. She felt the deep, pleasured rumble against her heart. "Celia. You never cease to amaze me. A model of efficiency. Ready for anything, as always."

She had gone out and bought the condoms a week ago. She'd intended to be ready—if and when. "Well. Hope springs eternal, as they say."

He scanned her face, his gaze wonderfully avid, as if he couldn't get enough of looking at her. "You *are* charming…."

"Why, thank you."

"And so pretty."

"Keep talking. I do sincerely like what you're saying."

But he had fallen silent. He cupped her left shoulder with his right hand, the gesture, somehow, stunning in its intimacy. Then his fingers moved.

She slanted him a suspicious look. "What are you doing?"

Her suit had a short semi-wrap jacket that buttoned on the left side. As she watched, he freed that button. And then the next one. There were only five in all.

"Aaron."

"Um?" Button number three gave way.

"I think we should go on to your bedroom now."

Oops. There went number four. She could see the scrap of bright red lace beneath—her lovely, naughty, meant-for-seduction new bra. He slid that last button free and gently edged the facing aside. "Celia, I am liking what I see here."

"Well, good." She grabbed that naughty hand of his, turned and started for the living room. "Where's the bedroom?"

He wouldn't budge. "Don't you think it's nice right where we are, under the skylight?"

She looked up. "The skylight I can live with—but not that elevator over there."

"No one will disturb us."

"You think."

"Celia—"

"The bedroom, Aaron. Please."

He was grinning. "I like you with your jacket unbuttoned and that gorgeous red lace peeking out underneath, with that just-been-kissed look on your face and a blush on your cheeks…"

"The bedroom?"

"I have to ask. To what do I owe all this red?"

She stopped tugging on his hand and simply glared at him.

Aaron relented.

Yes, he would have thoroughly enjoyed undressing her beneath the skylight.

But if she worried the whole time about Miles coming back, it would ruin her pleasure. He didn't want that. He decided he'd take her where she wanted to go.

Sparing one last rueful glance at the skylight above, he moved to take the lead. "All right. This way." He pulled her through the living room and down a hallway to the room at the end.

She hesitated in the doorway. "Oh. It's all white…"

It was, for the most part. He had a wide white bed with a white woven cotton headboard, a pair of white marble nightstands, one to either side, and a white art-deco-inspired limestone fireplace. No dressers or bureaus, since the room contained two walk-in closets fitted with all the drawers and shelves he could possibly need. There was also a sitting area, with a deep white couch and two matching easy chairs, a glass coffee table between them. And there were etched-glass mirrors, in varying shapes, here and there along the walls. Aaron liked mirrors, liked the way they added space, they way they glittered, amplifying the light.

As it happened, even the flowers on the nightstand to the left of the bed were white right then—calla lilies.

He led her over to the end of the bed. "Have a seat." She did, demurely, clutching her purse with its crucial load of condoms, her red hair and red clothes all the more vivid against all the white, her jacket gaping open in a most alluring way.

He felt…very young, suddenly. A boy with his first woman, starving to have her.

He turned from her, to pace himself. It was always better, when he wanted something badly, to take it easy, draw out the pleasure, to make himself go slow.

With his back to her, he shrugged out of his own jacket and removed his tie, tossing them over one of the white chairs. Then he went to work on his cuff links, dropping them into a carved ivory dish that waited on the glass table between the couch and the chairs.

He knew he couldn't stay turned away for too long. She was just insecure enough that she might take it all wrong. So after he'd unbuttoned his shirt and tossed it on the chair, too, he faced her again.

She looked up at him, eyes wide, mouth slightly parted—yearning. Yet unsure.

He undid his belt and slid it off, then went to the white ottoman not far from the bed. He sat, began removing his shoes. "So…"

Her sweet face went eager, and so hopeful. "Um?"

He wanted to take away that jacket, the scrap of lace beneath, to see her breasts, to touch them….

Soon.

But not yet.

"I think you should tell me what you've been up to."

"I should?"

He nodded, set his shoes beside the ottoman. "That suit, the hair, the shoes…" He went to work on his socks.

"Well, my friends came, this weekend. Jane and Jillian…"

He dropped the socks across the shoes. "That would be Jane Elliott, whose uncle, J. T. Elliott, was once the sheriff and is now the mayor."

"That's right."

"And Jillian's last name is Diamond. She's an image consultant, right?"

"That's it. Very good." A smile quivered across her mouth. He wanted to kiss it, that mouth, to taste that trembling smile.

And he would.

Soon...

He stood. Her eyes widened. He looked down at his own hands as he unbuttoned his slacks and casually stepped out of them. He put them with rest of his clothes.

All that was left was his silk boxer shorts. He looked at Celia again. "So your friends came. And the image consultant offered a little advice...."

She nodded. "That's right. Hair, nails, you name it."

"Ah," he said, slipping the waistband of his boxers over his erection and stepping out of them as he had the slacks, letting them drop to the floor.

He stood tall, facing her. She made a sweet, scared noise low in her throat. Her eyes were so big, they seemed to take up her whole face.

He wondered, at that moment, if she might be a complete innocent. It seemed a little difficult to believe. She was in her late twenties. Not many women were virgins at that age—not in his experience, anyway. Truth was, he couldn't think of one. However, if Celia just happened to be the last of the late-twenty-something virgins....

Well, he'd have to rethink this situation. He'd come to accept the fact that he wanted her. A lot. He was standing in front of her naked and way too eager to do what came naturally.

But he didn't make love to virgins.

"Celia."

"Um?"

"I have to ask this."

"Uh, what?"

"Is this your first time?"

She stared at him blankly. Then comprehension dawned. "Oh. With a man, you mean."

"Right."

"Uh. No. There was someone—well, two some-ones, actually. First, Derek Pauley, in high school. Remember him? He's still in the Comstock Valley, a farmer. Like his father was before him. Dairy farmers, remember? With very happy cows. Holsteins, I think they were, black and white with those big, soft eyes and—"

"Hold it." He gave her a smile. "That's all the info I need for right now."

"Oh. Well. Of course. Sure…"

When her voice trailed off, he said, very softly, "I just want to be certain you're okay."

"Oh. Oh, yes. I'm fine." She nodded madly, clutching that red purse for all she was worth. "Just so nervous, all of a sudden. It…well, this is really happening, you and me, here, in your bedroom, isn't it?"

"Yes, Celia. It is."

He went to her, half expecting her to jump up as he approached, to back away—or even bolt from the room. But she held her ground, there, on the bed.

He reached out a hand, carefully, and traced the line of that crimson hair with an index finger. "Maybe," he suggested quietly, "we can get what we need from that purse and then you can let go of it."

Her mouth quivered. "Um…"

"Is that a yes?"

She nodded again, this time more slowly.

He turned his hand over and waited. She blinked, twice, then she opened the purse, dug around in it, and came up with three condoms. She put the condoms in his open hand.

"The purse, too."

She handed it over. He went to the left nightstand, set the purse down on the outer edge of it and the condoms closer in.

When he got back to her, she stood. "I—"

"Shh…" He reached for her, slowly, easing his fingers beneath the warm fall of that shining hair, cupping the back of her neck.

She tipped her mouth up to him, whispered, "Aaron…"

"What?"

"Oh." She was frowning, as if whatever she'd meant to tell him had somehow escaped her. "Uh. Nothing."

He brushed his mouth against hers, "Just 'Aaron'?"

"That's all."

"You're sure?"

Her frown deepened. "You are teasing me."

"Maybe."

"You ought to stop that. It just makes me more nervous."

"Stop that and...?"

"Kiss me."

He brushed her lips with his again. "Kiss you?"

"That's right, Aaron. Kiss me. Now."

How could he refuse such a sweet command?

And why would he want to?

He settled his mouth against hers and he gave her just what she wanted, lightly at first, then deepening it a little, but being careful not to pull her into his naked body. She sighed, opening to his questing tongue. Her mouth was silky. Warm. Good. He tasted her to the limits of his control.

At the point where he knew he would grab her and crush her close, he lifted his head. Her eyes drifted open, the pupils wide, drugged with the promise of pleasure.

Yeah. She was relaxing, letting go, letting the nervousness fade away. He could feel the tension easing from the tendons at the back of her neck.

He let his hand go roaming, around to the front of her. "Soft," he said. "Touchable. Nice..."

He slid both hands between the open sides of the red jacket, guiding it over her shoulders and down her arms. She squirmed a little, her arms trapped behind her. He paused in the act of undressing her, his hands holding her arms, the jacket falling halfway down her back. He paused and he stole another long, drugging kiss.

This time, he dared to rub his chest against her. Her breasts were small and high and the red lace of that sexy bra was scratchy, arousingly so. She moaned into his mouth and arched her back, pressing harder, closer....

He raised his head again and he helped her to pull her arms from the sleeves of the jacket. He tossed it away, not caring where it landed. Then he wrapped one arm around her, to steady her, and with the other, he carefully guided the lacy cups of that bra out of the way, revealing two sweet, delicate white breasts tipped with coral-colored nipples.

"So pretty..." He lowered his head and captured one hard little bead.

She moaned and clutched his head. He worked that sweet, hard nipple, rolling his tongue around it, teasing it with his teeth—and sliding a hand around to the back of her at the same time, working the clasp of the bra until it gave.

He went on, kissing one breast and then the other, as he guided the satin straps down her shoulders. She straightened her arms for him, her body a bow, surging up to his mouth as he suckled on her.

The bra fell away. He lifted his head again and she opened her eyes, glazed now. So hungry.

As hungry as he was...

"Get rid of this, all of it...." His voice was gruffer than he meant it to be as he felt behind her for the hook and the zipper at the back of her skinny little skirt. She let out a small cry—and then she helped him, pushing his hands out of the way, unzipping it herself.

He shoved it over the singing curve of her hips, going on down with it, dropping to his knees before her, grabbing her pantyhose and the lacy red triangle that covered her sex from him and dragging them down. She teetered a little, but then rested her hands on his shoulders to kick off those pointy red shoes. Once the shoes were gone, he took her by the waist and sat her back on the end of the bed.

The panties and stockings were bunched just below her knees. He got them the rest of the way down, pulled them off the ends of her red-tipped toes and tossed the wad of nylon and silk over his shoulder.

She cried his name.

He glanced up at her, liking the sound of it, his name, so needful on her sweet plump mouth, which was bruised now, fuller than ever from his kisses.

"Lie down," he whispered.

With a tiny, hungry moan, she dropped back onto the bed.

He took her knees and eased them over his shoulders and he moved in, close. A long shiver coursed through her. He put his hand on her, on her white belly, which tightened in response to his touch. She lifted her head off the bed and looked down at him, that newly red hair falling along the wonderful pink curve of her cheek.

"Aaron..."

He touched the shining brown curls at the place where her thighs met.

She gasped. And she let her head fall back.

Gently, he parted her. She was moaning by then, pressing herself eagerly to his seeking mouth.

He tasted her, that most private part of her. It was slick and soft, ready for him. He ran his tongue along the secret folds, moving in all the closer, tasting her more deeply, pressing a palm on her belly, to hold her in place.

Her hips moved, slowly at first, hesitantly. Then faster, and faster, her body bowing up off the white quilt, her sex opening wider, inviting his tongue.

He accepted her invitation, deepening the forbidden kiss, loving the taste of her, the way she cried out, the way she pressed closer, ever closer, her body reaching, striving—seeking the soft explosion of fulfillment.

It came at last. With a wild cry, she went rigid. He drank in the tender pulsing that signaled her completion.

He stayed with her through the pulsing, until she went lax and easy, sinking into the bed with a final long sigh. Then, very gently, he eased out from under the sweet weight of her thighs. He moved up onto the bed with her, turning on his side away from her, as he reached for a condom from the three on the night table.

He had it on in seconds.

He felt her soft hand, touching his back, stroking. He rolled to face her. She stared at him, mouth soft, eyes glazed.

He went into her waiting arms.

Celia cried out when he entered her—a cry of wonder, of excitement, of pure physical joy.

Oh, it felt so good. So right, to have him inside her. He stayed up on his elbows and he looked down at her, watching her.

She stared right back at him, all her earlier fears

and anxiousness seared away by his kisses, by his wonderful, slow, delicious caresses. He moved smoothly, surely, settling deeply into her. She accepted him, her body opening willingly to accommodate him.

She thought, *I love you, Aaron. I do. I love you so....*

But she didn't say the words. She knew he didn't want the words. So she was careful, so careful, not to say them out loud.

He thrust in harder. She took him. She could take anything, all he could give. She wrapped her legs around him, pulling him closer, taking him deeper.

He closed his eyes first. His bronze lashes swept down and his head went back, straining, the tendons standing out on his powerful neck.

She watched him, her love a searing flame within her, as the slow, deep rhythm of their lovemaking intensified. He surged into her, faster. She went right with him, her body rising, the pleasure expanding, every nerve singing.

And it happened. He hit the peak on a final, hard, deep thrust. She felt that—felt him contracting in spasms within her.

And then, she was lost, too, her body shimmering, all of her shattering into a thousand bright shards. Behind her eyes, the world was a million points of glittering light cascading within a hot and velvety darkness. And she was inside it, a part of that wonderful light-scattered darkness, falling forever into eternity, through a magical night of a billion stars.

Chapter Twelve

Aaron's lady.

Celia heard them whispering. She knew what they called her.

She smiled when she heard it. Because she was proud that it was so.

It took a little over a week of the two of them together in this wholly new way before word got around. They were discreet—during business hours, anyway. But they lived where they worked. And sometimes, when Aaron would take her to dinner at the Placer Room or Casa D'Oro, well, they couldn't help the way they looked at each other, couldn't prevent the occasional tender caress.

They were surrounded, after all, by interested observers. By maids and floor supervisors, managers and waitresses, vice presidents and security personnel. Everyone at High Sierra made it their business to know what was going on with the boss. It was, after all, to their advantage to know.

They had known about Jennifer. And they had known about the dazzling string of beautiful women before her.

And it was inevitable that they would come to know about Celia.

They treated her with respect and a sort of tenderness, a protectiveness, that warmed her. Not that they hadn't all respected her before, when she was strictly Aaron's secretary and personal assistant.

But now, it was...different, the way they looked at her, the way they deferred to her, the way the chefs and waiters in High Sierra's restaurants would fuss over her, the way all the bartenders suddenly knew that the Cosmopolitan was her drink of choice.

Aaron's lady, after all, helped to keep Aaron happy. And that was good for everyone.

A few days after Celia and Aaron first made love, Jane called and demanded to know what was going on.

So Celia told her. And Jane said, "Well. Are you happy?"

"You know, it's like a dream..."

Jane made a small, irritated noise in her throat. "Stop evading. It's a yes-or-no question."

"Okay. I'm happy." And she was. She truly was.

"But you want more."

"I didn't say that."

"So...you *don't* want more?"

"The hard fact is, I'm not going to get more. And so I think it would be a good idea to be happy with what I've got."

"Snippy, snippy."

"Sorry. I didn't mean to be."

"Hey," said Jane softly. "Enjoy yourself. Okay?"

"I will, Janey. I *am.*"

Jillian called about fifteen minutes after Celia said goodbye to Jane. "I hear that you and Aaron are an item. And that you're loving it."

"That's right. I am."

"Good for you, Ceil. Still like your hair?"

"I love it."

"Does Aaron like it?"

"*He* loves it."

"I'm sorry. I've got to ask. What were you wearing, the first time he—"

"That cinnamon-red suit we picked out at—"

Jillian let out a moan of pure pleasure. "Oh, I knew it. You're a dream in that suit. I'm so pleased with myself."

Celia couldn't help smiling. "Jilly, I'm crazy about everything you did for me. You've come a long way from dyeing Jane's hair green."

"I have, haven't I—and what next, between you and Aaron?"

"I intend to enjoy myself, to savor every minute with him, for as long as it lasts."

"Guess what? That was going to be my advice, exactly. Have a great time."

"I will."

* * *

It was no hardship, savoring every minute with Aaron. He treated her like a queen, made love to her as if he couldn't get enough of her. And he showered her with jewels—an emerald bracelet, a platinum lariat necklace, a string of absolutely perfect ten-millimeter Mikimoto pearls. At first, she wondered if he had another assistant stashed somewhere, someone he wasn't sleeping with, someone he could instruct to go out and find charming, pricey trinkets for his latest lady.

But Celia did keep all of his personal accounts. And she figured out soon enough how he came by the gifts. He was bidding for them on the Internet.

That discovery pleased her—first of all, because *he* was choosing the gifts himself, thinking of her when he did it, looking for things he thought she might like. And also, well, it was just so *like* him to find gifts that way, now that his secretary was the person he was buying the gifts for. He could check in at the auction site periodically, see what else was available, raise a bid if he needed to—and all without leaving his desk.

Oh, it was a wonderful time, really, full of memories to treasure. They spent the days working together—and the nights wrapped up in each other's arms.

Two weeks went by in the blink of an eye.

Then, the first Monday in April, Caitlin dropped in unannounced.

Aaron's mother breezed into the office at eleven in the morning, wearing black velvet jeans, skin-tight, of course. For a woman in her fifties, Caitlin certainly was fit. Her shirt was Western-cut, as always—black, with lots of glittery yellow fringe.

Caitlin sashayed in and swung a leg up on the edge of Celia's desk. "Hello, baby doll."

"Hi, Caitlin. What a surprise."

"Where's my son?"

"Aaron isn't in right this minute, but—"

"Well, good. I didn't come to see him, anyway."

"Oh?"

"Thanks for doing my taxes. It's a major load off my mind."

"You're welcome." Celia knew what was coming. And it was.

"Now. Down to what matters."

"Yes?"

"Word gets around. The gaming industry's a small one in a lot of ways."

"Oh?"

Caitlin chuckled that sexy deep chuckle of hers. "Sweetie, you should see your pretty little face. Oh, yes. Waitin' for the other shoe to drop, as they say— and you're lookin' good, by the way. I like your hair. And you've changed your makeup, haven't you?"

"As a matter of fact—"

Caitlin beat the air with a hand—a signal that she didn't need to hear more. "Well, like I said. It looks good. And I might as well save the effort at subtlety. We all know I'm not. I'll just say it out straight. I heard about you and Aaron. That looks good to me, too—then again, you knew it would, since I told you so last month. What I want to know is, when's the weddin'?"

The wedding? Where had that come from?

Celia had expected Caitlin to find out about her new relationship with Aaron. And, judging by the things Caitlin had said to her three weeks ago, she'd been pretty sure that Aaron's mother would approve. But *marriage?* Surely Caitlin had to know enough about her own son to realize a wedding wasn't part of the equation.

"My sweet darlin', you look like someone just shot your dog."

Celia thought, at that moment, of Jane. Jane would tell her to be up-front and direct about this. And really, that was probably the best way to go. "Caitlin, you have to know that your oldest son is not the marrying kind."

Caitlin beat the air with her hand again, as if fending off Celia's words. "Sure he is. He just doesn't know it yet."

"No. Seriously, he's a very bright man and he knows how he feels."

"No. He doesn't. He knows what he *thinks* he feels. It's not the same thing. He needs to get what's good for him, whether he likes it or not."

"Caitlin, listen to yourself. Don't you remember what you told me a few weeks ago? How you were staying out of this, one hundred percent?"

"Well, sure. But you worry me a little. Sometimes I think maybe you haven't got the stomach for what needs to be done. And I can't help being me, and being me means not fooling around. I want to see some action, you know?"

"I swear, you have no shame."

Caitlin didn't even flinch. "That's right, I don't. I go after what I want when I want it, and I don't let anything stand in my way."

"Well, that's great. That's terrific. But this isn't about you, it's about Aaron. And me. And we'd like to run our own lives, if you don't mind."

Caitlin leaned forward. "Baby doll, I do mind, if you're gonna make a mess of things."

More than a little overwhelmed by all the glittery fringe and musky perfume, Celia leaned back. "It's just…"

"What?"

"Caitlin, this is not your business."

"Sure it is. He's my son and I want him to get what's best for him."

"That's for him to decide—and come on. You never settled down yourself. Why would you think your son would want to?"

"I'd like to think he's smarter than me. And besides, he's a man. A man needs a good woman. A man needs…a home base."

"Well, I'm flattered, sincerely, that you think I'm the right woman for Aaron on a permanent basis, but—"

The phone jangled to life. "Excuse me." Celia reached for it.

Caitlin slammed a hand down on the receiver. "Uh-uh. Leave it."

Celia sighed. "Caitlin. Let go of the phone."

"You've got voice mail. Get a little use out of it."

"This is so overbearing of you."

Caitlin just stared at her, black eyes gleaming. The

phone rang four times. When it was finally silent, Caitlin folded her arms over her impressive breasts. "You love him, right?"

"It's none of your business."

"I'll take that as a yes. So. You love him, you want what's best for him. Right?"

"As I said before, what's best for Aaron is for Aaron to decide."

Caitlin threw back her head and groaned aloud. "Listen. You marrying my boy will be the best thing that ever happened to him. You'll be doing him the biggest favor you ever did for anyone. And since you love him, it's natural you'd want to do right by him."

"He does not want to get married."

"I want you to get a ring on your finger."

"Well, as I've said a number of times now, what you want is not what matters here."

"Do whatever you have to do."

"I can't believe you're saying this."

"A baby would be nice…"

"Oh, Caitlin. That is so unacceptable."

"He'll thank you for it later."

"No, he won't. What are you thinking? He's not going to thank me for *tricking* him."

"Sure he will. Eventually."

"Caitlin. Whoa. Stop. Hold on."

Caitlin sat back a little. "What?"

"I am not going to manipulate Aaron into marrying me. It's wrong. And I won't do it. He doesn't want to get married. Ever. He's made that very clear."

Caitlin made a humphing sound. "Well, if you believe that, then what are you doing with him?"

"I beg your pardon?"

"Oh, don't go gettin' all huffy on me. You know what I'm sayin'. We both know that you *are* the marrying kind. You're a nice girl who wants a husband, like all nice girls do."

"That is *so* not fair."

"What's *fair* got to do with it? What's *fair* got to do with any damn thing? Haven't you heard, darlin'? Life is *not* fair."

"Fine. All right. You may have a point there. But that crack about nice girls…for your information, Caitlin, there are nice girls in this world who have more on their minds than getting a ring on their finger."

"Well, you could be right. Maybe there are nice girls like that. But you're not one of them, not when it comes to Aaron, and we both know it. One thing you learn in my business, it's how to read a face. And I can read yours, baby doll, every time you look in my son's direction—every time someone mentions his name. So don't tell me lies. You know you're no good at them. Don't you sit there and try to convince me you don't want to marry my darlin' boy."

"I didn't say that."

Caitlin tossed that hard black head of hair. "Hah."

"What I said was, *he* doesn't want to marry *me*."

"And I said, he *does*. He just doesn't know it yet."

"Caitlin, this conversation is going in circles."

"You're right." Caitlin swung her leg off the desk and stood, sucking in her stomach and poking out those big, proud breasts. She smoothed her velvet jeans—as if they could possibly have gotten wrinkled, tight as they were. "I'm goin' downstairs to have a look around the place, see how things are doing.'' She clicked her tongue. ''Drives Aaron crazy, when I do that—will he be back around here soon?''

''After lunch.''

''Hmm. You know what?''

''Caitlin, I don't like the look in your eye.''

Aaron's mother had the nerve to flutter her fake black eyelashes. ''I don't think I'll stick around.''

''But—''

''Let me speak. I want you to give a little thought to the things I've said to you.''

''Caitlin—''

''I'm not done. Give what I said some thought. And remember, if there's anything—*anything*—I can do to help you out with this, you just let me know. As for right now, I'm goin' down to the casino, gonna walk the floor a little, just enough so word will get back to Aaron that I'm as irritating as ever—gotta keep him guessin', after all.''

''No, you don't.''

''Sure, I do, sweetie pie. Aaron wouldn't know how to handle it if all of a sudden, I turned *reasonable* on him.''

''How do you know he couldn't handle it? Have you ever tried being reasonable?''

''No, and I don't believe I'll start now. What I *will* do is walk the floor a little, then head for the airport and catch a flight home.'' Celia knew there was a clincher coming. And there was. ''I'll let *you* tell him the real reason I came. That is, if you *want* to tell him. Because, baby doll, I promise you, he'll never hear it from me.''

* * *

Celia intended to tell him. She honestly did.

He returned to the office at two-thirty. One of his managers had already reported that his mother had been down on the casino floor. "Is she here?" he asked grimly, shooting a put-upon look at the shut door to his own office.

"No. But she was—at a little after eleven. When she left, she told me she was going down to the casino for a while and then she was going back to the airport to catch a plane for home."

He was scowling. "I don't get it. What did she want?"

Celia recognized the moment for just what it was: time to come clean.

But when she opened her mouth, evasions came out. "Well, she thanked me. For doing her taxes."

"That's all? She flew down here just to thank you for doing her taxes?"

Celia shrugged, letting him read whatever he chose to in the cryptic gesture.

He said, "I do not understand that woman. Never have, never will."

"I'd have to say, you're not alone."

He hitched a leg up on the desk—as his mother had done a few hours before. "Well. She's gone now. I think I'll just be grateful for small favors."

"Good idea."

He leaned toward her. Her midsection heated and her breath caught.

Just before his lips met hers, she made herself sit back. "Uh-uh. Not in the office."

"Celia."

"Yes, Aaron?"

"Admit it." His voice, pitched low for her ears alone, caused a long, delicious shiver to slip along the surface of her skin.

"Admit what?"

"You want me to kiss you."

"Oh, yes. I do."

He leaned forward again.

She put up a hand, between his lips and hers. "But not in the office."

He lifted an eyebrow. "Such admirable restraint." He stood. "Tonight." The word was a promise.

She nodded, slowly. "Yes. Please. Tonight."

She was thinking, I *will* tell him. Later. I honestly will.

He was coming to her rooms at eight. When he got there, she would pour him a drink and sit him down and tell him everything, all of it—from Caitlin's remarks in New Venice three weeks before, to everything she'd said that morning.

But every time Celia imagined herself doing that, she found herself wincing and squirming in her chair.

It was just too…embarrassing to go into it. No matter how she tried to put the words together in her mind, it made her feel *less* somehow, to tell him the truth about this. Because deep in her heart, she wanted exactly what Caitlin had said she wanted: to marry the man she loved.

But she had no illusions. She honestly didn't. They had a clear understanding on the subject of marriage. There wasn't going to be one.

And she didn't want to go into it. She didn't *need*

to go into it. There was no point in going into it. She
was a strong woman and she knew where she stood
with him, that what they had wouldn't last forever.

But while it did last, damn it, she had a right to
her pride.

Let Caitlin play her absurd matchmaking games.
Celia had made herself clear to Aaron's mother. She
was not, in any way, going along with the older
woman's schemes.

And she was not going to report to Aaron the ridiculous things his mother had said.

Let Caitlin do it herself—or not. It was nothing to
Celia. She was not saying a word.

The first thing she did when he came to her door
was to wrap her arms around his neck. "Welcome."

He held her lightly, grinning down at her. "I think,
maybe, you're glad to see me."

Shamelessly, she rubbed her hips against him.
"Um. I *know* you're glad to see me...."

His wonderful hands slid down her back and over
the twin curves of her bottom. He cupped her, pulled
her up snug and close, so she could feel even more
intimately how much he wanted her. "I suppose
you've got dinner waiting...."

"No. I thought you could use a little time to relax
first. I asked them to send it up at about nine."

"An hour."

"Um-hm."

They kissed, a deep, seeking kiss, right there, in
her entryway, with the door to the hall standing wide
open so anyone who walked by might have
seen them.

Neither of them cared about that. Why should they? Everyone knew they were lovers and they were on their own time, in her private space.

When he finally lifted his head, her whole body was humming. He scooped her up into his arms, kicked the door shut, and headed for her bedroom.

They went to Atlantic City that weekend, to look over a small casino/hotel Silver Standard was acquiring. Celia stayed by Aaron's side, doing her job, tending to the details, keeping things running smoothly.

And when they were alone, she went into his arms.

Saturday night, in bed in their hotel suite, he asked her when she'd be going on the pill. They had talked about it earlier, and she'd told him that she would.

She traced the line of his jaw with a lazy finger. "Well, I've been to my doctor...."

"And?"

She stroked his hair, lightly, at the temple. "I got a prescription. I also had it filled...."

"And?"

She kissed the cleft in his chin. "Now I have to wait until the Sunday after my next period to start taking them."

"And that will be?"

She thought for a moment, realized her period was due in the next few days. "Soon," she said. "Very soon..." He wrapped his arms around her and put his mouth on hers and for a while, she forgot everything but the magic of his kiss.

But their conversation had reminded her that her

period was due. She waited for the signs, for the bloated feeling and the cramping.

The signs didn't come.

By Friday, it seemed as if she thought of nothing else but the fact that she was late—and what that might mean.

On Saturday, she left High Sierra and went to a drugstore downtown, where she bought a home test. The instructions on the box said the test could determine pregnancy the day after a missed period. Back in her rooms, Celia went straight to the bathroom off her bedroom. She sat on the edge of the tub and opened the box.

Inside, along with the necessary equipment, she found a lengthy brochure containing detailed instructions, including the information that taking the test first thing in the morning minimized the possibility of getting a false negative result.

Carefully, Celia folded the brochure back into a tidy square and returned it to the box. She put the box in the cabinet under the sink.

Tomorrow morning, she thought. Tomorrow, I'll know.

That night, she and Aaron had dinner in the Placer Room, where the tablecloths were snowy white and the booths were half-moon-shaped, upholstered in glove-soft black leather. The walls were papered in stamped antique-gold foil. Aaron ordered a nice bottle of pinot grigio. After Aaron tasted it and nodded, the wine steward filled Celia's glass.

She looked at that full glass and knew she would

not touch it. That was the moment she understood her own intention. If the test tomorrow came out positive, she was going to keep the baby.

Oh, God. What would Aaron think about that?

She wasn't sure she wanted to know.

Aaron's estranged cousin, Jonas Bravo, the man they called the Bravo Billionaire, also had dinner in the Placer Room that night. He and his platinum-haired wife, Emma, sat three booths down from Celia and Aaron.

Aaron never so much as glanced their way, which didn't surprise Celia in the least. Caitlin and her brood had always lived as if the other Bravos didn't exist. After all, Aaron's father, Blake, had been disinherited and completely cut off from the rest of the family by the time he met Caitlin. And then, before her youngest, Cade, was even born, Blake Bravo had faked his own death and vanished. He took a second wife and fathered another son. But before that, he'd kidnapped his own nephew for revenge against the family that had scorned him.

In the end, thirty years later, Jonas Bravo got his brother back, and the evil Blake was truly gone—according to the newspapers, he'd died last May of heart failure in an Oklahoma Hospital.

New Venice had been abuzz with gossip as the story unfolded. A lot of folks had assumed that the branches of the family would reunite at last.

But it hadn't happened. For the Nevada Bravos, things stayed as they had always been. Caitlin and her sons continued to behave as though they were the only Bravos in the world. Which meant that Jonas and his lovely wife could eat dinner three booths down from Aaron and Celia and not so much as a nod of recognition would pass between the two men.

Emma Bravo, however, was another story. More than once, she caught Celia's eye. Each time she did, a big, friendly smile would spread across her pretty face. That smile was contagious. Celia couldn't help but smile back.

Aaron noticed the exchange of looks between the women. He said, very softly, "Celia, what are you up to?"

She felt angry with him, suddenly—mostly, she knew, from sheer nerves over what she'd learn tomorrow when she finally took that test. "Nothing. Just smiling at someone who smiled at me. Is that all right with you?"

He frowned at her. "What's the matter?"

She thought, *I'm terrified I might be pregnant.* She said, "Well, don't you think it's about time you and your cousin stopped ignoring each other? I mean, I understand, your mother is a proud woman. And she was loyal to your father's memory and refused to have anything to do with the family who cut him off. But now the truth has come out about Blake, don't you think everyone should forgive and forget?"

He picked up his wineglass and sipped, then set the glass down. "Celia." He spoke quietly, thoughtfully. "I have nothing at all against Jonas Bravo, or any other Bravo, for that matter. Yes, my mother used to say she hated them, back when Cade and Will and I were kids. But you know Caitlin, a drama queen if there ever was one. She never mentions them at all these days. We're all going along just fine. There's no animosity.''

"And no connection, either."

"Why does there need to be a connection?"

"Well, because you are *family* to each other."

He shook his head. "I know who my family is. My crazy mother and my two brothers. That's about all the family I can handle, believe me."

"But—"

"Celia." He caught her hand, kissed the back of it. "Stop." He gestured at her full plate. "Are you going to eat? You've hardly touched your food—or your wine."

Gently, she pulled her hand free of his. She picked up her fork and her steak knife and went to work on her filet mignon. His phone must have vibrated, because he murmured, "Excuse me."

"Of course."

He took the phone out and answered, first glancing at the display. "Tony, what is it?"

Tony Jarvis, she supposed, with some question or other that couldn't wait till later. "Yes," he said. "All right... That's fine. Go ahead."

Celia ate her dinner and promised herself she wouldn't bring up the subject of Jonas Bravo again. Aaron's relationship with his cousin was Aaron's business. She was on edge about the test tomorrow, and a contrary part of her was looking for any excuse to start an argument.

But really, she didn't want to argue with Aaron. She loved him and she intended to treasure every moment she had with him.

When he slipped his phone back into his pocket, she leaned toward him, till her shoulder brushed his arm. "Sorry..."

He put his hand on her knee beneath the tablecloth and gave it a tender squeeze.

Later, when they got to her place, Aaron asked again if something was bothering her.

She lied some more. "No. Why?"

"I don't know. On and off, all night, you've seemed...far away. Distracted."

She shut the door and engaged the lock. Then she turned into his arms and slid her hands around his neck. "Bring me back to the here-and-now."

His glance tracked from her mouth to her eyes and back to her mouth again. "This does look promising."

"Kiss me."

"You're sure a kiss will do it?"

"I think we really ought to give it a try."

"Like this?" His mouth came down on hers.

"Oh, yes..." She breathed the words against his parted lips.

He lifted his head. "More?"

"Please."

So he slanted his mouth the other way and claimed her lips again.

Oh, sweet heaven, the man did know how to kiss. He started undressing her, right there in her small entryway. She was naked in no time, at which point he began guiding her backward, toward the living room, leaving her little black slip dress, strapless black bra and panties, as well as her spike-heeled satin shoes in a mound on the floor of the foyer.

She'd thought they were headed for her bedroom. But he detoured to the living-room sofa. He pulled her over there and sat down and pulled her on top of him, so she sat astride his lean hips. Shameless, she rubbed herself against him, moaning at the feel of him, that ridge of hardness and heat beneath the zipper of his slacks.

She went to work on his jacket, getting it off, tossing it away, kissing him deeply as she worked at his tie.

"Can't wait..." he groaned against her mouth. He started working at his belt buckle.

She realized she was in the way. With a groan, she slid off him. They fumbled together at his belt. Once it was undone, she grabbed the end of it and slithered it free of the belt loops, tossing it to the floor. He unzipped his slacks. She pulled the elastic of his boxers out of the way, freeing him. Oh, he was so beautiful. So silky and big and hot...

She felt his warm breath against her ear. "Ride me..."

Moaning in pure delight, she slid one bare leg over him. Oh yes. She felt him, there, nudging the feminine heart of her. She was wet and open. So ready....

She lowered her body onto—

At the last possible second, she realized the huge mistake she was about to make.

She scrambled off him.

He swore. "What the—"

"Wait right there."

He groaned—and then he swore again. "Celia. What's going on?"

"You know. Protection."

He blinked. "Oh, God. Right."

They stared at each other.

It *had* happened before. The only difference between now and then was that tonight, she'd remembered in time to correct the mistake.

Worry jabbed at her again. Maybe it didn't matter at this point. Maybe tomorrow, she'd discover it was too late, anyway.

She pushed the worry to the back of her mind. It would still be there tomorrow.

And for now, well, better to proceed in a responsible manner.

He looked down at the evidence of his desire for her, pointing boldly north. Then he lifted his gaze to hers. "Where do you think you're going?"

"To get the—"

"Stop right there." He reached in his pocket and pulled out a foil-wrapped pouch. "Is this what you're looking for?"

A giggle of pure surprise escaped her. "Where did you get that?"

He grinned. "I've decided it's best to be ready at all times, in all circumstances."

"Ah." She looked at him, loving him—and wanting him so. It was going to be all right, she just knew it. Everything was going to work out fine. And for now, well, she couldn't resist the promise in those blue, blue eyes. She didn't *want* to resist.

Softly, she whispered, "Good thinking."

He was already rolling the condom down over himself. ''Get back here,'' he growled. Then he looked up at her, eyes so tender. ''Please.''

She climbed into his lap again. He whispered her name on a pleasured sigh, as she slid down onto the waiting length of him. Oh, it felt so good to be joined with him. It felt so right, so very fine....

He lifted her slightly, gathering her to him, first licking a circle around her left breast, then capturing it, tenderly drawing the nipple to a hard, aching bead. Celia felt the silken cord of arousal, that connection between her breast and her womb, shimmering, tightening, quivering like a drawn bow.

She let her head fall back and moaned low in her throat, riding him slow, in long, wet, lovely strokes. ''So good...'' she whispered.

He made a low noise that sounded very much like agreement.

And then he encircled her waist with his lean hands, pressing her down as he slid up harder into her, increasing the hungry, rolling rhythm.

Everything flew away.

She cried out.

He took her mouth, kissing her as fulfillment sang through her, a burning melody, fire-bright.

He got up to go at a little after two. She walked him to the door.

''Tomorrow,'' he said. ''Lunch?''

''Yes.''

''I'll call, around ten...''

''Okay.''

He gathered her into his arms and kissed her good-night.

Oh, the man could kiss. Her midsection was melting, her knees turning boneless.

A kiss like his should never end.

But it did. He left her. She returned to her bed.

She felt drowsy, at first, soothed and satisfied by their lovemaking. She anticipated a few hours of restful sleep.

But the drowsiness passed. Sleep never came. She waited, wide awake, until five. And then she got up and went to the bathroom and took the test.

It was positive.

And as she looked at the double pink line in the result window, it almost seemed that she could hear Caitlin Bravo's low, knowing laughter echoing in her ears.

Chapter Thirteen

Was she surprised?

No, she decided. Not really.

She felt kind of numb, actually. Numb, but calm.

And determined.

She did know one thing for certain right at that moment. She was keeping this baby.

Gee. Wouldn't Aaron be thrilled?

She recalled how he'd asked if she was pregnant all those weeks ago, when she'd first confessed her love to him.

Maybe that was how she'd break it to him.

Guess what, Aaron? I wasn't pregnant then. But I am now....

She tossed the test wand into the wastebasket and went back to her bedroom, where she dropped to the side of her tangled bed and looked down at her bare red-tipped toes.

She sat that way for perhaps five minutes, gathering her red robe close around her, hugging herself tight, thinking that she ought to *do* something—but not sure exactly what.

Maybe what she needed was a little good advice.

She reached for the phone, punched the auto-dial button for Jane—and then disconnected the call before it went through. What was Jane going to tell her?

The usual.

Honesty is the way to go here. Tell him the truth.

And surprise, surprise. Jane would be right.

But she didn't need Jane to rub it in, thank you very much. She knew she would have to tell Aaron that she was having his baby. What she didn't know was how she was going to make herself do it.

And how she would bear his reaction. That was another thing she didn't want to think about.

Really, she'd rather talk to Jilly than Jane right at the moment. Celia loved Jane dearly, but Jane was always so firm and uncompromising when it came to the tough questions in life. Jilly would be more easygoing, less judgmental—on this subject, anyway. Jilly was always more interested in those she loved getting what they really wanted, not so much of a stickler on truth and integrity.

Celia punched the button for her other best friend— and then cut it off in mid-dial as well. What advice would Jilly have for her? What to *wear* when she told him?

No. Jillian wouldn't have the answers here.

And besides, Celia didn't *need* answers. She knew what to do. She just utterly dreaded the thought of doing it.

She stared at the phone in her hand—and experienced a powerful impulse to call Caitlin, to scream rude, incoherent, hopeless things at her. And then to slam the phone down before Caitlin could say anything back.

Celia waited, clutching the phone, as that dangerous urge slowly faded away. When it was gone, she felt like a balloon with all the air let out of it—drained and limp.

Very gently, she hung up.

Then she took off her robe and got under the covers. She turned on her side and she drew her legs up close to her body and wrapped both arms around her knees.

All tucked into herself, seeking a comfort she didn't really expect to find, she closed her eyes.

The ringing of the phone jangled her awake.

"Huh?" Her eyes popped open. She was looking straight at her bedside clock. It was 10:02.

The phone went on ringing. Celia lay perfectly still, staring at the clock. After four rings, she heard the machine in the other room pick up the call. She watched the clock and saw the time change. 10:03. She closed her eyes and went back to sleep.

The next time the phone rang, she didn't even open her eyes. She rolled to her other side and wrapped the pillow over her head. She drifted off again.

The phone rang for the third time not long after the

second. With a groan, Celia turned over. The clock was waiting. Ten past twelve. Not even morning anymore.

She dragged herself to a sitting position and grabbed the receiver in mid-ring. "Hello," she grumbled into the mouthpiece.

"There you are." It broke her heart, just hearing his voice. "Still in bed?"

"'Fraid so." She gripped the phone much tighter than she needed to and told herself she was not going to burst into self-pitying tears.

"I called twice before. No answer."

"I confess. I was sleeping."

"Well, it's time you got up."

"Yes. Yes, I guess it is."

"How about if we—"

She cut him off. "Aaron."

A pause, then he asked, "What?"

"Do you think you could come here, to my rooms, in say, half an hour? There's something I have to tell you."

"Celia—"

"No. Really. I do need to talk with you. And I need to do it face-to-face."

He was quiet again. It was far from a comfortable silence.

"Aaron? Did you hear me?"

"Of course, I heard you."

"Will you—"

He cut her off. "I'll be there. Thirty minutes."

The line went dead.

Celia yanked the phone away from her ear and stared at it, unable to believe what she had just done.

What was the matter with her? She was maybe three weeks pregnant, tops. She'd only taken the test a few hours ago.

Yes, she did have to tell him. Sooner or later.

But right *now,* today?

Even Jane wouldn't have expected *that* of her.

With a groan of pure misery, Celia shook the phone at the far wall. The silly display of frustration did nothing to change the fact that in the next half hour Aaron would be knocking on her door, expecting to hear what she just had to tell him immediately.

She slammed the phone back in its cradle.

And then she flopped back on the bed. "*Why* did I do that? Why, why, why?" she asked of no one in particular.

Not surprisingly, she got no answer.

Aaron arrived at Celia's door twenty-eight minutes from the time he'd hung up the phone. He punched the buzzer.

The door swung back immediately, leading him to believe she'd been waiting right behind it. She wore flared black slacks and a red sweater. No makeup. Her face had that scrubbed-clean, innocent look. She smelled dewy and sweet. Fresh from the shower.

Conflicting urges tore at him.

He wanted to grab her and hold her and kiss that soft, plump mouth.

He also wanted to demand to know what the hell was going on. He'd sensed something wasn't right for

a few days now. Last night, he'd even asked her—
more than once, too—what was bothering her. She'd
said there was nothing.

But looking in her troubled face right now, he knew
for certain that she had lied.

And he was angry.

And strangely fearful, as well.

He didn't understand his own emotions in this. He
only knew that little Celia Tuttle mattered to him in
ways no other woman ever had. They worked together and they played together. They shared a bed
almost every night. He spent more time with her than
he ever had with any of the other women he'd been
involved with romantically.

He kept waiting to get bored.

But it wasn't happening.

In fact, he seemed to be moving in the opposite
direction. The more time he spent with her, the more
he *wanted* to spend with her. She'd become very important to him.

Too important, probably.

"Please come in," she said, way too formally, re-
minding him of the first time he'd been here, to her
rooms—that day in early March, when she'd confessed that she loved him.

They went to the living room. He took an easy
chair and she sat on the couch.

She folded her hands and looked down at them.

What? he was thinking. *Talk. Tell me what the hell
is going on.*

But he kept his mouth shut. The way he saw it,

she'd asked him to come here, said she had to talk to him.

So all right. Let her say whatever she had to say without any coaxing from him.

Celia knew very well that the ball was in her court. She'd gotten him here and it was her job now to tell him why. She cleared her throat. "Um, well, I..." and the words kind of petered out. She stared at her folded hands. She didn't want to look up. She didn't want to meet his eyes.

She didn't want to tell him what she knew she *had* to tell him.

And as she sat there, in that awful, yawning silence, it occurred to her that she...couldn't.

She could not tell him. Not right now, not today. She'd barely learned the truth herself. The baby— *their* baby—wouldn't be born for months and months.

Of course, Aaron would have to know eventually.

But he certainly didn't need to get the news this minute.

Didn't she have a right to a little time for herself? A little breather, where she could begin to deal with the enormity of what was happening in her life?

In the back of her mind somewhere, she could hear Jane chiding, *Tell him. He has a right to know. He's the baby's father. And honesty is always the best policy....*

Oh, shut up, Jane, she thought.

But that one word, *honesty* seemed to echo in her brain. Oh, yes. There *was* a central problem here— beyond the fact that they'd messed up a few times and forgotten to practice safe and protected sex. That central problem was all about a lack of honesty. On her part.

Which was ironic, since she had told herself she was being so straightforward, so up-front, so *truthful* in this love affair.

But the whole time, she'd been lying—lying to *herself.* She was exactly what Caitlin had accused her of being. A nice girl who wanted a good man to marry her.

Correction. A nice, *pregnant* girl. A pregnant girl who wanted her baby's father to marry her.

She looked up. He was waiting, jaw set, eyes watchful. He was on to her now. He knew for certain there was a serious problem of some kind. At this point, he wouldn't buy her denials for a minute, should she try to resurrect them. If she sent him away now without telling him about the baby, it would do serious damage to his opinion of her.

And she valued that, his high regard. Maybe he didn't love her, didn't feel the same searing joy and agonizing pain at the thought of her, at the very mention of her name, as she did when it came to him. But he did respect her. He *liked* her.

And she never wanted to lose that—his good opinion of her as a person—not if she could help it, anyway.

He kept on watching her, waiting for her to come out with it.

She stared back at him, into his eyes. As they regarded each other, it seemed to Celia that all her excuses and evasions, all her cowardly hopes for putting off this conversation, softened to formlessness and melted away.

She understood. There really was no backing out now. She had to do it, had to say it, now, today. She had called him here and sat him down and he had a right to hear the truth from her lips. He needed to know what was happening, and to know it now.

It was, after all, his baby, too. She couldn't turn back time, couldn't do the past over. She'd been careless and she was pregnant and the best she could hope for was to handle the situation with dignity and frankness.

She yanked her shoulders back and aimed her chin high. "Aaron," she said. "I'm pregnant."

He didn't move. He didn't speak—for a hideous count of ten. Then he opened his jacket, took his phone from the inside pocket and tossed it on the wheat-colored Berber that covered the floor. It took her a second or two to realize it must have been vibrating with an incoming call.

She said, "Please. If it's important, you can go ahead and—"

"Celia."

"Hmm?"

"Forget the damn phone call."

She gulped, nodded. "Okay."

"When did you find out?"

"This morning. I took a home test. The results were positive."

He tipped his head to the side, thinking. Then he asked, "How dependable is a test like that?"

"Very. They're accurate the day after a missed period. I'm four days late."

He was quiet again. Then he muttered, "Last night." His eyes accused her. "I kept asking you what was the matter."

"Yes, I know."

"But you said there was nothing."

"I lied."

"Why?"

"Because I wanted to take the test first. It could have been a false alarm. I didn't see any reason for both of us to worry."

He considered her words. After a minute, he nodded. "All right. That makes sense."

She realized she'd been holding her breath. She let it out, slowly.

He asked, "Now what?"

She told him the next thing he needed to know. "I'm going to keep this baby."

That got her one of his wry half smiles. "Why doesn't that surprise me?"

She forged on. "I'll raise the baby alone, if I have to. But I'd rather not. I believe that, if possible, a baby should have *both* of his—or her—parents."

"Ah," he said. "I see."

"You disagree?"

He lifted one shoulder, sketching a shrug. "Well, I'd have to say, that is the conventional wisdom. But what would I know about it? I was raised in a bar by a woman who never did manage to settle on one man."

"Aaron?"

"What?"

"I think you know where I'm going with this."

"Let's say I have a pretty good idea."

"Well, I guess I'll just ask you."

"Go for it."

"Aaron, will you marry me?"

"Yes, Celia. I will."

Chapter Fourteen

*Y*es.

He'd said yes.

Celia stood up. Then she felt a little dizzy. So she sat down again.

His answer was the one she'd hardly dared hope for. And not in the least what she'd expected. She didn't know *what* she'd expected, exactly. But it certainly wasn't a quick, firm "yes."

However, he *had* said it. He was willing to marry her.

Everything was working out, after all. And she should be happy. She should accept his answer and go on from here. After all, when a non-marrying man said he would marry you, the last thing you should do was question his decision.

But she couldn't help it. She *did* question his decision.

She cleared her throat. "Aaron, I have to ask. Are you sure you want to do that?"

He gave her a puzzled frown. "Didn't I just say yes?"

"Well, yes. You did. But, well, you know how you are."

He looked at her sideways. "And that is?"

"You told me from the first that we weren't going to be married."

He made a low, amused noise in his throat. "Under the circumstances, I've changed my mind."

"Ah. Well."

The look of amusement faded. "Well, what?"

"Well, that's good. But—"

He put up a hand. "Why not just leave it right there, with 'that's good'?"

"Because, now that I think about it, maybe you should take a little time, not rush into this. I'd like you to be certain that marrying me is what you want to do."

"Celia. You asked. I answered. I think we've about covered it."

"Well, I want you to have a little time to—"

"I don't need time."

She swallowed. "You don't?"

"No." He looked at her probingly. "Do you?"

"Well, of course I don't. This is what I want. To marry you. To have our baby…"

"Okay then." He stood. "We're in agreement." He came toward her.

She watched him, feeling edgy. Wary.

Oh, what was the matter with her? She'd gotten exactly what she wanted.

Why didn't she feel better about it?

He held out his hand. "Come on." After a slight hesitation, she put hers in it. His grip was warm. Firm. The familiar thrill shivered through her, the excitement when he touched her. Her inconvenient apprehensions faded a little.

He gave a tug and she was in his arms.

Oh, it did feel good to be there. She sighed and rested her head against his chest.

"Look at me." He took her chin and tipped her face up so that she had no choice but to meet his eyes. "I think you'll make a fine wife. I've always thought so. Whether I'll make much of a husband remains to be seen. But I'm willing to give it a try— for you. And for the baby."

She told herself she was content. They would do the best they could with the hand they'd been dealt. "About the wedding…"

"I'll leave that to you. I suppose it ought to be soon, don't you think?"

"Yes, I agree."

"And this *is* Las Vegas. Pick a chapel. Any chapel."

"Well, actually…"

He brushed a kiss between her brows. "I'm listening."

"I was thinking we might get married in New Venice. Something small and simple. Next weekend, if I can get everyone together. Just family and close friends.''

''However you want it, that's fine with me.''

She reconsidered the time frame. If they married next Saturday, that only gave her five days. No way it would be enough time. ''On second thought, maybe the weekend after next.''

''Whatever you say.''

''You are certainly agreeable.''

''You don't like me agreeable?''

''Well, I just want to be sure that—''

He cut her off by laying a shushing finger, so lightly, against her lips. ''Celia. I'll tell you what you can do.''

''What? Anything. Please. Just say it.''

''You can kiss me.''

''Kiss you? I'd love to, you know that. But that's not what I—''

''Celia.''

''What?''

''Shut up and kiss me. Will you do that?''

''Oh, I do worry, you know, that you—''

''Shh.''

She groaned and shut her mouth.

''Kiss me. Come on…''

She tipped her head back and presented her lips.

''That's better,'' he said, and brought his mouth down on hers.

They ended up in her bed, of course. And after that, she called Casa D'Oro and ordered them lunch. He

had some work he needed to catch up on, so he left
her at a little after three.

As soon as he was out the door, she called Jane.

Jane said, "Hello."

And Celia said, "I'm pregnant."

"Oh, no."

"Oh, yes."

"Celia Louise, what is the matter with you? I assumed you had sense enough to always practice safe
sex."

"I did, I *do*—well, *almost* always."

"*Almost* isn't good enough, and I think you know
it isn't."

"Janey. Please. I know I screwed up. A lecture is
the last thing I need right now."

"You're right," said Jane in a gentler tone. "Are
you okay? Do you need me to fly down there?"

"Thanks for offering. I'm fine—well, as fine as a
any woman who went and got herself accidentally
pregnant ever is."

"Do you know what you're going to do?"

"Have a baby in about eight and a half months."

"Ah. And when do you plan to tell Aaron about
this?"

"I already have."

That actually gave Jane Elliott pause. "Wow. Celia
Louise. Good going. You got right on it."

"Yes, I did."

"What did he say?"

"Before or after I asked him to marry me?"

Jane gasped. "You didn't."

"I did."

"Talk about being direct. I'm impressed. I truly am."

"Thank you," Celia said modestly.

"And his answer was?"

"Yes. He said yes."

Jane let out a Jillian-like shriek of pure delight. "Oh, Ceil. I'm so happy for you. I am. Happy and proud. You went out and you got what you wanted. It took you a while to do it, but you did tell the man you loved him right up front, no coyness. No games or denials. And now this. You were right there, right on the case, telling him the truth when you found out you were pregnant. Telling him what you wanted— marriage. And it's all worked out, hasn't it? Because, all along the line, you have told the truth. You have behaved with total honesty and absolute integrity."

Well, more or less, Celia thought, but didn't say. Jane was right—for the most part. Celia *had* been honest, or at least, she'd tried her best to be.

Jane asked, "When's the wedding?"

With a large measure of relief, Celia let the subject of her integrity drop. "Well, that's another thing I called about. We want it to be soon. Saturday after next, if possible. That's the twenty-eighth. Not a big production or anything, just family and close friends. And up home, there in New Venice and—"

"How about here, at my house?"

"Oh, Janey. You read my mind. But are you sure? It *is* short notice, and—"

"I'd love to do it."

They talked for another hour: about the guest list— small enough that Celia would simply call everyone and invite them personally—about the food and the beverages, the cake and the flowers. Jane said she'd contact Reverend Culpepper over at the Community Church and ask him to do the honors. If he wasn't available that particular Saturday, she'd ask her father, the judge.

"You call Jilly, right away," Jane instructed before she hung up.

"I will," Celia promised.

Jane said goodbye and Celia punched the speed-dial for Jillian.

"Ohmigod, pregnant." Jillian groaned. "What will you do?"

"I already did it. I asked him to marry me. And he said yes."

Jillian let out a gleeful cry. "Get *out* of here."

"No. It's true. The wedding's a week from this Saturday. At Jane's."

"Ceil, I gotta hand it to you. You do not fool around."

"So, will you be there?"

"Just let anyone try to keep me away—what about a dress? Have you found one?"

"Hey. I'm fast, but not that fast."

Jillian rattled off the names of three Las Vegas bridal boutiques. "All of them are wonderful. You'll love what they have."

"Thanks, Jilly."

"And if there's anything I can—"

"You know that there is."

"I figured as much. What?"

"Janey's got the list. She'll call you."

"All right. Ceil?"

"Hm?"

"Are you happy?"

"Ecstatic."

And she was, she kept telling herself, as she called her mother and her two sisters and three brothers. She was marrying the man that she loved. Of course, she was happy.

Celia's mother was her usual distracted self. "Celia. Wait a minute. Oh, it's so hard to keep track of all you kids these days…"

"What, Mom?"

"Well, it's just that I didn't know there was anything going on between you and your boss."

"We haven't been…together, as a couple, for all that long."

"Oh, honey. *Aaron Bravo?* I know you love your job, but—"

"The point is, I love *him.*"

"Oh. Well. If that's the case, then what can I say?"

"Congratulations?"

"Well, yes. That. And, Celia dear, you do have to realize, it is a shock. You, marrying one of those Bravo boys…."

Patience, thought Celia. "Mom. As I said before, I love him. And I'm marrying him."

"Hmm," said her mother. "Hmm…" Celia waited. Finally, her mother admitted grudgingly, "Well, I *have* heard that those boys have done well for themselves."

"That's right. They have."

"But that Caitlin is a wild one still. One man after

another and each one of them younger than the one before. I don't understand how she—''

''Will you come to my wedding, Mom?''

''You know your father and I hate to fly. All the inconvenience, and then, who *knows* what could happen these days? The world is not what it used to be and—''

''Mom. Will you come to my wedding?''

Her mother heaved a huge sigh. ''Oh, well, I suppose it's one of those things we really shouldn't miss.''

''That's right.''

''Okay. We'll be there.''

After her mother, Celia called her oldest sister, Annie.

''Aaron Bravo?'' Annie said, as if maybe she'd heard wrong. ''Celia, are you *serious?*''

''Well, no, Annie,'' Celia replied. ''This is all a big joke. Are you laughing yet?''

Annie backpedaled madly. ''Look. Celia. I'm sorry. It just surprised me, that's all. I know you work for him and everything, and I know he's made it big and all. But *I* went to high school with the guy. And he's one of those bad Bravos and…well, I don't know. My sweet, shy little sister *marrying* him? Who would have thought that would ever happen?''

''It's happening.''

''You're mad at me.''

''No. Honestly. I'm not. Can you come to my wedding?''

''Saturday, the twenty-eighth, you said?''

''That's it. It's in New Venice.'' Annie and her

husband John and their two kids lived in Susanville, California, now. "At Jane's. You remember Jane?"

"Of course I remember Jane."

"Great. Well, she lives on Green Street now, in the house that used to belong to her Aunt Sophie."

"I remember that house."

"The wedding will be there."

"Right. The twenty-eighth."

"At two in the afternoon."

"I'm going to say yes now. I can't think of anything that would keep us from it."

"Thanks, Annie. I know you guys are busy and this is short notice."

"Celia. I have to ask."

Celia didn't like the sound of her sister's voice. "Yes? What?"

"Well, he isn't in the Mafia or anything, is he? I think I heard somewhere that—"

"Annie. Please. Do you honestly believe I'd marry some Wise Guy?"

"Well, what do I know? I live in *Susanville*."

"Annie. Listen. Aaron's not in the Mafia. I swear to you."

"Well, good. Sorry. I had to ask."

After Annie, Celia called the rest of her siblings, leaving messages for Peter and Katie, reaching Tom and Janice. Tom said he'd be there. Jannie said she'd try.

And what about Caitlin? Celia found herself wondering once her own family had been called. What about Cade and Will Bravo? They should be called, too. She'd told Aaron she'd take care of inviting everyone. But really, he should be the one to tell his family he was getting married.

She asked him about it that evening, over dinner, at his place. He said, "Sure, I'll call my brothers. But do you think that maybe you could call Caitlin?"

"Aaron. She's *your* mother."

"Don't rub it in."

"Oh, very funny."

He waved a hand. "Okay, okay. I'll call her. First thing in the morning. How's that?"

She knew she should leave it alone then, let him call his mother and say whatever he wanted to say to her. But guilt was eating at her, gnawing away. She really should have told him about those private conversations she'd had with Caitlin, the one concerning how Caitlin so thoroughly approved of Aaron and Celia as a couple, the one about wedding bells and baby carriages. In fact, if she had any backbone at all, she would just go ahead and tell him right now.

But she didn't.

What she said was, "Do you plan to tell her about the baby when you call her?"

He set down his fork and reached for his wine. "I don't know. I hadn't thought about it." He sipped. "She's going to find out eventually, right?"

"Yes, you're right. Of course, she will."

He set his glass down. "Celia. Whatever's on your mind, I wish you'd just say it."

"Well, the truth is, I'd rather you didn't tell her I'm pregnant yet. I told Jane and Jillian, but I don't really want anyone else to know right now. Let's get married and get into the rest of it later."

"Fine. Works for me."

If only she didn't feel so guilty, so much like a conniving, scheming lowdown cheater. "Aaron, I've been thinking. What about a prenuptial agreement?"

He set down his fork again. "What? You're afraid I'm after your money?" He was grinning, of course. He thought he was so funny.

"Oh, stop it. You know what I mean."

The grin turned to a frown. "Celia, I have to say it. You're acting strangely."

"I'm not. I'm trying to be fair. Here you are marrying me because I slipped up and got pregnant. There should be a prenuptial agreement, one that makes it very clear I can't take you to the cleaners. I mean, you know, if it doesn't work out."

He slid his napkin in at the side of his plate, poured himself a little more wine and sat back in his plush, high-backed chair. "Tell me. Do you intend to take me to the cleaners—if it doesn't work out?"

"Well, of course not."

He stared at her over the rim of his glass. Then he set the glass down. "Don't you think I know that? Don't you think I know *you?*"

"Well, of course, but—"

"Listen."

"Uh. All right."

"Maybe I don't know a lot about marriage. Maybe I've never seen a good one up close. Maybe marriage is not a place I ever intended to go. However, given the circumstances, I *am* going there. But don't kid yourself. I would *not* go there under *any* circumstances with a woman I didn't trust absolutely. Only an idiot would do that. And I'm no idiot.''

He trusted her, absolutely.

Now, why did that make her want to burst into tears?

She set her own napkin by her plate and then reached out, hesitantly, touching the sleeve of the silver-gray cashmere sweater he wore. ''Oh, Aaron,'' she whispered. ''What a beautiful thing to say.''

He put his hand over hers. ''Forget the prenup idea.''

''All right. If you're sure.''

He pushed back the big chair and rose to his feet, pulling her with him, taking her mouth in a long, slow, sweet kiss. ''Let's go to bed,'' he suggested, when at last he raised his head. ''We're always in complete agreement there.''

He kept his word about calling Caitlin. He did it first thing Monday morning, in his office.

Celia knew he did because five minutes after he disappeared behind his door, her line rang. She picked it up and said, ''Aaron Bravo's office.''

And Caitlin said, ''Good job, baby doll.''

Celia experienced that urge again—the one that made her want to scream rude things and slam down the phone.

''Sweet cakes, you there?''

''I'm here.''

''I have to hand it to you, you got it done faster than I ever expected.''

"Well, Caitlin. I honestly do not know what to say."

"Oh, don't get a nasty tone with me. You know I'm on your side. You've got to be knocked up, right?"

"Knocked up. What a lovely way to put it."

"Answer the question."

Celia grimly kept her mouth shut.

Caitlin didn't seem particularly bothered by her lack of response. "I'm gonna be a grandma. Hmm. Am I ready for that? You know, I think I am. I surely do."

"Well, that's a load off my mind."

"Hah. So I *am* right about this."

Celia gave up. "All right. Yes, I am pregnant. But I did not intend to be. It was carelessness, that's all."

Caitlin chuckled. "Hey. What does it matter how it happened? Do you hear me complainin'?"

"I know that you think I tricked Aaron into this."

"Uh-uh. Don't you even imagine you can see inside my head. The point is, I'm happy about it. Very happy. I'm lookin' forward to the wedding, to havin' you for a daughter-in-law and to bein' a grandma at last."

Now, *there* was an image. Caitlin Bravo, a grandma—her own baby's grandma. Celia shivered at the thought.

"Sweetie pie." Caitlin's whiskey voice was all coaxing softness. "Don't be mad at me, now. You and I both know all I did was give you a few little shoves in the right direction."

"Caitlin, it was an *accident*."

"Whoa, darlin' girl, no need to shout."

"I am not shouting." Was she? She cast a guilty glance at Aaron's shut door.

"You eat right, you hear? No booze."

Could this be happening? Prenatal advice from Caitlin Bravo—who had married a kidnapping murderer and just recently ended a passionate liaison with a Fabio look-alike half her age?

"Don't let Aaron work you too hard. And if you need me, you just holler."

The line to Aaron's office blinked—saved by the red light. "Caitlin, I have to go."

"Sweetheart, wait." There was a plaintive note in that smoky voice. "You're not *too* mad at me, are you?"

Celia wasn't, not really. The person she was angry at was herself. "No, Caitlin. Of course not."

"I'll be good to you. My *son* will be good to you."

"I know that."

"See you at the wedding."

"Yes. See you there."

Celia punched the button that put Aaron on the line. "Yes, Aaron. What can I do for you?"

"I like the way you say that."

His teasing tone warmed her. She chided, sweetly, "Not in the office."

"Such integrity. It amazes me."

Integrity, she thought. There it is, again. My favorite word.

"Ready?" he asked. It was time to go over the calendar.

"I'm on my way."

* * *

Celia found her wedding dress the next day, on her lunch hour. It was knee-length and sleeveless, of ivory silk, tiny pearls embroidered at hem and neckline. A little hat went with it, complete with a small froth of veil. It was perfect for a low-key, friends-and-family-only afternoon wedding.

Jane called that day and on Wednesday, Thursday and Friday, as well, to report on her progress with the wedding preparations. Reverend Culpepper would preside over the ceremony. The cake had been ordered. The flowers were handled.

Celia had decided to forgo attendants. She and Aaron would simply stand before the reverend and say their vows. She wrote checks to the bakery and the caterer, the florist and the party supply store. It was all going smoothly—or so Celia kept telling herself.

Aaron treated her with tenderness and passion—and patience, when she couldn't help asking if he was *sure* this was what he wanted.

"I'm sure," he would say, a little more wearily each time.

Each time she asked him, she knew that she shouldn't have. That he'd answered the question over and over and if his reply didn't satisfy her, asking again wouldn't help.

But in the back of her mind, guilt went on nagging. Everyone thought she was so honest, so chock-full of integrity—and yet she'd lied to herself from the first in this relationship. She'd always wanted more than he wanted to give.

And she never had told him the truth about Caitlin.

She felt as if, somehow, by not telling Aaron of his mother's schemes, she had colluded with Caitlin. After all, in the end, what Caitlin had suggested had come to pass.

On Friday night, five days after Celia had proposed and Aaron had accepted, they went to his rooms for the evening. He'd had dinner sent up. It was waiting in the dining room.

He pulled back her chair for her. She saw the blue velvet jeweler's box just before she sat down. She knew by the size and shape of it what it had to be.

And right then, at the sight of that little blue box, she understood what she had to do.

He was still waiting behind her. He moved up close and whispered in her ear. "Open it."

She could feel him, feel the warmth and solidness of him so close. She wanted to press herself back against him, to turn in his arms and offer her mouth to him—to put off what she now knew was the inevitable.

"Open it," he said again.

And the moment of cowardice passed.

She picked up the box. Her hand wasn't even trembling. She lifted the lid.

It was as she'd expected.

An engagement ring. A platinum band and a huge square-cut diamond flanked on either side by a matched pair of slightly smaller triangle-shaped stones.

"Do you like it?"

Like it? It took her breath away.

And at the same time, she was thinking, *Diamonds. It always ends in diamonds....*

Her heart contracted.

Oh, she did love him. And he was a much better man than a lot of people realized, a man determined, no matter what, to do the right thing, to make the best of the situation he'd found himself in.

The ring sparkled, winking at her as it caught and reflected the light from the chandelier above the table.

It always ends in diamonds....

That wasn't his intention now, of course. She knew very well he'd never given any other woman a diamond *ring* when he said goodbye to her.

But then, in this case, he wasn't the one saying goodbye.

He put his hands on her shoulders, so gently. Oh, his touch was magic. How would she live without it?

"Celia." His voice was teasing. "Say something."

She turned in his arms, met those blue, blue eyes. "It's absolutely beautiful. And I can't accept it."

Chapter Fifteen

Aaron took her meaning.

Or at least, he thought he did.

But then again, maybe not. Who could say what Celia really meant lately?

He asked warily, "You don't like it?"

Those slightly slanted hazel eyes were dewy with unshed tears. "Aaron. I love it." She snapped the box shut. "But I—"

He put up a hand. "You know, you say that word a lot lately. *But* this, *but* that."

"I know. I'm sorry."

"Don't be. Just stop."

"I can't."

"Sure, you can."

"Aaron. Please. It's not going to work."

"It," he repeated, as if he didn't know what "it" was.

"This," she insisted. "Us. You know what I mean. It's not right. Not fair to you."

"Don't you think I should be the judge of what's fair to me?"

"No, not in this case."

"Why not?"

"Because you're only trying to do what's right."

"And that's wrong?"

"No. No, of course not. *You* have done nothing wrong. Nothing at all. It's *me,* don't you see? I can't *do* this. You said from the first that you didn't want marriage. And that hasn't changed. You just feel you *have* to marry me now."

He backed off a step. And he kept his arms at his sides. It was difficult not to reach for her, not to grab her and shake her until she said something that made a little damn sense.

"Thank you, Celia," he muttered, low. "Now I know how I feel."

"Oh, please don't be sarcastic."

He strove to keep his tone level and reasonable. "You were the one who brought up marriage in the first place. *You* asked *me* to marry you."

"Yes, I did. And I shouldn't have. It was a mistake, a...throwback reaction involving faulty logic. I thought, I love Aaron and I'm pregnant with his baby, therefore it follows that we should get married."

"Seems like sound enough logic to me."

"But it's not. Not necessarily. Not in our case."

"Why not?"

She pursed up her sweet mouth at him. "Oh, for about a thousand reasons."

"And those reasons are?"

"Well, first of all, the basic one. You don't love me."

Love.

He supposed he should have known that was coming. And hell, what was he holding back for? He was willing to take a chance on marriage with her, wasn't he? If he was going to go that far, why not go for broke? "Look, Celia. I—"

She was shaking her head. "No. Please. That's not what I want. Truly, it's not. Your saying something you don't mean isn't going to fix anything. My point is, this baby inside my body is making me face a few things I've never wanted to think too hard about before. And one of those things is, well, it's about what I really *am*, as a person, you know?"

He didn't. So he waited. He figured she'd go on.

She did. "What I am, Aaron, is *ordinary*."

"Ordinary."

"Yes. I am. Oh, I can wear bright clothes and dye my hair red and sleep with the glamorous, sexy, brilliant CEO of a Vegas super-casino. But at heart, I'm a small-town girl, a little shy, a middle child from a big middle-class family, a middle child who never got enough attention, but who still knows her mother loves her, still feels a bond with her sisters and her brothers."

It was nice to learn that she thought of him as glamorous, sexy and brilliant. But where was she going with this? What was the point here? "I'm not following. Because you're a small-town girl from a big family, you can't marry me?''

''That's right.''

''I don't—''

She cut him off. ''Aaron, I slept with two men before you and I—''

Where the hell did that come from? ''Wait. Slow down. Back up.''

''What?''

''Are you about to tell me there's some other guy in the picture now?''

She stiffened. ''Are you crazy? I love *you*.''

''Then these other men you're talking about are strictly past tense?''

''Well, of course they are.''

''Then Celia, why are you talking about them?''

She gave a desperate cry. ''Because I'm trying to *explain* myself to you.''

''Ah,'' he said, for lack of anything better. She was doing a truly terrible job of it, but he saw no percentage in pointing that out to her.

''Will you *let* me explain?''

''Absolutely. Please go on.''

''All right. I'll try.'' She blew out her cheeks in a frustrated breath. ''What I'm getting at is, those guys were nice, ordinary guys.''

''Okay…''

''They were nice, ordinary guys and they said that they loved me and wanted to marry me.''

''I see.'' He didn't. But it seemed the right thing to say.

''I told them no.'' She waved the ring box at him,

shook her head. "Both of my best friends married early. And got it wrong. But not me. I was *different.* Oh, I thought I was so special, that I was secretly meant for great things. But now, I'm realizing the truth. And the truth is, I didn't marry those other guys because I didn't love them. I didn't find love until you. And now I've found you, well, I want the things that any ordinary woman would want. I want you to be my devoted husband. I want our baby. I want us to make a home...."

He almost asked her why the hell she hadn't noticed that he was perfectly willing to give her what she wanted.

But he didn't. He didn't think it would do any good.

And then she said, "And also, well, I feel like a rotten, lowdown cheat all the time now and I hate feeling like that."

He forgot all about the big questions, the ones that centered on the nature of love and whether Celia Tuttle was or was not ordinary at heart. "You feel like a cheat. Why?"

She blinked. He knew then that he was onto something. Finally. "I just, well, there are things I should have told you that I didn't tell you and—"

"What things?"

"Oh, Aaron." She held out the velvet box. "Please. Just take this back. Take it back now." She pushed the box at him.

And that did it, somehow—her shoving his ring at him as if she couldn't wait to get rid of it.

Really, was there any reason to keep on with this?

If she wanted to break it off with him, fine. Let her have what she wanted. He was damn good at a lot of things, but dealing with the complex emotional needs of women wasn't one of them. He'd accepted that about himself early on, taken care to make it clear to all the women he dated that love and marriage and baby carriages were not part of the deal.

But then along came sweet Celia Tuttle, a nice girl from his hometown, the best damn secretary/personal assistant he'd ever had the good fortune to come across. He still didn't know quite how she'd done it. But she'd slipped under his defenses, awakened things inside him he hadn't even known were there. She'd made him start thinking that maybe, with her, things could be different.

He saw now how wrong he'd been.

And come on. Who said the baby meant they *had* to be married? Maybe this was a case of him thinking way too much like the ordinary guy Celia seemed so certain he wasn't. Why not approach the situation differently, why not think outside the box a little here? He could still make arrangements to take care of both her and their child, whether Celia was his wife or not.

He asked her one more time. "You're sure? This is what you want?"

She nodded, her lips pressed tightly together, unshed tears glittering in those pleading eyes.

What else could he do? He extended his hand. She set the small blue box in it. "All right. What things haven't you told me?"

She swallowed. And her gaze shifted away. "Now this is settled, I don't think we really need to—"

"I think we do. What things?"

"Aaron, I'd like a little time. I'd like to go home, for a few days, to New Venice, and I—"

"Fine. Do whatever the hell you want to do."

"Okay, I'll—" She started to turn.

He caught her arm. "Not yet."

"Aaron—"

"What things?"

"Let go of me."

He held on tighter. "You have some talking to do and you know it."

"Let go."

He held on and he waited.

And she gave in. "All right, all right. Fine. I'll tell you."

He loosened his grip on her arm. "Talk."

She pulled away, tried one more time to put him off. "Aaron…"

"*Now,* Celia."

"I…"

He waited. He would wait forever if he had to. But he'd get to the bottom of this before he let her leave that room.

The phone on the long table against the far wall chose that moment to start ringing. Celia stiffened at the sound and looked at him hopefully.

"Don't worry," he said, schooling his voice to a parody of tenderness. "I'm not going to answer it."

"Bu—"

He put up a hand. "Do not say that word."

She swallowed, looked away, then reluctantly back

at him. They waited for the ringing to stop. When it did, the room seemed preternaturally silent.

"Talk," he said. "Now."

And at last, in a small voice, she confessed, "It's about Caitlin."

He swore under his breath. "I should have known. What did she do?"

"Oh, Aaron…"

"Quit stalling. Give it up. You owe me this much, Celia. You know that you do."

"But if we—"

That did it.

He threw the box with the ring in it, threw it good and hard—aimed it an antique mirror on the wall several feet away and let it fly. The mirror cracked. The box flew open. He didn't see where it landed—or if the ring was still in it when it did. He didn't see and he didn't care.

Celia had fallen silent. When he looked at her again, she was watching him in wide-eyed shock. He was sorry he had frightened her. But the swift, violent action had achieved its intended result. She'd shut her mouth over the damned evasions.

With deliberate care, he moved away from her, around the curve of the oval table, to the place that had been set for him. Pulling out his chair, he sat, leaning back, ordering his body to relax, making it clear to her that he presented no threat.

And he didn't—as long as she told him what he wanted to know. "What about Caitlin?"

Celia had moved behind her own chair. He hid a

bleak smile. Did she imagine that chair could provide any kind of real barrier, if he wanted to get to her?

He asked again, "What about Caitlin?"

She cleared her throat. "Well, your mother just…from the first, from that weekend of your birthday, when she caught us in the back hall of the Highgrade together, she started in on me."

"Started in on you, how?"

"She said she knew there was…an attraction between us. And she was in favor of it. She said she was 'betting on me' in this 'game.' That was what she called what you and I had together, our love affair—a game." Her soft mouth quivered. He thought of how he was never going to kiss that mouth again.

He didn't like thinking that, so he ordered his mind *not* to think it. "What else?"

"Um, then later—you remember that day she came here and then just went home without seeing you?"

"I remember. What about it?"

"Well, the truth is, you weren't the one she wanted to talk to."

His mother's odd behavior that day had nagged at him. Now he understood. "She came to see *you.*"

Celia nodded. "She told me she'd heard we were lovers and that she approved of it. She asked when the wedding was going to be. I told her what I thought she already should have known—I mean, since you *are* her son, she has to be aware of how you feel about marriage."

"You explained that we weren't getting married."

"Yes, I did. And that was when she said I should…'do what I had to do,' I think was how she put it, to get a ring on my finger. She hinted that I should get pregnant to force your hand.''

''And did you?'' he asked, though he already knew the answer.

''No!'' she cried. ''I didn't. I swear.''

''Well, then. Why are you beating yourself up over this? My mother is my mother. You grew up in New Venice. You know what she is.''

''But I…I didn't *tell* you. And I *should* have told you. But I was too *ashamed* to tell you. Because I *did* want to marry you. I wanted to marry you right from that first day I figured out that I loved you. Your mother was right about that much.''

She was clutching the back of the chair now, as if she needed it for support. She lifted a hand and swiped at her eyes, dashing the traitorous tears away. ''I'm just…well, everybody keeps saying I have so much integrity. That I'm so honest and up-front and truthful all the time. But as you can see now, I'm not. Not at all…'' She gripped the chair again, in both hands, hard enough that her knuckles grew pale. ''I'm just so confused. I need some time, I really do, to try to sort all this out in my mind.…''

Aaron felt a powerful urge right then, to rise and go to her, to comfort her. But he knew she didn't want that—not from him anyway.

Her choice, after all, had been made.

He stayed where he was and told her gently, ''It's all right. Take some time off. However long you need.''

She was shaking her head. ''You have to see. It

really isn't going to work, for me to try to keep my job with you."

He supposed she had a point. "I understand. I'll find someone else. And I'll make financial arrangements for the baby."

Tears welled in her eyes again. "Thank you."

"I *will* want to see the baby. To be a part of his life."

"Yes. I know. I would never try to stop you from—"

It was enough for now. "Fine. We can work all that out later."

"Yes. Of course. That's good."

He stood. "Come on. I'll take you to your rooms."

She stepped back. "No. It's all right. I can get there on my own."

"You're certain?"

"Yes." She raked a hand through that silky red hair. "And listen, I don't want to leave you holding the ball on this. If you need me to stay a while, to find my replacement and—"

"No. I'll worry about that."

"Oh, Aaron. Are you sure?"

"Positive." He approached her slowly. She allowed it, though her eyes warned him not to touch her. He dared to put his hand at the small of her back. He felt her shiver and stiffen, but she didn't jerk away. "At least let me walk you to the elevator."

She gave him a brave and slightly wobbly smile. "All right."

They left the dining room, went down a short hall to the entryway with its round etched-glass skylight overhead. He pressed the button that summoned the elevator.

Seconds later, the door slid wide. The night elevator operator tipped his hat at them. "Mr. Bravo. Ms. Tuttle."

Aaron nodded and Celia did the same. She stepped into the car.

"Goodnight, Celia."

"Goodnight, Aaron."

The door slid shut and she was gone.

Chapter Sixteen

When she got back to her rooms, Celia went online and booked a flight home. Then she called Jane.

"The wedding's off."

"Oh, no."

"Oh, yes. I broke it off. I couldn't go through with it. I broke it off—and then I quit my job."

Jane must have known it wasn't the time to ask questions. "Come home. Stay with me for a while. Get your bearings."

"God. I was hoping you'd say that. That's all I want right now, to come home. I've got my plane ticket. But I wasn't quite sure where to go after I got off the plane. I was thinking I'd book a room at the New Venice Inn."

"My house," said Jane. "That's where you're staying."

"It's crazy, isn't it? All I want is to go home to New Venice, but no one in my family lives there anymore."

"I'm here."

"I know. And I'm so glad."

"Shall I pick you up in—"

"No. I'll rent a car."

"I don't mind coming for you, Ceil."

"I can get there on my own, and I'd prefer it that way."

"Well, all right. Just come straight to the house. If I'm not here, I'll be at the store."

"Jane."

"Hmm?"

"Please don't call Jillian. I'll do it, tomorrow. She's going to tell me I'm nuts. Maybe I *am* nuts. But I don't think I can bear to hear about it tonight."

"Whatever you say. Just come on home."

When Celia pulled up in front of the house on Green Street late the next morning Jane was there, waiting for her. Celia heard the screen door slam and then her friend was racing down the steps toward her, dark hair flying.

Celia popped the trunk latch and got out of the car.

Jane had her arms out. Celia went into them, hugging back as hard as she could, burying her face in the fragrant cloud of curly hair.

Finally, Jane took her by the shoulders and held her at arm's length. "It's good you're here."

"Yeah. Yeah, it is."

"Let's get your things."

They went around to the trunk. Jane pushed up the lid and grabbed the heaviest of Celia's three bags. Celia took the two smaller ones. They started up the walk, Jane in the lead.

They were halfway to the steps when Celia noticed the man standing in the shadows of the porch next door. He was tall and lean, in faded Levis and a dark shirt, lounging against a post, watching them: Cade Bravo. He nodded when she looked his way, one side of his mouth lifting in a slow half-smile.

Like Aaron, she thought. Not Aaron's smile exactly, but close....

Her heart felt too big, suddenly, to fit in her chest. It ached to be squeezed in so tight.

She realized she was lagging, and hustled to catch up.

Once inside, she turned to Jane and spoke in a carefully neutral tone. "I see Cade Bravo's come home at last."

Jane made a low noise of agreement—then changed the subject, which was just fine with Celia. "The blue room is waiting." Of Jane's various spare bedrooms, the blue room was Celia's favorite.

Jane led the way up the stairs and into the cozy room with its white-quilted twin beds and blue window treatments. She set the suitcase she was carrying on the nubby-textured blue rug. "I should get back to the store."

"No problem. I'll put my stuff away, get settled in."

"You're sure you don't mind if I leave you all alone?"

"Janey, I'm okay."

"I'll be home by six or so."

"No hurry. I'll be fine."

Saturday afternoon, sitting in Jane's kitchen at the round oak breakfast table, Celia used her cell phone to call the wedding guests—except for the Bravos. She'd leave that to Aaron, however he wanted to handle it.

Was that cowardice on her part? Probably. But it seemed presumptuous, somehow, to take it upon herself to call his family with this particular news. Add to that the fact that his family included Caitlin and, well, Celia simply could not face the prospect of talking to that woman right then.

It didn't take long to make the calls. Everyone was so understanding. They spoke to her quietly. With sympathy. They asked, "Are you all right?"

She gave the appropriate responses, she thought. She said she regretted how things had worked out, but she really did feel that it was for the best.

She didn't mention the baby.

Time enough for that later.

She called Jillian last, told her what had happened, that the wedding was off and she was staying at Jane's.

Jillian said just what Celia had expected her to say.

"Celia Louise, have you lost your mind?"

"Jilly—"

"I do not believe this. Tell me you didn't say it. Tell me I've heard you all wrong."

"I couldn't go through with it. It's that simple. He never wanted to marry me and—"

"Oh, please. As if Aaron Bravo is some babe in the woods. That man is no pushover. No woman would ever get him to do a thing he didn't want to do. If he agreed to marry you, he *wants* to marry you. The question is, why did you screw it up?"

"Jilly, I really don't want to talk about it."

"But you *need* to talk about it. You know that you do."

"No. I don't. Maybe eventually, but not right now."

Jillian sighed. "For the sweetest and shyest among us, you certainly can be stubborn as a bad-tempered mule."

"I have to go."

"No, you don't. You just don't want to hear what I'm telling you. You've made a big mistake and I want to know why and you just don't want to think about it."

"I have to go. I mean it."

"Okay, okay. Take care of yourself. Please."

"I will."

"Guess who came into the bookstore today?" Jane asked that night at dinner.

Celia shrugged. "Haven't a clue."

Her friend's dark eyes gleamed with teasing humor. "I'll give you a hint. Fabio meets the Terminator."

"Hans is back."

"It would appear so."

"Back with Caitlin?"

"Can't say for sure, yet. But ask me in a day or two. By then, the gossip mill will be churning. I'll have the whole lurid story."

For some insane reason, Celia felt defensive for Caitlin. "Why does it have to be lurid? They *are* both adults. Maybe she just *likes* him. Maybe *he* likes *her.*"

Jane frowned. "Ceil. Hey. I have no axe to grind here. Sincerely, I don't. It was an attempt at conversation, you know? A little humor—or so I thought."

Celia did know. "Sorry. I'm out of line. And not a whole lot of fun to have around, either." She gave her friend a rueful smile.

"It's okay," Jane said gently.

Celia cut another bite of chicken. When she looked up from her plate, Jane was watching her. "What?"

Jane picked up her water glass and took a thoughtful sip. "Well, maybe if you let yourself talk about it..."

Celia groaned. "Janey, I don't want to talk about it. I don't want to scheme or plan. I don't want to figure out my next move. I *have* no next move. I honestly don't."

"Did I suggest that you scheme or plan or figure out your next move?"

"No. No, you didn't. I'm sorry..."

"Stop apologizing. I just want to understand what *happened.*"

"I broke it off. I felt like a liar and cheat and I—"

Jane let out an outraged cry. "Well, that's just ridiculous. You are no cheat."

"Oh, don't defend me. Please. I did what I did and it's over now. I just want to rest a little, eat your wonderful food and take shameless advantage of your hospitality for a few days. Then I'll start thinking about finding another job."

"But you *love* him."

"Yes, I do. But it didn't work out."

"Celia—"

"Jane. Please. Can we leave it alone?"

They watched a video and turned in early.

Celia didn't sleep well. She lay in the narrow bed, staring at the blue walls, thinking of Aaron, missing him, telling herself she'd done the right thing.

And wondering why it all felt so wrong, why she couldn't stop Jillian's words from echoing in her head.

If he agreed to marry you, he wants *to marry you. The question is, why did you screw it up?*

Aaron wasn't sleeping well, either. He found he was angry and getting angrier.

He was angry at Celia, who had got what she said she wanted: him. And then decided she didn't want him, after all.

And even more than at Celia, he was mad at his mother, who never could seem to keep herself from barging in and messing up what would most likely have worked out just fine if only she'd had the common decency to leave it alone.

But she hadn't left it alone. And now Celia was gone.

He would have to get over her.

And he would. He'd get over her. He'd take care of business, get on with his life.

Last night, after Celia left him, he'd returned to the dining room and found the ring—on the floor, beneath a sideboard. It was undamaged. The box was there, too, a few feet from the ring. He put the ring in the box and put the box in his private safe.

Monday, he'd return it. He'd also see about getting the mirror he'd broken replaced. He'd see about replacing Celia, as well—professionally, anyway. The idea of taking another lover right then made him feel vaguely sick to his stomach.

And *that* made him angry all over again.

He told himself things would be back to normal soon. He told himself to forget it.

Forget Celia. Forget Caitlin. Forget both of them— for a while, anyway. Just put them completely out of his mind.

And the thought of doing that made him even madder.

Because he couldn't forget them, not really. One of them had given him life.

The other not only carried his baby—she'd also managed somehow to make off with his heart.

Chapter Seventeen

The Silver Unicorn Bookstore was closed on Sunday. Jane stayed home, with Celia. It was a gorgeous spring day, crisp in the early morning, turning warmer as noon approached. At around eleven, Jane suggested they sit out on the porch. They brewed a pot of peppermint tea and took it outside with them.

Jane got comfortable on the porch swing. Celia took the teak rocker with the needlepoint cushion. She closed her eyes and rocked slowly and told herself to appreciate the beauty of the day, to forget her problems for right now. There would be plenty of time to deal with them later.

But then she heard brakes squealing. She opened her eyes in time to see the gleaming black Trans Am come barreling around the corner from State Street.

The car screeched to a stop at the curb, right behind Celia's rented Chevy Corsica.

Caitlin.

So much for forgetting her problems.

Aaron's mother emerged from the low black muscle car, her raven hair big and hard and shining, her black jeans way too tight. Today, her shirt was black satin and her spangles dayglow green. Her scarf was green, too, tied at the side of her neck, the ends flowing jauntily along her shoulder. She slammed her door good and hard, hustled around the front of the car and marched up Jane's front walk.

At the base of the steps, she planted her feet wide apart and propped her fists on her hips. "Cade said you were over here—and that Aaron wasn't. I didn't believe it."

It appeared that Aaron had failed to call his family and let them know there would be no wedding, after all.

Jane stood from the porch swing. "Caitlin, why don't we all go inside and—"

Rising herself, Celia cut in. "It's okay, Jane. I'll handle this." Jane sighed and sat back down. Celia turned to Aaron's mother once more. "Believe it," she said. "We've decided not to get married, after all. The wedding is off."

"*What?*"

"Caitlin, you're shouting."

"Damn right, I'm shouting. And who is this 'we'? My boy decided the wedding was off? My boy said he wouldn't marry you?"

Celia turned for the front door. "That's all I have to tell you, Caitlin. Please go away."

"Wait. You get back out here. You get back out here now."

Celia pulled open the screen and pushed the front door inward. She crossed the threshold, shutting the door silently behind her.

Caitlin called Aaron at a little after noon.

"I just paid a visit to Jane Elliott's. Your woman was there. She told me the wedding was off. Is that true?"

He should have hung up on her. But he found himself imagining the great pleasure it would give him to wrap his hands around her neck and squeeze until her false eyelashes popped off.

"Aaron. Damn you, darlin', are you there?"

"Ma," he warned softly. "The last thing you want right now is my undivided attention."

She kept on shouting. "Aaron, you get home. You work things out with that sweet little girl. You hear me? Am I getting through?"

She was. "If I come home, Ma, I'll be looking for you first."

"Fine. Come on. You just come on. You think I can't deal with you? You try me, darlin' boy. I am ready for you, in spades, and that's a fact."

"All right, Ma," he said very quietly. "I'm on my way."

Aaron flew the Cessna. He arranged to have a rental car waiting when he touched down at the Comstock Valley airstrip.

He pulled into the parking lot behind the Highgrade at ten past four in the afternoon. A minute later, he was striding through the back hall, shouting his mother's name.

She was waiting in the bar for him, standing in front of the first pool table, arms folded across her chest. There were a couple of regulars there, bellies up to the bar—and Bertha behind it.

The Viking boyfriend was back. Hans stood well behind Caitlin, between the two pool tables, holding a pool cue and looking formidable, ready to rescue his aging lady love if it came to that.

"Out," Aaron said. "All of you."

The regulars drained their shot glasses and made themselves scarce. Bertha flipped up the hinged section of counter at the far end of the bar and slipped into the back room.

Hans stayed where he was.

"You, too, big guy. Get lost."

The Viking laid the pool cue on the table in front of him and folded his massive arms over his gigantic chest, so his pose was a mirror of Caitlin's. "I vill stay."

Caitlin shot him a look over her shoulder. "Go on, Hans. I can deal with this on my own."

"I said, I vill stay."

"Hans. I am fine. This is between Aaron and me. Please go."

Hans didn't move.

"Terrific," said Aaron. He was maybe three feet

from the bar. No effort at all to bend over and grab a stool.

"Aaron…" his mother warned.

She got no further. Aaron smashed the stool across the bar. The bar withstood the blow. But the stool broke apart. Aaron was left holding one of the legs. "Hans. This is private. Will you please get the hell out?"

"I despise violence and I don't vhant to hurt you," said Hans. "Don't make me."

Caitlin had already turned and was on her way around the pool table on the far side. "Hans. I mean it. This is none of your business and I want you to—"

Aaron threw the stool leg—not very hard. It hit Hans lightly in the chest and bounced to the floor.

Hans's chiseled Nordic features turned the color of an overripe tomato.

"Come on, then," said Aaron wearily, waving his hands in a come-and-get-me motion. "Let's go. Let's do it now."

"Hans!" shouted Caitlin.

But it was no good. Hans lowered his head and rushed, bull-like, at Aaron.

Aaron waited until the other man was almost upon him, then he leapt for the bar, sliding across it, swinging his legs over and landing behind it in one unbroken move.

It took Hans a moment to realize that his target had relocated. He staggered to a stop. "Huh?" And then he spotted Aaron. He threw back his huge blond head and let out what could only be called a battle cry. Then he dove for the bar.

Aaron was waiting for him with a fifth of Jose Cuervo Especial raised high. Hans hit the bar and Aaron hit Hans on the top of the head. The bottle shattered, sending shards of glass and good tequila flying everywhere.

"Ugh," said Hans. He looked at Aaron, his expression soulful. "Daht *hurt*." And then, with a groan, he collapsed across the bar.

Caitlin started swearing. She rushed to the Viking, who groaned some more and slowly raised his head again.

"Oh, sweetheart," Caitlin cried. "You okay?"

"Huh? Vhat?"

Caitlin wrapped her arms around Hans and sent her son a fulminating glare. "Let me take him in the back."

"Great. Go. Now."

"Come on, now. It's all right. Come on with me…." Caitlin led Hans around the pieces of broken stool, past the pool tables and through the door to the storeroom, leaving Aaron alone in the bar with glass in his hair and tequila all over his black leather blazer—not to mention the polo shirt beneath it. He brushed at the mess, wondering what the hell was the matter with him, anyway.

He never should have come here.

And he certainly shouldn't have taken his frustrations with Caitlin out on poor Hans, who'd done nothing in the least offensive—well, beyond falling for Caitlin in the first place, and then insisting on defending her. He wondered with a kind of bone-deep weariness when his mother would finally consider herself old enough to give up getting involved with inappropriate men.

Guilt started nagging at him. He looked around at the mess he'd made and decided he ought to at least clean it up. So he got the broom and dustpan from behind the bar and swept up the glass, then wiped up the booze that had spilled on the counter, and mopped up what had made it to the floor. After that, he went around by the pool table and picked up the pieces of the stool he had destroyed, setting them on one of the tables, ready to carry to the Dumpster out back.

When things were in reasonable order again, he sat down at the bar. Not two minutes later, the door to the back room opened. Caitlin came through it alone.

He rose from the barstool. "Is he okay?"

"Fine," she said tightly. "No thanks to you." She strutted toward him in those high-heeled boots of hers, stopping about a foot away, resting an elbow on the bar and slinging out a hip, in her best don't-you-mess-with-me stance. "All right. Go ahead. Lay it on me. Do your worst."

Aaron opened his mouth. And then closed it without making a sound.

He'd thought he had a lot to say to her.

But somewhere between smacking a stool across the bar and whacking poor Hans with a full tequila bottle, the whole trip home had begun to seem ridiculous, an exercise in futility, an excuse for breaking up the furniture and getting in a fight.

And now what?

The usual. He would shout at her. She would shout back at him.

It would just be the same-old, same-old, what they'd done all his life. Hotheaded Caitlin Bravo and one of her boys, going at it, shouting the house down.

He muttered, "What in hell is the point?" And he started to turn.

"Aaron. Wait."

Something in his mother's voice stopped him— something without pretense. Something raw and true and freighted with pain.

He turned. Even in the dim bar light, he saw the change that had come over her face. She looked older, very tired—and infinitely sad.

"Aaron. I only want the best for you. You know that, don't you?"

He grunted, shook his head. But when he spoke, it was gently. "Yeah. Yeah, I know that."

"I saw you two together, you and Celia, that night of your birthday, and I knew it. I knew she was the one for you. That in spite of everything, of all of it— your father, who never was any kind of father at all— and the way I raised you that never gave you much of anything to go by. In spite of yourself, and your determination not to let anyone get too close to your heart. In spite of all of that, you had found what matters, anyway. I didn't want you to blow it."

He considered her words, then shook his head again. "I don't think I did, Ma. I think you blew it for me."

"Oh." Her red mouth trembled. "Did I? Really? Are you sure?"

"Damn it, Ma. Don't start bawling on me. I don't think I can take that right now."

She sniffed, swiped her nose with the heel of her hand. "Yeah. You're right. Cryin' is a weak woman's trick." She smoothed those too-tight pants of hers. Then she sucked in a big breath, yanked her shoulders back and stood up tall. "I'm tougher than that."

He almost smiled. "You are. Tough as nails. There's no one tougher."

She put a boot up on the stool between them and leaned on the bar again. Then, uncharacteristically hesitant, she asked, "Celia was the one who called the wedding off?"

"Yeah."

"Did you...tell her you love her?"

"I started to. She stopped me."

Caitlin frowned. "And you let her do that?"

He stuck his hands in the pockets of his jacket, gave her a long, cold look. "Don't judge me. You weren't there."

Those false eyelashes swept down. She appeared to be studying the toe of her high-heeled boot, the one hooked over the rail of the stool.

He got tired of waiting for her to say whatever it was she had on her mind. "All right, Ma. Spit it out, whatever it is."

Her head came up and those black eyes were focused on him again. "I just think you ought to be lookin' at your own part in this."

"And that is?"

"Well, darlin' boy. You let her chase you until she

caught you. And you never really let her know for certain that you *wanted* to be caught. So she let you go. You say I blew it for you. Maybe I did. But only because you let it happen.''

Chapter Eighteen

A few minutes later, Aaron came out the back door of the Highgrade carrying the pieces of the barstool he had broken. He stopped at the Dumpster and tossed the pieces in. Then he turned for his rental car.

But he never got inside. About a foot from the driver's door, he found himself pausing, turning his head up toward the clear blue spring sky. He had an urge to walk.

He went around the side of the building and then down the alley between the Highgrade and Jane Elliott's bookstore. In seconds, he was emerging onto Main.

The old hometown looked good, he thought, as he started up the street. The trees were leafing out and the sidewalks were clean and someone had slapped a new coat of paint on Garber's Hardware Store.

He reached State Street in no time. And he turned onto it. It was right then, at that corner, that he realized where he was going—up to Green and to the right and then four houses down, to the Victorian with the cream-colored fish-scale shingles up under the eaves and the terra-cotta shiplap, with the green and red trim and the cute little tower tucked into the front porch.

He mounted the steps and rang the bell.

The heavy oak door had beveled glass in the top of it. After a moment, Jane Elliott appeared. She saw him through the glass and her dark brows drew together.

At first, he was certain she would turn away and leave him standing there.

But then she pulled the door wide. She didn't, however, unlatch the screen.

She moved up close, rested a hand on the doorframe. "Yes, Aaron?" she said in a low voice, but briskly. Her nostrils flared—must have got a whiff of the Cuervo all over his jacket and the front of his shirt. But she didn't let the fact that he smelled like the inside of a bottle throw her. "What can I do for you?"

"Is Celia here?"

She sent a furtive glance over her shoulder. "I..."

"She *is* here. Right?"

Jane faced him squarely again. "Yes. Of course, she's here. She's resting."

He longed to tear the screen wide, shove poor Jane aside, and go pounding up the stairs, shouting Celia's name. He asked, carefully, "Could you ask her if she'll speak with me?"

"Look, Aaron. I don't know if—"

Right then, they both heard the sound of footsteps on the stairs. He looked toward the sound and so did Jane.

"Jane. Who is—" Halfway down, she saw him. She froze, her hand on the railing. Her eyes were huge, her face so pale. That mouth he'd thought he might never kiss again formed a soft, startled *O*. "Aaron…"

He thought, I have to talk with you. *Please*….

But somehow, the words stayed trapped inside. And beyond whispering his name, she wasn't talking, either.

Jane broke the silence. "Listen. Aaron. Why don't you come in?"

He managed an answer, though he did not take his eyes off Celia. "Thank you. I will."

Jane unlatched the screen, pushed it wide. He ordered his legs to move. And then he was inside, standing by the door in Jane Elliott's entry hall, staring like a long-gone fool at Celia, who stared back at him, motionless, from the stairs.

Another silence descended. It didn't bother Aaron in the least. He was here, with Celia. He could *see* her. She was real. For the moment, it was all he needed.

All he could handle.

All he could possibly take.

Eventually, Jane said, "Look. If you two don't mind, I think I'll just leave you on your own for a little while. I have a few things I keep putting off over at the bookstore. You know how it is. There's always some little project or other just crying out to be done.'' She waited for one of them to say something.

Neither of them did.

Finally, Jane was forced to try again. "Celia? Is that okay with you? Do you mind if I go?''

Celia kind of shook herself. "Yeah, Jane. Great. See you later.''

Jane grabbed a purse from a narrow table against the wall. "Back in an hour or so.'' She went out the front door.

Time hung suspended. Aaron didn't mind. He was here and she was here and that was very, very good.

After an eon or so, Celia started moving again, coming toward him down the stairs.

Aaron drank in every line, every curve. She wore no makeup and her hair was smashed flat on one side. She had on a pair of gray sweatpants and a baggy Cal State Sacramento T-shirt. Her feet were bare.

She stole his breath and stopped his heart.

When she got to the bottom of the staircase, she stopped, her hand on the newel post. *Come on,* he was thinking. *Don't stop there.*

She must have read his mind. Her bare feet brushed the gleaming hardwood floor as she came toward him again.

At last, she was standing right in front of him.

She sniffed. Frowned. "Aaron? What is that smell?''

He hung his head. "Tequila.''

She reached out a hesitant hand, touched the still-damp front of his shirt. His heart turned over in his chest. He wanted to grab that hand, hold on tight, never let go. At the same time, he didn't dare move.

He confessed, still staring at the floor, at her beautiful bare feet. "I stopped by the Highgrade before I came here. There was a little altercation. I broke a bottle of tequila over Hans's head and got it all over myself in the process."

"Oh, Aaron..."

He jerked his head up and looked in her eyes again, searching hungrily for clues to her true state of mind. He wasn't sure what he saw. She looked...disappointed. Yes, that was probably it. Disappointed in him.

He hated himself. "I have no excuse for what I did. I was angry. I took it out on poor Hans...."

"Angry at me?"

"Yeah. And at Caitlin."

Her soft fingers brushed his jaw, stroked back into his hair. God. He did love that. The feel of her hand in his hair.

"Your mother does love you. Very, very much."

"I know. But her love is damned hard to take sometimes."

He thought he saw a tiny smile twitching at the corners of that tender mouth. But then it was gone. She ran her finger down the side of his neck, making his pulse race and his body burn. "You don't seem angry now."

He couldn't stop himself. He caught her fingers, kissed the tips of them, one by one. "Celia..."

"Oh," she said. "Oh, Aaron…" She pulled her hand free and stared up at him. What the hell was she thinking? If only he knew.

She seemed troubled. Or maybe anxious. "I have some things to say to you."

His pulse thudded hard in sudden dread. "What things?"

"Well, I've been thinking, the past two days…"

"Yeah?"

She turned from him. It took all the will he possessed not to reach out and grab her. She went to the stairs and sat on the bottom step, drawing her legs up, wrapping her arms around them, then shyly patting the empty spot beside her. "Sit by me?"

He approached with caution. She looked up at him, anxious—yes, he was sure of that now. She was anxious. He didn't know why she thought she had to be anxious.

They were working it out, weren't they? That was why he was here.

But then again, maybe she'd decided *she* didn't want *him*. Maybe that was what she'd been thinking about these past two days.

Maybe— No. Better not do that, not jump to any conclusions about what was happening here. Better to wait. See what she had to say.

He turned and dropped down next to her. "All right. What?"

She gathered her legs in closer, rested her sweet soft chin on her knees. "Well, my friend Jillian said something. When I told her the wedding was off. She asked me if I was crazy. I was expecting that—I mean, because she knows how I love you.''

His heart soared. She still loved him!

And she was still talking. ''Also, Jilly knows about the baby. Naturally, she'd question why I would break it off with you. But she said something more. She said that you weren't the kind of man who would let himself get roped into doing something he didn't want to do. That you never would have agreed to marry me unless you *wanted* to marry me.''

''I hardly know this Jillian. But I like her. A lot.''

She laid her cheek on her knees and looked at him wistfully. ''You mean, she's right?''

Words were lost to him again. But he managed a nod.

''Ah,'' she said. Did she look happy? He wanted to think so. She lifted her head, faced forward again and stared off into the middle distance. ''Jillian said I needed to ask myself why I would break it off with you, when marriage was obviously what *both* of us wanted. She said I should ask myself why I would want to screw up what we had together.''

He leaned into her, just a little, brushing against her, then pulling back. ''And *did* you? Ask yourself?''

''Yes, Aaron, I did.''

''And did you come up with an answer?''

''I think so.''

''And was it, maybe, that you had chased me and caught me and asked me to marry you? And you wanted more from me than the lukewarm yes I gave you?''

She turned her head his way again and blinked at him, owl-like. "How did you figure that out?"

"My mother does have her moments."

She drew back a fraction. "Caitlin told you that?"

"She did."

"Well," she said, looking surprised and pleased. "What do you know?"

Did she lean toward him? Or did he make the first move?

He couldn't have said. He only knew that they were leaning toward each other. And then, at last, their lips were meeting.

They kissed for a long time, sitting there on the bottom stair, neither quite daring to reach out with their hands yet, each craning toward the other, mouths fused but otherwise not touching.

At last they pulled apart—but not too far. Only a few inches.

And he said, "I love you, Celia Tuttle. You are everything I didn't know I was looking for. I think we can have a terrific life together. Please, please, will you marry me?"

She didn't answer. Not in words. But those hazel eyes were shining and her mouth was softly parted.

That mouth was too much of an invitation to resist. So he kissed her again, this time pulling her into his arms. She kissed him back. With all the sweetness and passion he'd learned to love in her.

She turned in his arms, sighing, and ended up stretched across his lap. He lifted his head and she opened lazy eyes, raising a hand to stroke his hair at the temple. "Did you hire my replacement yet?"

"There is no one who could replace you, and you know it."

"Good. I like my job. We'll have to make some changes. Later. But not right away."

He said gruffly, "I suppose you'll want to get a house, stop living at High Sierra, now we're having a family."

She shook that mussed red head. "No. I like where we live. And our baby will be fine there. Maybe eventually, we'll have to get a house like regular folks. But not for a while…"

He wondered at the musing look on her face. "What are you thinking?"

"Oh, about being ordinary."

"*You* said that. I didn't."

"Aaron. It's okay with me. There's nothing at all wrong with being ordinary."

How could he disagree? If Celia was ordinary, then ordinary was just what he'd needed all his life.

"Okay," he whispered. "You are incredibly, fascinatingly, enchantingly *ordinary*."

She beamed up at him. "Thank you—and I was also thinking about Caitlin. And you…"

"What about Caitlin—and me?"

"I was thinking that Caitlin is big and bold and sloppy and loud. And you are so fastidious at heart."

He grunted. "I reek of tequila. I just beat up my mother's boyfriend. That's fastidious?"

"You've been frustrated lately."

"Yes, I have."

"But at heart, you are a fastidious man. I think you grew up wanting some order in your life. And you got it by keeping love out. I've made things a little bit messy for you.''

He thought about that for a moment. Then he nodded. "Maybe you have. But I'm not complaining— and Celia, you know you haven't said yes yet.''

"That's right. But I will.''

He bent close again—and kissed her nose. "That's good to hear.''

"Where's my ring?''

"In my safe at High Sierra.''

"Will you let me have it, after all, when we get home?''

"You know that I will.''

"Funny…''

"What?''

"This is one time in your life when diamonds will be the beginning and not the end. And right now, it occurs to me, I want to rethink the wedding….''

This information did not surprise him. "However you want it, that's how it will be.''

"Now I'm thinking we should have it in Vegas. At High Sierra.''

"That's doable.''

"And I want to invite your cousin Jonas and his wife….''

He swore under his breath.

She chuckled. "*I* will invite them. You won't have to do anything but be nice to them if they agree to come.''

"You are relentless.''

"Well, yes.'' She looked much too pleased with herself. "I guess I am.''

"Say yes to my proposal. And mean it. Say yes now."

"Yes, Aaron. I will marry you."

"Say you love me."

"Oh, I do. I love you with all my heart."

"Now kiss me."

And she did, pulling his head down and parting her lips with a tender, eager sigh. Aaron gathered her in and returned her kiss—passionately, fully, without reservation.

A non-marrying man? Not anymore. Aaron Bravo had the only woman for him held close in his arms.

And he was never, ever letting go.

*   *   *   *   *

Mercury Rising

CHRISTINE RIMMER

For my nieces Lily and Tessa and Morgan,
with all my love.

Chapter One

"Mom?"

Virginia Elliott turned from the window. "Ah. Thank you, dear." Jane gave her the fresh-cut blush-pink roses she'd just wrapped in a cone of newspaper. "So lovely..." Virginia brought them close, breathed in their scent. "You do have a way in the garden. Your aunt Sophie would be proud."

Jane's beloved Aunt Sophie Elliott had been a single lady all her life. When she'd died, nearly three years ago now, she left Jane her beautiful old house and the gorgeous garden surrounding it.

Her mother turned back to the window. "I notice your new neighbor is at home."

"Yes." Jane kept her voice and her expression as bland as a clean white sheet. "He does travel a lot, though."

Virginia had the roses in her left hand. Her right strayed to the pearls at her throat. She fondled them, ticking them off like the beads of a rosary. "He was out there, on the side porch, just a moment ago." Each word was heavy with disdain.

Jane resisted the urge to say something sarcastic. *Well, Mother. It* is *his house. I suppose he has the right to be out on the porch.*

Word around town was that Cade Bravo owned an ostentatious new house in Las Vegas and a condo in nearby Lake Tahoe. He'd taken the small town of New Venice completely by surprise when he'd bought the Lipcott place next-door to Jane's. A run-down farmhouse-style Victorian seemed the last place he would ever want to live.

But the house wasn't run-down anymore. Renovations had gone on for months. Finally the various work crews had picked up and moved on and the new owner had taken up residence.

"At least he had the grace to respect the integrity of the original home," Virginia said grudgingly, hand still at her pearls.

Jane thought he had done a beautiful job with the old house. It looked much as it must have when it was first built, at the turn of the last century, a house a lot like Jane's house, one that harkened back to simpler, more graceful times, with an inviting deep wraparound porch and fish scale shingles up under the eaves.

Virginia muttered, "Still. One of those Bravo boys living on Green Street. Who ever could have imagined such a thing?" Green Street was wide and tree-lined. The charming old houses on it had always been owned by respectable and prosperous members of the New Venice community, people from well-established local families—the Elliotts and the Chases, the Moores and the Lipcotts.

True, Cade Bravo had surprised everyone by prospering. In that sense, he fit the profile for a resident of Green Street. Was he respectable? Not by Virginia Chase Elliott's exacting standards. But then, in Virginia's thoroughly biased opinion, no Bravo was—or ever could be—considered respectable.

"Does he bother you, honey?" Her mother was looking right at her now.

"Of course not."

"He was always such a wild one—the worst of the bunch, everyone says so. Takes after that mother of his." Virginia's gray eyes narrowed when she mentioned Caitlin Bravo. Her hand worried all the harder at her pearls. "I suppose he's got the women in and out all the time."

"No. He's very quiet, actually, when he's here—and you should get those roses home. Cut an inch off the stems, at a slant, and—"

Her mother waved the hand that had been so busy with the pearls. "I know, I know. Remove any leaves below the waterline."

Jane smiled. "That's right. And use that flower food I gave you."

Virginia sighed. "I will, I will—and how is Celia?"

Celia Tuttle was one of Jane's two closest friends. Her name was Celia Bravo now. A little over two months ago, at the end of May, Celia had married Cade's oldest brother, Aaron.

"Happy," said Jane. "Celia is very, very happy."

One of Virginia's eyebrows inched upward. "Pregnant, or so I heard."

"Yes. She and Aaron are thrilled about that."

"I meant, a little *too* pregnant for how long they've been married."

Jane shook her head. "Mother. Give it up. Celia is *happy.* Aaron loves her madly. They are absolutely adorable together, totally devoted—and looking forward to having a baby. *I'd* like to find a man who loves me the way Aaron Bravo loves his wife."

Her mother made a prim noise in her throat. Jane folded her arms and gave Virginia a long, steady look heavily freighted with rebuke.

Virginia relented. She waved her hand again. "All right, all right. Celia is a sweet girl and if she's happy, I'm happy *for* her."

"So good of you to say so."

"Don't get that superior tone, please. I don't like it when you do that—and I know, I know. Celia is your dearest friend in the world, along with Jillian." Jane and Celia and Jillian Diamond had been best friends since kindergarten. "I ought to have sense enough never to say a word against either of them."

"Yes, you should."

Virginia stepped closer, the look in her eyes softening. She reached out and smoothed Jane's always-wild hair in a gesture so tender, so purely maternal that Jane couldn't help but be soothed by it. Jane did love her mother, though Virginia was not always easy to love.

"You haven't mentioned how your date went Friday."

Jane gave her mother a noncommittal smile. "I had a nice time."

Virginia looked pained. "My. Your indifference is nothing short of stunning."

Indifference. Sadly that pretty much summed up Jane's feelings about Friday night. It had been her second date with that particular man. He taught Science at the high school and Jane had met him over a year ago now. He'd come into her bookstore looking for a good manual on Sierra birds and a well-illustrated book on weather patterns. He really did seem the kind of man she'd been looking for: steady and trustworthy, kind and wise. A man who had sought to be her friend first. He'd told her he admired her straightforwardness, said he respected her independence and valued her intelligence. Jane believed him when he said those things.

And he was nice-looking, too, with thick brown hair and a muscular build. There was nothing *not* to like about him. Jane *did* like him. She also knew in her heart that liking was all she felt for him.

Was she asking too much in daring to want it all—decency and steadiness *and* a kiss that turned her inside out?

Probably.

"Gary Nevis is a great guy, Mom. I just don't think he's the guy for me."

"Now. Give it time. You might discover there's more there than you realized."

"Good advice," Jane agreed without much enthusiasm.

"And on that note, I'll take my roses and go home."

Jane walked her mother out the door and down the front steps.

"A beautiful summer we're having," her mother said as they proceeded down the walk toward the car at the curb.

"Oh, yes." Jane turned her face up to the warm ball of the August sun. "A splendid summer." Northern Nevada's Comstock Valley was, in Jane's admittedly biased opinion, the best place in the entire world to live. A place where the pace of life was not too hectic, where you knew your neighbors, where people were always forgetting to lock their doors and it never mattered because nothing bad every happened. Here, folks enjoyed reasonably mild winters and summers where daytime temperatures tended to max out in the low eighties.

At the curb, about twenty feet from the low, celadon-green sports car parked in front of Cade's house, Jane took the roses and held the door open while her mother got settled into her Town Car, sliding onto the soft leather seat and taking the sunscreen out of the windshield, folding it neatly and stowing it in back.

"Here. Give me those." Virginia took the bundle of fragrant pink blooms, turned to lay it carefully on the passenger seat to her right, then smiled up at her daughter once more. "Thank you for coming to church with me."

"I enjoyed it."

"And for the lunch."

"My pleasure."

Virginia lifted her cheek for a kiss.

Jane fondly obliged. Then she stepped back and swung the door shut. Her mother fumbled in the console for a moment, came up with the key and stuck it in the ignition. A moment later, the big car sailed off down the street, turning at the corner onto Smith Way and rolling on out of sight.

Jane turned back toward her house. She got about two steps and paused to admire the scene before her.

Her house was Queen Anne-style. It had a turret with a spire on top, touches of gingerbread trim in the eaves and a multitude of cozy nooks and crannies.

Her garden stole her breath. It was late-summer glorious now, a little overblown, like a beautiful woman just past her prime. The Jack clematis that climbed the side fence was in full flower. Black-eyed Susans thrust their gold-petaled faces up to meet the sun. The big patch of lacy-leaved cosmos to the right of her walk was a riot of purple, white, lavender and pink.

Among the cosmos, on pedestals of varying heights, Jane had mounted a series of gazing balls, one blue, one pink, one green, one that looked like a huge soap bubble, crystal clear with just the faintest sheen of mother-of-pearl. The cosmos partially masked them. They peeked out, smooth reflective spheres, giving back the gleam of sunlight.

Oh, it was all so very lovely. If she didn't have her dear aunt Sophie anymore, at least she had a house and a garden that filled her heart to bursting every time she took a minute to stop and really look at it.

Jane let out a small laugh of pure pleasure. Enough with basking in delight at the beauty that surrounded her. She needed to put on her old clothes and her wide straw hat and get after it. With the bookstore closed, Sunday was prime time for working in the yard. She had the rest of the day completely to herself—and the tomatoes and carrots out back cried out for harvesting.

She started up the walk again—and spotted Cade Bravo, just emerging from the shadows of his porch.

She hadn't meant to look toward his house, she truly hadn't.

But somehow, she'd done it anyway. And as her glance found him, he emerged into the sunlight, those long, strong legs of his moving fast, down the steps, along the walk.

The sunlight caught in his hair. Oh, he did have beautiful hair—not brown and not gold, but some intriguing color in between, hair that made a woman want to get her fingers in it. He kept it short, but it had a seductive tendency to curl. Jane secretly thought it was the kind of hair a Greek god might have, hair suitable for crowning with a laurel wreath.

He waved, just a casual salute of a motion, long fingers to his forehead, so briefly, then dropping away as he moved on by.

"Hi, Cade." She gave him a quick cool smile, ignoring the shiver that slid beneath the surface of her skin, pretending she didn't feel the heat that pooled in her belly, that she didn't notice the sudden acceleration of her pulse rate.

Turning away in relief and despair, Jane made for the haven of her house.

Chapter Two

Cade got past Jane and went on down the walk. He had hardly glanced at her, just given her that quick wave and moved on by.

He knew that was how she wanted it. So fine. Let her have what she wanted.

It wouldn't have been such a bright idea to try to get her talking right then, anyway. He was on edge. Who could say what dangerous things might slip out of his mouth? The sight of Virginia Elliott, staring at him through Jane's dining-room window, fingering her pearls and scowling, had pretty much ruined his day.

Cade got in his car, slammed the door and started the engine. He wanted a drink. But he didn't want to sit by himself in the house he probably never should have bought, pouring shots and knocking them back.

Drinking alone was just too depressing. So he was headed for the Highgrade, a combination saloon/café/gift shop/gaming establishment on Main Street. Headed for home—or at least, the closest thing to home he'd every known. He'd grown up there, in the rambling apartment above the action, on the second floor.

Flat-roofed and sided in clapboard, the Highgrade was paneled inside in never-ending knotty pine. Slots lined the walls and the air smelled of greasy burgers, stale beer and too many cigarettes.

Okay, there had to be better places for a man in need of cheering up to go. But even on Sunday, he knew he'd find a few die-hard regulars in the bar. They wouldn't be big talkers. He'd be lucky to get a few grunts and a "Hiya, Cade." But technically at least, he wouldn't be drinking alone.

It was a very short drive to Main Street. Cade swung into the alley between the Highgrade and Jane's store, Silver Unicorn Books.

Jane. The name echoed like a taunt in his brain.

Seemed he couldn't turn around lately without being reminded of her. Ubiquitous. That was the word for her.

And don't laugh. Yeah, maybe he hadn't been to college—like Jane. And like both of his brothers. But he could read. And set goals. He tried to learn a new word for every weekday. Five new words a week. Times fifty-two. Do the math. Two hundred sixty new words a year. Including ubiquitous, which was another word for Jane.

Because she was *everywhere.* She had the store

next to his mother's place. One of her two closest friends had married his brother. And she lived in the house beside his.

Yeah, yeah. If living next to her bothered him, he shouldn't have bought the damn house in the first place.

But he'd had that itch to move back home. And he'd scratched it by buying the old Lipcott place. How the hell was he supposed to know what was going to happen to him as a result of buying a damn house? How was he going to know ahead of time that proximity would breed awareness? And that awareness would develop into a yen.

It just wasn't the kind of thing that he'd ever imagined could happen to him. Uh-uh. Cade Bravo didn't brood over lovers—or over women he wished would become his lovers.

Why should he? In spite of his lack of formal education, women liked him just fine. He'd never had to put up with a whole lot of rejection. Most women were willing to look at him twice. And besides, he'd always been a guy who took life as it came. If a woman didn't respond to him, well, hey, guess what? There'd be someone new on the horizon real soon.

He'd never been the type to pine and yearn.

Or at least, he hadn't until now.

Cade parked his car in one of the spaces reserved for family at the rear of the building and went in through the back door.

Caitlin Bravo had owned the Highgrade for over thirty years, since before Cade was born. The way Cade understood it, his bad dad, Blake Bravo, had set her up with it. The old man had given her three sons and the Highgrade and then vanished from their lives, never to be seen by any of them again.

In fact, Cade had never seen his father, period— not in the flesh anyway, only in pictures. It was no source of pride to him that he was the only one of Caitlin's three sons who had his daddy's eyes. Silvery eyes. Scary eyes, a lot of folks thought.

And let's lay it on the table here, the old man had been a pretty scary guy.

Blake Bravo had faked his own death in an apartment fire not all that long after he'd planted the seed that would one day be Cade. And later, once everyone thought he was dead, he had kidnapped his own brother's second son, claimed a huge ransom—and never returned the child.

The way everyone figured it now, in hindsight, Blake must have put some poor loser's body in his place when he burned that apartment building down. And somehow, he must have managed to falsify dental records. He'd been out on bail at the time, up on a manslaughter charge after killing some other luckless fool in a barroom brawl.

Getting dead had made it possible for him to beat the manslaughter rap without even going to trial. One clever guy, that Blake Bravo.

The good news was, Blake was really and truly dead now. He'd died in an Oklahoma hospital a little over a year ago. Embarrassed the hell out of Caitlin, to learn that the dead guy she'd always considered the love of her life had lived an extra thirty years and then some beyond what she'd known about.

Inside the Highgrade, things were hopping on the café side. It was usually that way on Sundays after church. Caitlin, in skintight jeans and a spangled Western shirt, was playing hostess, leading people to the booths, ringing them up at the register when they were ready to go. She saw him and gave him a wink.

He went the other way, into the comforting morose silence of the bar.

Bertha was bartending. Big and solid with carrot-colored braids anchored in a crown around her head, Bertha didn't talk much. She had a good heart and a ready smile. Cade had never known a Highgrade without Bertha Slider working there.

"Hey, honeybunch." One look in his face and Bertha knew what to do. She put the bottle of Cuervo on the bar with a shot glass beside it, set out the lime wedges and the salt, poured the beer chaser.

There were two other guys down the bar a ways. Cade saluted them and got the expected pair of grunts in response. He fisted his hand, licked the side of it and poured on the salt. Then he knocked back the first shot.

It was no good, he realized about an hour later. He'd only had a couple of shots, after all, hadn't even gotten himself to the stage where his lips started feeling numb.

And he didn't want any more. Didn't want to get drunk.

Things had gotten pretty bad when a man didn't even have the heart to pour a river of tequila over his sorrows. He tossed a twenty on the bar, said goodbye to Bertha and got the hell out.

He knew he shouldn't have, but he went back to his house. Somehow, while those two shots and that one beer to chase them hadn't made him even close to drunk, they *had* broken through his determination to put the book-peddling temptress next door out of his mind. He stopped in front of his house and turned off the engine and just sat there behind the wheel, staring at her front yard where flowers of every kind and color twined the fences and lined the walk.

He didn't see her. She must be in back. He knew she was out in that yard of hers somewhere. It was her gardening day.

Sundays, as a rule, she went to church with her mother. And after that, she would go out and work in the yard. Sometimes she wore a huge, ugly straw hat. But sometimes she didn't. Sometimes, she'd go bareheaded, anchoring that wildly curling coffee-colored hair in a tumbling knot on her head. Always, for working in the yard, she wore baggy old clothes that somehow, to him, seemed all the more provocative for what they didn't reveal.

Yeah, all right. He knew her habits. He knew her ways.

He'd observed her going in and out of her house morning, afternoon and evening, headed to and from that bookstore of hers, all that hair loose on her shoulders, snaky tendrils of it lifted and teased by the wind.

She often left her windows open. He could hear her in there sometimes, talking on the phone in that soft alto voice of hers. Her laughter was low, musical...warm.

The sound of her had the same effect on him as the sight of her. It made him think of getting her naked and burying his face in all that hair—of listening to that gorgeous voice of hers pitched to a whisper, saying wicked things meant for his ears alone.

He knew damn well she had a wild side. He also knew she kept it under strictest control. Ask anyone. They'd tell you. Since Rusty Jenkins died seven or eight years back in a botched convenience store robbery, Jane Elliott had strictly walked the straight and narrow. She'd gone to Stanford after Rusty died, got herself a nice liberal arts degree. She had her garden and her auntie's house and her cute little bookstore on Main Street. She dated only upwardly mobile guys with steady jobs. She was thoroughly practical, completely down-to-earth and obstinately sensible.

Cade, on the other hand, had made his money in poker parlors up and down the state and later, in the big tournaments in Las Vegas and L.A. And yeah, he'd been in a few tight scrapes with the law—most of them while he was in his teens and early twenties, back when Jane's uncle, J. T. Elliott, who was now the mayor, had been the sheriff. He also had that rep as a lady-killing charmer. And yeah, all right. He'd admit it. The rep was mostly earned.

Jane Elliott, unfortunately, was the one sort of woman a guy like Cade didn't really have a prayer with—and he knew it. She was the kind who'd been there and done that and learned from her mistakes. If he had any sense at all, he'd forget her.

But hey. Who said sense had a damn thing to do with it?

He was suffering, and it was bad. And since his brother had married Jane's friend Celia, it had only gotten worse. Now, he and Jane sometimes ended up at the same social events.

And don't think he hadn't tried to make use of the opportunity those events provided. He'd been no slouch. He'd tried all the preliminary moves a man will use on a woman who attracts him. He'd stood a little too close—and she had backed away. He'd struck up achingly casual conversations—which she concluded quickly and politely before they even really got started. When there was food available, he'd offered to bring her a plateful. What he got for that was a cool smile and a "Thanks, Cade. I'm not hungry right now."

Once, there was dancing. He asked her to dance. She surprised the hell out of him by following him out onto the floor. He held her in his arms—for one dance, and one dance only. Her spectacular breasts rubbed against his chest. The scent of her hair almost drove him insane.

The minute the music stopped she thanked him and pulled free.

Before she could escape, he'd suggested, "Hey. How about one more?"

For that, he got a wry twisting of her wide mouth and a maddeningly arousing low chuckle. "I'm not really a big one for dancing, Cade."

He knew she wasn't interested—or if maybe she

was interested, she would never give her interest a chance to become anything more.

He'd had enough women come on to him over the years to realize when one was *not* coming on, when she wasn't even willing to sit back and relax and let *him* come on to her.

It was probably nothing short of hopeless, the yearning inside him that tied him in knots.

So why the hell did it keep getting stronger?

He knew where this had to lead. That the moment was fast approaching when he would come right out and ask her. Give it to her point-blank: *Jane. Will you go out with me?*

He'd just been putting it off for as long as he could stand it. After all, he knew what would happen when he asked her. She would turn him down flat.

The day was really heating up. Cade shrugged out of his leather jacket, tossed it on the passenger seat.

Then he got out of the car. This craziness had to end.

He would ask the question now, today. She'd give him her answer.

And then, just maybe, he could get over Jane Elliott and get on with his life.

Chapter Three

Jane had picked the ripest tomatoes. They waited in a basket on the porch steps. She'd pulled up a bucketful of carrots, shaking the fragrant black soil off of them and sticking them just inside the back door, ready to clean up later, when she was done outside for the day.

For about thirty-five minutes, she'd been squatting among the rows, digging up persistent dandelions and other irritating weeds. Her back was feeling the strain.

With a small groan, she stood, pulling off her grimy gardening gloves, dropping them at her feet. Sweat had collected under her straw hat, so she skimmed it off and raked her hand back through her unruly hair, letting the slight afternoon breeze cool her off a little. She grabbed the boat neckline of her old shirt and fanned it. It felt wonderful, that cool air flowing down her shirt. Then she put her hand at the base of her spine and rubbed a little.

Oh, yes. Much better....

"Jane."

She froze. She didn't have to turn and look to know who it was. She knew his voice, would have known it anywhere. Deep and soft and rough, all at the same time, the voice she sometimes heard calling her in her dreams.

In her dreams, she always called back, *Yes, oh yes!* And sometimes, in her dreams, he found her and took her in his arms. Just before he kissed her, the dream would fade. And then, usually, she would wake. She would stare at the ceiling and fight the urge to go to the window, to see if the lights were on at his house.

She hadn't heard him come through the back gate. How long had he watched her?

Her legs felt kind of shaky. And a flush crept up her cheeks. But she couldn't stand there, looking off toward the back fence forever.

He had to be faced.

She turned. He was waiting maybe fifteen feet away, not far from her back porch. In those wonderful, deliciously frightening silver eyes of his, she could see what he planned to say to her.

She supposed she had known it was coming. She opened her mouth, to get it over with, to tell him no before he even got a chance to ask the question. But she shut it without speaking.

Something had happened in his face. Something tender and vulnerable, something that yearned as she yearned.

All right, whatever he felt for her deep in his secret heart, he was going to have to get over it. Just as she fully intended to get over him. Cade Bravo was not Rusty Jenkins—thank God. But he was close enough. A wild-hearted Bravo man, a lady-killer who lived the gambler's life, dangerous to love for any woman.

But especially for a woman like Jane who'd let love—or desire, or lust or whatever you wanted to call it—almost annihilate her once and had sworn never to let anything like that happen again, a woman who had a nice, stable life now and was not in the market for anything even remotely resembling a tumultuous affair.

What Jane sought in a man, Cade Bravo didn't have.

And yet, to be fair to him, she had to admit he'd handled himself with courtesy and tact. For months, he had kept his distance. Yes, she'd known he watched her. But how could she blame him for that, when she was doing the same thing herself? Watching him right back, wishing it might be different…

He'd done all the right things whenever they ended up at the same party or get-together. He'd let her know he was interested. But he hadn't pushed her. The minute she'd made her reluctance clear, he had backed off.

And now, when he was finally making a real move, he had a right to a little courtesy from her. He deserved to be treated with respect.

Nervously she fingered the brim of her straw hat, aware of the moisture between her breasts and beneath her arms, of the way her hair clung to the back of her neck, of the bead of sweat that was sliding down her temple, almost to her cheekbone now. "Listen." She lifted one hand, carefully, and wiped away that bead of sweat. "Would you like to go inside? I've got some iced tea in the fridge. I could maybe even dig up a beer, if you'd prefer that."

Those silver eyes regarded her. They saw down into the depths of her. They saw things she wished they didn't.

"Inside?" he asked softly. The one word meant a hundred things, most of them sexual, all of them dangerous.

Too late to back out now. She bent, picked up her dirty gloves. "Yes. What do you say?"

He took a moment to answer. She found herself watching his mouth—the mouth she never quite got to kiss in her dreams. The mouth, she reminded herself sternly, that she had better start forgetting about. And soon.

"Yeah," he said at last. "Iced tea sounds great."

Another silence, between them. A silence that felt like a standoff. She wanted him to just turn and go up the three steps to her back porch, go on in ahead of her. She didn't want to have to approach him, to move past him, to lead the way, with him at her back, watching.

But of course, he wouldn't go ahead of her. It was her house, her responsibility to show a first-time guest inside.

"Well," she said, and forced her feet to move.

Neither of them seemed capable of looking away. She advanced and he just stood there. And then, when she came even with him, she closed her eyes, briefly, breaking the hold of his gaze. She moved by, went up the steps. He followed. His tread was light, but she felt every footfall, pressing on her, in some deep, private place. She paused to pick up her basket of tomatoes, to drop her gloves at the edge of the step. Then she went on, pulling open the door and standing back.

He went in, and she followed, onto the service porch where her washer and dryer and laundry supplies lined one wall and her bucket of dirty carrots waited on the edge of the doormat to be cleaned.

The porch half bath was through the door to her right. She wanted to go in there, rinse off her sweating face, run a comb through her hair. But no. Not right now, not with him standing here, waiting. Better to show him on in first.

She had dirt on her shoes. "Hold on a second…"

He said nothing, just stood to the side a little and watched as she set down the tomatoes, shucked off her gardening clogs, got rid of her slightly grimy socks, tossing them in the wicker laundry basket on top of the dryer. Her pale feet seemed very bare— defenseless, without her socks. A few evenings ago, she'd given herself a long, lovely pedicure, buffing and pumicing and stroking clear polish on her toenails at the end.

She despised herself right now because she was glad that she had.

Swiftly she slipped on a pair of sandals and picked up the basket again. "Okay." Her voice was absurdly breathy and urgent. "This way." She moved ahead again, opened the inner door and went through. He followed.

They entered what she thought of as the family room. Bookshelves lined the walls, the blind eye of a television stared from a corner and the furniture was a little bit worn and very comfortable. She took him through the open doorway to the kitchen and gestured at the bay window and the round oak table in front of it. "Make yourself comfortable." She set the tomatoes on the counter. "And if you'd give me one minute?"

"Sure."

She retraced her steps, through the family room and out to the service porch, then on into the half bath at last. She shut the door, rested her head against the wood, closed her eyes and let out a long, shaky sigh. Then she drew herself up and turned to face the mirror above the sink.

Her eyes were wide, haunted-looking. Twin spots of hectic color stained her cheeks.

This was awful, impossible, wrong. Had she learned nothing from the mess she'd made of her life once? It certainly didn't feel like it, not with the way her heart was pounding, the way she burned with hungry heat.

She might as well have been seventeen again, that first time she snuck Rusty into her parents' house. Seventeen, with her parents gone—off somewhere. She couldn't remember where, but it would have been two separate places. Her mom and dad didn't go out together much. But wherever they were, neither of them had a clue what their bright, perfect, well-behaved daughter was up to. That she had Rusty in the house.

Yes. She had Rusty in the house and she knew that he was going to kiss her. And she knew that he wouldn't stop with just kisses.

And she was glad.

"Oh, God," she whispered low.

She flipped on the cold tap and splashed water on her face, grabbing the hand towel, scrubbing at her cheeks as if she could wipe away not only the water, but the heat in them, the evidence of her own insistent, self-destructive attraction to the wrong kind of man. She got a brush from the drawer and tugged it angrily through her hair, trying to tame it. Failing that, she found a scrunchy in the other drawer and anchored the mess in a ponytail, low on her neck.

"There," she whispered to her reflection, "Better. Really. It's really okay." Swiftly she tucked her raggedy shirt more securely into the waistband of her baggy old jeans.

And then there was nothing else to do but get out there and deal with him.

He was sitting at the table when she reentered the kitchen, but he'd turned his chair out a little, so he could comfortably face the doorway to the family room. He wore faded denim and worn tan boots and his skin looked golden in contrast to his white T-shirt. He was Brad Pitt in *Fight Club,* Ben Affleck out of rehab. He was a young Paul Newman in that old Faulkner movie, *The Long Hot Summer,* the barn burner's son looking for more than any woman ought to give him. He was sin just waiting to happen.

And *why,* she found herself wondering? *Why me?*

What did he see in her? Not that there was anything *wrong* with her, just that she simply was not his type. Not gorgeous, not glamorous, not a party animal.

And look at her wardrobe. Eddie Bauer and L.L. Bean—and, times like right now, when she'd been gardening, various little numbers one step away from the ragbag. Cade Bravo's women wore DKNY and Versace. They probably all bought their underwear at Victoria's Secret.

It made no sense. No sense at all.

But then, it had been the same with Rusty. Attraction of opposites. A good girl and a bad boy, tasting the forbidden, doing what they shouldn't do.

And loving every minute of it.

At least, for a while.

"Iced tea, you said?"

"Great."

"Sugar? Lemon?"

"Plain."

Her refrigerator had an ice maker in the freezer door. She got a pair of glasses from the cupboard and stuck them under the ice dispenser, one and then the other. The cubes dropping into place sounded like gunshots in the too-quiet room.

She got out the tea, poured it over the ice, filling both glasses. Normally she liked sugar and lemon. But no way she was fooling with any of that right now.

She put the tea away, picked up the two glasses and carried them to the table, setting his in front of him, then sliding into a chair.

"Thanks," he said.

She gave him a tight smile and a nod in response. Then, not knowing what else to do, she sipped from her tea—too bitter, not tart enough.

She set it down in front of her and looked at it. She was afraid to look anywhere else, and that was a plain fact.

"Jane."

He was waiting, she knew. For her to look at him.

Better get it over with. She dragged her gaze upward, and she met those silver eyes again.

And he said it. "I want to go out with you. Dinner. A show. It doesn't matter to me. Whatever you want, that's what we'll do."

She looked at him, into those eyes. "Thank you. For asking me." The words came out flat, without intonation. "I'm sorry. But no. I can't go out with you."

He didn't look surprised. "Can't?" He was mocking her.

She couldn't blame him for his scorn. *Can't,* in this case, was a coward's word. And a lie. "I won't. I won't go out with you."

"Why not?"

She shut her eyes, dragged in a long breath, then looked at him again. "Won't you just take what I said? Take *no thank you,* and let it be?"

He smiled then, more or less. At least the corners of his mouth hitched upward. "I will, if that's all I can get. It's not like I really have a choice. But you're honest, or you try to be, and—"

"How do you know that?"

"Does it matter?"

It did matter, a lot, for some reason. "I'd like to know how you know that about me, that's all."

"Jane. How could I not know?"

"You mean you've been watching me."

"What? That's news? It offends you, that I like to look at you, that I listen when people talk about you?"

"Who? Who talks about me?"

"Oh, come on. Your buddy Celia's married to Aaron. It's a story she likes to tell, how she fell in love with my brother and you told her to be honest, to let him know how she felt, that honesty was always the best policy. Is that right? Did that happen?"

She nodded, feeling vaguely foolish for making a big deal out of not very much. "Yes. All right. It happened."

"And your other friend, Jillian, she said Celia should wear sexier clothes and brighter colors, make him notice her as a woman first before she told him she was gone on him."

Jane couldn't help smiling at the memory. "And Celia did both—told the truth *and* bought a few new clothes."

"Yeah. And look at them now."

"Yes," she said carefully. "They're very happy." They lived in Las Vegas. Aaron was part owner and CEO of High Sierra Resort and Casino, on the Strip. Celia was his secretary and personal assistant—and now, his wife as well.

Cade said, "And I haven't forgotten what I asked in the first place. Did you think I would?"

Yes. All right. Maybe she had. She regarded him warily, her mouth firmly shut.

He asked again, "Why won't you go out with me?"

Jane looked through the bay window at her backyard, wishing she was out there, deadheading mums and geraniums, digging up more dandelions, working that long, tenacious central root up out of the soil. Anything but this, having to tell this man *no* when her body and her wayward heart wouldn't stop crying *yes*.

"Well?" he prompted.

She looked at him again and she spoke with defiance. "You know why. You're from town. You know about me. I had a bad marriage. A really bad marriage."

"I didn't mention marriage, Jane."

"Well, of course you didn't."

"Did you want me to?"

"Did you plan to?"

He grunted. "No. As a matter of fact, marriage wasn't what I had in mind."

"Exactly. And that's another reason for me *not* to go out with you. We want completely different things from a relationship."

"Do we?" His eyes said things she shouldn't let herself hear.

"Nothing is going to happen between us," she said, slowly. Firmly. With much more conviction than she actually felt. "What I want from a relationship, you're not willing to give."

He lifted an eyebrow at her. "You're saying you want to get married again?"

"Yes, I do. And I want a *good* marriage this time. When it comes to a man, I'm looking for an equal— an equal and a best friend."

That fine mouth curved, ever so slightly, in another one of those almost-smiles. "Well, all right. Let's be friends."

She did not smile back, not even marginally. "You're not taking me seriously."

"Yes, I am. You want a man to be your friend. Fine. Let's be friends."

It was a trap. She knew it. They'd play at being friends. And eventually, they'd make each other crazy enough that they'd give in to what was really driving this. And she should be insulted, that he would sit here in her kitchen and pretend to offer friendship when they both knew what he really wanted from her.

But she wasn't insulted. She was too excited to be insulted. She just wanted to say yes—Yes, yes, *yes*. Whatever he wanted, however he wanted it.

"No." She had to push the word out of her mouth. "I won't be your friend."

His long hand cupped his glass of tea. He stroked, wiping the moisture clinging to the side of the glass, so it slid down and pooled on the table. "Why not?"

She looked away from that stroking hand, made a low, tight sound of disbelief. "Because I really don't think that my friendship is what you're after."

She was looking at his hand again. Slowly he turned the glass in a circle, smearing the puddle of moisture at the base of it. "You don't, huh?"

She yanked her gaze upward and glared at him. "No, I don't. Are you going to tell me I've got it all wrong?"

There it was again, the smile that didn't quite happen. "Let me put it this way. I'll try anything once, friendship included."

She felt vaguely ridiculous, to keep on with this, to make all this effort to be truthful when she didn't *feel* truthful, when she knew he was teasing her, making fun of what she said. But she did keep on. Because however pointless it felt to tell him these things, she believed they were things that had to be said. "I want marriage, a good marriage. I want a steady man, a man who'll stick by me, a man who'll be true."

He had that golden head tipped to the side, as if he were considering whether or not to say what was in his mind.

"What?" she demanded. "Just say it. Say it now."

He lifted one hard shoulder in a shrug. "Okay. How long's it been, since Rusty died? You were, what, twenty?"

She had to clear her throat before she could answer. "Twenty-one. It's been six years."

"You run into any steady men, since then? Any true, good men?"

"Yes. Yes, of course, I have."

"You dated a few of them, of those good guys, those solid guys?"

"That's right. I did."

"So what happened? How come you're not with one of them now?"

Silently she cursed him. For knowing her secret

truth, for hitting it right on the mark. "It didn't work out, that's all."

"You're looking away again. Let's have some truth, Jane. Let's have it out straight."

She snapped her gaze back to collide with his and she muttered between clenched teeth, "You're being purposely cruel. I've had enough of that, in my life. Cruelty. From a man."

He leaned her way, just a little, enough that she felt him, encroaching, not quite enough to make her move back. "Listen," he said in a low voice. "I'm not him. Not Rusty. Yeah, all right, I've had my run-ins with the law. I've made trouble. I'm not exactly a solid citizen. And I've got no interest in getting married. But I've never held up a damn convenience store. I earn my way. I pay for what's mine. And the kind of cruel I'm guessing Rusty Jenkins was to you, I'm not and would never be. Get out your stack of bibles. I can swear to that."

Her lips felt dry and hot. She licked them.

His gaze flicked down, watched her do that. "God," he whispered.

And she forgot everything, but the sound of his voice and the shape of his mouth. All at once, they were leaning in, both of them. She smelled him, smelled the heat and the maleness, the clean cotton scent of his T-shirt. She felt his breath across her cheek.

Just before their lips could meet, she shoved her chair back and jumped to her feet. "No." It came out every bit as desperate-sounding as she felt. "No, please…"

He sat back, draping a hard arm over the back of the chair, looking up at her through lazy, knowing eyes. "I wasn't sure. About you, about how you felt. Sometimes, when a man wants a woman, it's easy to imagine reactions that aren't really there. But it's there, isn't it? It's as bad for you as it is for me."

She clenched her fists at her sides. What could she say to that? What could she tell him? The truth was unacceptable. And she was not a woman who told lies. "Nothing is going to happen between us. It's…not what I want. Please understand."

"Not what you want?"

"You know what I mean."

"Oh, yeah. I think I do." The gleam in those pale eyes told it all. He knew what she meant, all right. All the *wrong* things she meant. Her good intentions were nothing to him.

"You're purposely misconstruing what I'm saying."

"You're not saying what you really mean."

"I am. Yes. I'm not going to go out with you. Nothing is going to happen between us. You'd better forget me. And I'll forget you."

He shook his head. That smile that wasn't quite a smile was back on his sinfully beautiful face. "How long's it been, since this started, this thing between us, this thing that you keep telling yourself is going to just fade away? Months, anyway, right?"

"What does it matter? I want you to go now."

He didn't budge from that chair. "It matters because you've been fighting it, right? And don't think I haven't been fighting it, too. I have. I mean, come on, I got your messages. Loud and clear. You know the ones. *Get back. Keep away. Don't come near.*''

"But here you are, anyway." She was sneering. She couldn't seem to stop herself. "Sitting in my kitchen."

"You invited me in."

"And I also asked you to leave, not two minutes ago."

He chuckled then. "Jane, Jane, Jane…"

"Stop that!" She realized she'd shouted, brought the volume down to a whisper of rage. "Don't you laugh at me."

His face had gone dead serious. "I'm not. You know I'm not. I'm just telling you the truth. Being honest, the way you say you want it. I don't think this is funny at all. The truth is, I want you. You want me. You deny it. I deny it. But it keeps on. It's kept on for months. Ignoring it is not going to make it go away."

She had no reply for that. He was right. They both knew it. "Look. I mean it. I'd like you to leave now."

"Fine." He gathered those long legs up and stood.

She stepped back, clear of him. His body could not be allowed to touch hers—even accidentally, in passing.

He gave her a look that burned and chilled at the same time. "I suppose you want me to go out like I came in. Through the back. That way, there's less chance someone might see that I was in here, less chance your mother might hear about it."

She drew herself up. "The implication being that my mother somehow runs my life?"

"Admit it." His voice was way too soft. "You don't want her to know I was here."

It was Jane's turn to shrug. "Okay. It would make it easier on me if she didn't know—which is a very good reason for you to go out the front."

He frowned. "I don't get it."

"I invited you in here. I'm not ashamed that I did. If my mother finds out, well, okay. She finds out."

"She hates me—hates all us bad Bravos. You know that, don't you?"

She did. "My mother is difficult. Her life didn't work out the way she would have liked it to. She has a tendency to take out her disappointments on others. It's sad, really. She needs love so much, yet she's always pushing people away."

He wore a musing look. "You surprise me."

"Because I know my own mother?"

"I guess. I had you pegged differently, when it came to her."

"Maybe you had me pegged wrong."

"Maybe so."

"The point is, I'm a grown woman. I've done nothing wrong here. Neither of us has. And I won't live like a guilty child."

He studied her for a moment, then he let out a hard breath. "Whatever. But I still think it's best if I just leave through the back." He started to move past her.

"Wait." She reached out. He froze, his eyes daring her. She continued the movement, lifting her reaching hand to smooth her hair. The gesture didn't fool either of them. She had almost touched him, had stopped herself just in time.

She dropped her hand. "This way."

"Hey. Relax."

"You'll go out the front."

He seemed amused. "Is that an order?"

"Just a statement of fact."

"Okay, no problem. I can find the door myself."

"No. I will see you out."

He looked her up and down, his gaze sparking heat everywhere it touched. "So damn well brought up, aren't you, Jane?"

Was that supposed to be an insult? "Yes, I am."

She turned for the open doorway, but instead of going straight, into the family room, she went left, entering the central hall. He came along behind. It seemed to take a very long time to reach the front door.

But at last, they were there. She grabbed the door handle and pulled the door wide, unlatching the screen, pushing it open. He went through, out onto her porch, down the steps, into the sun that found the gold in his silky hair and reflected off his white T-shirt, so that she blinked against the sudden blinding brightness of just looking at him.

At the bottom of the steps, he paused and turned to her. "Thanks. For the iced tea."

He hadn't taken so much as a sip. "You're welcome."

"I'll have to think about this. What you said. What you meant."

"Don't. Please. Just let it go."

He looked her up and down again, as he had done back in the kitchen, slowly, assessingly, causing heat to flare and flash and pop along the surface of her skin, making that heaviness down in the center of her, that willingness in spite of her wiser self.

"You probably shouldn't have invited me in."

It had seemed the decent thing to do. "Maybe not," she confessed.

He turned, took a few more steps, then turned again, so he was walking backward away from her, not quite smiling, in that way of his. Her heart lifted. For a fraction of a second, he was only a man she found attractive, walking away from her, but reluctant to go.

"Pretty," he said, reaching out his left hand, brushing the surface of one of the gleaming glass spheres tucked among the cosmos. The gold bracelet he always wore caught the sunlight and winked at her.

She smiled at him.

He saluted her, the way he had that morning, two fingers briefly touching his forehead. Then he turned toward the street again and continued down the walk.

She closed the screen and shut the door and told herself that whatever he hinted at, nothing would happen. She'd ended it before it had a chance to begin.

Chapter Four

Cade left town sometime the next day.

When Jane got home from the bookstore Monday night, his house was dark. The green Porsche was nowhere in sight. At a little after noon, on Tuesday, Jane spotted Caitlin on Cade's porch, picking up the mail and papers as she always did whenever he went away.

Wednesday, at a little before five, Gary Nevis dropped in at her store. He bought a book on western wildflowers and asked her to have dinner with him Saturday night.

She looked into his handsome, friendly face and felt like crying. He was just what she was looking for. Except for one little problem. He didn't fill her fantasies.

And he never would. That *thing,* that spark, that whatever-it-was. With Gary, well, it just wasn't there.

In the back of her mind, Cade's taunts echoed, *You run into any steady men, any true, good men? You dated a few of them, those good guys, those solid guys? So what happened? How come you're not with one of them now?*

She turned Gary down, softly and firmly. She could see in his eyes that he understood the extent of her refusal. He wouldn't be asking again.

She'd already been feeling low. After that, she felt lower still.

She arrived home at a little after nine that night. The house next door remained dark. No green Porsche crouched at the curb.

Jane went to bed around ten, drifted off to sleep and then woke at a little after three. She lay there, staring into the darkness, until she couldn't bear it for another second. Finally she gave in. She got up and looked out the window.

Big surprise. His house was dark. She went back to her bed and turned her pillow over to the cool side. She punched it to fluff it a little. Then she resolutely closed her eyes.

Sleep was a long time coming. Sometimes her mind could be every bit as unruly as her hair.

Thursday at four Jane held her biweekly Children's Story Hour. She had a presentation area in the rear of the store, with a mishmash of chairs and benches—and also with a lot of plump pillows in the corners for folks who preferred to sit on the floor. She held the story hour there, as she did the various readers' groups she hosted, the occasional musical evening and any speaker or workshop events.

As it turned out, the story hour was just what she needed. She read some Dr. Seuss and a little Shel Silverstein and then a few chapters from *Charlie and the Chocolate Factory.*

Her heart lifted as she looked out over the small, wide-eyed faces, and she felt a smile breaking through the gloom that had been dogging her since she told two men no—one she wanted and one she didn't, one who was all wrong and one who was just right. Reading to the kids always raised her spirits, brought hope to life again.

Someday, she *would* find the right guy. She would marry again, this time well and wisely, marry a man who not only turned her bones to water, but who also loved and respected her, a man who would never hurt her, a man who wanted children as much as she did.

Jillian Diamond came bouncing into the bookstore at a little after six on Friday.

Jillian had her own business, Image by Jillian. She taught her clients how to dress for success. She also wrote a column, "Ask Jillian," for the *Sacramento Press-Telegram.* She'd already spoken at Jane's store once, back in March. Lots of folks showed up and Jillian had really wowed them. She was funny and she had some quirky and fascinating ideas. Jane had prevailed on her to do it again.

For her talk this time, Jillian wore a short, sleeveless, fitted sheath in a geometric print and a pair of white patent go-go boots. Her gold-streaked brown hair curled loosely around her arresting face. Her gray eyes sparkled beneath those startlingly dark, thick brows.

"Janey, I made it. Have to tell you, though, I had my doubts. What is it with Highway 50, anyway? Is there ever a time when half the lanes aren't blocked off for repairs?"

"Sure. That would be in the middle of winter, when *all* the lanes are closed due to ice and snow." They hugged.

Jillian smelled of her favorite perfume, Ralph Lauren's Romance, and also of Cheez Doodles. She was carrying an open bag of them. She stepped back from the hug and popped one in her mouth, then held out the bag to Jane.

"No, thanks."

"I stopped by the house and left my suitcase and stuff." Jillian gobbled more Cheez Doodles. Jane wondered how she did it. Jillian ate whatever she wanted and she never worked out and she weighed just what she'd weighed the day they graduated from New Venice High—which was about one-fifteen, soaking wet. In go-go boots.

"Oh, I am starving," said Jillian. "And I'm in a burger kind of mood. Let's go next door."

Next door. To Caitlin Bravo's place.

"To the Highgrade?" It came out sounding grim, though Jane truly hadn't meant it that way. Really, there was no reason to avoid the place. Cade wouldn't be there. He wasn't even in town.

"Janey. Sometimes you are a total food snob."

"I am not. I love a good burger as much as any-body."

"Then what is the hang-up here?" Jillian slid a glance at Madelyn, Jane's clerk, who was busy ring-ing up a sale at the register. Then she leaned close and whispered, "A Mommy Dearest issue?"

"No, nothing like that." Until the day Jane turned eighteen and eloped with Rusty, thus declaring her independence from Virginia Elliott in a very big way, she never would have dared to upset her mother by entering Caitlin Bravo's place of business. But all that was years ago. Now, Jane ran her own life and al-lowed no one to tell her where she could or couldn't go. She often headed over to the café next door for a sandwich—or she used to, until recently, when she'd become increasingly worried she might run into Cade there.

Jillian's thick brows were all scrunched up. "Well if there are no, er, family issues involved and you love burgers, why not?"

"Good question." Jane tried to sound breezy. "If you want to eat there, it's fine with me."

Jillian stepped up to the register and offered the rest of her Cheez Doodles to Madelyn. "Enjoy." She brushed the orange dust from her hands and turned back to Jane. "Let's go."

Caitlin was there to greet them. "Well, look who's here." She emerged from behind the cash register counter in the Highgrade's central game room. "What's up?"

Jillian told her. "I'm speaking next-door at Jane's tonight."

"Speaking of what?"

"Having It All and Loving It. How to Please Both Yourself and Your Man."

Caitlin chuckled her low, naughty-sounding chuckle. "Well. I'd say that about covers everything."

"Drop over if you get a chance."

"Sweetie, I just might take you up on that—and right now, I suppose you two want to eat?"

"You bet." Jillian's eyes were shining. "I'm starved. For a bacon and Swiss burger, I think. With onion rings and a chocolate shake—but I'll have a look at the menu, just in case something else jumps out at me."

Caitlin's false eyelashes swept down. When she looked up again, it was straight at Jane. "We've missed you around here lately."

"Oh, well, things have been really busy."

"I'm still counting on you to do your story lady gig at the picnic Labor Day." The Labor Day picnic was an annual event in New Venice. The town merchants went all out for it. There were horseshoes and shuffleboard, live bands, beer on tap for the grown-ups, a clown show and face-painting booth for the kids—among other things. Caitlin was heading up the picnic committee this year.

"I'm looking forward to it."

"Good. And don't be a damn stranger. You can drop in for a sandwich anytime and be back at your store in twenty minutes flat. I will personally expedite your order.''

"Thank you. I'll remember that."

"Don't thank me. Just come around more often."

"Yes. I will. Honestly."

"This way." Caitlin led them through the open doorway to the café and straight to a corner booth. She gestured at the big laminated menus, which were tucked upright between the sugar dispenser and the napkin holder. "Have a look." The orange sequins on her tight black shirt glittered aggressively with every breath she took. "I'll send Roxy right over." She strutted off.

Jillian picked up her menu and spoke from behind it, out of the corner of her mouth. "God. Best butt I've ever seen on a woman over forty-five."

Jane whispered back. "She is one of a kind."

"And I swear, she's a 38-D. Just like you. And not saggy, either."

"Fascinating," said Jane dryly. "What are you having?"

"I'm looking, I'm looking…."

"Right." Jane studied her menu, which had a knotty-pine fence on the cover—no doubt to go along with the Highgrade's extensively knotty-pine decor. Inside, a cartoon miner with a big hat, baggy old jeans and a pickax slung over his shoulder, grinned and pointed at the various menu selections. "The club sandwich is always good."

Jillian wasn't listening—or looking at the menu. "I don't see the Viking Hunk." The Viking Hunk was Caitlin's on-again, off-again lover, Hans. He was about Cade's age, had long blond hair and looked like he'd walked right off the cover of a steamy romance novel.

Jane shrugged. "You're right. Hans hasn't been around lately. I think I heard he's left town again."

"Ah, the course of true love never did run all that smooth."

"Here comes the waitress. Quit mangling Shakespeare and figure out what you want."

They ordered and the food arrived quickly. Jane concentrated on her sandwich and tried not to remember....

That engagement party Caitlin had thrown here for Aaron and Celia back at the beginning of May. The place had been packed for that. There had even been other Bravos, specifically the famous Bravo billionaire, Jonas, from Los Angeles, and his wife, Emma. Jonas was Cade's cousin and his presence had surprised every one. For over thirty years, Caitlin and her sons had lived as if no other Bravos existed. But Celia—and Jonas's wife, Emma—were working to change all that.

"Hey, Jane." Cade's voice had come from behind her. It was friendly, slightly teasing, nothing in the least pushy about it. Still, she felt pushed, way down inside herself. Pushed and pulled at the same time.

She'd turned and put on a smile. "Hello, Cade. How are you?"

"Doin' okay. Did you eat yet? I was just going to go and fill myself a plate."

"Thanks, but I'm not all that hungry right now."

Those strange, beautiful eyes went from molten silver to ice. "Right. Not hungry."

She spotted her excuse to escape him on the other side of the room. "Oh, there's Jilly. I've been looking for her..." She left him, weaving her way quickly through the press of people, a slight shudder moving through her at the thought that might follow her, perhaps become more insistent....

But he didn't.

And then, a few weeks ago—she'd seen him in here again. He'd been in the game room, kind of lounging against the wall, chatting with Donny Verdun, who ran the convenience store at the corner of State and Main. She'd tried to slide on into the café without him spotting her.

But no such luck.

Two minutes after she sat down, there he was, standing by her booth, asking her how she'd been doing, those eyes of his looking into hers, telling her things his mouth wouldn't dare say.

She'd come very close to rudeness that time, insisting she was in a hurry. Could he please send the waitress over right away?

"Sure, Jane. I'll do that." And he was gone.

She'd felt small and mean then—and strangely bereft. After that, she'd decided maybe it would be better if she stopped eating at the Highgrade for a while.

"Yoo-hoo, Janey. Are you there?"

She blinked and looked down at her hands. At some point, she had picked up the tube of paper that had covered her straw. She was wrapping it absentmindedly around her index finger. "What?" She yanked off the flattened tube of paper and dropped it on her plate beside her half-eaten club sandwich.

"You should see your face. Dreamy." Jillian set down her milkshake and leaned in close. "There's someone, isn't there? At last, after all these years. Come on. Tell Jillian. Who is he?"

"Oh, Jilly. Eat your Swiss and bacon burger. We can't sit here all night."

Later, back at the bookstore, Jane kept half expecting Caitlin to walk in. But she never appeared.

Jane closed up at ten. She'd walked to the store that morning. Since Jillian, who never walked anywhere if she could help it, had driven over from the house in the afternoon, Jane rode home with her.

They stayed up till a little before two, drinking wine at first and then switching to herbal tea around midnight.

They talked about the things they always talked about. The bookstore. Jillian's career. Celia.

"I called her last Saturday," Jane reported. "She sounded great. I forgot to ask her about the Labor Day picnic, though."

"Where you are playing story lady, right?"

"Right. I know Aaron's helping out, hiring the bands for it. But I still don't know if he and Celia are planning to be here for it—and how about you? Will you come this year?"

"Yeah. I could probably be here. I'll let you know."

The next morning, Jillian slept in.

Jane had to open the store at ten, so she was up at

eight. She sat at her kitchen table with the morning sun pouring in the bay window and sipped her coffee and told herself that life was good.

And maybe Cade would stay away for weeks this time, the way he used to, back before his house was finished.

She smiled a sad little smile and sipped more coffee. Yes, that would be good for her. It really would. But whether he stayed away or not, she would get over this impossible, unhealthy attraction. No doubt about it. It was only a matter of time.

Jillian left early Sunday morning.

And Jane's mother called. "Hi, dear. How about church?"

"I'd love it."

"Why don't we just meet there?" Virginia suggested. "I'm running a little late."

When Jane left the house, she saw Cade's powerful green car parked at the curb next door.

He was back.

Her heart felt like something was squeezing it. Then it started beating way too fast.

Get over it, she told herself as she got in her van and started it up. *He lives here and he's going to be here a lot of the time. Accept it.*

And forget him.

"How about a sandwich and some iced tea at my house?" Jane offered, as she and Virginia walked down the church steps toward the cars waiting at the curb.

"Wonderful," said Virginia.

Her mother followed her home.

The first thing Jane noticed when she turned onto her street was that the green Porsche was gone again. Good. She got out of her van and waited for Virginia to park.

They started up the walk together.

Jane saw the object on the porch—on the mat, right in front of the door—at about the same time her mother did.

"Jane. What *is* that?"

Jane didn't answer. She walked a little faster. Soon enough, they both stood on the porch, looking down at it.

Virginia said, "Why, it's so beautiful. It looks like an antique."

"It is an antique," Jane said softly, staring down at the gorgeous thing. "I'm almost certain of it. An antique mercury glass gazing ball and vase, in one." The silvery-gold ball sat on a central glass platform, with a clever little trough all around it where the flowers would go.

"A gazing ball? Like the ones in your garden?"

"Not quite," Jane said dryly. "My guess is that this is the real thing."

"The real thing. How so?"

Jane gestured toward the gazing balls that gleamed among the cosmos along her front walk. "Those you can find in just about any garden shop. They're made of a single layer of glass treated with some sort of transparent opalescent paint."

"And this?"

"It's an old technique. They would flow real mercury between two layers of glass. They don't make them like that anymore, though. They haven't in decades." Jane had read about such treasures in the various books on rare glassware she kept in her store. She couldn't resist. She had to know for certain. "Here. Hold these a minute, will you?" She handed her mother her keys and her small purse. Then she knelt and oh-so-carefully slipped her fingers beneath the vase.

"Yes." She grinned.

"Yes, *what?*" Virginia demanded.

"I can feel the stopper underneath. They would have to use a stopper, to hold in the mercury." She lifted it. "And it's heavy. Mercury is heavy. That means it still has its original filling."

Her mother was frowning at her. "It's filled with real mercury?"

"That's right. And that's very rare. Most of the old pieces like this have been drained, with reflective paint injected in the mercury's place."

"Better not drop it," her mother said warily. "Just what we need. Mercury all over the place."

"I'm not going to drop it." So beautiful, Jane thought. She stood again, carefully, cradling the precious vase close to her body.

"Who could have left it here, do you think?" Virginia was intrigued—and suspicious, too.

Jane shrugged and made a noncommittal noise, evading her mother's question, coming perilously close to telling a lie.

Because she knew very well who had left it there.

If she closed her eyes, she could see him now, walking backward down the walk, the sun gleaming golden in his hair, reaching out to brush those long fingers across one of the shining globes tucked among the flowers.

"Jane?" her mother prompted. "I asked who would leave something like this on your front porch."

Jane considered telling her mother the truth. But it would only be inviting more questions—not to mention an excess of outraged noises at the very idea that Cade Bravo would dare to offer expensive gifts to Virginia Elliott's only daughter.

She settled for shrugging again. "Open the door, Mom. Let's go inside and I'll make our lunch."

Chapter Five

Jane set the golden vase carefully on the narrow table near the front door.

"It must be valuable," Virginia said.

"Yes, I'm sure it is."

They both stood back for a moment, admiring it. It reflected light so beautifully, with the shiny golden surface—veined in places, after years and years—and that layer of quicksilver trapped beneath. It seemed almost magical, managing somehow to be opaque *and* transparent *and* reflecting all at once. It was all curves, too, distorting in a fascinating way what it mirrored, so that, staring into it, Jane's entry hall became a strange and fantastical otherworldly place.

"And you don't know who left it on the front mat?" Her mother sent her a quizzing, narrow-eyed look.

Jane made another noncommittal sound.

"That means you know, but you're not telling," said Virginia, her tone accusing now.

Jane gave her mother a smile. "Lunch will only take a few minutes. Let's go on in the kitchen."

They ate at the oak table by the bay window. Twice more, Virginia tried to pry from her daughter the name of the person Jane believed had left the vase. Finally Jane decided she'd had enough.

"Mom, by now you must have gotten the message that I don't want to go into this. I'd appreciate it if you'd just leave the subject alone."

"Well, but why wouldn't you want to talk about it? It makes no sense that you'd be so touchy about something like this."

"If I'm touchy, it's because I've asked you to let the subject drop—and you haven't."

"But—" Virginia began, and then had the grace to cut herself off. She shook her head and conceded in a thoroughly wounded tone, "Well, all right. I won't say another word about it."

"Thank you. More iced tea?"

"Yes. I suppose. One more glass."

Virginia left about a half hour later, with a bouquet of blood-red roses and three grocery bags, one each of tomatoes, string beans and zucchini. Jane felt marginally guilty loading her poor mother up with all those vegetables. There were only the two of them, her mother and her father, at home now, after all. And her father rarely showed up to sit down to dinner with his wife.

Clifford Elliott was district judge and he sat on the

boards of various trusts and charities. And then there were all the organizations he belonged to, the Masons and the Knights of Columbus, to name just two. Both he and Virginia liked to say that he "kept very busy." The fact that he was away so much and didn't share his wife's bed when he finally did come home was one of those things that simply wasn't talked about.

Virginia said, "Belinda's coming Wednesday." Belinda was her housekeeper. "I can share some of these beautiful vegetables with her. And I'll make some zucchini bread. It freezes well." Jane helped her mother carry it all out to the car.

The Porsche was back again. Cade must be home. Good. She had a thing or two to say to him. She kissed her mother's cheek and stood waving as Virginia drove off.

Once the Lincoln turned the corner, Jane headed for her house again. She marched up the walk, mounted the steps and went inside. The outer door closed automatically behind her.

Leaving the heavy oak inner door standing open, she went for the vase, which gleamed, breathtakingly beautiful, on her entry hall table to the right of the door. She paused, caught again by the absolute perfection of it as a gift meant specifically for her, for Jane Elizabeth Elliott.

She knew a sharp pang of regret. She wanted to keep it. A lot.

But she couldn't keep it. And she knew it.

Gathering it gently into her arms, surprised anew at its weight, she turned for the door again and circled back around it, cradling the vase with great care. She planned to ease through the screen with a nudge of her shoulder.

What she hadn't planned on was Cade.

He was there, standing on her welcome mat, looking at her through the screened top half of the outer door, holding an enormous bouquet of bright yellow daisies.

She gasped and almost dropped the vase.

And he grinned.

She could have shot him. Luckily for both of them, she didn't own a gun. She glared at him through the screen.

"Hello, Jane."

She said nothing, simply turned again and retraced her steps around the door. Carefully she slid her burden back onto the narrow table, breathing a sigh of relief to have it out of her arms and in a place of relative safety once more.

He was still waiting. He had to be dealt with. She smoothed her hands down the front of the sleeveless linen dress she wore, half hoping he might just turn around and leave, knowing at the same time that if he did, she'd only end up having to go after him. She had to confront him and she knew it. She must return his gift and make it clear, once again, that whatever ideas he had in his mind about her, he might as well give them up, because ideas were all they would ever be.

She forced her feet to move, around the open door again, into the doorway behind the screen. "I was just coming over to talk to you."

He looked at her, a long look, a look that blasted

her defenses, a look that stripped her down to flesh and sensation and the longings she kept trying so valiantly to deny. "You plan to let me in?"

The word *no* did occur to her. But she didn't say it. Instead she pushed on the screen. He stepped back, until she had it all the way open. Then, just like last Sunday, he was inside.

He held out the daisies. "I know you've got all the flowers you need. But I wanted to get you some anyway. It seemed only right to get them to go with the vase."

He looked so tender. So hopeful. So infinitely woundable. And she'd always had a weakness for daisies....

She stepped back, put out both hands in a warding-off gesture. "I can't take them. You know that. And I can't take the vase."

He gave her another of those long, assessing, knee-weakening looks of his. She clutched desperately for all the reasons she could never, ever go out with him, reminded herself frantically, *This is the guy that Rusty used to idolize.*

She could almost hear Rusty's voice now. "Man, that Cade Bravo. Did you hear the latest? Your uncle locked him up again this week—for being drunk and disorderly." Or "Cade Bravo got picked up for speeding. He was drunk, too, from what I heard. Got himself another DUI. He told old J.T. off, too. No one tells Cade Bravo what to do...."

Once, on a dare, Cade had run down Main Street naked. Nobody in town had ever forgotten that, the day Cade Bravo streaked Main.

And then there were all the women. Cade had always had a way with the women. People whispered that he had got Enda Cheevers pregnant, back when he and Enda were both in high school, and then refused to marry her even when Enda's father came after him with a shotgun. And another girl, Desiree Lott, had carved his name on her forehead with a pocketknife to prove her love for him. The story went that Cade had told her she was crazy and then refused to go out with her again. Desiree had a breakdown and had to be sent away.

And then, as he got well into his twenties and no longer lived in town, he'd return now and then with some new, drop-dead gorgeous woman on his arm. Never, that Jane knew of, had he brought the same woman home twice.

He was not, by any stretch of a vivid imagination, the kind of man she was looking for. She had to remember that.

She had to stay strong against his tender, I-am-so-vulnerable looks, his for-her-and-her-alone gifts. Of course, he would have the tender looks down pat. And he would know the ways to please a woman, know just what to do to get a woman to want him.

He ought to know. After all, he'd had enough practice at it.

Cade turned and set the flowers on the hall table, a few inches from the vase.

"Cade," she said to the back of his golden head. "I am serious. I told you, last Sunday, how I felt. I told you—"

He turned on her then, a seamless, catlike move-

ment. "No." Those silver eyes burned through her.
"You didn't say how you felt. You didn't say how
you felt at all."

"All right. Maybe I put that wrong."

"Oh, I don't think so."

"Listen. Whatever I might have felt, I did say *no*.
I said—"

"I remember. You said nothing would be happening between us."

"That's right. And I said it more than once, too."

"Yeah, Jane. You did."

"Then if you know that, if you admit you remember my telling you that—"

"What?" he demanded.

So she told him what. "Why are you here? What
are you up to? Leaving presents, *expensive* presents,
on my doorstep while I'm away at church, so I can
find them when I come home, with my *mother*—and
don't tell me you didn't realize that, didn't know that
my mother would be right beside me when I found
that vase."

"Wait a minute." He was shaking his head. "No.
No, I didn't know your mother would be with you
when you got back home."

"Oh, please. You know very well that I go to
church with her most Sundays. And you also know
how my mother feels about you. So you must have
thoroughly understood the position you would be putting me in."

"Jane. You're twisting what happened."

"No, I'm not. You left that vase on my porch on

Sunday while I was at church and you know I always go to church with my mother.''

''All right. I should have—''

''Oh, no. Don't give me any *should haves.* Just tell me. Why did you do that?''

''I wanted you to have the vase. I thought I'd just leave it there, let you find it. A surprise. You left on your own this morning. I thought you'd be coming back the same way. And then I thought there should be flowers. So I went out and I got them. And when I came back, your mother's car was there. I waited till she left. And here I am.''

Now, how had he done that? Made her feel like a complete jerk for doubting his motives? And why had she even brought up her mother? It should not be an issue. There was no reason to quiz a man about his motives unless she *cared* about his motives, unless why he did what he did was important to her.

He stuck his hands in the pockets of his snug black jeans. ''Look. I saw that vase in the window of an antique store in Tahoe. I knew it was perfect for you. I knew you would want it. I just…wanted you to have it.''

Oh, this was awful. How had this happened? She felt like an ungrateful, hard-hearted bitch. She swallowed. ''Cade. Truly. I can't accept it.''

''Was I wrong?'' His jaw was set, his eyes narrowed to silver slits. ''Are you going to tell me that you *don't* want it?''

She backed off a step and crossed her arms beneath her breasts. ''What I want isn't the issue here.''

He took a step forward. ''Sure, it is.''

"Stop. I mean it. Just stay right there."

He shrugged. "Okay. I'm not moving."

She spoke with great care. "The vase is beautiful. So are the flowers. But I'm sorry. I can't accept them."

His thick, silky lashes drooped down and when he looked at her again, everything was changed. His eyes had gone lazy now—lazy and knowing. "Sure, you can."

"No, I—"

"Jane. It's a gift, and that's all. I don't expect anything in return for it. So there's only one question here. And that is, do you like the damn vase?"

"No, Cade. That's not the question. That's not it at all."

"Yes, it is."

"No."

"Do you like it?"

Neither of them had taken a step since she had ordered him to come no closer to her. So why did she feel as if he'd backed her into a corner?

She went ahead, gave an honest answer. "Yes. I do like the vase. And the daisies. Very much."

Something sparked in his eyes. A gleam of triumph. "You want to keep them."

"Don't put words in my mouth."

"Just admit it. You want them."

He had trapped her again. Either she lied—or she admitted how she coveted his gift. He knew very well what she thought of telling lies. But an admission would only encourage him. "I'm not admitting anything."

"So all right. You want them."

"I didn't say—"

"Damn it. It's a vase. Some flowers. No big deal. Give us both a little pleasure. Take them."

Give us both a little pleasure.

It was an innocent enough remark, in context. Still, the hidden meanings in it caused a hot shiver to slide over her skin. "Listen to me, Cade Bravo." She spoke perhaps more strongly than she should have, her voice going just to the edge of shrillness. "I won't take any gifts from you. I'm not going to go out with you. You just have to accept that. You just have to leave me alone."

Something happened in those silver eyes, a veil going down. There was not even a hint of a smile on those lips now. His face was closed against her. She had that feeling again, the same as in the Highgrade that day when he tried to get her talking and she brushed him off so curtly—that sinking feeling.

That feeling of loss.

He said, very gently, "All right, Jane." And then he turned and went out the screen door.

"Cade!" she called after him. He was halfway down the steps and he didn't so much as pause. "Take your vase and your flowers."

He didn't stop. He didn't turn. He went on down the walk.

"Cade, please."

But he was already gone.

Chapter Six

Jane almost grabbed the vase and chased after him. But what good would that do? He'd only refuse to take it. They'd end up at the same standoff they'd reached just now.

Or worse.

She had to face it. Each time she confronted him, she felt the pull of attraction more powerfully, as if their arguing with each other fed the fire between them. She had to be careful. She could end up going down in flames.

No. She couldn't go rushing after him. She had to settle down a little, get her mind thinking rationally. She stared at the long, narrow table to the right of her open front door, at the bouquet of yellow flowers and the shining golden vase.

All right. Somehow she had to find a way to make

him take back the vase. It didn't matter what he said, about wanting her to have it, no strings attached. Maybe he meant what he said. She would never know for certain. But it simply *felt* dishonest, for her to take his special gift to her and then say no to his advances.

However, she would keep the flowers. They weren't especially expensive and they were perishable. He could hardly return them to the florist for a refund. Keeping them, treating them with care and respect, seemed the graceful thing to do.

Jane took the daisies into the kitchen, filled a big yellow pitcher with water and flower preserver and then arranged the bright flowers, stripping off leaves where necessary, fresh-cutting the stems at a slant. When she was done, she found herself smiling just to look at them, so sunny and cheery. She put them in the center of the kitchen table and then she went back to the front hall and quietly closed her front door.

The next day, when she came home from the bookstore during her lunch break, Cade's low, green car was nowhere in sight. There was no one in the house, at least not that she could see.

She went inside and got the vase and carried it over to his place. Gently she set it by the front door. And then, her face flushed and her silly heart beating way too fast, she ran back to her house. She raced up the steps, yanked back the screen, darted inside and shut and locked the front door behind her.

As if there was some danger. As if locking her door for her lunch hour would keep her safe from him.

When she finished her light meal of fruit and cheese and came out again to return to the store, his car was still gone. And the gold vase still waited on his porch. She hesitated a moment, on the sidewalk in front of his house, worrying that maybe someone else would come by before Cade. That they would see the vase. And take it.

But that was highly unlikely in New Venice, where burglaries were virtually unheard of. No. The vase would be fine where it was. He'd discover it soon enough. There was nothing to worry about.

That night, when she got home, his car was gone. And so was the vase.

Well, good. He must have been home, at least for a little while. Maybe he'd gone on over to Tahoe, to that antique store where he'd found the vase in the first place. He'd sell it back to the dealer. That would be that.

She made herself dinner. After she ate, she took a long, scented bath and then she got into her big old four-poster bed, propped herself up against a pile of pillows and called Celia. Her friend answered the phone on the third ring.

"You busy?"

"Jane. Hello."

Jane heard murmuring. Celia must have put her hand over the receiver. Yes. Celia's soft voice, then Aaron's low rumble.

"You're busy," said Jane.

"No. Not for you. I'm never busy when it's you."

"Hah. Right."

For a long time, before Celia and Aaron became an item, when their relationship was strictly profes- sional, Celia was constantly working. Jane would call and leave messages and Celia would forget to call back.

"I'm a settled, married woman now," Celia said. "I return my calls and take time for my friends."

"But if you and Aaron were—"

"He's always got work to do. You know that. He's already left the room. But don't worry. He'll be back. In a half hour or so—and how are you?"

"Doing all right. How's the baby?"

"Just fine, according to my doctor. But I'm getting fat. Aaron says I'm not. He says I look beautiful. I think I'll keep him."

"A wise decision."

Celia talked about the plans she and Aaron had made. They were going to keep living on-site, at High Sierra, the resort and casino that Aaron ran. They were planning to add a nursery to Aaron's penthouse suite, and Celia was starting to think about hiring a nanny. She loved her job as Aaron's assistant and she planned to go back to work a few weeks after the baby was born.

Celia did sound so happy. There was a lightness, a certain note of joy in her voice now. Jane was glad for her, and yet a little sad, too. A tiny bit envious, though she knew it was small-minded to feel that way. Celia had a husband she adored who loved her passionately in return. And a baby on the way.

Jane put her hand on her own stomach, remembering…

But no. The past was a place it was better not to visit. There were some tender memories there. But such terrible pain, way too much fear…and a gaping hole of loss.

Jane said, "Hey. I heard your husband was handling the bands for the Labor Day picnic this year?"

"That's right. You won't believe who he got." Celia mentioned three different groups. All big stars.

"Wow. I am impressed."

"Has my man got the juice, or what?"

"No doubt about it. And I keep forgetting to ask. Are you two going to be there?"

"Absolutely. We wouldn't miss it. I've already booked us a beautiful room at the New Venice Inn."

"You know you can always stay with me."

Celia sighed. "You know I love to stay with you. But big plans are afoot here."

"Meaning?"

"I'll explain. In a minute—and what about Jilly? Do you know? Is she coming, too?"

"I think so. She didn't give me a definite, but it was close enough."

"*Yes.* That's what I want to hear. It's going to be great. Triple Threat strikes again." Triple Threat was the three of them, Celia and Jillian and Jane. It had been a joke between them, since middle school. They'd called themselves the Triple Threat, when in reality they were three nice, middle-class girls who turned in their homework on time, obeyed their mothers and never cut school.

Jane said, "Now tell me about these big plans."

Celia laughed. "More progress on the Bravo front."

"I'm listening."

"Jonas and Emma will be there."

"At the picnic?"

"That's right. And that's not all. Get this. Marsh Bravo, his wife, their daughter and their baby son are coming, too. I've booked them all at the New Venice Inn, with us. Bravos will be taking over the place for the Labor Day weekend."

"Marsh. That's Cade's half brother, the one who lives in Oklahoma, right?"

There was a silence. Then Celia repeated, "*Cade's* half brother?"

Jane's face felt hot. What a stupid slip. "Well, I meant, *you* know. Aaron *and* Cade *and* Will's half brother."

"Janey, you're backpedaling."

"Oh, well, fine. Whatever. So tell me. What happened with Marsh Bravo?"

"Janey—"

"Come on, tell me. I want to know how this happened."

Celia gave in and let the slip-up pass. "Well, I got Aaron to call him. Marsh lives in Norman, which is near Oklahoma City. His wife is named Victoria, goes by Tory. They were glad to hear from us. Turns out Marsh has no brothers or sisters, except for Aaron, Will and Cade."

"Well, I think that's wonderful. That he called them. That they're coming out here."

"Me, too. I've really wanted this, to see Aaron get to know the other branches of his family at last."

Jane agreed that it was a very good thing. Then Celia asked how the bookstore was doing, how Jillian's latest visit had gone. Jane answered all her questions.

And then, a few minutes later, they were saying goodbye.

Jane picked up the novel she'd been reading, opened it to her place and stared blindly down at the page. She blinked, tried to focus, read a few lines.

But it was no good.

She couldn't concentrate.

She turned off the bedside light and sat in the dark, staring at the open door to the upstairs hall, telling herself she was not going to get out of that bed.

Then she pushed the sheet away and padded to the window.

His lights were on.

He was home.

Her heart did something ridiculous inside her chest.

God. She was hopeless. A totally, completely, utterly hopeless case.

Cade saw the light in her bedroom go out. He wondered if she had as much trouble sleeping as he did lately. He hoped so. He hoped she thought of him. He hoped she suffered like he was suffering. Hoped she was driving herself crazy trying to get him off her mind.

He sat in his completely remodeled den, which was housed in the turret on the side of the house next to hers, and he channel-surfed for an hour or two. There was nothing of any interest on any of the seventy-plus channels available to him. Next to him, on the side table by his reclining chair, sat the gazing ball vase she had left at his door that day. Now and then, he would glance at it, see his own face, bizarre and distorted, all nose and mouth, see the flash and flare as it cast back the images from the TV.

Around eleven, he got up and grabbed his keys and drove over to the Highgrade.

Caitlin was behind the bar. "Something eatin' you, my darlin'? You don't look so good."

"I'm fine, Ma. Give me a draft."

She leaned across the bar at him. He smelled that musky perfume of hers. The top half of her Western shirt had starbursts of purple sequins sewn on it. "Uh-uh. You got a moody look. What's the problem—love or money?"

"Back off, Ma. I only want a beer."

She turned, tapped him a tall one, and set it in front of him. "So what's the good word for the day?"

He drank, then saluted her with the half-full glass. "It's Sunday. I only do the word thing on the weekdays."

"So give me Friday's word then."

He drained the glass, set it on the bar. "That would be *loquacious*. Means long-winded. Chatty. Talkative. All the things I'm not tonight."

Caitlin chuckled. "'Nother beer?"

He nodded. She filled his glass again. He carried it into the back room, where he found a game of seven-card stud in progress. He pulled up a chair.

By three in the morning, when the game broke up, he was up a little over a thousand. He drove home, where the rooms were big and empty and the house next-door was dark.

He went straight to the den where the golden vase was waiting.

In the morning, when Jane went out to get the paper, she found the vase back on her porch. He'd put it well to the right of the door, so that she wouldn't damage it by accident when she pushed the screen wide. She didn't see it until she'd picked up the paper from the bottom step, glanced over to see that his car was there, at the curb by his house, and turned back to go inside again.

At the sight of the vase, gleaming silver-gold, back on her porch all over again, her heart kicked crazily against her ribs. Her pulse went racing. Her skin felt hot.

Ridiculous. Absurd.

She slapped her paper against her thigh and went inside, leaving the vase right where it was. She ate her breakfast, read the news over a second cup of coffee and dressed for work.

When she left the house, she left the vase, too, in the exact spot he had put it, on her porch, to the right of the door. At lunchtime, it was still there. She set her mind on ignoring it.

Which, of course, was much easier said than done. The mind, after all, will always find its way to any place you tell it not to go.

That night, at eleven-thirty, she ran out of the energy to keep pretending there was no antique vase on her front porch. She got out of bed and put on her clothes—dark clothes, as a matter of fact, clothes suitable for skulking—and went downstairs.

The vase was still there, right where he'd left it. She looked out at the curb. No sign of his car. Over at his house, the porch light was on, the windows dark.

She knelt and picked up the vase and carried it over there and left it in the same place she'd left it the day before.

The next morning, it was back on her porch.

Jane sighed at the sight of it.

And then she waited, until that night when his car was gone. She took it back over and left it at his house.

The next morning, Wednesday, when she went out to get her newspaper, there it was. She saw it and she smiled.

And right then it occurred to her that it was becoming a game with them—sneaking his gift back and forth between their houses, each so careful to return it when they knew the other wouldn't catch them in the act.

A game. She was playing a game with Cade Bravo.

She utterly disapproved of herself.

And as of right now, she was opting out. She picked up the vase and took it inside and then went out to her garden and clipped an armful of flowers. She arranged them in the fabulous vase, quite artfully, she thought. And then she put the vase in the place of honor in the center of her dining-room table.

A little later, at the store, she made some calls to a few antique dealers in Tahoe. On the fourth call, she hit the jackpot. The dealer remembered the vase.

He'd sold it just the Saturday before, to a gambler flush from some tournament down in L.A.

Yes, she thought. That would be Cade.

She explained that she was considering buying it, asked if he could tell her how much she ought to pay. If he could let her know what he'd sold the vase for, she suggested, that would be terrific.

"Sure," he said, and named a figure.

To double-check, she called more dealers. In Sacramento and in Reno. To each, she described the vase and asked if they were familiar with such a piece. She managed to talk two of them into giving her an educated guess as to the vase's value. Both of those estimates weren't all that far from the amount the dealer in Tahoe had quoted her.

So she made out a check to Cade Bravo.

She chose a nice card from the card rack at the store. It had a picture of the seashore and two children, a boy and a girl, building castles in the sand. Inside she wrote,

> Cade,
> I've decided to keep the vase. I've called several dealers and I'm reasonably certain I'm giving you a fair price for such a beautiful piece. My check is enclosed.
> Sincerely,
> Jane

She slipped the check inside the card and put the card in its matching envelope, sealed it, addressed and stamped it. Then she left Madelyn to mind the store for a few minutes and ran across the street to the post office. She felt quite pleased with herself as she dropped the envelope in the mail slot. She had taken a bad situation and turned it around, made it all right.

Things should settle down now, she told herself. She'd solved the problem. She'd paid for what she took from him.

Yes, she felt a little jittery the next couple of days, a little on edge. It was that waiting-for-the-other-shoe-to-drop feeling. Sometimes she wondered what he would do next.

But Thursday passed. And Friday. And nothing happened. By Saturday morning, she was telling herself that the problem was solved. He'd accepted the fact that they couldn't go on playing silly, pointless mind games with each other, sneaking onto each other's porches when the other wasn't looking. Her buying the vase from him was a reasonable solution. He would cash her check and that would be that.

Saturday, his car was again in front of his house and her mail was waiting when she walked home for lunch. She carried it inside with her. Three catalogs, a couple of bills and an envelope addressed to her in a bold, round hand. There was no return address, but the letter had been mailed from in-town, according to the circular U.S. post office stamp.

From Cade.

She knew it without having to open it. She dropped the rest of the mail on the long table by the door and took the letter into the dining room, where she put it down a few inches from the silvery gold vase.

She glared at that envelope, considering. Maybe

she shouldn't even open it. What good could it do her, to find out what was inside? Most likely none at all.

Then again.

It could be something totally innocent, couldn't it? A simple acknowledgment that he'd received the check.

She let out a scoffing sound. Right. Cade Bravo doing something totally innocent.

Not in this lifetime, girlfriend.

She swore, low, a word that her mother would have gasped to hear. And she grabbed the envelope and ripped it open.

There was a card. A card very similar to the one she had sent him. A beach scene. Two children, a boy and a girl. The boy wore shorts and a striped shirt. The girl, a sleeveless white lace dress and a straw hat with a turned-back boat-style brim. They stood very close, the boy holding a conch shell to the girl's ear, their bare toes just touching in the wet sand.

It was lovely. So sweet, their young faces, seen from the side. You could almost hear the boy whispering, "Listen…"

And the girl had her eyes cast down, lost in the sea sound coming from the shell.

Jane's hand was shaking. She opened the card, found her check waiting there. She moved it out of the way to read what he'd written.

Jane,
What's this? You don't owe me any money.
Hope you are enjoying the vase.
Cade

It was too much. It had to stop.

Clutching the card in her hand, Jane whirled for the front door. She barreled through the screen, letting it slam behind her. When she got to his door, she punched the bell three times in quick succession. When he didn't immediately answer, she fisted her hand and banged on it good and hard.

It opened.

And there he was. Wearing khaki pants, no shoes, and a short-sleeved cotton shirt—unbuttoned.

He had one of those torsos you could scrub your laundry clean on. A real, true honest-to-goodness six-pack of a stomach. Jane stared at it, and blinked, and forced her gaze upward.

Into those silver eyes. "Jane. What a surprise."

"I'd like to come in, please. I don't want to stand here on your front porch and say what I have to say to you."

He stepped back and bowed her over the threshold.

Chapter Seven

He led her to the ground-floor turret room, next to the entry hall, a nearly circular room with windows all around, a room where the furniture, arranged in the center, was big and inviting-looking, mostly camel-colored leather, with a couple of fat easy chairs in an attractive plaid. The tables were mismatched, pleasingly so. The afternoon sun streamed in the tall windows, reflecting warmly off the shining pale wood of the floor.

The room gave her pause. Jane had been in the house once or twice over the years, while the Lipcotts owned it. She'd always thought of it as dark to the point of being oppressive. There had been mahogany paneling, hadn't there? And dark hardwood floors? Cade had opened it up inside, made it friendlier, brighter, more welcoming than before.

Not that it mattered.

She hadn't come here to admire the decor.

He gestured at a big leather sofa. "Have a seat."

She backed up to it—then decided no way she should sit down for this. She stood tall and waved the card at him. "What is this, Cade?"

"Well, Jane. It's a card."

"Oh. Oh, right. A card. It's a *card.*"

"Jane—"

"Don't you speak."

He threw up both hands in an I-give-up gesture. Then he dropped to one of the plaid easy chairs and sprawled there, looking insolent and challenging and maddeningly sexy, with his shirt gaping open around that impossibly hard washboard belly, feral eyes watching her.

She glared down at him. "I am so furious, so livid. So *damn* mad."

"Hey. I can see that."

"Don't you smirk at me."

"Jane—"

"And stop interrupting me. Let me say what I came here to say."

He shrugged, slung one lean leg up on the arm of the chair, rested an elbow on it—and kept his mouth shut.

Now, she could talk. She could tell him off.

Trouble was, all of a sudden, she had no idea where to begin.

He lifted an eyebrow at her, but other than that, he didn't move, didn't make a single sound.

She let out a long, weary breath, thought, *What am*

I doing here, adding fuel to this dangerous fire burning between us?

It was a moment of insight. She saw herself clearly and what she saw wasn't good. She was keeping this thing between them going every bit as much as he was.

Confronting him thrilled her.

And her life, in the years since the disaster of her marriage, had been distinctly short on thrills. She'd told herself she liked it that way. Certainly, at first, she had. But what about now? What about the past few busy, contented—and just a little bit lonely—years?

A deeper, more painful truth dawned. When this silver-eyed charmer finally gave her what she said she wanted—when he left her alone for good—she was going to feel dumped, brokenhearted. Forlorn.

It didn't matter what happened today, or where they went from here. If it ended right now, with whatever they said to each other in this light-filled room, she would miss him. Terribly. Miss the excitement between them, the awareness, the connection of the attraction they shared.

Somehow, without her even realizing it was happening, it had become too late. Too late to tell him off and turn around and walk away and forget him.

When he stopped pursuing her, when he finally lost interest, she would suffer. She would have to go about the painful process of getting over him.

For some reason, her legs didn't feel all that trustworthy. She stepped back and lowered herself to the end of the sofa where she'd refused to sit just moments before. In her right hand, she still held the card he'd sent her. She stared at it, at the two innocent children, the wild surf beyond, and she heard her own voice murmuring, "Oh, I don't...how did this happen? I didn't mean for this to happen...."

She looked up. He was still there, still slouched and waiting, his lean, tanned bare foot hanging over the arm of the chair. He was also still silent, as she'd ordered him to be.

She set the card on the low table between them. Her throat felt tight and dry. She swallowed. "Once I told Rusty to shut up. He hit me."

Oh, God. Had she really said that?

She must have. Something flared in his eyes. His mouth tightened, but he didn't speak.

She sat forward. "Go ahead. Please. Say it."

"I've said it before. I guess you weren't listening. I'm not Rusty."

"No," she said. "You're not. I know you're not. He, um, he hit me a lot."

Cade moved then, swinging his leg to the floor and leaning toward her as she leaned toward him. "I've been in fights. Well, you know that. I've had a chip on my shoulder, I guess you could say. But I never hit a woman, Jane. Never in my whole damn life."

"I believe you. I do." She swallowed again, nodded. "He idolized you, Rusty did. It was always 'Cade Bravo this, Cade Bravo that' with him. I guess I'm holding that against you, a little."

"Jane. I hardly knew him. He was your age, right?"

"Um-hmm."

"Five years younger than me, just another kid with a bad attitude hanging around town. I have to admit, I took a little notice when I heard how he got shot trying to hold up that that Speedy Mart over in Reno, but only to think what a damn fool he was."

"I was the fool. For falling for him, for running off with him, marrying him…" She paused, pressed her lips together in regret and self-disgust. "Just your everyday, classic act of rebellion. Against my mother, against all her rules and restrictions. And against her unhappiness, too, with her sham marriage to my father…well, you know about that, right—I mean, at least about my father and Caitlin?"

He sat back in the chair again. "I heard the rumors. That Caitlin and your father had a thing going years ago."

"I can tell by your voice, by the look on your face, you don't believe there was any affair."

He shook his head. "Caitlin has her standards, hard as that is for some folks to believe. She's been with a married man or two. But never when she *knew* that they were married. As soon as she found out they had wives, they were outta there. She would have known your father was married from the first. So my bet is, she wouldn't have let herself even get started with him."

Jane dragged in a long breath. "I think you're right. That she wouldn't. And she didn't."

He actually looked surprised. "Wait a minute. You know what happened, then?"

"I think so, yes."

"Your mother told you?"

"Hardly. My mother's always…referred to it. Always hated Caitlin, made cruel remarks about her. But she would never talk about what actually happened."

"Your father, then."

"No. My father and I don't talk much. We never have. I wouldn't know how to ask him something like that. I wouldn't know where to begin."

"Then who?"

"My aunt Sophie. I could ask her anything. And I did."

"Ah. And what did Aunt Sophie say?"

"That my dad had a thing for Caitlin. That he went after her and she turned him down. More than once. That she told him to go back to his wife. So he left my mother. Caitlin still wouldn't have him. He came back home and picked up where he left off. My mother accepted his return. But that's about it. They're not close, not in any sense. And my mother won't let go of the idea that it was all Caitlin's fault."

"And she also considers all Bravos guilty by association."

"It's her problem. I know that."

"But?"

"Well, it does make it all the more…difficult, between you and me."

He grunted. She sat back a little, leaned an elbow on the arm of the sofa, looked away and then back at him.

"Go ahead," he said. "You were talking about Rusty."

"It was probably a mistake."

"It's all right. Tell me."

"I think I've said too much already."

"I don't. I think you should go on."

"No. Really. You don't need to hear any more."

That almost-smile came and went on his lips. "Maybe you need to say it."

That made sense. Too much sense. "Yes. All right. Maybe I do."

He nodded. And then he waited.

And soon enough, she was talking again. "I was so crazy for him, for Rusty..." Her voice faded off. She was thinking, *Crazy for him, just like I am for you.*

She blinked, went on. "I thought it was love. What did I know? I was only seventeen when it started. And then, after we got married, I was so sure I could make it work. I *wanted* it to work, desperately wanted to prove myself, as a grown woman, as a wife."

"Yeah, and what did Rusty want?"

A tight sound escaped her. "To get high, to have a good time, *all* the time—with me, while it was new between us..." Again, she wondered, *Should I be saying this? Is this wise?*

He prompted, softly, "But then?"

And wise or not, she told him. "For Rusty, being with me got old. There were other women and there was too much drinking and there were way too many drugs. And the more he got high, the meaner he got. He beat me down. More than my mother ever did. It was physical and it was psychological, too, what he did to me. I went from being crazy in love with him to trying to appease him to being flat-out terrified of him. When he died, I was…broken. It took a long time, before I felt whole again.''

There was a silence. She heard a car going by on the street outside, and the jeering call of a blue jay perched on the fence between their two houses. The jay took flight.

And Cade said, ''What else?''

She sat straighter, folded her hands in her lap. ''What do you mean?''

''There's something else you almost said. But you held it back.''

How had he known? ''You know a lot about women, don't you?''

He made a low sound in his throat. ''I read faces for a living. I count cards, I remember the order of play—and I watch the other guy, I try to spot his tell. You know what a tell is?''

''A gambler's term, isn't it? The little things a player might do, little gestures and looks, that give his hand away.''

''Right. Just now, it was something that happened before you said 'broken.' Your eyes shifted, your mouth got tight. You were going to say more. But you changed your mind.''

''I think I've said more than enough.'' She stood. ''Don't you?''

He let his head drop against the back of the chair and looked up at her, a look both lazy and measuring. ''How the hell would I know if you've said enough? I don't know what it is you're not telling me.''

''It's not important.''

''Jane. Shame on you. That was an outright lie.''

He was right again. Her cheeks burned. "Yes. It was a lie. What I didn't say *is* important—to me. And I don't *want* to say it. I've said enough." She felt so strange, so raw around the edges, and bewildered, too, like someone suddenly awakened from a sound sleep in a dark room by a bright light glaring full in her face.

She had come storming over here to tell him off—and ended up sitting on his sofa, pouring her heart out.

And now, truly, it was time to go. She told him as much. "I should go now. I have to get back to the store."

He stayed where he was, resting back in that comfortable chair, looking up at her with—what? A sort of friendly intimacy. He asked, "Will you keep the vase? Please. As a gift."

Somehow, it didn't even seem like an issue anymore. "Yes," she said. "I will take the vase. As a gift. Thank you."

He smiled then, a real smile, and he straightened in the chair, gesturing at the coffee table as he rose to his feet. "Take your check."

She picked up the card, slid it in the side pocket of her skirt and then turned for the entrance to the front hall. He followed behind her, to the door.

Before she went out, she couldn't resist turning to him again. "I…"

"Yeah?" He looked hopeful. He didn't *want* her to go.

And really, a few minutes of small talk…how

could that hurt? "I like what you've done. To the house."

"I'm happy with it."

She backed up enough that she could lean against the door. "I heard you had other houses, in Las Vegas and in Tahoe."

"I sold the Vegas house. Lately I'm not there enough to justify the expense." His focus kept shifting—from her hair, to her eyes, to her mouth, as if he couldn't decide which part of her he wanted to look at the most. "And yeah, I have a condo in Tahoe. It's on the market."

She was thinking that she liked it, the way he looked at her, as if he couldn't get enough of looking at her. She liked it a lot.

And wasn't it her turn to talk? "So, you're really settling in here?"

"For now." His gaze had stopped roving. He looked right in her eyes. She stared back—and then couldn't resist looking down a few inches, watching his mouth move as he spoke.

He said, "I'm not a big one for settling in, long-term. I like to keep mobile."

Mobile, she told herself. *He likes to keep mobile. He doesn't want to settle down.*

She got the message. It was pretty hard to miss. He was telling her again, as he'd told her before. Whatever happened between them would not include forever.

She should go.

She stayed right where she was.

He added, "I know folks wondered, that I would buy a house like this."

"Yes, they did wonder." She smiled, leaned more fully back against the door.

"Did you?" he asked.

She was staring at his mouth again. She shook herself. "Did I what?"

He smiled. Slowly. He knew exactly what kind of effect he had on her. Patiently he asked again, "Did you wonder what bad Cade Bravo was doing, buying an old Victorian on Green Street?"

"Not really. After all, *I* have a house on Green Street. And I love it. It's not so hard for me to believe someone else might feel the same."

He moved in closer, rested a hand on the edge of the door, not far from her shoulder. "And your mother—she's pretty outraged, right? 'One of those horrid Bravo boys, living on Green Street!'"

Jane almost laughed. He'd hit Virginia's reaction so precisely.

Cade did laugh, the sound low and sexy and warm. "I nailed her, right?"

"Unfortunately, yes."

He was very close. She could smell him, soap and man and a faint hint of aftershave. "Jane..." And heat. Somehow his body gave off a scent of heat. He whispered, "You gonna let her stop us, let her keep us from each other?"

Dangerous, she thought. She was looking at his mouth. So dangerous. So tempting. So exactly what she longed for. She realized she was biting the inner side of her lower lip. She made herself stop that. "It's not only my mother."

"What else?"

"You know what. We don't want the same things."

"That's right." The very sound of his voice was like a tender hand, stroking. "We want different things. *I* want *you*. *You* want *me*."

"Very funny." She wasn't laughing. She felt kind of hypnotized, her mind slow and thick, but in such a thoroughly lovely way. "That's not what I meant. You know it's not. I meant, in life. We want different things in life."

"So?"

"So it can't...go anywhere. You said that yourself. You're not a man who wants to settle down."

"Is it so necessary, for me to settle down, for a love affair to *go* somewhere?"

"Not as long as you're having that love affair with someone who isn't me."

"But, Jane. I thought you understood. I don't want to have a love affair with someone who isn't you."

"You say that now."

"And I mean it. Now."

"But later—"

"I keep trying to tell you. Forget about later. Later can take care of itself."

"Haven't we been through all this before?"

"Yeah. We're still working on it."

"You mean *you're* still working on *me*."

"Jane, Jane. You have a cynical mind."

"No, I'm realistic. And I have goals. I have hopes

and dreams. I want a good husband. I want babies...."

"There you go with the good, steady man again. The one you keep finding over and over—the one who bores you to death." He tipped his head to the side, as if considering. "Then again, the babies are news. You never mentioned them before."

"I know it's all funny to you. But to me, it's—"

"Shh." He put up a finger, near her lips, but not quite touching them. It seemed, though, that she could feel it—feel that finger, on her skin. "Listen," he said. "I know I'm not what you're looking for, not in the long-term. Not marriage material, not your steady, dependable guy. Not Mr. Right in anyone's book. But I'm here, now. There's this...thing between us. You're single, so am I. It's our damn business what we do behind closed doors."

Her mind seemed to be on hold. Her body was burning. She couldn't help thinking, *He's right. Why not?*

She tried to argue, to call up the principles she made a point to live by. "Cade, it wouldn't be right. Wouldn't be honest."

He swore, a whisper of an oath. He was close enough that his breath stirred her hair. "Tell me you don't feel this—the pull between us."

She let out a small moan. "I can't tell you that."

"Damn right you can't. You'd be lying, if you did. Because it *is* honest, what we feel for each other. Maybe it doesn't come with a lifetime guarantee. But it's palpable. It's real."

"Palpable?" she whispered, surprised that he would choose such a word.

"Yeah. That's right. Palpable. Capable of being touched or felt. My word for Friday."

She was enchanted. "Your...?"

"Every day, Monday through Friday, I learn a new word. You think that's funny?"

"No. No, of course not."

"I didn't go to Stanford, but I'm not stupid, Jane."

"Oh, I know. I know you're not."

He had a dent in his chin—a cleft. All the Bravo boys had it. She imagined herself lifting on tiptoe, pressing her lips there, on the cleft in his chin. He was clean-shaven today, no shadow of beard to make his skin rough. It would be smooth, if she kissed him. Smooth and hot...

He lifted a hand.

It was a crucial moment, a moment of choice. She could slide away.

Or stay, feel his touch.

She didn't move. He laid that hand against her throat. A long shudder took her.

He whispered, "Oh, yeah..."

And then she was lifting her mouth with a starved, low cry.

"Say it," he commanded, his face against her hair. He breathed in, deeply, through his nose, as if he craved the scent of her. "Say what you want."

"A kiss. I want you to kiss me...."

"I'm nuts for you, Jane." He said it in the most lovely, tender, incredulous way.

"Oh, Cade..."

He made a low sound in his throat and pulled back enough that she could see how his eyes crinkled with humor at the corners. "That's it? All I get? *Oh, Cade?*"

"Words seem to have failed me."

"I've left you speechless."

"Well, let me put it this way. If you don't kiss me soon, I think I might explode. It could get very messy. You wouldn't want that."

"Kiss you?"

"That's what I said. Please. Kiss me."

"All right, Jane. I'll do that."

"Now, please."

"Yes, ma'am."

Chapter Eight

His mouth touched hers—so lightly, brushing, back and forth, back and forth.

Jane could hardly believe it: her forbidden dreams of him, coming true at last. Her forbidden dreams only better, because the kiss that never happened in her dreams was happening now. She let out a moan and she slid her hands up, over that hot, hard chest of his, to clasp the back of his neck.

He chuckled against her mouth.

And she yanked him closer with a needful groan.

He didn't object. His wonderful mouth went soft over hers and his body pressed in tight, pinning her against the door.

Jane sighed in delight, kissing him madly, letting her hand glide downward again, along the side of his neck, back to the front of him.

Oh, he was glorious. She traced the shape of him, that deep, strong chest, the wonderful ridges of muscle at the top of his belly, then around, edging under the open side of his shirt, to where the skin stretched taut over the bones of his rib cage. And she didn't stop there. Oh, no. Her fingers danced on, until they caressed the tight curves at the small of his back.

He moaned then, as she scooped at the tender hollow of his spine. And he pressed in even harder, grinding against her, leaving no doubt as to how much he wanted her.

Oh, and she wanted him! So very much. The response of her body to his left her breathless. Arousal moved through her in waves, hollowing her out, leaving that marvelous liquid inner softening. It had been so long, since she'd felt this joyful eagerness, this wonder, this longing. This need...

She moaned again as his tongue found hers. He cupped her face in his hands and he held it, tipped up to him, pressing her harder against the door, drinking the kiss from her mouth.

She was lost in it, in all of it, in the taste and the scent of him, in the feel of him touching her, of *her* touching him. Time stopped. The whole world was right there, captured between them, in the magic of that kiss.

He pulled away in stages, keeping his body pressed to hers, lifting his mouth slightly, then coming back again to kiss her deeply, then retreating, then returning. All the while, he rubbed against her, a sexual friction that drove her wild.

At last, with a low sound that was half regret and

half promise, he opened his eyes and looked down at her. "Jane."

She made a noise, a questioning one. It was all she could manage right at that moment.

"What now, Jane?"

She slumped against the door, drugged with pleasure, longing for more.

"I could carry you upstairs and take all your clothes off and kiss you all over."

She swallowed, licked her lips. "Hmm."

"What does that mean?"

"Hmm. Uh. Well," she said, as if a few garbled sounds constituted some kind of answer.

"Don't tell me. Speechless again."

That was about the size of it. She stared at him for a long time, thinking that this was very nice, just leaning against the door, looking at him, imagining what might happen next.

"What?" he demanded, then shook his head. "All right. I get it."

Since she didn't know what he was talking about, she wisely said nothing.

And he said, "I don't get to seduce you right now."

She thought, *You've already seduced me.* But she didn't say it. It seemed way too dangerous a truth to give him when he hadn't even asked for it.

He added with tender indulgence, "Right now, you have to get back to your store."

Ah. Her store. For a while there, she'd completely forgotten she had a store. "That's true. I do."

"You should see your face. All soft, skin flushed,

mouth swollen. I like it. A lot. I was getting real worried I'd never see you like this.''

She touched his chin—touched that tender Bravo cleft and then his lips, swollen as hers. ''I swore this was never going to happen…''She stroked the side of his face, let her fingers brush the silky hair at his temple. ''But here we are, after all.'' The sad truth intruded. She dropped her hand to her side and added ruefully, ''For a little while, at least.''

He put a finger under her chin, lifting her head to make her look at him. ''Hey. Don't be thinking about it ending. It's barely begun.''

Easy for him to say. She frowned. Slowly the sensual haze was fading, rude reality intruding.

He stepped back. ''What? What is going through your mind?''

She stopped using the door to hold her up, stood straight and brushed at her skirt, not so much because it needed smoothing as for an excuse to look away. ''I'm sorry. It's just that, when I let myself think about it, I get doubtful again.'' She made herself meet his eyes once more. ''I can't help it. There was a time I didn't look ahead, didn't consider what would happen, later, after it was over. I didn't let myself see what a mess it would be.''

''Damn it, Jane. This is now.''

''I know, but a person learns from experience and—''

He cut her off. ''Look. Who knows what will happen this time around? Who the hell can say how it will be?'' The silver eyes narrowed. ''Wait a minute.

You're backing out, aren't you? That's what's happening here.''

"No. I didn't say that.''

"You don't have to say it. It's written all over your face.''

"Hey," she said, softly. "What's going on here? Are we arguing again?''

He took another step away. "Yeah. Kind of looks like it, doesn't it?''

There was a long, edgy silence.

Then Cade said, "What do you want to do, Jane? Say what you want.''

"A little time, okay? A little space, to think this over. That's what I want.''

"How long?''

"You would have to ask that.''

"Damn right. I want to know.''

"A couple of days?''

He shook his head. "Great. Tomorrow is Sunday. You can go to church with your mother. She can remind you of what a rotten, hopeless loser I am.''

"You are not a loser. From what I've heard, you do pretty well.''

He grunted. "That's supposed to mollify me, right—and yes, *mollify* was one of my words two or three months ago.''

"Well. Are you mollified?''

"Slightly.''

"Good. And my mother won't remind me of anything—not about you, anyway. I won't be discussing you with her.''

"Well, that's something. I guess.''

She laughed. And then she sighed. "Just a couple of days. Please. I really need them."

"Are you asking me or telling me?"

She wrinkled her nose at him.

"I get it. You're telling. The *please* was just to soften the blow."

"I need to think about this."

"Just admit it. You're telling."

"Okay, I'm telling."

He looked at her, a long look. "Monday night? Can you make up your mind by then?"

Oh, no, she thought. *Monday is way too soon.*

But who was she kidding? She already knew what her answer would be. Really, this was only a last-ditch attempt to put off the inevitable, one last to chance to give herself a serious mental talking-to. She could certainly do that by Monday.

"Monday," he said again. It wasn't a question.

"All right, Cade. Monday."

"Fair enough. I'll come to you. After you get home from the store."

"I'll be there."

Another silence elapsed. There was heat in it, this time, heat and the memory of his mouth on hers, of his hands on her skin, his body pressing in....

She said, "I should go."

"Yeah. Guess so."

She turned and pulled open the door and got out of there.

Jane called Jillian that night but got her answering machine. She hung up without leaving a message.

Then she called Celia. They talked for twenty minutes or so about nothing in particular.

Celia kept asking if Jane had something on her mind.

Jane evaded. Which was doubly reprehensible, in her own eyes. First, because evasion was just next-door to lying. And second, because she'd called her friend with the intention of mentioning what was going on with Cade.

Of asking, *What do you think? What should I do?* Of saying, *I want him so much, but it would only be temporary. An affair. And I know it. And that's not what I'm after.*

And actually, she decided as she went on evading, she had a pretty good idea of what Celia would say, anyway. Celia would come off like a Nike ad.

Go for it. Or was that *Just do it?*

Whatever. Celia would tell her to go where her heart led her. That's what Celia had done, when she fell for Aaron. Aaron had made it very clear to her that he would never marry her.

And look at them now. In the end, Aaron had gone on his knees to Celia—and been happy to be there.

Then again, Celia had known it was love, when she went after him. She really had followed her heart.

If Jane went after Cade, would she be doing that? Following her heart? Hah. Jane had to admit it felt more like something a little lower down.

It felt like lust. A serious case of it. And it was. No doubt about it. Lust was a big part of it.

Was it the only part?

Jane was ashamed to admit that she couldn't be

sure. Couldn't really trust her own battered heart, the heart she had trusted once—and look where that got her. Married to a violent, drug-abusing criminal.

But that wasn't fair. Cade kept telling her he wasn't Rusty. And he wasn't. She knew that.

And hey. There was another bonus with Cade. No chance of her ending up in a bad marriage with him. No chance of a marriage at all.

He'd made that painfully clear.

And she didn't *want* to marry him—did she?

No, of course not. She just plain *wanted* him. As he wanted her.

She said goodbye to Celia and hung up the phone. The night stretched ahead of her, long on indecision and yearning, short on sleep.

Virginia picked her up for church the next morning. As usual, Jane invited her mother in for lunch afterward.

Virginia remarked on the mercury glass vase. "Well, I see you've kept it, whoever gave it to you. Do you know for certain now who that is?"

"Yes, Mom. I do."

"And?"

Jane had her answer ready. "It's a *secret* admirer, Mom," she said lightly. "Which means I can't tell you."

"Oh, that's ridiculous. A ridiculous excuse. I don't approve of this. Of all this mystery."

"Sorry to hear that."

"You're not going to tell me anything, are you?"

"No, I'm not. Iced tea?"

"I don't like this."

"You said that already. Do you want iced tea or not?"

Virginia left at a little after one. Jane went out into the garden and worked until three. The day was just too hot to go on any longer—in the nineties, without even a hint of a breeze.

Sweat was running off her when she gave up and went inside. She was careful, very careful, not to look toward Cade's house. She doubted he would be there anyway. She hadn't seen his car, when she walked Virginia out to the Lincoln.

But she was strictly not looking at his house, not looking for *him*. Until tomorrow. When she would tell him…whatever she would tell him.

And yes, she did know that she was being more than slightly silly, that not looking at his house wouldn't help her with her decision, that it made no difference where she looked, she'd still have to figure out what to do about Cade, what to do about this longing that refused to go away after months of denial, after sleepless night upon sleepless night of telling herself that it would fade.

She went inside and she stripped off her clothes and she stood in the shower—yes, a *cold* shower. When she got out, she was all goose bumps, shivering like mad.

But the longing was still there.

She still wanted Cade.

And that night wasn't any better than the night before.

By Monday morning, she was actually glad she

hadn't told him she had to have longer to make her decision. She was as ready as she'd ever be, she realized that now.

Sometimes, a person had to make like a Nike ad, to behave decisively in spite of the indecision in her heart. She couldn't hang on the edge of her own longing forever. At some point, she had to make the leap.

At noon, she called his house and left a message. "Hi, Cade. It's Jane. Would you call me at the store as soon as you get in?" She rattled off the phone number. "Thanks." And she hung up.

Then she ran to the bathroom and took a shower. She shaved everything that needed shaving. She slathered lotion all over herself and spritzed on scent, reapplied her blusher and mascara and lip gloss. She dressed with care, in her best, most seductive underwear, in a silk chemise-style dress that clung to her curves and would be very, very easy to take off.

She was ready—or as ready as she'd ever be—to become Cade Bravo's lover.

She spent the afternoon jumping every time the phone rang. And every time it rang, it *wasn't* Cade.

By the time she went home, she was certain that *he* was the one who had made a decision. He'd decided he'd be better off not to get involved with her, after all.

On Green Street, the blinds were drawn in his front windows. His car wasn't there. Her feet felt like a pair of lead bricks as she dragged herself up the walk.

Why was this happening to her? All she'd wanted was a nice, steady, average guy.

But no.

She had to go and fall for an impossible Bravo charmer, a guy who'd never held a steady job, who'd run naked down Main Street, who'd made love to more beautiful women than Jane cared to count, who'd come waltzing into her life, bearing a vase with mercury trapped inside it, an armful of yellow daisies—and a relentless determination to break down the walls around her heart.

And all right, all right. It was not specifically her heart he was after. She understood that. And accepted it.

Finally. Now that it was too late.

At seven thirty-five, she was standing at the window in the front parlor, staring out, telling herself she was acting like an idiot. He wasn't coming home tonight, and standing here watching for him to come strolling up her walk wouldn't change what wasn't going to happen.

She was hungry. She should eat.

And yet she just stood there, staring out, watching the street, hearing the cars coming near, watching them pass by, listening as the engine sounds faded away.

At seven forty-two, she heard a car pull up next door. The car stopped. The engine went silent.

She went straight to her entry hall and out her front door. The screen banged shut behind her as she ran down the steps and out into the fading light of the late-summer evening.

He saw her when she was halfway down the walk. He'd emerged from the car. He wore baggy green pants, a white T-shirt, with a short-sleeved shirt unbuttoned over that. He also wore a look of real pleasure at the sight of her.

He came right for her. They stopped, maybe two feet from each other, at the end of her front walk.

"I couldn't stand hanging around here waiting," he said low. "I know a place in Tahoe where I can always pick up a game."

"I thought you weren't coming."

He smiled then. "Ah. Kept you guessin'."

"You did, you rat."

There was one of those moments, where they just stood there and gazed at each other like a couple of lovesick fools.

Finally he asked, "Does this mean I get to come in?"

She reached out and took his hand, reveling in the shiver of excitement that went through her as he twined his fingers with hers. "Come on," she said, and pulled him up the walk.

They barely got in the door before he was kissing her.

She didn't object. She wrapped her arms around his neck and she lifted her mouth, sighing with pleasure when his lips met hers.

Chapter Nine

Cade couldn't believe it.

He was in her house. He had his arms around her. Her mouth was open under his, her naughty tongue was playing teasing games. He could feel those incredible breasts of hers, soft and full against his chest. The scent of her, of her smooth white skin and midnight hair, was all around him.

It was happening. At last. Jane was in his arms....

He tangled his fingers in that fabulous hair and fisted his hand, pulling carefully, losing her mouth as her head went back and she gave him her pale neck. He kissed her, in the warm hollow of that smooth throat, his lips on the pulse there, her heartbeat swift against his mouth.

"Nice dress," he said, nuzzling that little hollow between the wings of her collarbone.

She sighed.

The dress had a string around the wide neckline, a string that tied in a bow at the front. He untied the bow. Presto. The neckline loosened in a very accommodating way. He pushed it down, over her shoulders.

"Let me help you," she whispered and she licked his ear.

"Great idea." He stepped back a few inches and watched as she kicked off her low-heeled blue sandals and then pushed the dress free of her arms and down over the fine, full twin question marks of her hips.

The dress dropped to the floor. She looked down at it, then back up at him.

Oh, yeah, he thought. *Oh, absolutely....*

Her bra was navy-blue satin. Her little panties were a match. He drank in the sight of her—all that wonderful hair, those soft brown eyes. Pale skin, with a blush on it. A smile that invited him...

And those breasts. He'd always liked her breasts. There probably wasn't a man who wouldn't. The midnight-blue bra pushed them up so that they looked like they were going to overflow the top of it, spill right out—and into his waiting hands.

She had full hips and rounded thighs and a curving belly. She was not a small woman. She was tall and there was flesh on her, a certain lushness about her. He liked that. A lot. Liked the very naturalness of her that spoke of how comfortable she was, living in her own skin.

So different from the majority of the women he'd known—mostly knock-your-socks-off types who put beaucoups of effort into the way that they looked. To Cade, more and more, over the years, all that effort seemed to smack of desperation.

Jane wasn't like that. Jane was simply Jane. Smart and real and soft, with hair as wild as the side of her he was finally getting to see—and to touch.

On the other hand, he thought, hiding a grin, he *had* seen desperation in Jane. But only to get away from him.

He said, with real enthusiasm. "All this, and we're only a few feet from the front door."

She sighed. "Life is good."

"We're going to need a bed. Very soon."

She looked at him from under her lashes, sending a bolt of pure lust zapping through him. And she murmured, "There's something else we need. I suppose I should have thought of it...."

She was right. "Condoms."

She nodded.

He had plenty. Over at his place.

If he went to get them...

Damn. He could see it all now. He'd come racing back over here with a handful of little foil-wrapped packets, only to find her fully dressed, a scowl on her face and "I've changed my mind" on her lips.

"Jane?"

"Hmm?"

"I've gotta ask."

"Anything."

He liked the way she said that. "If I leave for three minutes, will you promise not to change your mind about this?"

"I promise," she whispered. "I'm not going any-where."

"Good." He pulled the door open, then couldn't resist turning back for one last look. Incredible. She slayed him. She'd damn well *better* be there when he got back. "Stay right there. Don't go anywhere."

"Where would I go? I'm almost naked."

"Stay that way."

"Oh, I will," she whispered. "I promise, I will."

He took off at a run, the screen slamming behind him, down her walk, up his, onto his front porch. He stuck the key in the lock and let himself in—remembering just in time to disarm the alarm. Then he was taking the stairs two at a time, racing into the master suite, grabbing what they needed.

He was down the stairs, out the door and running up her walk again in what felt like ten seconds flat.

The inner door was open a crack. He yanked back the screen and shoved the door inward and—

She wasn't there.

He knew a stark second or two of hot fury born of his long-term state of frustrated lust. He wanted to break something, to snap something in two. He saw himself throwing his head back, screaming her name.

But then he got it—she'd left him a trail: her dress over there and a sandal beyond that. That midnight-blue bra draped over the landing halfway up, back strap trailing onto the stair right below.

He let out the breath he hadn't realized he was holding. And he shut and locked the door.

Then he followed where her clothes led him, pick-ing up each item as he got to it, starting with the

dress, which was soft and silky and—he couldn't resist pausing to bury his nose in it—scented of her. He
reached the first sandal, scooped it up. And he
mounted the stairs, stopping on the landing to pick
up the bra, hooking an index finger under one of the
shoulder straps, lifting it—still warm from her body—
twirling it on the end of his finger. Because she had
left it there. Because he could.

Directly ahead of him, on the wall of the landing,
was a framed portrait of a high school-age girl with
Jane's hair and eyes, but dressed in the tight-waisted,
full-skirted style popular way back in the 1950s. Cade
knew who she was. Jane's aunt Sophie. She used to
drive one of those old narrow, high Volkswagen
buses and she taught English at New Venice High.
Everybody knew you didn't mess with Miss Elliott.
She was tough and smart and funny, too. Always one
step ahead of a troublemaker like Cade.

He went on, up the second half of the stairs. The
other sandal was waiting for him at the top. He bent
and grabbed it.

Then he saw the blue satin panties, in front of the
first door opposite the stairs, to his left. He moved to
them swiftly, scooping them up and laying them over
his arm with the dress and the bra.

The door to the room in front of him was open.

It was a large bedroom, with walls papered in roses
on a blue ground, walls trimmed out in cherrywood—
the window frames, the plate rails, the fireplace, too,
which was on the wall opposite the doorway where
he stood. A pair of comfortable-looking easy chairs
faced the fireplace and there were a number of shut

cherrywood doors—to closets and the bathroom, more than likely.

The bed, a big old four-poster, piled high with pillows and covered with a pale crocheted spread, stood on his right, footboard out, headboard against the wall. It had matching nightstands, little tables with lamps on them, one to each side. On the far side of the bed, the wall opened up into the turret, which was smaller than the one at his place, but otherwise much the same, a pentagon of windows looking out on her yard and his yard and Green Street beyond.

Jane stood there, in the turret. Naked.

She was staring out the central window, through the white lace curtains that covered the glass. Outside, the day was fading, but not yet completely gone. The sun had dropped well below the rim of the mountains. Behind her, to her left, on the turret wall nearest the fireplace, a compact spiral stair led up to another room above.

She was a study in shadow. He took a good, long look—because he could. Because she didn't turn or say a word or signal him in any way that she even knew he was in the room with her.

He liked everything he saw. From the dark mass of her hair, to the smooth shape of her shoulders, the incurving waist, the rising swell of her hips. It was all good—all of her, all the way down to her pale bare feet.

Good and…somehow not quite real. It almost felt like this was all some magical, impossible dream he was having.

He ached to get his hands on her, to prove to himself that this really was happening. At the same time, he could have stood there, just looking, forever.

She still hadn't turned toward him.

He looked down at himself. Definitely overdressed.

He went and set her clothes on one of those easy chairs by the fireplace, placing the sandals side by side on the rug. He took off his own shoes and socks, tucking the socks inside the shoes, placing the shoes next to her sandals. He removed his shirt, pulled the T-shirt over his head and laid both on the chair arm opposite her dress.

She still hadn't turned, had given zero indication she knew he was there, in her room with her. But by then, he was certain she knew damn well. He smiled to himself, and took the handful of condoms out of the pocket he'd stuffed them into a few minutes before. He set the condoms on the chair cushion long enough to remove his pants and his boxers and toss them on the chair arm with his shirt.

Then he grabbed up the foil pouches and approached her, stopping no more than a foot behind her.

"Jane."

She didn't answer, not in words. But she did turn her head to the right, her chin down, a move that acknowledged him, accepted him—and invited him, too.

He transferred the contraceptives to his left hand. Then he smoothed the veil of her hair aside, so he could see the tender smile on her lips, the way her dark lashes lay like fans against her cheeks.

She looked back out on Green Street again. "I've

stood here, in this exact spot, a lot in the past few months.'' She spoke softly, to herself, it seemed, as much as to him. ''I've stood here with all the lights off, looking at your house, telling myself to stop acting like an idiot. But then not stopping. Staying right here. Looking for signs that you're at home—for the glow of a lamp in a room, for just a glimpse of you through a window…''

''I've done that myself, looking for you.''

''I know you have.''

They were silent. It was a good kind of quiet—surprisingly comfortable. And yet exciting, too. He felt the promise in it, the anticipation.

And from her, he sensed willingness. The willingness to have him, here, with her now. It soothed something down inside him, made a calmness beneath the urgency—after all the bleak months of wanting and waiting—to lay his claim on her at last.

He stepped in even closer, lifting his hand to touch her again, running the backs of his fingers down the side of her throat, out along the warm, silky skin of her shoulder, down her arm. He felt a shiver move through her as his knuckles skimmed her flesh. That shiver pleased him.

He touched her wrist, sliding his hand on down to cradle hers, the back of her hand nestling against his palm. She readily opened her fingers enough that he could slip his between them.

He moved in closer still, wrapping his other arm around her. ''You think this'll be enough?'' He opened his hand.

She looked down at the condoms. "What? Only seven?"

He chuckled. "I can always get more."

"Well, okay then. We'll manage."

He closed his fist around the condoms as she touched the gold bracelet that gleamed on his wrist and he whispered, "World Series of Poker, No Limit Hold'em. Two years ago."

"That's the big one, right?"

"Yeah. At Binion's, downtown Vegas. Winner takes the gold bracelet—and over a million in prize money. The money goes...wherever money goes. But no winner will ever let go of the bracelet."

"I remember when you won." She was smiling. He could hear it in her voice. "Made the front page of the *Record.*"

"Yeah. Big news in New Venice, local loser makes good..."

"I read that article. Nowhere in it were you called a loser. And it *is* a big thing. You should be proud."

He brushed a kiss against her neck. "Yes, ma'am."

"I am serious."

"So am I."

"Serious in yes-ma'aming me, or seriously proud?"

"Both."

"Hmm. All right. I can live with that answer."

"Glad to hear it." Her bare shoulder looked especially inviting right then. He kissed it.

Sighing, she let herself lean back, all those shadowed curves and hollows, soft and warm and smelling so good, settling close, resting against him. He released her hand and brought that arm around her, too, pulling her closer still, feeling her quick indrawn breath as his arousal tucked itself against the small of her back.

"Remember," she whispered after a moment, "that time you asked me to dance? At that party for Celia and Aaron, the one put on by his company, in Las Vegas?"

He remembered all right. He accused, gruffly, "You made me crazy."

"Well, I knew that wasn't any gun you had in your pocket."

He nuzzled her hair. "You're such a comedian."

"You were trying so hard not to hold me too close."

"Hard," he said. "That would be the word for it." He cupped one of those heavy breasts. She groaned. He liked the sound of that. A lot. Her nipples were dark, puckered with excitement. He ran his thumb over one and she gasped.

And that did it. He couldn't resist sliding his hand down, over the curve of her belly, into the dark, thick curls between her white thighs.

She stiffened, gasped again.

"Jane," he whispered, brushing his lips against the side of her face, into her hair, along her cheekbone, at the hollow of her temple. "Jane, Jane, Jane..."

The stiffness left her. She went easy in his arms, parting her legs a little, giving him access. He insinuated one finger between the protective folds of tender flesh. She dragged in a ragged breath, moaned a little, leaned more fully back against him, lifting the mound of her sex a little, offering it to him.

"Yeah," he whispered against the wild tangle of her hair. "Oh, yeah…"

For a while, he teased her, running his finger up over her belly, and down, caressing the side of her waist, the flare of her hip, sliding his palm along the outside of her thigh. He petted her, rubbed the heel of his hand against her, but he held back from parting her, from delving in.

For a while….

And then, when he did touch what she was offering him, he found her as he wanted her. Wet and ready. He dipped a finger in, and then another. She was moving by that time, her hips rocking, making little moaning sounds, her head rolling back and forth against his chest, her hair electric, crackling, clinging to his skin.

He wanted…more. All of her. To touch her. To hold her. To *know* her. All over.

The condoms in his left hand hindered him. He let them go. They spilled to the rug at their feet. She laughed, low in her throat—and then she cried out as he touched her more deeply than before.

He turned her, guiding her around to him, and he moved his hand forcefully in her. He looked in her eyes. They were wide, dazed, far away. And yet also right there, with him, with what he was doing to her, with the sensations he roused in her.

She whispered his name, low.

"Yeah," he said, stroking her deeply, in rhythm with her rising need. "Say it again. Say my name…"

Her eyelids quivered shut.

"No. Come on, Jane. Look at me. Say my name...."

She made a frantic, wild sound. And her lids fluttered open, her brown eyes met his.

"Yeah," he said, then asked gently, encouragingly, "Yeah?"

And she gave him what he wanted. "Cade," she whispered, the sound hot and husky. "Oh, Cade..."

And then she cried out again. Her body bucked wildly. He felt the contractions around his fingers, her climax rolling through her. He held her, going with it, following her body's cues with his hand.

Her knees buckled at the end. She moaned, dragging at him, wanting to go down. He had no problem with that. He went down with her, onto the rug, among the scattered condoms.

Her pleasure quivered on the crest, then slowly faded to afterglow.

They rested, stretched out there, together, on the rug in the turret, with the spiral staircase turning toward the ceiling above them and the summer night falling beyond the windows. He kept his hand on her, in her, feeling that softening, so that her inner body itself seemed to have melted, gone completely liquid. He knew that going into her would be the sweetest thing, the warmest, most welcoming thing.

And he also knew he couldn't wait too long, let the afterglow fade down too far, let her body begin to close itself against him. He wanted her that way, in that perfect state of readiness, the first time he entered her.

With some regret, he pulled his hand from her. She sighed, softly, looking at him in the dazed and open way of a woman satisfied, a woman ready for whatever would come next. He couldn't resist licking his own fingers, tasting her, scenting her, there, on his hand.

She watched him do that, her pupils widening, lips going lax, infinitely soft. He reached out, slid his hand, still wet from her and from his own mouth, into her hair, cupping the back of her head, bringing her to him.

He kissed her. It was all one—his mouth, her mouth. And the taste of her, passing between them, from his tongue to hers.

Still kissing her, he reached over her and picked up one of the condoms. To deal with it, he had to surrender her mouth.

She watched him as he slid it on, looking so open and soft and easy, on her side now, where he'd pulled her when he kissed her, raised up on an elbow, that glorious hair tumbling down her shoulder, veiling her arm and one ripe, full breast.

Was this real? He wondered again, at the two of them, here at last, doing all the things he'd known, deep inside himself, were never going to happen.

She was his now—or she would be, very soon. *His.*

He realized what he felt for her was something different. Something new to him.

It was a need to claim, to make something private, between them. Something they shared only with each other.

He wondered what was really going on here, inside his head…and his heart.

Strange. To find himself thinking about his *heart*.

He'd always believed himself immune to the urges that a lot of other men felt. Never had he wanted to make a bond with a woman, to make something between them that would last beyond the moment, beyond the wanting and the taking, beyond the sweet mutual gift of sexual release.

But with Jane…

No. He pushed the dangerous, half-formed thought away. Now was not the time for it. He would think about it later.

Right now, there was Jane. *All* of Jane. To be tasted and enjoyed.

She reached out a hand. And she touched him, curving her fingers around him, at the base. He groaned—and he was damned lucky he didn't lose it right there.

And then she was rising up, sliding one of those slender white feet across his belly, gliding on top of him, capturing him between her smooth, full thighs. She rose higher, up on her knees, one leg on either side of his hips.

He looked at her above him, at the wild tangle of her hair, at her soft, flushed face as she stared down at him through lazy, slitted eyes. He didn't dare look any lower. He groaned, let his head drop back.

And she lowered herself onto him.

Paradise.

No other word for it. Paradise on earth, to be inside

of Jane, her wet heat surrounding him, those fine thighs gripping him…

She moved.

He knew he would die.

''Wait.'' He made a ridiculous, garbled sound as he grabbed for her, pulling her down tight onto him, holding her there. ''I can't…''

She moaned. He opened his eyes in time to see her raise her arms and lift her hair, tossing it, inky and wild in the gathering darkness. He watched her head fall back, her white neck stretching.

''Oh, you can…'' She lowered her head again, her eyes meeting his, moving, rocking on him, though he tried to hold her still. ''Cade. You know you can…''

''Jane…''

''Oh, yes. Oh yes, you can…''

''Wait. Jane.''

''Come on, you can. You know you can.''

He made more pleading sounds. And then he couldn't help it. He wanted her moving every bit as much as he needed her still.

He stopped restraining her, let her have him, let her do what she wanted, move as she willed. He dared to look up at her, at all of her, as she rose and came back to him, sliding away and then claiming him fully, her heat and wetness drawing on him one second, then almost lost to him the next.

He let his hands slide upward over her rib cage, his thumbs under her breasts, pleasured by the fullness of them, the womanly weight. He claimed them, cupping one in either hand, loving the size and softness of them, the way the hard nipples pressed into his palms.

He moved with her, wildly, and then slowly, and then faster again. He felt his climax coming long before it took him, rolling toward him, like a huge, wild, obliterating wave.

The wave broke, at last, and he took her hips again, hard, stilling her, pressing himself up into her as he came. She fell then, her upper body dropping against him, her inner muscles contracting as she whimpered in his ear, finishing right with him, going over the moon, beyond the rainbow, past the most distant star in the summer sky.

He wrapped his arms around her and held her tight. He wasn't letting go of her. She had too much that he wanted.

She thrilled him.

And at the same time, she felt like something he hadn't even known he'd been looking for, like the answer to the question he'd been asking himself for over a year now, to what had started with his buying the house next-door and nagged at him all the harder as he found himself noticing her, realized he was attracted to her—hell. More than attracted to her.

That he hungered to get his hands on her.

That he wanted her, bad, in a bed. Or on a floor. It didn't really matter where. Anyplace. As long as she was naked against him.

And that was it, or so he'd thought.

An itch that needed scratching. More powerful, maybe, than the itches that had gone before. But workable. Something that would leave him in peace eventually—and maybe even sooner if he could just get his hands on her, put an end to the mystery. Prove to himself that she was only a woman like any other woman.

But now, well, his attitude had changed.

Everything was different.

Because she was so much more than that, more than her beautiful lush white body, more than an itch he yearned to scratch.

What was it, this thing he felt with her, when they talked, when they laughed together, when he held her—and when he didn't?

Maybe it was crazy, maybe it was next-door to nuts, edging up to downright impossible.

But being with Jane Elliott felt to him like coming home.

Chapter Ten

For a long, lovely time, Jane lay there, using Cade for a mattress, lying limp against his hard chest. She listened to his heartbeat, smiling dreamily to herself, feeling utterly satisfied.

But eventually, a muscle in her calf started twitching. And she noticed that the old wool rug was digging into her knees. She tried to slide to the side.

Cade made a noise of protest deep in his throat, "Uh-uh," and held on.

She kissed him, right next to his ear. "I can't lie on top of you, squashing you, forever."

"Why not?" he growled. The question must have been rhetorical, because as soon as he asked it, he let her go.

She stretched out on her back beside him and felt for his hand. He gave it, bringing hers to his lips, kissing the back of it, then settling their joined hands on the rug between them.

Again, there was stillness. It surprised her, how comfortable she felt with him, how natural and unforced. Really, she'd never felt that way with anyone—well, except maybe Ceil and Jillian. And with them, it was about friendship, which was a whole other thing than this.

Finally she turned her head to smile at him. "Hungry?"

"A little. You?"

Her stomach chose that moment to growl. "A lot."

Cade wanted a shower, so Jane showed him which door led to the master bathroom. He disappeared beyond it. It was fully dark by then. She got up and switched on a lamp and gathered up the scattered condoms, leaving them on the little table to the right of the bed.

Then she joined Cade in the shower. There were kisses. And caresses. Jane thought it a very satisfying way to get clean.

After that, Cade put on his pants and Jane pulled on a robe and they went downstairs to make sandwiches and pour themselves a couple of big glasses of milk. They carried the food back up to her bedroom and got up on the bed where they sat, cross-legged, facing each other, munching away.

Cade said, "That's your aunt Sophie, that picture on the stairs, right?"

Jane chewed and swallowed and grinned at him. "My grandfather Elliott had that painted, the year she

graduated from high school. She was something, Aunt
Sophie. Did what she wanted and lived her own in-
dependent life. And she always…supported me.'' She
gestured widely, indicating all that surrounded them.
''I mean literally, of course. This was her house and
her money made it possible for me to open my bookstore. And more than that, she always made me feel
that she was totally on my side. Even during the worst
of times, even when I ran off and married Rusty, Aunt
Sophie never turned her back on me.''

He tipped his head to the side, studying her. ''But
other people did turn their backs on you, right?''

She bit her lip, shrugged.

He knew. ''Your mother?''

She nodded.

''That's cold.''

Since Caitlin Bravo's stormy relationship with her
sons had always been a subject for the New Venice
gossip mill, Jane couldn't resist asking, ''Are you trying to tell me that Caitlin never got fed up with you?''

''No. If I told you that, it would be a lie. And if
I'm going to hang around you, I've got to stick with
the truth. Right?''

She wasn't sure she trusted that gleam in his eye.
She said, carefully, ''The truth would be much appreciated.''

''Don't hedge. The truth is expected—isn't it?''

''Yes.'' She frowned. ''But why does that sound
like a trick question?''

''A trick question? From me?''

She laughed. ''That's what I said. And about
Caitlin…''

"All right. Yeah, sure. She got fed up with me. She would yell and throw things and call me—and my brothers—some pretty ugly names. And then, with her, there was also the problem of her just *being* her. That meant all the men. And the way we lived, over the bar. Yeah, okay. We might have done some pretty crazy things, the three of us—me especially. And I guess a lot of it was just par for the course, natural that we'd be wild, considering the kind of life we lived with her. But still…"

"What?"

"Well, deep down, we always knew she'd kill for us if she had to. She'd die for us without so much as batting those false eyelashes of hers. Never, no matter what stupid, crazy stunt we pulled, would she ever have turned her back on us."

Jane found she could almost envy him—to grow up knowing that kind of passionate devotion from a parent. So strange. She'd always felt a little sorry for those bad Bravo boys. They weren't outcasts in town, exactly. But they came pretty close. And now, listening to Cade, she realized that those boys had had something in Caitlin that pampered, well-behaved, well-brought-up and well-to-do Jane Elliott had never known. They'd had a parent who loved them unconditionally.

Jane did want to be fair, though, to her own parents. "My mother and father didn't cut me out forever. They got over it, eventually—over my running off with Rusty. We reconciled."

He had that watchful look. "When was that?"

She sat back a little. She didn't like this—his sudden watchfulness, or the sharp turn the conversation had taken, edging way too close to territory she had no desire to enter.

She said, carefully, "My parents and I reconciled before Rusty died."

"When you lost the baby?"

She stiffened—and then she told herself to relax. It wasn't all that surprising, that he would know about her miscarriage. She'd been in the hospital. Word had gotten around.

He said, as if in answer to the question she hadn't even asked, "I think I heard about it—about the baby—when I heard about Rusty getting himself killed."

"You heard what?"

"That Rusty was dead. And that it had to be all the rougher on you, since you'd just lost a baby a few months before."

"Well." She swallowed. "Yes. That's right. That's what happened."

He seemed to be waiting for her to tell him all of it.

But she didn't want to tell him all of it. She didn't want to go into it. The horror of her marriage to Rusty Jenkins was behind her now. She wanted to leave it that way.

Cade said, "That was it, right? It was about the baby, the other day, at my house. When you said you were *broken,* but didn't say exactly why?"

She pressed her lips together, nodded. "Yes. That was it."

"So..." He let the word trail off, clearly waiting for her to say more.

She asked, too sharply, "What?" She was thinking about honesty, about the whole truth that she simply didn't want to share.

"You made up with your parents." His tone was gentle. "They stood by you in the end."

"Yes, they did."

"But they hurt you, too, a lot, when they cut you off for marrying the wrong guy."

"That's true. But I hurt them first. I knew they wouldn't approve of Rusty, so I made sure they never knew about him. Then, out of nowhere, as far as they were concerned, I ran away and married him. They felt betrayed. Tricked. And really, I did betray them. I tricked them every time I snuck out to meet him, every time I invited him over when I knew they wouldn't be home."

He said nothing, only looked at her. A probing kind of look. Then he turned and picked up his milk from the bedside table. He drank from it and set it back down. She wondered what he was thinking.

He didn't make her wonder long. "I gotta ask. Is that what'll happen with us?"

"What do you mean?" she said, as if she didn't know.

He gave her a look that said he knew that *she* knew exactly what he'd meant. Then he went ahead and clarified, "Am I going to be another big secret you keep from them?"

It was a yes or no question—and she answered with

evasion. "This is a completely different situation. I'm a grown woman now."

"What does that mean, Jane? Will you tell them about us, or not?"

She turned and picked up her own milk from the night table behind her. When she faced him again, he was waiting with one eyebrow raised.

She blew out a breath. "You said it yourself, the other day, when you were trying to talk me into doing what we just did a little while ago. That you're single and so am I and it's our business what we do behind closed doors."

Her answer hadn't pleased him. His mouth was tight. "Behind closed doors. So that's what we're up to here. No one's gonna know, right? We'll be sneaking between our houses, getting in a quickie when we're both sure no one else will be dropping by. When we get invited to the same places because of Aaron and Celia, we'll act like we hardly know each other. We'll smile and say hi and then turn and walk away."

She took a sip of milk and then set her glass back down. Carefully. "Cade. I didn't say that."

Something flashed in those silver eyes, something dangerous. "Then let's go out. To Bennett's Steak House. You and me. Tomorrow night." Bennett's was arguably New Venice's best restaurant. It was on Main, across and down from Jane's bookstore and the Highgrade.

Stalling and not liking herself very much for it, Jane picked up the second half of her sandwich. She stared down at it, thinking that if Cade took her to

Bennett's, it would be all over town within a day or two. Everyone would know that something was going on between Jane Elliott and wild Cade Bravo. Did she want the whole town to know? It wasn't going to be pleasant, when the story got back to her mother....

"Forget it, Jane."

She blinked and looked up at him. "I didn't—"

"You hesitated. Way too long. You know you did. So just forget it." He turned and set his empty plate on the nightstand behind him.

"Cade. Please…"

The look on his face said it all. She had hurt him. And he wanted the subject dropped. Now.

Jane sat up very straight. "Cade, I'd love to go to Bennett's with you tomorrow night."

"Yeah, right."

"I would. I *will*."

"Jane?"

She sat forward, eagerly, hoping he'd give in and give her another chance on this issue. "Yes?"

He looked…sad. And a little bit tired. "Let it go."

"But—"

"I mean it." His voice was soft. His eyes weren't. "Let it go."

What could she say? "Yes. Yes, all right." She'd blown it and she knew that she had. Her appetite had vanished. She dropped her sandwich on the plate and put the plate on the nightstand behind her.

When she faced him again, he was still looking at her.

She made herself meet those eyes of his, feeling awful, wishing she could turn back the clock, have

him ask her out all over again. This time, she
wouldn't mess up. She'd answer yes straight out, no
hemming and hawing and putting him off.

Oh, what was the matter with her? In recent years,
she'd prided herself on how much she'd changed and
grown since the disaster of marrying Rusty.

But now she couldn't help wondering, where was
the change? Where was the growth? Here she was,
making love with a man again at last. Loving every
glorious, erotic minute of it. And then stalling at the
idea of being seen in public with him, worrying about
what her family might say.

"Jane." He touched her bare knee, gently, reas-
suringly. "It's okay."

"No, it's not. But you're kind to say so."

He took the facing of her robe, which had fallen
away, and smoothed it over her knee, tenderly, pro-
tectively. Then he caught one end of the sash she'd
tied around her waist and gave it a tug. Her robe fell
open.

"Hey," she cried, her mood lightening when she
saw the gleam in his eye. "What's going on here?"

"Nobody calls me *kind* and gets away with it."

"Oh. Well. I'm so sorry."

"Prove it."

Oh, I will, she thought, as she scooted backward,
giggling. She'd blown it once. She wouldn't blow it
again. The next time he asked her out, she'd give him
an unequivocal yes—in fact, she'd *do* the asking, if
he took too long to try again.

He leaned forward, moving to his knees. And she

leaned back, uncrossing her legs. He settled between them. It felt really good to have him there.

"About your aunt Sophie." He was resting on his forearms, kissing her eyelids, her eyebrows, the bridge of her nose…

"Mmm?" She wrapped her arms around him—and her legs, too.

"I really did like her."

"You did?" She ran both hands down the glorious musculature of his bare back. He was still wearing his pants. They'd have to do something about that soon.

He nibbled her earlobe. "Yeah. Had her for bone-head English, in tenth grade. She called me charming and incorrigible."

"Aunt Sophie was no fool." She groaned as he slid down her body—just low enough to latch onto her breast. He drew on the nipple. She groaned some more.

He lifted his head and winked at her. "I had to look up incorrigible. And it wasn't easy, let me tell you. At first, I thought she had said 'encourage-able.' But I could tell by her tone that couldn't be right. I knew it was some other word—but I had no idea how the damn word was spelled."

"That was Aunt Sophie," she whispered breathlessly. "Always finding clever ways to motivate her students." He lowered his head to her breast again. She cried out. "Oh! Oh, yes…"

And then he was moving again…lower.

And lower…

Jane gave herself up to the incredible things Cade Bravo knew how to do with his mouth and his hands.

* * *

Cade opened his eyes. It was still dark. He stared up at the ceiling. Not his ceiling. Jane's.

He was at Jane's. With Jane. In Jane's bed.

He rolled his head and looked at her. She looked good. Soft and sweet, her dark hair all tangled and wild on the pillow. Sound asleep.

The digital clock on her side of the bed glowed at him through the darkness: 3:10 a.m.

Time to get out. Now. While she was still sleeping.

Carefully he turned on his side, facing the edge of the bed, away from the woman sleeping so peacefully beside him. In one slow, even movement, he slid out from under the blanket and lowered his feet to the floor.

Chapter Eleven

Jane woke to morning light. Memories of the night just past came flooding in. She blushed. Her body felt…well used. Well-satisfied. A little bit tender in certain places, but in a very nice way.

She was smiling when she turned her head toward *his* side of the bed.

Empty. She sat up. "Cade?"

No answer. She tossed back the covers and checked the bathroom.

Not there.

Without a stitch on, she ran down the stairs, checked the family room and the kitchen and the parlor and the central hall. In the dining room, the gorgeous vase he had given her gleamed on the table.

But no Cade.

She ran back upstairs and pulled on some shorts

and a shirt, then raced down again, flying straight for
the door, flipping the latch, hauling it open, banging
through the screen.

His car was gone.

She sank to the porch steps, hung her head and
stared down at her bare feet.

Well, all right. He had left. He had a right to leave.
It wasn't exactly considerate behavior, but it was certainly nothing for her to get crazed over. She had no
claim on him.

Just the opposite. She'd as good as turned him
down when he asked her to dinner. And she'd made
it pretty darn obvious she hoped her mother and father
would never know what was going on between them.
She had probably hurt him. And she had no right to
expect him to be here this morning.

But wait a minute.

Jane flipped her sleep-snarled hair back off her face
and sat up straight. He did have a garage, on the far
side of his house, in back. Maybe for once, he'd decided to use it. Maybe he'd gotten up and gone somewhere and come back and parked in the garage and...

Jane let her head hang down again and rediscov-
ered the view of her feet. ''Oh, give it up, you fool,''
she muttered aloud. He was gone. Out of here. Not
at home.

Still....

Well, she might as well check—just in case. She
got up and padded down her walk and up the driveway south of his house. There was a window on the
north-facing wall of the detached garage. She peeked
in it.

No Porsche.

So all right.

He really had left.

"Deal with it," she said out of the side of her mouth. "And for heaven's sake, stop talking to yourself."

She trudged back down the driveway and up the walk to her house. When she got to the door, she went in without letting the screen bang shut behind her.

It wasn't too bad. At first.

She got the coffee brewing and she took a shower and she ate her breakfast and walked to her store.

As her lunch break approached, she was aware of a rising feeling—of hope, of anticipation. She walked home fast, feeling breathless and giddy—until she turned the corner onto Green Street and saw that the Porsche still wasn't there. She dragged herself the rest of the way home.

Caitlin, behind the wheel of the shiny black Trans Am she'd owned for at least a quarter of a century, drove up just as Jane was slogging up her front walk. The black car slid to a stop at the curb in front of Cade's house.

Jane lingered on her walk, watching as Caitlin got out of the car. The bright midday sun caught the sequins on her shirt so that they glittered boldly. The ends of the bright bandanna she always tied around her neck waved jauntily in the breeze.

"Hey," Caitlin called. "How you doin', Jane?"

"All right. You're here to pick up Cade's mail?"

"Yeah, sweetie." Caitlin came around the front of the low black car and started up Cade's front walk.

Jane just had to ask. "Uh, Caitlin?"

Caitlin stopped. Turned. "Yeah, darlin'?"

"Well, I was just wondering. Um, is Cade gone then, for a while?"

"Who knows? I'm his ma—and that's about all. He calls and asks me to keep an eye on things when he goes. And then he calls when he gets back. I don't get the details, like where the hell he is or how long he plans to be gone."

"Oh. Well, of course. I understand."

Caitlin was frowning, her head tipped to the side. "You all right, hon?"

Jane smiled instead of answering. "You have a good day, now."

"You know," Caitlin reminded her, "you promised you'd come in the Highgrade and see me sometime."

"I did. And I'll get over there. For lunch. Real soon."

"Don't let me down."

"I won't. Sincerely."

Caitlin waved and went on up the walk. Jane did the same, telling herself that she could stop getting her hopes up every time she came home. If Cade had asked Caitlin to watch his house, chances were he'd be gone for several days.

Her hopes were stubborn, though. That evening, her silly heart beat faster as time to close up approached. She pretty much ran all the way to Green Street.

When she saw that he wasn't home, she trudged the rest of the way to her front door.

She called his house. He didn't answer, of course, since he wasn't there. She left a brief message, asking him to please call her back as soon as he got the chance.

Then she called Celia. They talked for an hour. It was the same as the last time she'd called her friend. Celia kept asking if she had something on her mind. And Jane kept evading. Somehow, she just couldn't bring herself to talk about Cade. Though she wanted nothing so much as to unburden her aching heart, somehow, she could not get the words out.

She kept herself from calling Jilly. She knew it would only be more of the same, with Jilly sensing something was up, urging Jane to tell her what, and Jane changing the subject. More half lies and evasions. No. She was better off just not going there.

Wednesday was about the same as Tuesday. Hope sprang up in the morning, at noon, and when she came home at night. Each time hope was crushed flat when she saw he was still gone.

Thursday came and went. She had her story hour in the afternoon. Even the beautiful, eager faces of the children didn't help much. She felt glum.

Bleak and empty.

Friday was the same. He didn't come home. He didn't return her call.

She called him again, late Friday night. Left a second message saying basically the same things she'd said in the first call. Only her voice was different. She could hear the change as the words escaped her lips.

She sounded sadder. And vaguely desperate. She hung up wishing she hadn't called.

By Saturday, she realized she was mad at him. Really mad. He was driving her crazy, staying away like this. Surely he must have some system for picking up his messages. He must know she had called him. Why didn't he call back? What was the matter with him? Had he no consideration at all?

Doubt began to gnaw at her. Maybe she'd read him all wrong. Maybe she hadn't hurt him at all. Maybe this was just the classic situation of a man getting what he wanted from a woman and moving on.

It felt awful, to think that.

But she did think it. How could she *help* but think it, with the way he was behaving, disappearing from her bed, from her house, from her *street?* Not returning her calls, gone for days and days...

She almost had a fight with her mother on Sunday. All morning, Virginia kept after her, nagging her. "Jane, is something the matter?" "You don't look well. Are you sick?" "You have circles under your eyes, honey. Aren't you sleeping well?"

Jane had given the usual answers. "I have some things on my mind." "No, I'm not sick." "And no, I haven't been sleeping all that well. But it's nothing for you to worry about."

"But what is it that I'm not supposed to be worrying about? And really, if you're not sleeping well, that *is* something for your mother to worry about. Sleep is very important. Sleep-deprived people can suffer all kinds of difficulties. Exhaustion can make a person careless. You could be in an accident. You could—''

It was right about then that Jane shouted, ''Mother, enough!''

Virginia subsided into injured looks and one-syllable remarks. Finally she left.

Jane had never been so glad to see her go.

Sunday afternoon, Jillian called. She'd gotten an offer to write a piece on Labor Day in the wine country. She wouldn't make it to the picnic after all. Jane told her she would be missed. And Jillian said that Jane sounded strange. Was something wrong?

Jane changed the subject and ended the call soon after that—and then felt glummer that ever.

Really, she did need to talk to someone eventually. She could use a little support. Maybe some good advice.

But every time she had the chance to bend a sympathetic ear, she turned it down. Why?

For some unknown reason, right then, she thought of Caitlin, remembered how she'd promised Cade's mother twice now that she'd get over to the Highgrade for lunch.

Tuesday, Jane left the bookstore at one-thirty. When she entered the Highgrade, the lunch rush was over. She found Caitlin at the register counter, looking through a stack of receipts. Cade's mother glanced up. A pleased smile lit up her face.

''Well, darlin'. It's about time.'' She came strutting out from behind the counter, all flash and fire and shimmering spangles. ''You come on with me. We'll get you a nice booth and I'll make sure you get your food on the double.'' She was already leading the way into the café.

And right then, Jane admitted to herself that lunch really was not what she'd come here for. "Caitlin…"

Cade's mother turned. One black eyebrow lifted. "What's up, sweet stuff?"

"I wonder, do you have a few minutes? Could we talk alone?"

Caitlin didn't even hesitate. "Why, sure. My office okay?"

"Great."

"Want a Coke?"

"I'd love one."

"Wait right there." Caitlin vanished into the café and returned a minute later with two tall red plastic glasses filled to the brim, and a couple of straws. "Here you go." Caitlin handed Jane her Coke and her straw. "Right this way." They went down the long central hall that led to the back parking lot. Caitlin ushered Jane through the second-to-last door on the right. "Have a seat."

The room was windowless and purely functional. There were metal file cabinets and metal shelves against the walls. A big green metal desk dominated the room, with a comfortable-looking leather swivel chair behind it. Two guest chairs faced the desk. Jane slid into one of them.

Caitlin went around the desk and dropped into the swivel chair. She cleared a space on the cluttered pad, peeled her paper off her straw and stuck the straw in her Coke. She sipped, long red nails gleaming as she held the straw. "Ah. Nothin' like a tall, cold Coke."

Jane sipped her own drink. "You're right. Thanks."

The two of them set their glasses on the desk at the same time. Then Caitlin leaned back in her chair. "Well, okay. What's goin' on?"

Jane's mouth went dry. She had one of those what-am-I-doing-here moments, a split second where she couldn't believe she'd come here, had no idea what in the world she wanted to say.

Caitlin sat forward again. Behind the false fringe of all those black lashes, her midnight eyes were shining bright. "Come on. It's okay, whatever it is. There ain't a thing you can say that I can't handle, honey-bunch."

All of a sudden, in the tilt of Caitlin's head and that gleam in her eye, Jane saw Cade, saw the resemblance of mother to son, though she had never really noticed it before. Cade was lean and rangy, with those silver eyes and that almost-blond hair. And Caitlin was all curves, with inky curls and eyes to match. But really, they were a lot a like. Smart and wild, the both of them. Determined to take life by storm, to live strictly on their own terms.

Jane said, "This is probably inappropriate, for me to be here, asking for your advice, but—"

"Is that what you're doin'? Lookin' for advice?"

"Yes. It is."

"And you don't really think I'm the right one to ask?"

"I only mean that you and I hardly know each

other. And then there's all that old stuff that happened, between you and my father.''

Caitlin picked up her Coke again and sipped from it. ''You know, I think sometimes that what happened way back when is never really gonna be known by anyone. Those of us that lived it, we each have our own version of it, all duded up and turned around to suit the lies we think we have to tell ourselves to get by.''

Jane leaned in. ''I do understand what you mean. We both know my mother, after all.''

Caitlin sipped more Coke. ''Your mother's not a very happy woman. Never has been. And I can tell you this much. I did not take your father to my bed. I promise you, I didn't.''

''Oh, I know you didn't. My aunt Sophie told me what happened.''

Caitlin chuckled. ''Miss Sophie Elliott. I always liked her.''

Jane smiled. ''Cade said he liked her, too.''

''Ah,'' said Caitlin softly. ''Cade did, did he?'' She looked at Jane steadily. Jane did not look away. Caitlin set down her glass and rested her hands on the arms of her chair. ''You're not really here to talk about what happened more than twenty-five years ago, are you?''

Jane swallowed. ''No. I'm not.''

Caitlin was frowning. ''You know, I told myself, that with you and Cade, I was going to stay out of it, that I would let you two work it out for yourselves.''

Jane wasn't quite following. ''With me and Cade?''

Caitlin cleared her throat. "Fact is I kind of messed it up, a little, between Aaron and the baby doll."

"The baby doll?"

"Your friend. Aaron's wife. Celia. I was gonna stay out of that, too. But I didn't. I had to get in there and do my bit. And what I did didn't help. But, well, you can see that they worked it out in the end. So no permanent harm was done. And this is a different situation, anyway, right? I mean, with Celia I kind of butted in. I went after her, tried to get her to let me help. But this time, you're the one comin' to me. Right?"

Jane still wasn't sure she was following. Still, she gamely replied, "That's right. I am."

Caitlin beamed. "You know, I gotta admit, it gives me a real charge, that you're here, that you see me as someone to talk to about this. Someone who is very much on your side. Because I am on your side. One hundred percent."

"Caitlin?"

"Yeah?"

"May I ask you something?"

"Shoot."

"Are you saying you know, about me and Cade?"

"Well hon, I'm not blind."

"So he hasn't…talked about me?"

"With *me?*" Caitlin waved her red-tipped fingers in front of her face. "I told you the other day. I'm just his ma. I look out for his place when he asks, I'm always here, if he needs me. But I don't get told a damn thing."

"Well, then how do you know that he and I—"

Caitlin swore under her breath. "Oh, come on. My vision's twenty-twenty. I see what goes on. I see the looks you two give each other, the kind of looks that could burn a buildin' down. Cade is crazy for you, and you're crazy for him. And whatever I can do to help you with that, well, here I am. Ready to do it. So drink that Coke and talk to me."

"I..."Jane picked up her Coke, then set it back down without taking a sip. "Oh, Caitlin..."

"Yeah?"

"You know about me—and about Rusty Jenkins?"

"I know you ran off and married him. That he was big trouble. That he put you through hell."

"Caitlin, I swore to myself I'd never make that kind of mistake again. But now, with Cade..."Jane's throat felt tight. And there was pressure behind her eyes. No way, she thought. I am not going to sit here and blubber like a baby. She gulped—to clear her throat, to force the tears down.

"With Cade, what?"

"Oh, Caitlin, he left. Out of nowhere. And now I miss him. So much."

"Well, of course you do. You love him."

Jane blinked. "I do?"

Caitlin only nodded.

Jane thought she ought to argue. But she didn't. She was thinking, is that it? Love? I love Cade....

The words echoed in her mind. They didn't sound so outrageous. Or incredible. They sounded kind of good.

Kind of like the truth.

And if they were the truth, well, what did that say

about her, about Jane Elizabeth Elliott, about how much she'd learned from the bad things that had happened to her?

"Oh, but Caitlin. Is there something *wrong* with me? All over again, I'm gone on a totally unsuitable kind of guy. I mean, ever since Rusty, I've been determined to be honest and straightforward and to find myself a straight-ahead guy. And what's happened? I end up in a one-night stand with my gambling, ladies' man next-door neighbor and now I'm carrying a torch for him." Jane shifted in the chair, suddenly angry. "And where *is* he anyway? Can anyone tell me? He's been gone for a week now, just locked up his house and vanished into thin air. Is he okay? Has he gotten himself into some kind of trouble?"

Caitlin was just sitting there, elbows on the arms of her chair, red-tipped fingers folded over her middle, listening. Watching.

Jane let out a hard breath. "Well?" She gestured, broadly, with both hands. "What? What do you think? What should I do?"

"If you'll shut up for a minute, I'll be glad to tell you."

Jane sank back in the chair. "Yes. All right. I'm listening. I am."

"Good." Caitlin waited.

Jane sat very still and didn't say a word.

Finally Caitlin spoke. "I could get real insulted, you know, at you comparin' my Cade to that loser, Rusty Jenkins."

Jane felt hot color rising to her cheeks. "I never

said that Cade was as bad as Rusty. I don't think that.
Sincerely. I would never—''

"Jane."

"Hmm?"

"Quiet."

Jane pressed her lips together and nodded to show
just how quiet she intended to be.

After a minute, Caitlin continued. "I think you
need to take a long, hard look at the facts here. My
boy has not been in any real trouble in years. He's
doin' damn well and I am proud of him. Yeah, he
gambles. He gambles for a living. For him, it's a job.
A job he likes. A job he happens to be damn good
at. And as far as him bein' a player with the ladies,
well, okay. Maybe he has been. The ladies like him.
And he's always liked them right back—until the past
year or so. Until he bought that house next to you.
Since then, I haven't seen him look at any woman
but the woman you see when you look in your mirror.
Cade is…struggling now, searchin' for something
more in his life than bright lights and a party all the
time. He's come back home, he's livin' a decent life,
trying to make a real place for himself."

"But where *is* he?"

"Well, if I knew, I'd tell you. But I don't. And
maybe that's not the question, anyway. Maybe what
you should be askin' yourself is what you said or did
that made him pick up and leave."

"What *I* did?"

Caitlin gave Jane a long, knowing look.

Jane admitted grudgingly, "Okay. Maybe you're
right. Maybe it's my fault that's he's disappeared.

Maybe I said a few things I shouldn't have—or maybe I didn't say what I *should* have said fast enough. But couldn't it also be that you've read him wrong, when it comes to me? Couldn't it be that he's spent a night with me and that was all he wanted from me, so he's gone?''

''Oh, come on. Do you think that? Do you really think that?''

''Caitlin, I don't know what to think.''

''I'll bet you don't. You're confused, aren't you?''

''That's right. I am.''

''You don't know what to think. You don't know what to do. You are pretty much on the fence.''

''Well, yes. That's right. I suppose I am.''

''And that's most of your problem, the way I see it. One way or the other, you need to get off the damn fence. And all right, all right. I am no expert on the subject of true love. I've been married once—to a no-good murderin' bigamist, a child-stealin' con artist who lived a damn sight longer than he had any right to. Somehow, after Blake Bravo, I never felt up to tying the knot again. But I've seen a lot of what goes on in life. And I've learned that when it comes to love, *somebody's* got to go for it, to stand up and say, 'This is what I want and I'm gonna fight for it.'''

''And, in this case, that somebody ought to be me?''

Caitlin had to think for a moment before she answered that one. ''Well, hon. Between you and Cade, it's hard to say. Sounds to me like neither of you really knows what you're doin' in this love affair of yours. But maybe, if you want my son to be with you for more than one night, you're gonna have to put in a little effort here. You're gonna have to show him that *you* want to be with *him*. You're gonna have to give him a few solid reasons why it'd be the smartest thing he ever did if he settled in on Green Street to spend his life with you.''

Labor Day dawned cloudless and warm, with the promise of a hot afternoon to come. At nine in the morning, Jane arrived at Wildwood Park, a rambling hundred acres of trees and grass, with a creek meandering through it. The park boasted a half-acre's worth of children's play equipment, a set of baseball diamonds and a large number of picnic areas, each with a table and benches and a barbecue consisting of a grated iron box on a fat steel post.

Jane went straight to the small stage that had been set up for her the day before. She had four half-hour segments planned. For each, she would read stories from the Brothers Grimm.

With a little help from a few talented parents, she'd created a three-sided backdrop with cottages and livestock and the occasional fairy and elf crouching in the underbrush in the foreground. Off in the distance, at the end of a winding road, stood a magical pink castle. The castle had a moat and drawbridge, banners flying and knights at the ramparts.

Jane had dressed to fit the theme. She wore a long sky-blue skirt and a white puff-sleeved blouse with a wide drawstring neck, a lace-up black leather corset over the blouse and black ballet flats on her feet. Her hair she more or less tamed into a pair of fat braids.

Privately she thought of the getup as Snow White meets the milkmaid.

The kids loved it. At ten, one and three, they sat spellbound as she read to them—rapt, yet always ready to shout the answers to any questions she threw their way. And between her performances, whenever they saw her hanging out with Celia and Aaron and all those visiting Bravos, they would wave and call out, "Story Lady! Hello, Story Lady!"

At her final 5:00 p.m. performance, she had an audience of about two dozen. She sat on a three-legged stool in front of the backdrop of cottages and castle. The kids crowded in around her, their parents watching, ranged in a semicircle a few yards beyond the children.

Jane read *Rumpelstiltskin* and *Snow White and Rose Red.* She was halfway through *The Frog King,* when she glanced up and saw Cade standing just beyond the semicircle of parents.

Chapter Twelve

Jane almost fell off her three-legged stool. Her heart seemed to stop in midbeat—and then started pounding again, way too hard, way too fast. He looked …eager. And tender, those silver eyes gleaming. And so *tan,* in a short-sleeved white shirt—unbuttoned, as usual—and a pair of loose cargo-style khakis, one of those Abercrombie and Fitch-style necklaces of wooden beads around his neck. He also looked…fine. Healthy. Unhurt.

She *had* been worried he might have got himself into some kind of trouble. But wherever he'd been, he'd come back in one piece.

It had been six days since Jane's conversation with Caitlin. Since then, she'd had a lot of time to mull over the things Cade's mother had said to her.

Jane had come to a few conclusions, after all that

mulling. Most important, that Caitlin was probably right on two counts, at least. That this just might be love. And that when it came to love, at least one of the two people involved had to go for it.

A smile trembled its way across her mouth. He smiled back. Warmth flooded through her.

One of the children, Elissa Lumley, who had a halo of frizzy red hair around her freckled heart-shaped face and an opinion on every story, chose that moment to tug on Jane's arm.

"Story Lady, the princess has to take the ugly frog back to her palace. Because he got her golden ball for her and she *promised*. A person *always* has to keep their promise."

The other children chorused agreement.

"Ah." Jane put on a serious expression and made a show of clearing her throat. "Well. Shall I read on and find out what happens?" She dared another glance at Cade.

He was gone.

Gone...

She nearly jumped from her stool, gathered up her sky-blue skirts and took off after him.

But no. Not now. In a few minutes. As soon as she'd finished up here.

Elissa still had her small hand on Jane's arm. The child wore a Barbie watch. It was 5:22. Eight more minutes, then, to the end of *The Frog King,* and the Story Lady could retire for the afternoon.

"Story Lady, did you hear us? We were all shouting, but you weren't edzackly listening."

Jane heard a chuckle or two from the ring of parents. They must have taken note of her reaction to the sight of Cade. Some of those parents were folks she'd known all her life, people who would be wondering out loud to each other about just what might be going on between Jane Elliott and the baddest of the bad Bravo boys.

A voice in her head—a voice that sounded a little like Caitlin and a little like her dear aunt Sophie— demanded, *Well so what? Let them wonder.*

That advice sounded pretty good to Jane.

She bent close to Elissa and spoke in a stage whisper. "Oh, I am so sorry. What did you say?"

"We said you should keep reading."

"Well, all right. I'll do that." She held the big storybook high and pointed at the picture of the beautiful, spoiled princess turning her back on the poor, ugly frog. "Oh, well what do you know? It looks as if the princess doesn't plan to keep her promise to the frog...."

About twenty minutes later, Jane found Cade sitting at a picnic table near the bandstand with Caitlin and Will. One of the big-time musical groups Aaron had managed to get for the picnic was well into a second set. People sat drinking beer and soft drinks from plastic cups and eating barbecued chicken and ribs slow-cooked in the big iron barbecue drums brought in on flatbeds for the occasion. Or they danced on the wooden dance floor that had been specially set up in honor of the day.

Jane caught Caitlin's eye and signaled with a lift of an eyebrow. Caitlin couldn't take the hint fast enough. All at once, she was standing, pulling on her second son's arm. Will got up and let Caitlin lead him away.

Jane moved in closer, until she was standing right behind Cade. There were people all around them. She knew that some of them were watching.

Well, okay. Let them watch.

Since she'd caught him checking out the Story Lady, he'd acquired a straw cowboy hat—along with a tall glass of beer. Jane stared at the back of his hat, not quite sure what to say to him, how exactly to begin.

The band finished the song it was playing. And Cade said, quietly, without turning, "What can I do for you, Jane?"

His tanned arm lifted. He drank from the cup. He still did not bother to turn around. If she hadn't seen his face, back there in the circle of grown-ups as she read to the children, she never would have guessed how glad he was to see her. He certainly didn't seem all that eager to turn around and talk to her now.

Jane moved in closer. She put her hands on his shoulders—oh, that did feel lovely, all that heat and lean, hard muscle. She had sincerely missed having her hands on him.

He stiffened—but at least he didn't pull away. The band started up again.

Jane bent close, breathed in the scent of his skin, and spoke into his ear. "Would you come for a walk with me?"

He turned his head then, slowly, and looked at her,

those silver eyes shaded by the brim of his hat. "People are watching, Jane."

She shrugged. "I asked you if you'd come for a walk with me. Someplace a little quieter. Where we could talk."

"Talk about what?"

The band was doing a very credible rendition of "Lady Marmalade." The lead singer, who wore a sexy dance-hall outfit and could belt it out with the best of them, kept the volume high. Jane was more reading his lips than hearing him. "It's too loud here. Please. Come with me...."

He took his sweet time making up his mind. But then at last he got up. She stood back so he could disentangle himself from the space between the picnic table and the bench. Once he was standing, he swallowed the rest of his beer and pitched the empty cup into a nearby trashcan.

She reached for his hand. He allowed her to take it, hesitating the tiniest fraction of a second before twining his fingers with hers. She stepped closer, and wrapped the fingers of her free hand around his arm.

He looked down at her with obvious suspicion. "What's going on, Jane?"

"We'll talk about that. This way." And she led him off into the trees.

Jane knew a place down by the creek, where the willows grew close and the loud music would be blocked by all the greenery and the steepness of the bank. It took them several minutes to get to it. They didn't speak the whole way. Jane didn't really care. Her hand was in his hand, she held onto his arm.

She was *with* him, at last, after two whole weeks of missing him, of longing for him, of thinking of all the things she should have done differently that final, beautiful night before he picked up and left. They saw people they knew, exchanged smiles and nods. Jane noted the knowing gleam in more than one pair of inquisitive eyes. Only a blind woman would have missed those swift looks of surprise, which were instantly followed by too-friendly smiles.

There would be talk, and lots of it, by the time the day was through. Jane would give them until tomorrow, at the latest. By then, someone would just *have* to tell Virginia Elliott who they'd seen holding hands with her only child.

A narrow path led down the bank to creekside. Jane half slid to the bottom, getting dirt in her little black shoes. Cade led the way, holding tight to her hand to help her keep her feet.

By the time they got to the water's edge, she was laughing. She stumbled and fell against him.

"Watch out." He caught her, his expression reluctant, his arms around her anything but.

She looked into his face and then she just couldn't help herself. She slid her hands up that hard chest and hooked them around his neck. "Oh, it's so good to see you."

He swore.

She grinned. She was pressed up close enough to know he was just as happy to see her as she was to be with him.

She sighed. "Listen. Please."

"What?" He growled the word as his eyes scanned her face, tracking from her mouth, to her eyes, to her nose, to the tip of her chin.

"I want you to take me out to Bennett's. How about tomorrow night? And as far as me telling my parents about us..."

"Yeah?"

"I don't think I'll have to. They'll know very soon. They might even know right now, the New Venice grapevine being what it is. They're both here today— not together, of course. But they're here. Someone is bound to tell them they saw us just now, holding hands, looking like a lot more than casual acquaintances."

He regarded her narrowly. "You're willing then, to have your mother know about me?"

"I am. And if her simply finding out isn't enough for you, I'll go further."

"Yeah?"

"I'll make a formal declaration of my intention to be seen in public with you on a regular basis. I'd do it this evening. However..."

"I knew it." He took off his hat, dropped it onto a nearby rock. "There's a catch."

"Um-hmm."

"Hit me with it."

"I'm hoping to be very busy this evening—all night long, as a matter of fact. So how about tomorrow? I'll give her a call and—"

Apparently he'd heard enough. His mouth swooped down.

Jane responded with utter abandon. She lifted her face to him, moaning aloud. Their lips met. Their tongues danced together and their bodies pressed close.

Oh, it was magical. The two of them, here in the moist coolness by the creek, hidden among the willows, kissing for all they were worth.

He lifted his head. She stood on tiptoe, to steal one more quick, mouth-to-mouth caress. Then she kissed his chin. And his neck. He nuzzled her throat, nibbled the hollow a little lower down.

And then, with a sigh, she went still, her head on his shoulder, enjoying the feel of his body against hers. She ran her fingers down his hard brown arm. "You're so tan...."

He chuckled. The sound echoed pleasingly against her ear. "One thing about livin' from hotel to hotel, there's always a pool to take advantage of between poker games. I swim. I sit in the sun. I use the gym. Believe it or not, I read."

"I believe it."

"And then there's my ongoing effort to improve my vocabulary. It's a life of endless excitement. Too bad we all know how I'll end up."

"How?"

"Busted. With a melanoma."

"Well, as far as the melanoma goes, you could try a little sunscreen."

"Doesn't fit my image."

"Put it on in your room. No one has to know."

"Hey. That's a thought."

"And as far as your ending up busted, well, who

says so? Caitlin tells me you're very good at what you do.''

''You've been talking to Caitlin about me?''

''Yes, I have. Does that bother you?''

After a moment, he grunted. ''Not really. She can drive Aaron up the wall, but she and I have gotten along pretty good in the last few years. We understand each other, I guess you could say.''

''And Will?''

''What about him?''

''How does he get along with her?''

''Looks good on the surface. But who can say about Will? He's the deep one. Plays it close to the vest—and what did Caitlin tell you about me?''

''All good things.''

''I'll bet.''

She tipped her head back to meet his eyes. ''You could have come home, right? Between those poker games.''

''Yeah. So?''

She pretended to punch him in the arm. ''So I missed you. A lot.''

He frowned, but she could tell it was mostly for show. ''Your signals were mixed the last time I saw you.''

''I'm working hard on that.''

''I've noticed.'' He was hiding a grin, she could see it. ''And a homecoming like this is worth staying away for a long, long time.'' She shifted from one foot to the other. He frowned again. ''What?''

''Dirt in my shoes.'' She stepped back enough to slip off one shoe and then the other, shaking them out in turn. He obligingly gripped her free hand, helping her keep her balance on the sloping bank. "There," she said, as she slipped the second shoe back on. "Much better."

He was looking her up and down. "Nice getup. Like something from an old Disney movie."

"That was the idea."

"I like the braids. They make you look so sweet."

"Don't kid yourself."

He chuckled. "Also, they make me think of *un*-braiding them. And that lace-up thing. I *really* like that. And you know how I feel about little strings at the neck of your shirt. Very efficient."

"I am so glad that you approve of my costume."

The teasing light left his eyes. "So what happens now?"

She faked a look of surprise. "I get to decide?"

"Hey. I'm only the guy. We all know who runs the damn world."

"It's a relief to see you've come to understand the way things work at last."

"I'm not joking, Jane. What happens with us now?"

"Well, right now, I thought we'd go back to the picnic. Enjoy the evening. It's starting to cool off a little, which is nice. There will be dancing under the stars."

"You and me? Dancing? *Together?*"

"Exactly."

"More than one dance?"

"That's what I was thinking."

"This is what is called a breakthrough, right?"

She nodded. "We'll mingle. With your brothers and my best friend. With your mother and the Bravo relatives who came to town for this event. With my mother and my father, too, if we happen to run into them."

He winced. "Your mother."

"You can handle it."

He looked at her probingly. "You'll be with me. That's what you're saying."

"That is exactly what I'm saying. And then later…"

He had that part down. "We go home together."

"Yes. Where we can talk. In depth."

"And more than talk. In depth."

"Yes."

He had that look again—the glad one, the he'd had on his face when she glanced up and saw him while she read to the children. She knew her expression mirrored his.

He said softly, "I like it."

She grabbed his hat and held it out to him. "Well, then. Let's get started."

They danced. Repeatedly.

And they hung out with Cade's long-lost relatives.

Around seven, they loaded up a couple of plates and shared a table with Emma and Jonas Bravo. Jonas, who ran a multibillion-dollar corporation in L.A., liked to gamble for relaxation. He admired Cade's gold bracelet and asked Cade if he had any tips for a dedicated amateur.

Cade laughed. "The tips are always the same.

Don't bet what you don't have. Never draw to an inside straight. Know when it's time to get up and walk away—all the clichés. Which are clichés because they're true.''

Emma Bravo, who was a successful businesswoman in her own right—not to mention gorgeous, with platinum hair and a sweet Texas twang—leaned Jane's way while the men talked gaming.

She confided that she and Jonas were expecting. ''In April of next year.'' Emma patted her flat stomach. ''I still can't believe it. Neither can Jonas. He says he's the happiest, luckiest man alive. I love it when he talks like that. Proves to me all over again that he is not the man I married.''

Jane frowned. ''*Not* the man you married?''

Emma laughed and leaned closer. ''You should have known him before I married him and went to work on him. He was a mess. Well, I mean, emotionally a mess. To most of the world he looked like the walking definition of success. Rich as they come. Powerful. All that. But inside, he was lonely and unhappy. He wouldn't let anyone get close.''

''What happened?''

''Love happened.'' Emma beamed. ''I know it's corny, but love can do miracles. It truly can.'' Emma caught her husband's eye across the table. The look they shared brimmed with abiding affection—and considerable heat.

A few minutes later, Marsh Bravo, Cade's half brother from Oklahoma, joined them. His wife, Tory, was at his side, carrying their baby son Russell. Not far behind was their ten-year-old daughter, Kim and

Jonas's three-year-old adopted sister, Mandy, whom Jonas and Emma were raising.

Kim and Mandy had been to the face-painting booth.

"See me," said Mandy proudly, marching over to Jonas and holding up her small face. Fanciful, glittery flowers and butterflies perched on her cheeks and twined along her temples. "I am so beautiful."

"You are gorgeous," Jonas agreed. "You are absolutely dazzling." He grabbed her and tickled her and she squealed in delight.

After the meal, Cade led Jane out on the dance floor again. They swayed together to the music. Jane decided that right then, at that moment, she was the happiest she'd ever been her entire life—so far.

When the band took a break, they went back to sit down. Jane had barely settled at the table when Celia and Aaron appeared.

Celia marched right up and grabbed Jane's arm. "Come on. Right now."

"Ceil. What the—?"

"With me. Now."

Aaron let out a deep laugh. "She's a demon when she gets like that. You're better off to just do what she says."

Jane cast Cade a sheepish glance. He grinned and shrugged.

So Celia dragged her off to the baseball diamonds. They climbed the bleachers and sat in the top row, alone but for a few giggling teenagers a lot lower down.

"Now," said Jane. "What?"

"Oh, puh-lease. I don't believe this. I've been asking you what's wrong for weeks now. And you've been changing the subject on me."

"Ceil, listen—"

"Have you told Jilly?"

"About?"

"Oh, you know very well what."

She did know. And she also felt a little bit guilty for not telling her friends. "Cade."

"Duh."

"No, I haven't told Jilly."

"Well, that's something. At least I'm not the only one you don't trust."

"Ceil—"

"I'm hurt. I am. I trusted *you,* now didn't I? Back when Aaron hardly knew I existed? Back when I was sure he was never going to see me as anything but the best damn personal assistant he'd ever had the good sense to hire?"

"Ceil—"

"I told you—and Jilly—all about my hopeless case of unrequited love for the boss. I listened to your advice. And I took that advice. I don't necessarily expect you to do the same. But to *tell* me when I ask if something is bothering you, I do expect that. Especially from you, Jane. From Ms. Honesty-is-the-best-policy, Ms. Everything-starts-with-the-truth."

"You're right."

"I also—what?"

"I said, you're right. I should have told you."

"Well. Humph. At least you admit you were wrong."

"I was. I've been…confused."

"It's been going on for months, hasn't it?"

"If you mean the attraction between us, yes."

"Oh, I knew it. The minute I saw you with him today, everything fell into place. The way you'd always changed the subject whenever anyone asked about your new neighbor. The way you two would look at each other—and then look away."

"Yes. All right. All that did happen. But we weren't…together. We never spoke beyond the usual hi-how-are-yous."

"Until?"

"A few weeks ago."

"And? Oh, come on. Talk to me. You can spare a few minutes to bring me up to speed."

So Jane filled her friend in on the events of the past few weeks.

When she fell silent, Celia gaped at her in disbelief. "You talked to *Caitlin?* And it *helped?*"

"Yes, I did. And she was wonderful, really. She's a very smart woman."

"No argument there. She's smart as they come. But she wasn't any help at all to me. In fact, to be painfully honest, it was very much the other way around."

"She mentioned that."

Celia grinned. "But it all worked out in the end."

"She said that, too."

"And now, I adore my mother-in-law. She's one of a kind and I wouldn't trade her for the world—and you haven't said if you're thinking along the lines of Caitlin being *your* mother-in-law."

"You're right. I haven't said."

Celia pretended to pout. "And you're not going to, right?"

"How about if I keep you posted?"

"As if I have a choice. You'll tell me when you're good and ready, and we both know it. And I do hope you're not letting old garbage—that would be spelled *R-U-S-T-Y*—get in the way of things now."

"Maybe I was. But I'm not anymore."

"Good. Oh, Janey. I'm so glad to see you *glowing* like this. You're positively radiant. It's about time— and I just have to ask. About your mother…"

"She's not going to be a problem."

"You're sure?"

"I am absolutely positive. She can have all the fits over this that she wants. But in the end, she'll have to accept the fact that this is my life and it gets lived my way."

Chapter Thirteen

As the sunset faded and the first stars began to gleam in the darkening sky, Caitlin ordered the lighting of the paper lanterns that had been strung from tree to tree across the dance floor. Celia had brought along a new camera, a fully digital one. She took an album's worth of pictures. Jane and Cade were included in several of them, standing side by side, holding hands, grinning right into the camera.

"I want copies," Jane told her friend.

"Don't worry. You'll get them. Cross my heart."

Later, Jane and Cade took some time to wander over to the midway area across the creek. There was a Ferris wheel and a Tilt-A-Whirl, a carousel and a tunnel of love. With a toss of a coin, Cade won her a carnival glass fruit bowl.

They had their fortunes told by a gypsy who called

herself Madame Zuleika. She said the future looked bright, full of riches, of love and laughter—and babies, too. The fortune-teller did bear a strong resemblance to Mary Lou Garber, whose husband owned Garber's Hardware on Main. But neither Jane nor Cade let that bother them. They decided that when it came to predictions of good fortune, it didn't matter if a real gypsy—or the hardware store owner's wife—made them.

Jane hadn't seen her mother all day, and as the night drew on, she doubted that she would. Around ten, though, as she and Cade were once again swaying together on the dance floor, she spotted her father. Clifford Elliott, looking somber and aloof as always, stood with her uncle, the mayor, over by the Forest Service booth, where picnickers could get free posters of Sierra flora and fauna, as well as flyers on campfire safety.

Cade saw them, too. "Don't look now," he whispered in her ear. "But your father and my favorite ex-sheriff, J.T., are lurking over by the Forest Service booth."

"I know," she whispered back. "Don't be scared."

"You'll protect me?" He nuzzled the ear he was whispering in. "You won't let your uncle arrest me?"

She sighed and stroked the back of his neck with a fond hand. "I'll protect you. With my life." The song ended. She took his hand. "Come on."

He hung back. "Wait a minute. You're not planning to—"

"We should say hello."

"Jane…"

She looked at him from under her lashes. "Please?"

He muttered something that was probably profane, but then let her lead him off the floor.

Jane had inherited her stature and coloring from the Elliott side of the family. Her father was tall, with a deep chest and broad shoulders and dark hair now streaked with silver. Her uncle J.T. also had the dark, imposing look of an Elliott, with the same thick salt-and-pepper hair. But J.T. had always enjoyed a good meal. His stomach hung over his belt.

Her father saw them first. Jane had to give him credit. Except for an almost imperceptible narrowing of those dark Elliott eyes, her father gave no indication that the sight of his daughter with one of Caitlin's sons had any effect on him at all. Her uncle J.T. didn't dissemble quite so well. When he saw them, he scowled.

Cade muttered, "Are you sure about this?"

She sent him a smile, squeezed his hand and pulled him onward.

"Dad," Jane said brightly. "Uncle J.T. How are you two? Having a good time?"

Her father coughed officiously. And then he forced out a few words. "Hello, Jane. Yes. It's a beautiful evening. The picnic seems quite a success." He nodded at Cade—stiffly. But that didn't necessarily mean anything against Cade. Her father did a lot of things stiffly.

J.T. took his tone from his older brother, wiping

the scowl from his face and forcing a politician's smile. "Well. Yes. Ahem. Hello, you two."

Cade said, "Real nice to see you, Judge. You, too, J.T."

Jane asked, "So, Dad, have you seen Mom?" Cade squeezed her hand then. She got the message: don't push your luck.

He was probably right. But she felt reckless tonight. She felt powerful and bold—and strong in her determination to break down facades, to meet old demons head-on and vanquish them totally, once and for all.

Her father didn't miss a beat. He was, after all, a master of evasion when it came to questions about his wife. "Not recently, no."

"She did come to the picnic?"

Her father's mouth twisted in a sour approximation of a smile. "She always does, now, doesn't she?"

"Well yes, Dad. As a rule, she does. But I'm asking if you've seen her here, today. I mean, I know you didn't come with her, since the two of you never go anywhere together unless you absolutely have to, but still, maybe you—"

"Jane," Cade said. And that was all. Just her name. But the sound of it stopped her cold. She looked at him. He stared right back. She saw reproach in his pale eyes.

Her father said, quietly, "If I see her, I'll tell her you're looking for her."

Jane thought about the night ahead, the one she and Cade would spend at her house. She didn't want her mother interrupting them. "No. It's all right. Just tell her I'll give her a call tomorrow."

"I'll do that."

Cade wrapped it up. "Well. Great seeing you…"Jane's father and uncle nodded, and made a few more polite noises. Then Cade led her away to the booth where the beer was on tap in big steel kegs. "Beer?"

"Yes. Thanks."

He bought them the drinks and then led the way to a table under a big oak tree a couple hundred yards from the dance floor. They sat side by side, facing the distant bandstand and the dancers gliding in pairs under the golden glow of the paper lanterns. Cade set his hat on the table and took a long drink from his cup.

Jane sipped from hers. "All right," she admitted after a minute. "I went a little too far."

He slanted her a look. "That's right. You could find a better time and place to talk to your dad about his problems with your mother."

She looked into her beer. No answers there. "Sometimes I just get so tired of it, of the phoniness of it, the way that they live. I don't know how they stand it. I don't know how they—"

"Jane."

Morosely she sipped more beer. "What?"

"It's not your life. It's theirs. You're all grown up now and the way your folks live doesn't have a hell of a lot to do with you."

She knew he was right. "Sorry." She scrunched

up her nose. "I admit. I can be a little overbearing, now and then."

He faked a look of shock. "You? Never." Then he reached over to brush a loose strand of hair off her cheek. "Hey. It worked out all right. They took seeing us together pretty damn well, I thought."

She leaned a little closer. The oak tree shadowed them, made the picnic table seem a private place created for the two of them alone. "Yes. It did go well."

He leaned closer, too. "I have to admit, though, it was never your father I was worried about."

"Cade." Now she was whispering. Their faces were so close. Their lips almost brushed as they spoke.

"Yeah?"

"It's going to work out."

"You seem so sure."

"I am. After all, Madame Zuleika said so, didn't she?"

"Yeah. Yeah, I guess that she did...."

"I think you should kiss me."

"You know what? I do, too."

He moved that extra fraction of an inch. And their lips met.

The kiss started out sweet—and swiftly got steamy.

When they came up for air, he said, "I think it might be time to head on home."

They went to her house. She followed in her van behind the black Chevy extended cab pickup he'd bought because, he said, he was tired of the Porsche, that his legs were too long for it.

Inside, by the front door, on the long table where Jane had recently put a fresh arrangement of flowers in the mercury glass vase, they left a straw cowboy hat, Jane's small shoulder bag and the carnival glass fruit bowl.

Halfway up the stairs, on the landing beneath Aunt Sophie's portrait, they paused for a kiss—the kind of kiss that just never seems to end. By the time they moved on, they were both naked, their clothes strewn about on the stairs and the railing. Holding hands, they ran up the rest of the way and straight to the master suite.

They fell across the bed, laughing and eager. He tickled her and she tickled him back.

And then, he was over her, looking down at her. The nearly full moon poured silver light through the turret windows. His face was so still, so serious.

"What?" She touched his mouth, his cheek, stroked the line of his jaw. "Tell me…"

He laughed again, but it was a distant, self-mocking kind of sound. "I don't believe this."

"What?"

"I want you. I want to get inside you. I want to go over the moon with you."

"But?"

"I want to talk to you first."

She blinked—and then she laughed in pure delight.

He pretended to glare at her. "Oh, great. Laugh at me. Go ahead."

"I'm not. You know I'm not." She kissed the end of his nose. "I love that you want to talk to me." She squirmed out from under him and then turned on her side to face him, sliding a leg between his two hairy ones, cradling her head on her bent arm. "Okay. Talk."

"Well…"

"Hmm?"

"It's partly…why I left three weeks ago, and why I stayed away."

"Okay."

"I didn't even want to go."

That was lovely to hear. "You didn't?"

He shook his head. "I woke up and you were right there, beside me. And I only wanted to stay."

"But you left anyway."

"I was thinking that I had to get real, you know? That it wasn't going to work, with us. Not in the crazy, impossible way I'd suddenly realized I wanted it to work. That the problem with us was, I didn't know a damn thing about how to keep it going long-term with a woman. And you couldn't help me out with that because you didn't want to get anything going long-term with me."

Looking back on her own behavior that night, she could understand completely how he'd come to that conclusion. She made a small, sad sound deep in her throat.

"Hey," he said softly. "I'm not telling you this so you'll start beating yourself up."

"I know. I said what I said that night. I can't go back and do it over. But I also can't help wishing that I'd done it differently, that I'd been braver, bolder. More decisive, more what I always say I want to be—more honest."

He gave her a rueful grin. "You *were* honest. You'd made it clear from the beginning, what you were looking for in a man. And you'd told me that I didn't have what you were looking for—not by a long shot, not in my wildest dreams."

She let out a groan. "You know, I can't believe you stuck around for as long as you did."

"Where the hell was I gonna go? I was already gone. Long gone. On you."

"Oh, Cade…"

"It's all about irony, see? And yes, that was one of my words. At some point so long ago I couldn't say exactly when. Irony being…" He paused, his brow furrowed. And then he continued, reciting from memory, "Irony being *the incongruity between the actual result of a series of events and the normal or expected result*—and yes, incongruity was another word for another day.

"But back to irony. The way I get irony is, it's what happens when things don't turn out the way you'd think they would, given the way they've always turned out before. Irony can be pretty damn funny."

Jane spoke up then. "But not when it's happening to you personally."

"You got it. And the irony with us was that *you* were supposed to be the one who would want to make things permanent. *I* was the guy who would never, ever settle down—and more than that. Because for months and months, while I ached for you and thought that I was never going to get my hands on you, I kept telling myself that if I only could have you, just once, I would be all right. I would get over

you. It had pretty much always worked that way before—and yeah, all right, what that says about me
isn't so great. I've been with too many women and I
haven't been with any of them for very long."

"So you always expect that it's not going to last."

"Right. But I could tell, I knew, that night when I
woke up beside you. This time it wasn't going to turn
out the way I expected. I'd had you. And it was great.
And I wasn't thinking about moving on. I was thinking long-term. I mean, what the hell was that about?
I *never* think long-term. And you—when it came to
me anyway—were thinking anything *but* long-term.
You didn't want to be seen on a date with me. You
hoped you could keep your parents from finding out
what was going on between us."

"Oh, Cade. I'm so sorry, about the way I acted
then. But now is not then. You know that, don't
you?"

He touched her chin with a finger and then kissed
her, once, a brush of a caress, his mouth to hers. "I
know. But I'm talking about that night, about why I
did what I did. I'm saying that waking up beside you
early the morning after was one of those lightbulb
moments. It hit me. I was going to get hurt. It was
only a matter of how much. I needed some time, to
think about the trouble I was in, some time to consider damage control. I had to go. Before you opened
those big brown eyes of yours and I started drowning
in them again. Before you touched me, before you
smiled at me, before you made me forget all the reasons I needed to get the hell out."

"So you got the hell out."

"Yeah. I did."

"Did you get my messages?"

"Yeah. It hurt me. To hear your voice. I wanted to come racing back here, to fall at your feet. I kind of despised myself for that."

"Why?"

"Oh, come on, Jane. You sound just like a woman."

"You men have way too much pride. And you did come back," she reminded him tenderly. "Finally."

"Yeah. I guess we both knew that would happen, too. That I'd be back. What I didn't know was that you had made a few decisions. The good kind of decisions, ones that went in my favor."

"I got help—from a very wise woman."

He laughed then. "Right. My mother."

"Don't laugh. Caitlin *is* wise."

"You don't know her like I do."

"What she told me was very wise."

"Maybe. And all right. I guess with all she's been through—and all the major mistakes she's made—she ought to be wise."

His lips were so soft. She had to kiss them again. She moved closer, pressed her mouth to his. He wrapped his arms around her and pulled her on top of him.

It was the moment, and she knew it. The moment to say it.

She lifted up just enough that she could look his eyes. "Cade Bravo, I love you. I am absolutely gone on you. I want you and only you, for the rest of my life. I want you so much. And I want…"

He smoothed her wild hair. "Yeah?"

She closed her eyes. "Oh, I shouldn't say this…"

"Yeah. You should. Come on. Say it."

So she did. "Your babies. I want that, Cade. A lot. I want children with you."

Chapter Fourteen

Babies.

It was a little more than Cade had bargained for. He knew a sudden and violent urge to jump from the bed and run down the stairs, grabbing his clothes from the landing as he went by, racing out into the summer night and away from this woman and all she offered—all she *demanded*—as far and as fast as his legs would carry him.

But then, if he did that, he would end up where he didn't want to be. Which was away from Jane.

She squirmed in his arms, rolling off of him and canting up on an elbow. "Oh, Cade. You're too quiet. I scared you, didn't I?"

He gave her a dark look. "You don't ask much, do you?"

"I did. I scared you."

"Jane. Come on. Don't you think this is all happening pretty fast?"

"Well, yes. I guess it is." She gave him a big, beautiful smile.

He looked at her sideways. "I mean, *babies?*"

"Yes, Cade. Babies."

"Right away?"

"Well, no..." He knew then, by the way she let that *no* trail off that *right away* was exactly when she wanted them. But she wasn't going to push that. "Not if you want to wait a while. I *will* wait. If you need more time."

He put his hand in her hair again, speared his fingers in it. He loved the feel of it. So warm and soft and *alive.* He captured a dark, twisting curl and guided it until it wrapped itself in a silken spiral around his finger.

He found he was thinking of what she'd always refused to tell him. Carefully he let loose of that curl, caught another one, guided it around his finger, too. "What's this about?"

Her dark brows had drawn together. "What do you mean? I was just telling you what I hope for. But if it's not what you want—if it's never going to be what you want—I'd like to know upfront, that's all."

"Is it really all?" He let that second curl go. "Is it everything you're trying to tell me?"

"I don't—"

"Look. You say you want babies—right away, if I'm willing."

"Yes. I do."

"But you haven't said if you can even *have* babies anymore."

She stiffened and jerked back. Those big dark eyes filmed over with sudden tears.

He felt like a thug, someone with no class at all. "Jane—"

"No." She swiped at her eyes with the back of her hand. "Don't apologize. You have every right to ask me that."

"But I could have done it in a better way."

"What better way? There is no better way. It's not your fault, what I did. What happened in the past. And the answer is yes. I *can* have babies. Or at least, the doctors *said* there should be no problem."

He wanted to touch her, to pull her close, to make it all better somehow. He reached for her.

"Wait." She put out a warding-off hand and scrambled to sit up. "I just…need a minute."

He did as she asked, keeping hands off, pulling himself against the pile of pillows at the headboard and keeping his mouth shut. He looked at her. That was always a great way to pass the time. She was so pretty in the pale moonlight. She'd grabbed a pillow and held it against herself, as if it could comfort her— or maybe, right now, she just needed some cover, to be a little less naked as she drummed up the courage to tell him the things she found so hard to say.

She sat with her legs crossed. Her hair fell in thick, untamed curls on her bare white shoulders. Her eyes were so troubled now. She clutched that pillow for all she was worth.

She sucked in a shaky breath and let it out fast. "I just…well, I'd like you to tell me—"

"Anything."

"How did you know?"

"Jane. Two and two generally adds up to four."

"But—"

"I know he beat you. I know you ended up in the hospital and lost your baby. It wasn't a big stretch to figure out what put you in the hospital."

"And there *was* talk, right? Back when it happened?"

"Yeah. I think I heard something. I don't remember what, exactly. Or who I heard it from." He put his hand on her knee, half expecting her to jerk away.

She surprised him. Her hand settled over his. For a moment, there was only that, the connection of touch. Then she pulled away and he let go, too.

She spoke in a small voice, holding that pillow to those beautiful breasts of hers, not meeting his eyes. "I'm still ashamed when I think of it. I like to imagine myself as strong, you know? A strong woman…"

"You *are* a strong woman."

She looked at him. And she swallowed. "I was five months pregnant. We had this fight. I don't even remember what started it. But at the end of it, after he'd hit me in the face a few times, he shoved me backward. I landed on the floor. I turned over, as quick as I could, tried to curl into myself, to protect the baby. But he just circled around me. He kicked me in the stomach."

Cade thought it was probably a very good thing

that Rusty Jenkins was already dead. "And you lost the baby."

She nodded, swallowed again. "He walked out. I managed to crawl to the phone and dial 911. They came and took me to the hospital—and yes. There were questions. Suspicions. On the part of my parents, of Celia and Jilly, of Aunt Sophie and the nurses and my doctor. Reports were filed. But I wouldn't admit it, wouldn't say what he'd done to me—and more important than me, to our innocent baby. I was too afraid of him. I knew better than to tell what he'd done. I knew that if I told, he would find a way to get to me. A way to hurt me and hurt me bad."

"So you said nothing."

She nodded again. "And then the time came when it didn't matter anyway. Rusty was dead. It was over, all in the past."

"Good," he said flatly.

"Was it? I don't know. Yeah, he was gone. And I didn't have to live in fear of him. But it was also too late, you know?"

"Too late for…?"

"To stand up to him, to make him face a few consequences for what he'd done. He was dead. There was no need anymore to tell anyone. A dead man has no consequences left to face."

"You're saying your parents never knew?"

"Oh, they knew. They guessed. But I never told them outright."

"You never told *anyone* outright?"

"No. I did tell. Eventually. I don't think I could have gotten over it, could have gotten on with my life, without getting it out, without talking about it to people I could trust. I was in counseling for a while. My counselor knew. And Aunt Sophie. And Celia and Jillian, I told them, a few years ago. I…well, I always planned to tell the man I married.''

He smiled at that. "Right. That steady, solid, dependable guy.''

She gave a low, sad little laugh. "Yeah. That one.''

He reached out, took the satiny edge of the pillow she held and gave it a tug. She let it go. He tossed it over his shoulder. And then he held out his hand to her.

With a small cry, she came to him. He pulled her in, guiding her down, tucking her against him spoon-fashion, so he could wrap his arms around her and bury his face in all that dark, sweet-smelling hair.

She let out a long sigh. "It's the worst regret in my life. That I didn't stand up to him. That only the accident of his death set me free of him, gave me a chance to start over.''

He stroked her hair, her shoulder, the long, soft curve of her arm. "It happened like it happened. But don't sell yourself short. You would have found a way. To face him down. To get free of him.''

"Maybe. But I'll never know for sure.''

He whispered, "Hey.''

"Um?''

"Forget the regret. You're alive. He's not. And the way I heard it, he more or less engineered his own death, with that stupid botched holdup attempt. He got what he deserved. And you didn't have to risk his murdering you to make it happen.''

"I didn't stand up to him."

"Jane."

"What?"

"Sometimes the cards go against you. Sometimes you don't have a prayer. You've got a losing hand. So you fold. You let it go."

"But I—"

"Jane. Let it go."

She made a noise of reluctant agreement. He pulled her in closer, resting a hand against her belly, then moving it upward, to cup one full breast. She sighed, snuggling her bottom up closer, making him all the more acutely aware of what he wanted to do to her.

Very soon now.

He smoothed her hair out of the way, kissed the tender skin on the side of her neck.

It was all like some dream, in a way. Coming home, expecting that the best he was going to get from her was a lot of sneaking around and maybe a few more bouts of great sex.

And instead…this.

An evening right out in the open, the two of them, side by side. The truth about that SOB, Rusty, at last.

Her telling him she loved him. And wanted his babies.

Love.

Now there was a hell of a concept.

Was that it, what he felt for her?

How would he know, for certain? How could he say?

He knew he was…looking. Had been for a while

now. Trying to find something solid. Something that would last.

And with her, he did feel something different than ever before. A deeper kind of wanting. A sort of hopefulness for the future.

But could it really last, like she said, for their whole lives?

"Jane?"

"Hmm?"

"About you and me…"

He could feel the sudden stillness in her. "Yes?"

"I…well, I'm willing, all right? To give it a try."

She started wiggling then. He supposed he'd known she would. She wouldn't stop until she'd turned over and could look into his eyes. She stroked a hand down the side of his face. "Give what a try, Cade?"

"You and me. The baby thing."

"Ah." She ran the back of a finger along the line of his jaw. "The baby thing…"

He reminded himself that there was something he'd better make clear to her before those wonderful hands moved any lower. "Listen."

"Mmm?" Her eyes were dreamy.

Too dreamy. "I mean it. There's something I want you to understand."

She blinked. "Okay."

"You know the story, of my father. Met my mother when she was seventeen, supposedly married her, gave her three sons—then faked his own death in an apartment fire, disappeared from our lives. Went off to do a lot of evil and illegal things."

"Yes. I remember. I've heard all the stories."

"The key word is *supposedly.*"

Her eyes changed as understanding dawned. "Are you saying that Blake Bravo never actually married your mother?"

"You got it."

"But she had three children with him."

"That's right. And we have our suspicions about that, my brothers and me."

"Suspicions?"

"Yeah. The only thing we can figure is that she kept having babies to try to force him to marry her."

She sat up. "Oh, no. Not Caitlin."

That made him chuckle. "Why not Caitlin?"

"Well, because. Caitlin makes her own rules and doesn't let anyone tell her how to live her life. She would never do something so calculating, just to get a man's ring on her finger."

"Jane. You don't know my mother as well as you think you do."

"Oh, please. I just can't buy that she would do that. And not only because it's so manipulative, so scheming."

"Caitlin can be manipulative, Jane."

"But it's *pitiful,* too. She had to have seen the hopelessness of it. I mean, if he didn't marry her after Aaron, what made her think he would after Will—or you?"

"Good question. But then, we're talking about Caitlin. Most of the time, her motives are a black hole to the rest of us."

"I'm sorry. I still can't believe she would—"

"Jane. Face it. She just might. You can't let your-self get too carried away with some fantasy idea about my mother. She's no angel. And she never has been. And whatever her reasons for having Blake Bravo's kids without having his ring on her finger, she did it."

"But...she's Caitlin *Bravo.* That's been her name as long as I can remember."

"Eventually she just started calling herself that, and after a while, it stuck. And she gave my brothers and me his last name when she filled out the birth certificates. So yeah, we really *are* Bravos. But the fact is, Caitlin McCormack and Blake Bravo never officially tied the knot. And folks called us *those bad Bravo boys* and also *those little Bravo bastards.* In both cases, what they called us was the truth."

Her eyes were soft with sympathy. "Oh, Cade. I'm so sorry. I always thought it was...just an expression, you know?"

He hooked his hand around the back of her neck and brought her sweet face down to his. "Here's an-other truth for you, Jane. If you had some idea about being the single mom of my baby, get over it. I'm not bringing any bastards into this world. You get my drift?"

"I...yes. Well, of course. I don't want that, either. Honestly I don't."

He let go of her then. He hauled himself to a sitting position and pulled out the drawer in the nightstand by his side of the bed. As he'd expected, the remain-ing condoms from that other night were there. He took one out. "Say what you want about all the women I've been with. One thing I've always done right.'' He shoved the drawer shut and held up the little foil pouch. ''And that's *not* getting anyone pregnant.'' He saw the gleam in her eyes then. And he knew what she was thinking. ''Go ahead. Say it.''

''What about Enda Cheevers?''

He glared at her. ''What about Enda?''

''Well, everyone says—''

''You know, I hate that. What everyone says. Did it ever occur to you that what everyone says might not be true?''

''Cade, I'm only—''

''I don't give a damn what people say. That baby of Enda's wasn't my kid. If you think back, maybe you'll remember how she left town not long after the incident between me and her daddy and her daddy's shotgun.''

''Yes. I remember.''

''She ran off with the baby's father, an encyclopedia salesman from Bend, Oregon.''

''Oh,'' Jane said. He could see she was embarrassed at how eagerly she'd believed all the rumors. Good, he thought. She ought to be embarrassed.

He said, ''I've never done what my daddy did. And I never will. I'm not givin' any small-minded people an opportunity to call an innocent kid a damn ugly name.''

She was looking at him sideways, kind of nervous—and kind of hopeful, too.

He caught her hand, turned it over and set the condom in her palm. ''So it's your choice.'' He curled her fingers over it. ''We use that. Or we don't. If we do, well, that's okay. We can take a little time, to be sure about all this, before we jump right in to having a family.''

''And…if we don't use it?''

''Then you get a chance at what you say you want. My baby. And you marry me. Tomorrow.''

Damn. Had he really said that?

Apparently yes, judging by the dazed expression on her sweet face. She stared for an endless two or three seconds—and then she let out a sharp, surprised laugh. ''*Marry* you?''

He wondered if he should be insulted. But no. He couldn't blame her for being surprised. He was pretty stunned himself at what had just come out of his mouth.

''Well,'' she said.

''Well, what?'' It came out sounding gruff.

A big smile broke across that mouth he always longed to kiss. ''Well, great. Works for me.''

He frowned. ''That was a yes, right? I mean, is that a yes?''

''Of course it is.''

''You're sure?''

''I am. This is exactly what I want.''

''It is?'' It occurred to him right then that they were both stark, raving nuts. He couldn't believe what he'd suggested. And she should damn well have had sense enough to hesitate, at least.

But she wasn't hesitating. Far from it. Her eyes were shining—and not with tears. ''Oh, yes. It's just what I want—what I didn't quite dare to propose myself. Oh, Cade. You are so much braver than I am.''

"Uh. I am?"

"Yes. Oh, yes. You are." She tossed the condom over her shoulder.

He watched it go flying. It hit the nightstand on her side of the bed, bounced off and dropped to the floor. "Hey. Get serious, Jane. Are you *sure?*"

"Yes. I am sure."

"But—"

She threw her arms around him, pressed all those womanly curves and hollows against him. "No buts. We're doing this. Too late to back out now."

"I can't think when you do that."

She tipped her head back and grinned at him. "When I do what?"

"Throw yourself on me, all naked like that."

"Well, good. Don't think. Just kiss me and make love to me and forget about everything but how good it feels."

He grabbed her waist in both hands with the idea that he would push her away a little. Bright move. Once he had a hold of her, there was only one option: to pull her closer. "Damn you, Jane."

"Are you getting cold feet on me?"

"I'm not what you wanted. I'm not—"

"Oh, yes. You are. You are just what I wanted. What I've needed. What I've been looking for. I know that now."

He had to admit, he liked the sound of that. "Me? You've been looking for *me?*"

"Yes, I have. And you know that other guy—that nice, steady, dependable guy? The guy I never found?"

"Yeah?" He wasn't sure he wanted to talk about that guy. But he asked anyway, "What about him?"

"I never found him because I never *wanted* to find him. Because he wasn't for me."

Well, all right. This *was* getting interesting. "How do you figure that?"

"He wouldn't have been good for me. And I certainly wouldn't have been good for him. We would have bored each other silly."

"Oh, yeah?"

"Yeah. Because I have this tendency..."

He stroked his hand down the full curve of her hip. He couldn't help himself. Her body held endless enchantments. Just to look at her, to touch her, to feel her quiver beneath his hands....

She moaned.

He gave her train of thought back to her. "You have this tendency..."

"Ah. Yes. I do. A tendency to play it safe. To get stuck in a rut. To be stodgy and self-righteous. To be humdrum."

"Humdrum. As in boring?"

"That's it, that's what I said."

He definitely did like the way this conversation was headed. "And that means you need..."

"...someone to shake me up a little, someone to remind me that life is not only safety. There has to be risk. Adventure. Chances taken."

He cupped her bottom. It was a beautiful bottom. Fit just great into his hands. He bent enough to nibble on the tender curve where her shoulder met her neck.

She made a small sound of surprise and delight. Then she said, with enthusiasm, "Oh!"

"Lots of deep thoughts going on here, Jane."

"Oh, yes. If I can only…"

"What?" He sucked on that soft, white skin.

"Remember…"

"Yeah?"

"What I was talking about…"

He lifted his head, just enough to note with satisfaction the love mark he'd left at the base of her throat. He touched it, rubbed it, with his thumb. "You said there has to be risk."

She moaned some more. He really liked that. Hearing her moans.

"Yes," she whispered, breathless. Sighing. "That's right. Risk. I think—" She gasped as he caught her earlobe between his lips, worried it, then lightly nipped it with his teeth.

He reminded her, "You were saying?"

"Mmm…"

"You said, you think…"

"Yes. I do."

"You think *what?*"

"That there was a reason I fell for Rusty."

"Rusty," he muttered, running his tongue along the ridge of her collarbone, "should burn in hell."

She groaned. "I try not to judge him."

"Well, I'm not that noble, Jane. I judge him. And I say he should burn in hell."

"Well—oh!—that's how you feel. I can't tell you how to feel."

"That's right."

''But I mean—'' She cut herself off with another of those sweet moans of hers.

''You mean what?''

''Well...'' She caught his mouth, kissed it, then started talking again. ''It was all wrong—''

''What?'' He asked the question—then tried to catch her mouth again.

She canted her head back, avoiding his kiss in order to answer. ''Between me and Rusty, it was all wrong. Rusty was in no way the right man for me. But I see...an important urge there.''

''An urge.''

''That's right.'' She brought a hand between them and traced his lips with the pads of her fingers. ''Such a beautiful mouth...''

''What about this urge, Jane?''

''This urge?''

''With Rusty. You said there was an urge. An important urge.''

''Ah. Right. It was an urge to...take chances. To invite a little risk.''

''A *little* risk?'' He dipped his head and ran his tongue down her throat.

''Okay.'' She grasped his shoulders, made a low, purring sound. ''I went overboard. I was seventeen, when it started with him. My life was so...locked up. I felt hemmed in, on a treadmill, everything gray and dull. I saw my life stretching ahead of me, antiseptic and constructive, with no excitement, no *fun*.''

He lifted his head and met her eyes. ''Because of your parents?''

She nodded. ''Especially my mother. Her expectations for me were crushing me. Their life together was a lie. I wanted to be free of them. With Rusty, I broke out.''

''Yeah, in a big way.''

''I *said* it was all wrong. Rusty ended up being the wrong risk, a bad chance I never should have taken. He killed our baby. He almost killed me. But the basic urge—the urge to break out, to play it some other way than safe—I think I was onto something there.''

He considered her words for a moment, and decided they made sense. ''Okay. I see what you mean.'' Her lashes fluttered down. He caught her chin in his hand and tipped it up to him. ''Jane…''

''Mmm?''

''We've been talking, Jane. We've talked a lot.''

''Yes, we have.''

''I'm kind of tired of talking now, for a while. Okay?''

''Oh. Yes. That's fine.''

''You gonna kiss me now, Jane—some slow, long, deep kisses? You gonna let me kiss you back?''

She licked her lips. He figured that was answer enough. He guided her down among the pillows as he covered her mouth with his own.

Chapter Fifteen

Late in the night, Cade woke.

His first thought was a question: What am I doing here? But then he looked over and saw Jane sleeping, her face soft and defenseless as the babies she said she wanted to have with him.

Looking at Jane, he found himself thinking it would be all right. They would make it, somehow. She really did seem sure that he was what she wanted, that what they could build together would be something worth having.

For the most part, he agreed with her. He had this feeling of rightness, when he was with her. This feeling that the world was a better place than he'd known it to be before he found her. That there were more possibilities than he'd realized. That with Jane, he'd always be looking forward to coming home. And that he wouldn't ever be lonesome when he got there.

There was going to be a lot to deal with, though. Like how she would handle it when her mother cut her off again. And he didn't kid himself. Virginia Elliott was going to go seriously sideways when she found out her daughter had hooked up with another bad boy. And not just any bad boy. Uh-uh. Much worse. This time, Jane had picked herself a bad boy with Bravo for a last name.

And then he couldn't help asking himself, was Jane really ready to marry a guy who didn't pull a nine-to-five? A guy who took off for days and sometimes weeks at a time in order to bring home the bacon? A guy whose income could be spotty, to put it mildly?

Did she really want to have her babies with a guy like him?

Jane stirred. She yawned. She looked so cute when she did that. He felt her soft hand, reaching for him under the sheet.

She found him.

He pushed his doubts to the back of his mind and moved into her waiting arms.

They got up at daylight. Cade headed for the shower and Jane went downstairs, to get the coffee started and to collect their clothes from the stairway.

A few minutes later, she joined him in the shower stall. They stayed in there until the water turned cold.

Downstairs at a little before eight, Jane scrambled some eggs and he made the toast and they sat at her breakfast table with the morning sun pouring in the bay window, sipping coffee, talking about their wedding—or more accurately, *she* talked about their wedding. He listened and he agreed, happy just to watch her as she made her plans. Her face had a glow about it. And the morning sun made her hair shine, catching those hints of brown and red in the dark strands.

She still seemed sure—that she wanted to marry him and that she wanted to do it that day.

"I need to go over to the bookstore," she told him. "I've got to make a few arrangements with my clerk. And I want to call Jilly. And Ceil, too—I think she said she and Aaron were staying in town until this afternoon. And I want to talk to my mother."

Cade knew a few bad words he wouldn't have minded muttering about then. He held them back. He picked up his coffee mug and saluted her with it. "That'll be interesting." He sipped.

The happy glow had left her face. She looked bleak. And determined. "It has to be done. Yes, this is sudden. But I want to make it very clear to everyone. We're proud and we're happy and we're not sneaking around. I'll call her right after breakfast and tell her that we're getting married."

He set down the mug. "Hold on a minute."

She stiffened in her chair. "Why?"

"Think twice."

"About what?"

"Your mother's not going to like this."

Her lips flattened out. "Too bad. It's not her choice to make."

"Hey," he said softly. "Relax. I'm on *your* side."

She raked a hand back through all that gorgeous

hair. "I just don't think we can afford to back down when it comes to her. Sooner or later, she's going to have to accept our marriage."

"No, she's not. It may be our choice to get married. But it's her choice how she deals with it."

"Whatever. We *are* in agreement that there's not going to be any sneaking around, right?"

He gave her a nod.

She gestured, emphatically, with both hands. "So then, one way or another, my mother is going to hear about our marriage. And I think it's important that she hear it from me—and before the fact."

"I'm not arguing."

That shut her up. For about half a second. "You're not?"

"No. I'm just saying you should tell her to her face. Not on the phone, not unless you have no other choice."

She finally caught on. And she looked damn sheepish. "You know, you're right. I'll call her. Say I need to see her right away. How's that?"

He couldn't help smiling. "Sounds good to me."

"Oh. And my father. I'll call him, too—I think that's acceptable, that I tell him over the phone. Don't you?"

"Sure."

"And we can't forget Caitlin. You'll call her, won't you?"

"Be glad to."

"Anyone who wants to come, fine. We can caravan."

"You know that means Caitlin for sure, don't you?"

"No problem. I'd love to have your mother at our wedding."

"Fair enough. And I'll see if I can get hold of Will."

"Yes." She leaned across the table and kissed him. She smelled of coffee and Ivory soap. Wonderful smells. He couldn't get enough of them.

She dropped back into her chair and sipped from her mug again. "I can be ready to go by eleven. Is that okay?"

"It's good with me."

"How about Tahoe?"

"Fine."

"We'll be there in no time. We'll get the license and then we'll find the nearest chapel."

He laughed. "This is what they mean when they say a hasty wedding, right?"

"Oh, maybe. I don't know. I don't care. I only know that before tomorrow comes, we'll be married. And I'm glad."

He held out his hand.

She reached across and took it. "We'll just come on home, after the ceremony. Is that all right with you?"

"It's fine with me."

"Maybe in a few weeks—whenever we can both spare the time—we'll plan for a wedding trip."

"I'd like that."

"Oh, Cade. We're going to be very happy."

"You sound pretty damn certain."

"I am. I truly am."

* * *

The doorbell rang as they were clearing up the breakfast dishes. Jane knew who it would be.

Cade seemed to know, too. He grabbed the dish towel and dried his hands. "Listen. I'll go out the back, all right? You talk to her, break it to her as easy as you can manage it. She could have a damn heart attack, if the first thing she sees when she walks in your door is me."

Jane knew he had a point. It would probably be better if she talked to her mother before Virginia actually saw them together.

But then again, why cater to her mother's sad, sick little prejudices?

"She'll live," Jane said, closing the dishwasher, taking the towel from him to dry her own hands. "And remember, the whole idea here is that we're not going to sneak around."

The doorbell rang again.

"I don't like it," Cade said. "You should talk to her alone first, tell her what's going on. Give her that much. I'll just go to my place. You bring her over there if and when you think she can handle the sight of me."

She hung the towel on the hook beneath the cabinet. "It's not right, Cade. Listen to yourself. *If and when she can handle the sight of you?* I hate that. That's not fair to you."

"Yeah, well. Where was it that you got the impression life was gonna be fair?"

"But—"

"Look. All the time I was growing up, there were big scenes. Big confrontations. Caitlin screaming and the three of us shouting right back at her. They did nothin' for nobody. Just made raw edges, you know, the next time we rubbed up against each other. Why ask for that if it's not absolutely necessary? Why not cut your mother as much slack as we can afford to in this? Over time, maybe, she'll get used to me. I'm not counting on it, but I'm hoping. I don't want to give her any excuses to hate me any more than she already does. I want to know that we did what we could, that we broke the news to her in the most gentle way possible."

She stared at him, thinking what a good man he was—at heart, where it really counted. No wonder she loved him. And maybe he was right. And even if he wasn't, they couldn't stand here all morning debating the issue. "Okay," she conceded. "I'll talk to her first—if it is actually my mother at the door."

Again, the bell rang—three times in succession—insistently, impatiently.

"It's your mother," said Cade flatly.

"I'll bring her over to your house in a few minutes."

"I'll be there." He turned for the door to the service porch.

It was her mother all right. And she was fuming. Jane could see her through the beveled glass in the top half of the front door. Her eyes were narrowed, her mouth pinched up tight, her back ramrod-stiff.

Someone must have already told her that Jane had spent last evening at Cade Bravo's side.

Jane slid back the dead bolt and pulled open the door. Her mother grabbed the outer door, yanked it wide and stepped inside.

"Jane." Virginia Elliott made the name both an accusation—and a rebuke.

"Hello, Mother." Jane brazened it out by forcing a pleasant tone.

Her mother didn't bother with pleasantries. "Jane, I have heard the most...well, I don't know what to say. I just—"

"Mom. I'm glad you came over."

"What? Glad? I don't—"

"I have the coffee made. Come on back to the kitchen." Jane put her arm around her mother's thin shoulders and attempted to shepherd her down the central hall.

"I don't want..." Right then, Virginia caught sight of Cade's hat on the long table. "Whose hat is that?"

"Mom—"

Virginia jerked free of Jane's guiding arm. "I asked you a simple question. You can just answer it. Whose hat is that—there, on that table?" Virginia blinked. "And that vase? That strange golden vase. You would never tell me who gave you that vase. I think you should tell me now."

Jane stepped back. She felt regret—mostly for Cade's sake. He'd wanted her to handle this delicately. But there was just no way to do that. Her mother was irrational in her fury. And it was only going to get worse.

"Tell me," Virginia demanded. "Tell me now."

Jane made one last try. "Are you sure you wouldn't like a cup of coffee?"

"Stop babbling about coffee. I have no interest in coffee. Is that Cade Bravo's hat on your table there? Did he give you that vase?"

Jane drew in a long breath and let it out with care. "Yes," she said. "Right on both counts. It's Cade's hat and the vase was a gift from him to me."

"Oh, my God," said her mother. "Oh, my sweet Lord."

"Mother—"

"Everyone is talking, you know. Lotty Borghesian. And Edna Reese. They both called me. I didn't believe it. How could I believe it? I told myself, Jane wouldn't do this, Jane wouldn't be so foolish, not now. That's all behind her, all that craziness over the wrong kind of boy."

"Mom. I'd really appreciate it if you'd settle down, if you'd pull yourself back from the brink."

The veins in Virginia's neck stood out in sharp relief. She wasn't wearing her pearls so she couldn't fool with them. Instead she clutched her thin hands to fists at her side. "Settle down? Pull myself back from the brink? What are you talking about? What is going through that mind of yours?"

"What is going through my mind is that I hope you don't take this too far. I hope you don't say anything I'll find too hard to forgive."

"You hope *I* won't say anything *you* can't forgive?"

"Yes, Mother. That's what I said. I'm so sorry, that

you have this…obsession with Caitlin Bravo and anyone related to her. But I can't and won't live my life
by your obsessions. I am in love with Cade Bravo.
And I'm marrying him. Today."

Virginia gasped as if she was having trouble getting
enough air. "What? Today? You can't be serious."

"Oh, but I am. We're getting married in Tahoe this
afternoon. You're welcome to come, if you promise
to behave yourself, to treat Cade—and his mother and
his brothers—with respect and courtesy."

Virginia groped her way backward. She reached the
chair by the entrance to the front room and slowly
lowered herself into it. All the outrage seemed to have
left her. Now she looked horrified, crushed. And desperate.

"Jane." She leaned forward, all urgency. "You
can't do this. You can't ruin your life a second time.
Oh, what is the matter with you? There have been
nice men, in your life. *Good* men."

"Mother. Cade *is* a good man."

Virginia waved her hand as if batting off flies.
"What happened to that science teacher? He was a
fine—"

"Mother. Get it through your head. I'm marrying
Cade. Today."

"Oh, that's impossible. You *can't.*"

"I can. I am."

"Oh, my Lord. Oh, no. Oh, please. Cade Bravo is
Rusty Jenkins all over again. You have to see that.
You have to see that you have a real *problem* here,
when it comes to men, that you have some…fatal

weakness, for the wrong kind of man. You're not able to—''

A fatal weakness? It was enough. It was way too much. ''Mother.''

''Oh, Janey. Oh, honey…''

''I want you to listen to me.''

''Jane—''

''No. Stop.''

''You simply cannot—''

Jane put up a hand. ''Are you listening?''

''But I have to make you—''

''Stop.''

''I have to—''

''Stop!''

Her mother made a whimpering sound, then started to speak again.

Jane didn't allow that. ''Not. Another. Word.''

Virginia drew in a ragged breath, shut her mouth, and nodded.

Jane said, slowly and clearly, ''I love Cade Bravo. He is not Rusty Jenkins all over again. And if you were capable of looking at this situation reasonably, you'd see that he's not. I said it once and I'll say it again. I'm going to marry Cade. Today. I spoke too hastily, I realize, in inviting you. You're *not* welcome at my wedding, Mother. I love you, but you'd only make trouble. And I just don't need that. Not today.''

''Oh, Jane.'' Her mother stood and reached out pleading arms. ''Don't do this.''

Jane stepped back. ''Go on home now, Mother. I have a lot to do this morning. It's my wedding day.''

Chapter Sixteen

Jane stood on her porch and watched her mother drive away. Then she went over to Cade's.

He had the door open before she got all the way up the walk. With a small cry, she ran to him. He met her on the top step, enfolding her in his strong arms. She hugged him tight, pressing her face into the side of his neck, feeling his morning beard, rough against her cheek. He rocked her gently, from side to side, holding on as tight as she was.

Finally she pulled back.

He asked, "Not so good, huh?"

"Disaster. But then, I guess I knew it would be."

He lifted an eyebrow at her. "Are you trying to tell me that your mother won't be coming with us to Tahoe?"

"I told her I didn't want her there."

"Ouch." He guided an unruly curl of hair away from her mouth. Then he took her hand and pulled her down with him, to sit on the steps. "What did she say, exactly?"

Jane gave him a wry look. "Are you sure you want to know?"

"Good point. Forget I asked."

She leaned her head on his shoulder. They were quiet for a moment, just sitting there on his front step, staring down his front walk. Above them, the sky was clear and blue. Not a cloud in sight.

Finally he said, "Maybe someday..." And then he didn't seem to have the heart to finish the sentence.

She braced her elbow on her knee, cupped her chin in her hand and looked up at that gorgeous blue morning sky. "Well. One good thing."

"And that is?"

"I love you, and it's a beautiful day for a wedding."

"That's two things."

"Yeah, it is." She beamed him a big smile and then got to her feet. "We'd better get busy."

He leaned back on his hands and looked up at her. "We're out of here at eleven, right?"

Was that going to be enough time? "Oh, I don't know. It's after nine now. Could we aim for one o'clock, do you think? I not only have to decide what to wear, I've got to have a little time to—"

"One is great."

"You'll call your mother and—"

"Jane. I've got my orders. Now get lost and give me a chance to carry them out."

Jane spoke with her father before she left for the
bookstore. It took more than one call, but she finally
reached him at the county courthouse. He wasn't exactly pleased, but at least he didn't shout at her or
plead with her to change her mind—or tell her she
had a fatal weakness for the wrong kind of man.

"You're an adult now, Jane. Your life is your own.
I only hope you know what you're doing."

"I do know what I'm doing, Dad."

"Then I wish you and your new husband the best."

He was taking it so well, she considered inviting
him along for the ceremony. But then she felt just
uncomfortable enough at the idea that she didn't do
it.

Really, the man was like a ghost in her life. A
father *figure* and not much else. A good provider,
always busy. It seemed to her that she thought of
him…from a distance. Standing off to the side, not
really involved in her life in any meaningful way.

He had stood by her bed, when she lost her child.
She remembered him, looking down at her, a worried
frown on his face. But she didn't remember him
reaching out, to offer a hug or a loving kiss on the
cheek, to smooth her hair or squeeze her hand the
way most people's fathers would.

He'd been there for her graduation from Stanford,
too. Had he hugged her then? Not that she could remember. He'd congratulated her, told her he was
proud of her. She'd seen the approval in his eyes.
She'd been pleased, she remembered. And satisfied.

Just as now she was satisfied to have his good

wishes for her marriage. She simply didn't feel close enough to him to want him there to walk her down the aisle.

Jane called Celia from the store. She and Aaron were still in town, at the New Venice Inn. They'd just returned to the inn to pack their own suitcases after seeing off the various Bravo relatives.

Celia shouted for pure joy when she heard the news—and quickly made plans with Aaron to re-schedule their flight back to Las Vegas. They'd stay at the inn another night. And they'd follow Jane and Cade to Tahoe.

"Oh, Janey. I'm so happy for you. Have you called Jilly?"

"I was just about to."

"Does she know, about you and Cade?"

Jane sighed.

Celia said, "Do it now."

"Okay."

"Call me back."

"I will, I will." The line went dead and Jane dialed Jillian's number. She got a machine. She tried Jillian's cell phone. No answer there, either. So she left another message.

She called Celia again. "I couldn't reach Jillian. I left her two long messages, on her home phone and her cell, telling her all about what's going on."

"She'll be sulky when she hears you've been holding out about Cade."

"Oh, I know it."

"Not to mention heartbroken when she finds out she missed the wedding."

"Hey. You don't have to rub it in."

"Yes, I do. I'm still a little mad at you. You really should have told me."

"Sorry, Ceil. Truly, honestly, utterly sorry. Please accept my heartfelt apologies."

"I love it when you grovel. It happens so seldom—and don't worry. Jilly will be disappointed. But she'll live. And we'll take lots of pictures."

"Oh, that's right." Jane hadn't even thought of who was going to take pictures. Whatever chapel they chose would no doubt have portrait options. But she wanted lots of candid shots, too. "Bring that new camera of yours."

"I plan to."

"We're leaving for Tahoe at one. But you know, I was thinking, if you got to my house by noon—"

"Good idea. I'll help you get dressed. We can work with your hair—and by the way, what are you wearing?"

"I haven't decided yet. We'll figure out something."

"This is the part where we really need Jilly."

"We'll manage," said Jane. "Somehow." She felt a definite lump in her throat. "Ceil?"

"I'm here."

"Yeah. You are. And it means a lot. It's always meant a lot."

"Triple threat," said Celia, softly.

And Jane repeated, "Triple threat."

About ten minutes later, Caitlin burst in the front door of the shop. "Where's Jane? Jane, honey, where the hell are you?"

Laughing, Jane emerged from behind one of the center bookshelves. "I'm right here, Caitlin. You don't have to shout."

"I'll shout if I want to. I'll shout the place down. Get over here, come on." Caitlin held out her arms.

Jane found herself crushed against her future mother-in-law's lush, sequined bosom, that musky perfume Caitlin always wore making her head spin.

"Oh, I am so damn happy," Caitlin announced, hugging all the harder. "I am one happy woman." Caitlin grabbed Jane by the shoulders and held her at arm's distance so she could look at her. "My daughter-in-law. I don't believe it."

Jane laughed. "What? Should I pinch you?"

"Cade said I could go. Is that true? Can I go?"

"We'd love for you to go."

"Oh, I am so happy."

"I think you mentioned that already."

"Have you noticed? My sons choose the absolute best women to marry." Caitlin cast a meaningful glance toward the register, where Madelyn was busy ringing up the first sale of the day. "Come here a minute." She pulled Jane back among the shelves and whispered, "I've got my fingers crossed that you're not gonna let any *troublemakers* mess things up for you."

Jane squeezed Caitlin's arm. "Don't worry. Please. I've already talked to the troublemakers."

"And?"

"Consider them dealt with."

Cade was upstairs in his bathroom squirting shaving cream into his hand when the doorbell rang.

He stuck his hand under the faucet to rinse off the froth of white stuff. Then he grabbed a towel.

The doorbell rang for the second time as he was zipping up his pants. He reached for the first shirt he saw—the one he'd worn yesterday—and made for the stairs, pulling it on and buttoning it up as he went.

The bell rang once more just as he was hauling open the front door.

Virginia Elliott stood on the other side.

"Please," she said. "I must speak with you."

Chapter Seventeen

The woman was neat and tidy as ever, not a hair out of place, her navy blue slacks and white shirt without a single wrinkle. But her gray eyes had a wild look in them, a burning look of furious determination.

Even without that scary look in her eyes, she would have made Cade damned nervous. She always had made him nervous. He couldn't remember her ever saying so much as a single word to him until five seconds ago. But whenever she looked his way—on the street when he was younger, through Jane's windows in the last several months—he'd seen the disapproval and disgust in her eyes, in the set of her narrow jaw, in the cold curl of her thin lips.

Today was the same as always—only more so.

"Mrs. Elliott," he said carefully, not wanting to

set her off if he could avoid it. "I'm sorry. Jane's not here."

"I didn't say I was looking for Jane. I want to talk to *you*." She cast that disapproving glance downward, toward his bare feet. Then she snapped her gaze up again. She didn't quite meet his eyes. She appeared to be studying the stubble he'd yet to shave off his jaw. "May I come in?"

No, he thought. *Bad idea. Go away.*

But he couldn't quite bring himself to shut the door in her face. She was Jane's mother. Someday, maybe, he'd find a way to get along with her. And he knew that Jane loved her, that Jane didn't really want to cut her off.

"I *said*, may I come in?"

He stepped back and gestured toward the entrance to the turret room.

"Thank you," she said, in a way that he knew didn't really mean Thank you at all. She entered his house and she hurried ahead of him to the room he'd indicated, the low heels of her well-made shoes tapping an angry rhythm across his floor.

She wouldn't sit down. She went to the circle of windows in the turret and stood with her back to them, as if she feared a surprise attack and wanted a view of the entire room, including the only way in or out. She had a little navy-blue purse with her and she held it in front of her, as if it was going to protect her from his evil self.

As if his evil self had any interest at all in getting near her. He stayed several feet away from her, near the leather sofa in the center of the room.

She didn't mince words. "I'm here to do whatever I have to do—beg you, *pay* you, whatever it takes—to convince you to leave my daughter alone."

Why the hell had he let her in here? "Mrs. Elliott—"

She jerked up a hand, fingers splayed, palm out. "No. I'm not finished. Please let me finish."

He felt kind of sick to his stomach. He didn't need this. He had enough damn nagging doubts of his own about what he and Jane were doing. He didn't need this smooth-haired, wild-eyed mother of hers making it worse.

"You know it can't work," Virginia Elliott said. "You know you're only going to break her poor heart. You're not a man who is cut out for marriage. You're only going to drag Jane down. She has a fatal weakness, for men like you. We both know that. What I'm sure you don't know, is what she's been through, all she's suffered."

There was a silence. One that echoed like a shout.

He realized she wanted him to speak now, to tell her how he didn't know what she was talking about. "As a matter of fact, Mrs. Elliott, I do know."

Her thin mouth pinched up tight. "You know." She scoffed the words.

He replied levelly. "That's what I said."

"She told you—the truth about that monster, Rusty Jenkins? About how he beat her? About how he killed her baby?"

"Mrs. Elliott—"

"I asked you a question—two questions, to be specific."

"Fine. Yes. She told me. About Rusty. And about how she lost her baby."

"Well," she said tightly. "Well, all right, then. All right then, you know."

"Yeah. I know."

"Then what *are* you, what kind of man are you, to go and ruin her life all over again?"

He opened his mouth—and then shut it without speaking. What the hell could he say to a loaded question like that?

And she was on a roll anyway. "I know, Cade Bravo, what you are. You are the child of an unholy union between a murderer and a—"

"Don't," he said very softly.

She must have seen in his eyes that he meant what said. Because she left that particular sentence unfinished. But *she* wasn't finished. Not by a long shot.

"All those women you've been with," she sneered. "The way you gamble to make your living, the brawls, the drunken crazy antics that have landed you in prison."

He couldn't let that pass. "Jail, Mrs. Elliott. I've been in jail. Never in prison."

"Oh. Well, all right. Jail and not prison. The point is, you've been arrested. The point is you're a drunk and a no-good and you'll end up betraying my daughter with some other woman. You'll end up breaking her heart and beating her up, just like—"

"I've heard enough."

"I am not finished."

"*I* am. I want you to go."

"I want you to—"

He took a step toward her. She let out a cry and held out her little blue purse, clutching it with both hands, an absurd makeshift shield against him. "Stop. Don't come near me."

"Just get the hell out. Get the hell out now."

She grabbed the purse close to her and she let out a cry. "I am begging you. Please. I can pay you. I can—"

He took another step.

She dashed to the side, circling the outer perimeter of the turret, keeping well away from him, quickly reaching the wide doorway that led to the front hall. He actually dared to hope she'd keep going. But she just couldn't do that, couldn't leave bad enough alone.

She turned in the doorway, her face twisting up into something that looked a lot like real agony. "Why?" she cried. "Why do you have to do this? Why do you—"

"Because I love her."

He said it and swallowed. Hard.

By God. It was true. He did. He loved Jane.

It had finally happened. To him. To Cade Bravo. He understood what love was now. Because he was in it. He was in it deep.

He said it again. "I love her. I love Jane."

"If you do," said Virginia, drawing her thin shoulders back and aiming that sharp chin high. "If you really do love her, then you'll realize you're no good for her. You'll want the very best for her. You'll let yourself see the parallels here, between yourself and Rusty Jenkins, between now and then. You'll see how much the same it is, the way it's all happening so suddenly, out of nowhere, you two running off to get married, right away, today.

"She has to do it that way, don't you see? She can't allow herself time to think about what she's doing. If she gave herself some time to think, we both know she'd change her mind."

"No," he said, hating the fact that what he was hearing made a sick kind of sense. "You don't know what you're talking about."

"Don't I? You think about it. And you'll see that I know what I'm saying. And when you see that, maybe you'll surprise us both. Maybe you'll do the right thing. Maybe you'll get out of her life and give her a chance to find a better man, the *right* man, the kind of man that she deserves."

Chapter Eighteen

Jane got back to her house at ten-thirty. She'd made all the calls that needed making. Madelyn had agreed to handle the shop by herself for the rest of the day and to stay for the book club meeting that evening.

Now the question was what to wear? And what about her hair? It was always a challenge. Maybe she could pile it up on top of her head somehow, or maybe try a few braids, little ones, at her temples, and pull the rest of it back and—

Jane let out a laugh. Her hair was something better handled with help. She could wait until Celia arrived to figure out what to do with it. Right now, she'd better make some clothing choices, then maybe she could indulge herself just a little with, say, a twenty-minute soak in a scented bath. And then she'd have to get to work on her makeup.

Cade's new black pickup was there, in front of his house.

She smiled to herself. And where else would it be? Right now, he would still be inside, getting ready. For their wedding.

Their wedding.

She could hardly believe it. She was marrying Cade Bravo. By tonight, she would be his wife.

Sometimes life could be so strange. So amazing.

So thoroughly wonderful.

She was seriously tempted to run over there, just for a minute, to steal a few quick kisses. But with the two of them, kisses always led to other things. And they had their whole lives ahead of them, together. There would be plenty of time for those other things that kisses led to. Right now, she had a lot to do and a limited time to do it in.

She got out of her van and ran up her front walk. The cosmos, which were getting a little bit past their prime now, seemed to turn their fading faces to her as she went by. The gazing balls twinkled, catching and reflecting the bright glare of the sun.

Inside, Cade's hat was still on the long front hall table, next to the vase he had given her. The flowers needed replacing. She'd have to cut some fresh ones.

Not today, of course. No time today.

But maybe tomorrow.

When she'd be Mrs. Cade Bravo.

She said it out loud, "Mrs. Cade Bravo. Jane Bravo." She liked it. It sounded good. She smiled some more, at herself this time.

She'd always thought that when she married again,

she'd keep her own name. Or maybe hyphenate. But now that she was actually headed for the altar, she didn't want to do that. It seemed important, to take Cade's name, because of who she was and who he was. Important that everyone understand she was proud to be his wife, to stand at his side.

Proud to be a Bravo.

Yes. It was the right choice, to take his name.

She shook herself—and laughed again. Here she was on her wedding day, with a million things to do, standing here staring at her beautiful mercury glass vase, thinking about cutting fresh flowers, pondering her choice to take Cade's name. Time to get cracking.

She headed for the stairs.

She had her foot on the bottom step when the front door opened behind her. She turned at the sound.

"Cade." She started for him, her happy smile blooming wider than before.

Two steps later, she was hesitating.

He hadn't shaved. He still wore that wrinkled shirt from yesterday. And his expression...

"Cade, what's happened?"

One corner of his mouth curled up. But it wasn't anything resembling a smile. It was more like a grimace, a look of pain.

She hurried toward him. "Oh, what's the matter? What's—"

He stuck his hands in the pockets of his rumpled pants and backed up a step. "Don't."

That single word said volumes. She stopped a few feet from him, midway between the stairs and the door. "What? Talk to me. Please."

"I've been giving this whole thing some serious thought."

Oh, this wasn't good. Not good at all. "All right." *Stay calm,* she thought, *stay reasonable.* "What have you been thinking? Tell me. I'm listening."

He glanced away, then dragged his gaze back to meet hers. "Look. It's not going to work, okay?"

"It?" she asked, as if she didn't already know, as if she couldn't see in those silver eyes exactly what he was trying to tell her.

He swore and let out a hard, impatient breath. "It. Us. Getting married. It was a crazy idea and it's not going to work. We're better off to call it quits here and now, before we go all the way through with it and make things that much worse."

She clasped her hands in front of her—in order to keep from reaching for him. "What happened? Something happened, didn't it?"

"Nothing happened." He said it too fast. She knew he was lying. "I had a little time to think, that's all, a little time to realize that we got carried away last night—that *I* got carried away, bringing up marriage. I never in a million years imagined you'd say yes."

In spite of the way her heart was aching, that almost made her smile. "But Cade. I *did* say yes."

He glared at her. "And you should have had sense enough not to."

"Cade..."

"Damn it. Will you stop that?"

"Stop what?"

"Just don't look at me like that, all right?"

"What is going on? What *happened?*"

"I told you. Nothing."

"But that doesn't make sense. When I left here this morning, you were all for the two of us getting married."

"I had my doubts, even then."

Now he told her. "If you had doubts, you could have shared them with me."

"Damn it, Jane. I'm sharing. I'm sharing right now. Just...accept what I'm saying, all right. We're not getting married. I'm calling it off."

"But—"

She cut herself off when she heard him mutter, "And you should be grateful."

She made herself count to three before she replied to that one. "Excuse me? I should be *grateful?*"

He made a low, impatient sound and rammed his fists deeper into his pockets. "Yeah. Grateful. I'm keeping you from making the second biggest mistake of your life."

She let out a wild laugh.

He scowled. "It's not funny."

"Sorry. I think it is. And thank you so much for *saving* me from myself."

"Go ahead. Razz me. You know I'm right."

"I don't know any such thing. And if marrying you would be my second worst mistake, I assume you mean the worst was marrying Rusty?"

"That's right. I'm bad. But I'm not *that* bad."

What was going on here? She still did not get it. "We've been through this. I though we settled it. You are nothing like Rusty."

"There are parallels. We both know it."

"What do you mean, parallels? You're not a criminal, you don't have a drug problem. You never hit a woman. I was eighteen and didn't know my own heart, when I married Rusty. Now I'm just about a decade older. I know what love is and I love you. I see the wonderful, steady, straight-ahead guy inside you, the guy you really are, the one you've worked so hard to be."

"You see what you want to see."

"No. I see what's really there. Maybe I thought there were parallels, for all those months I refused you, all those months I went against what my heart was trying to tell me. But now I know that was only on the surface. Deep down, where it counts, you're the right guy for me. And I truly do believe I'm the woman for you."

His expression had changed, softened. He was listening, *hearing* her. Hope struck sparks inside her, sparks that caught and flared.

He said, "I'm gone a lot. I have to go where the game is. You wouldn't like that."

"We could work that out. I can live with it. If you'd only be true to me, I'll get along, when you're not here. Lots of people have good marriages where one person travels. Salesmen. Truckers. They make it work."

"My income's not steady. I've been flat broke more than once."

"So? We'll get by. I'm hardly destitute. Together, we'll be fine." The urge to reach for him was powerful. She held it in check. "Oh, Cade. I'm not trying to tell you it's going to be a fairy tale. But it *will* be worth it. I know. I know it in my heart.''

He whispered her name. Hope flared even brighter, until it lit up the world.

But then he blinked. He shook his head. ''No.''

The shadow of loss encroached again. And she found she was pleading. ''Oh, no. Don't do this. Please, please don't do this....''

But his face was set now, his eyes hardened against her. ''It's the right thing.''

''It's not.''

''Jane. Face it. It *is* the same as with Rusty.''

''No, it's not.''

''Think about it, about the way it's happening. Us running off, eloping to Tahoe. Everything done in a big hurry. No time to think, no time to reconsider. It's way, way too fast.''

''Time,'' she said, grasping at straws now—and knowing it. ''Time. Is that it? You're scared and you need a little time to—''

''Jane. Give it up.''

''No. I won't. I can't. I don't understand.''

''Sure, you do. You just don't like it.''

''It doesn't add up. I know you called Caitlin. You told her we were getting married, told her she could come with us to Tahoe. Why would you do that, if you were having serious doubts?''

''I didn't come to my senses until after I'd called her, that's all.''

''No. I don't buy that. I don't—''

''Jane. Enough. Someday you'll look back and feel nothing but relief that I did this.''

"That's not true."

"You'll admit to yourself that you've got a fatal weakness for guys like me and you'll—"

"Wait." She had it. She understood.

"What?"

"A *fatal weakness*. That's what you said."

"Yeah. So?"

"You've been talking to my mother."

"Jane—"

"You have. I know you have. She said those exact words to me, too. She said I had a *fatal weakness* for the wrong kind of man."

He glanced away again. Away, and then back. "Jane…"

"Uh-uh. Those are her words I heard coming out of your mouth. She got to you. She got to you good. And you let her." That really hurt. "Oh, Cade. How could you listen to her? How could you *believe* her? She's a fanatic, the way she hates Caitlin—and anyone connected to Caitlin. She's the next thing to a mental case over it. You have to see that. You can't let her—"

"Jane. It doesn't matter, who I talked to, what was said."

"Oh, yes it does. It matters a lot."

"No. I mean what I'm telling you. It's over. Goodbye." He started to turn.

Desperate, she cried out, "But what about last night? What if I'm pregnant?"

That stopped him. He faced her once more and looked her up and down. And then he grunted. "Nice try."

"Don't you *grunt* at me. I thought it was important to you, that your babies have your name."

"It was only one night, Jane. We both know it's damn doubtful you're pregnant from one night."

"But it *is* possible."

"Fine. If it turns out you're pregnant, all right. I'll marry you."

She could have strangled him. "Oh, hey, mister. Don't put yourself out."

"Bye, Jane." He turned again for the door, reaching to grab his hat off the long table as he went by.

She couldn't bear it. She rushed for him, caught his outstretched arm. "Oh, wait!"

"Damn it, Jane." He jerked free.

The action caught her off-balance. She staggered into the table. Before she could steady herself, the table lifted on two legs and Cade's hat, the carnival glass bowl and her beautiful mercury glass gazing-ball vase were sliding to the floor.

The hat and the bowl landed without incident.

The vase hit with a crash and shattered. Glass flew. Mercury slithered everywhere.

"Oh, no," Jane whispered. "Oh, no, no, no..." She had found her feet. It only felt as if the world had dropped out from under her.

Cade bent, grabbed his hat and slapped it against his thigh. A few bits of broken glass tinkled to the floor. "Keep me around." He settled the hat on his head. "See what else gets broken."

She was done, she realized. Finished. Out of reasons why he should stay. She stared into those hard silver eyes. She was thinking that, under no circumstances, was he going to see her cry.

Finally she nodded. "All right. You want to go, then go."

He didn't wait around for her to change her mind.

Chapter Nineteen

Once he was gone, Jane stood in the foyer staring
at her shut door and let herself cry, let the tears stream
down her face, let the hard sobs take her.

After a while, she got tired of just standing there
bawling. So she picked up the carnival glass bowl and
carried it to the kitchen. She left it on the counter and
then she went out to the service porch and got a pair
of rubber gloves and a broom and a dust mop.

Sobbing as she worked, she picked up the half-dead
flowers first, then the scattered shards of glass. She
swept up the smaller pieces and blotted up the water.
Finally, she put on her rubber gloves and chased the
mercury around the floor, rolling the beads with her
dustpan to join with the other beads, gathering the
slippery, silvery stuff until she had one slinky, quiv-
ery mass of it. She coaxed the mass onto her dustpan

with the edge of a ruler and then she managed to transfer it to a Mason jar.

Still crying, sniffing and sobbing, tears running down her face, she screwed the lid on the jar. Then she held it up and stared at the quivering quicksilver inside, thinking how what she saw was just like Cade, that he was a silver-eyed charmer. Hazardous material. So hard to hold.

By then, it was eleven-thirty. She took off her gloves and washed her hands and her face. She blew her nose and combed her hair. When Celia and Aaron arrived at five minutes of noon, she was sitting at her kitchen table, staring out the bay window.

She heard the knocking at the front door, but she didn't answer. She knew eventually her friend would just come on in.

"Omigod, what's happened?" Celia cried when she and Aaron entered the kitchen. Jane turned and looked at her.

Celia said, "Aaron, darling. I think Jane and I need to be alone now."

He turned to go.

Before he could take more than a step, Jane said, "Aaron. I need a favor."

"Anything."

"Cade invited your mother to come with us to Tahoe. It's not going to happen. I wonder if you could—"

"No problem. I'll cut her off at the pass."

She thanked him and he left. Then Celia held out loving arms. With a heavy sob, Jane went into them.

Celia made tender noises and held on tight as Jane indulged herself in another good cry.

But she couldn't cry forever. After a while, she blew her nose again and splashed cold water on her face. Celia made them some green tea and they sat at the table, sipping, while Jane told all.

"Something has got to be done about that mother of yours," Celia said when the sad story was through.

"Tell me about it."

"What are your plans?"

"I'm going to have a talk with her. It may be my *last* talk with her. But I'm going to get a few things straight with her. I just need to ask my father a few questions first."

Celia blinked those big hazel eyes. "Your father? You *never* talk with your father."

"I know. But I'm talking with him now. I want to hear his side of what happened way back when. I heard the story from Aunt Sophie. And I'm reasonably sure she got it right. My mother is never going to talk about it—except obliquely, always blaming Caitlin. Caitlin will only say that she never slept with my father. I believe her. But I want to hear it from him, too. I want to hear what he says happened. I want to understand how my mother could hate another woman so much that she'd be willing to ruin her own daughter's happiness for the sake of that hatred."

Celia winced. "I've gotta ask."

"Go ahead."

"Well, so how's this going to help you get Cade back?"

"It probably won't. I guess maybe I'm hoping for the impossible. That I'll learn something from my father that will help my mother see the light. That I'll get her to admit to Cade how wrong she was."

"Jane. I have to tell you. I can't see that happening, ever."

"Yeah, okay, neither can I. But I have to try."

Her father kept an office on State Street. He agreed to meet with her there that evening at six.

She sat in the green leather guest chair opposite his mahogany desk and she told him that Cade had broken it off with her after Virginia had been to see him.

Her father sat back in his huge button-tucked swivel chair. "I'm sorry that it didn't work out as you'd hoped."

Did she buy that? Hardly. "Are you, Dad?"

"Well. As I told you on the phone this morning, you're an adult and you are fully qualified to make your own decisions. The time is long past when I felt I could tell you what choices to make."

"Maybe you should tell that to my mother."

"Jane. You know very well I can't tell your mother anything."

Jane felt all the old resentments bubbling to the surface. She wanted to ask what it *was* with them? Why did they stay together? How could they live the way that they did?

But that wasn't why she'd come.

"I have a few questions for you, Dad. I'd really appreciate honest answers. It would help me to understand what's really going on here."

His severe expression got bleaker than ever. "What is it, Jane?"

"I want to know about you and Caitlin Bravo. I want to know what happened between you. And I want to know why my mother never forgave Caitlin for it."

Her father said nothing for several endless seconds. Jane thought he was going to tell her that he wanted her to leave.

But then he said, "Your aunt Sophie told me she'd explained it all to you."

Jane sat up straighter. "Wait a minute. Aunt Sophie *told* you that she told me?"

He actually chuckled. It was a pretty rusty sound, but then he didn't laugh often. "I confess. I knew you were close to Sophie. And I never did seem to know where to start when it came to trying to communicate with you. So now and then, I would ask my sister—how you were doing, what was going on in your life. You know your aunt. She never pulled any punches." His dark eyes were so sad. "I miss Sophie. A lot."

Jane had thought she was cried out, that she couldn't shed another tear if she'd wanted to. Still, she felt the tightening of emotion in her throat, the pressure behind her eyes. "I miss her, too—and yes. Aunt Sophie did talk to me about it. She said that you fell for Caitlin, but that Caitlin refused you, told you to go back to your wife. So you left Mom and tried again to get Caitlin to give you a chance, but Caitlin still sent you away."

Her father shrugged. "That's about the size of it.

It was a tough time. I did love your mother, but she was…difficult. So high-strung. A perfectionist. And distant, a lot of the time. And then she had you. You were everything to her. Once you were born, she had nothing left to give to me. I started going to the High-grade. Caitlin was kind to me. She would listen while I yammered on about how miserable I was, how my wife didn't have any time for me…'' He closed his eyes and let out a long breath. When he opened them again, Jane could see he didn't intend to say much more. "It was a long time ago. In the end, I went back to your mother. We patched it up, more or less. Now, we get along well enough. We're used to what we have together. And to what we don't have.''

"But of the three of you, Caitlin is clearly the in-nocent one. You're telling me she never encouraged you, right?''

"That's right. She was kind to me. And she lis-tened to me. At the time, I wanted to believe that she saw me as a man, that she was attracted. But looking back, no. She was a good bartender with a big heart. She felt sorry for me.''

"Then why does Mom blame her?''

"Surely that's obvious.''

"Not to me.''

"Your mother has way too much pride. If she blames herself for driving me away, then she's got to swallow her pride and deal with her own shortcom-ings. She's not ready for that. On the other hand, with all that pride of hers, if she blames *me,* she'd have to divorce me.''

"And being the wife of Judge Clifford Elliott is very, very important to her."

Her father didn't respond to that. There was no need to. They both knew it was true.

Jane said, "You're saying that Caitlin's her scapegoat."

"That's right." He sat forward. "And what good does hearing all this do you, really?"

"I don't know, Dad. I just wanted to understand."

"I'd like to give you some advice. I don't expect you to take it, but for once I'd like to be able to say I told you the things I really thought you should know."

"Please. I want to hear it."

"Leave your mother alone now. Just…stay clear of her. Don't do the most tempting thing. Don't feel you have to confront her or tell her off for what she did to you. And please don't imagine you're going to change her, to get her on your side when it comes to the man you love. It won't happen."

"But I thought—"

He shook his head. "No. You're not going to change her. Only she can do that. Eventually she'll come to you. Because in spite of how misguided she is, she loves you. Very much. When she does come to you, you'll have some tough choices to make. But right now, leave her alone. Right now, you have something else you should be dealing with."

Jane answered softly. "You know, Dad. You're right."

"I must admit, the more I think about it, the more

I become accustomed to the idea of you and Cade Bravo together.''

Jane gulped down those pesky, persistent tears. ''Oh, Dad. You do?''

He nodded. ''He's cleaned up his act in the past few years.''

''He has. He truly has.''

''Seems to me someone like him might be just right for you. Where is he now?''

Jane shrugged. She supposed he'd left town again. His truck had vanished from the curb in front of his house. ''I *will* find him. Somehow.''

''That's what I like to hear.''

''And, Dad, when I do, when I work all this out, will you walk me down the aisle?''

''I thought you'd never ask.''

Jane's phone was ringing when she got back to her house. She didn't want to talk to anyone, so she let the machine get it. The machine was in the kitchen. But she'd left the volume up, so she heard Caitlin's voice all the way from the front hall.

''Jane? Damn it, Jane. Pick up…''

Jane sighed and moved toward the voice on the machine—not to answer it but to get a glass of iced tea from the fridge.

''Jane. You listen to me, Jane. What the hell is going on? Nobody's telling me a damn thing. As usual, I'm the mushroom in the crowd, kept in the dark. Fed a lot of crap. Aaron comes over here at noon and tells me the wedding's off. *What?* I said. *Why?* Aaron doesn't answer. He just orders me to stay put, to leave you alone, to mind my own business. Says you want it that way. That the baby doll is with you and you're going to be fine...."

Jane opened the fridge, took out the tea.

"Fine? *Fine?* How can you be fine, if you love my son and you were on your way to Tahoe and now you're *not* on your way to Tahoe, you've called it off. Or *he's* called it off. Not that I would know. And don't think I didn't ask him."

Jane got down a tall class, stuck it under the ice chute in the refrigerator door. For a few seconds, the clatter of the cubes drowned out whatever Caitlin was saying.

But then Jane could hear her again.

"...wouldn't tell me squat. Just said, 'Mind your own business, Ma. It didn't work out for Jane and me.' Then he heads for the back room and gets himself a game going. He—"

Jane grabbed for the phone. "Caitlin. Caitlin?"

"'Bout time you picked up."

"He's there, is that what you're saying? Cade is there? At the Highgrade?"

"Well, hell yes, he's here."

"Don't let him go anywhere."

"Honey, he's in the middle of a card game. A herd of mean mustangs couldn't drag him away."

Five minutes later, Jane entered the Highgrade through the back door. She raced down the long back hall. When she emerged into the central game room, she spotted Caitlin just coming out of the café, grabbing menus to seat the next group of customers who waited on the long bench opposite the high desk with the cash register on it.

Caitlin spotted her and pointed toward the entrance to the bar. "Through there, to the back room." Caitlin smiled at her customers, "Come on, folks. This way."

Jane went the other way, into the dimly lit bar.

Bertha Slider was serving the drinks, her gray-streaked red braids wrapped in a corona around her head. A few regulars sat on the stools, hunched over their drinks. They glanced her way, shrugged and went back to nursing whatever it was they were drinking.

"Hey, Jane." Pinky Cleeves, who'd been in Jane's class in school, raised her pool cue in a salute. Jane gave her nod.

Jane spoke to Bertha. "The back room?"

Bertha tipped her crown of braids toward a door deep in the shadows beyond the second pool table. "But I wouldn't interrupt, if I were you," she said under her breath.

"Thanks for the warning." Jane turned for the door. She felt the sudden silence as she strode the length of the room. The regulars were watching. Neither Pinky nor her opponent had turned back to their game.

Jane reached the door, raised her hand to knock— and changed her mind. She grabbed the door handle and gave it a turn.

In the smoky recess beyond, five men sat at a round felt-topped table. One of them was Cade.

"Hey," one of the other men said. "Close the damn door, will ya? We're busy in here."

"Yeah," said another. And another added, "Do it now."

The first man shouted, "Close the door! What are you, deaf?"

Cade didn't say anything. There were several tall stacks of poker chips in front of him. He still wore the rumpled clothes from yesterday. That straw cowboy hat shadowed his eyes.

Jane said, "I want to talk to you, Cade. I'm not leaving until I do." He just sat there, unmoving. She could feel his eyes on her beneath the brim of the hat. Jane cleared her throat. "I wonder if you gentlemen would mind getting out?"

There was a silence. A couple of the men mumbled profanities and grumbled some more about how she ought to get out and shut the door.

But then one of them laughed. "Hey. I'm about bust anyway." He threw his cards down. "You can make it up to me later, Bravo."

Cade made a grunting noise. It could have meant anything.

The man scooped his few chips into his hand and turned for the door. "Er, 'scuse me, ma'am." Jane stepped out of the way and he moved past her into the main part of the bar.

The other men—except Cade, who maintained a nerve-racking silence—muttered a few more rude epithets. Then a second one stood up. And the third. And the fourth. Each took a moment to collect the chips in front of him. Then, one by one, they filed out, headed for the cage at the end of the bar. Bertha was back there now, with the light on, ready to settle up.

As soon as the fourth man left the small room, Jane stepped in and pulled the door shut behind her. Cade just sat there, across the table, regarding her coolly from beneath the brim of his hat. Jane had her back against the door. Her heart was beating too fast and the smoke in the room stung her eyes.

Oh, what was he thinking? Why didn't he say something?

And right then, he did. "I was winning that game, Jane."

She drew herself up. "Too bad. That game is over."

"Oh, is it?"

I love you. Please say you love me back...

No such luck.

"Go on, Jane. Go home. We've got nothing more to say to each other. I'm no good for you and it's time we accepted that, time we started getting over each other."

"No. No, it isn't. What it's time for is time you stopped acting like an idiot, Cade Bravo. It's time you told me you love me. Time you admitted that your heart is mine."

"You're living in a fool's dream."

"No. No, I'm not. I've been thinking. And I think I've finally figured it out. What happened, with my mother. How she got to you, what she said."

"Jane—"

"Oh, come on. You can take it. You can listen to my theory."

"There's no point in—"

"She rubbed it in, didn't she? How much you're like Rusty? How I've got this big *problem* with falling for messed up men. How it's the same, our eloping, and my running off with Rusty. She got you doubting. She got to that hurt kid inside you, the one who had to listen to folks calling him a little bastard. And then she got you to admit that you love me. And *then* she told you that if you really *did* love me, you'd leave me alone."

He didn't move. And he didn't speak.

She said, "I do know. That you love me. I wish you had told me, instead of my mother. But it doesn't matter, if you say the words. Or if you don't. I know you love me. As I love you. And walking away from me isn't going to change that. Leaving me isn't going to make it all better. It's only going to break both our hearts."

He moved then. But only to throw down his hand.

She stepped forward.

"No." He shoved back his chair and stood.

She knew he was going to go, walk around the table, right past her—and out of the room. She put out both hands. "Listen. Let's talk this over. Please. Let's not be so hasty. Let's settle down, here."

He muttered her name. He was shaking his head.

Desperately she cast about for a way to keep him there. "How about this? How about I play you? Three hands. Uh, blackjack, okay? I mean, I know how to play that. Sort of. I do."

He said her name again—and she could have sworn he almost smiled.

"Look. Just sit down. Just shuffle and deal. Here's the thing. Here's my offer. Two out of three hands. If I win, you marry me."

"And if I win?"

"I'll leave." For now, she amended silently. I'll leave *for now*.

He pushed his hat back a little and gave her one of those long, slow sizing-up kind of looks. Then he dropped to his chair again. He began gathering up the cards.

She sat across from him, her heart pounding like mad, watching him shuffle—oh that was a thing of beauty, the way that man could handle those cards.

"Cut."

She did.

He put the bottom half on top and took the first card—a two of diamonds—and placed it face-up at the bottom of the deck. Then he dealt four cards in quick succession, one face down to each of them, a second facedown to her and one face-up to himself. His card showing was an ace of spades.

She peeked at her own. A six of clubs and a ten of hearts. She knew a little bit about odds. And she'd read somewhere that you shouldn't ask for another card if you had sixteen already. But he had an *ace*.

She said, "Hit me."

When he dealt her a queen of hearts, she uttered a very bad swear word.

He smiled at her then—and turned over his first card. King of clubs. Twenty-one.

"How did you do that?" she demanded. "Did you cheat?"

He gave her a patient look. "*You* want to deal?"

"Uh. No. You go right ahead."

He did. And it happened all over again. That time he had the ace of hearts showing. She got a seven of diamonds and a nine of clubs. She stayed, that time.

And he flipped over his bottom card. Jack of spades.

And that was it.

He gave her a crooked smile. "It's over, Jane."

"You did cheat, didn't you?"

He shrugged. "Better pay up."

What else could she do? She stood. "I would like to say one more thing, before I go. I want to say, again, that I love you. And I'm sorry for the rotten things my mother said to you. But I am not my mother and I know the kind of man you really are. A good one. And a steady one. And the only one for me. And as soon as you're willing to admit that I'm the only one for you, I do sincerely hope you will come over to my house and knock on my door." She turned.

And he said, "Hold on a minute..."

And something snapped inside her.

She whirled on him, fed up with fighting for him when all he did was turn her down. "*What?*" she shouted. "What the hell do you want?"

And he grinned at her. "Care to try for three out of five?"

She stared. And then she gulped and then she

asked, very carefully, "Are you saying what I think you're saying?"

"I'm saying you're right. I'm saying I love you. I'm saying let's do it. Let's get married."

"Oh, God. You mean it."

"You're damned right I do."

She let out a cry of pure joy and she ran around that table and threw herself into his waiting arms. He gathered her close and his mouth came down on hers and when they finally came up for air, she said, "Tahoe. Tomorrow. No backing out."

And he said, "However you want it, Jane. That's how it will be."

Epilogue

Jillian called that night. When she heard the news she got in her car and she drove straight to New Venice. The next morning, she did wonderful things with Jane's hair.

They all caravanned to Tahoe, Cade and Jane in the lead, with Aaron and Celia and Jillian in the next car, Caitlin and Will in the Trans Am, and Jane's father in his Cadillac taking up the rear.

The rumor mill went wild. Everyone said that Jane Elliott had made the same big mistake all over again, taken another thoroughly unsuitable mate. They said it would never last.

But Jane didn't care what they said. She knew that in Cade Bravo she'd found much more than she'd ever dared dream of. She'd found a man she could count on, her very best friend—and a lover who set her body on fire. She knew that their union would last them both a lifetime.

As for Virginia, Jane refused to speak to her for two full years. But then the first baby came—a daughter they named Sophie Elizabeth. Cade couldn't stand it. He went and got Virginia and brought her to the hospital.

Jane was adamant. "I don't want to see you or talk to you," she said, "until you apologize to my mother-in-law." And she turned her face to the wall.

Virginia Elliott held out for three more days. And then she went to the Highgrade and asked to speak with Caitlin. No one ever knew what words passed between those two women in Caitlin's small dark office in the back of the saloon.

But after that, Virginia and Caitlin were always civil to each other. Jane allowed Cade to bring Virginia to the house on Green Street—Aunt Sophie's house, which was the one they had decided to live in—and Virginia Elliott held her first grandchild at last.

After that, folks said, there was a change in Virginia. A softening, a new gentleness. A mildness of spirit folks found very appealing. Clifford began spending more time at home.

Cade Bravo remained a professional gambler. He won and lost three fortunes in the next forty years. He loved his work and he loved his wife—and he loved the five children she eventually gave him.

And when Cade taught their grandchildren how to play blackjack, he also told them the tale of how their grandma gambled for his heart—and lost.

"Well, Grandpa," said silver-eyed ten-year-old Cait. "If she lost, how come you got married anyway?"

"Sweetheart," Cade replied. "Your grandpa is a lot of things. But stupid isn't one of them."

* * * * *

1207/14/MB121

NEW from

MILLS & BOON®

Blaze

2 sexy reads in 1 scorching hot volume
ONLY £4.99!

From January 2008, Blaze will bring you two
stories in one super-sexy volume.

Look for
The Mighty Quinns: Marcus by Kate Hoffmann
and *Relentless* by Jo Leigh

On sale 4th January 2008

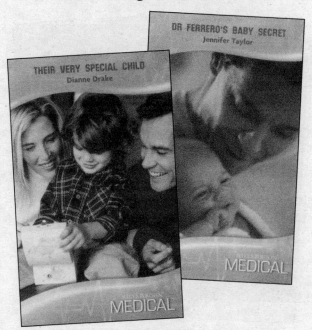

Celebrate 100 years of pure reading pleasure with Mills & Boon®

To mark our centenary, each month we're publishing a special 100th Birthday Edition. These celebratory editions are packed with extra features and include a FREE bonus story.

Now that's worth celebrating!

4th January 2008

The Vanishing Viscountess by Diane Gaston
With FREE story The Mysterious Miss M
This award-winning tale of the Regency Underworld launched Diane Gaston's writing career.

1st February 2008

Cattle Rancher, Secret Son by Margaret Way
With FREE story His Heiress Wife
Margaret Way excels at rugged Outback heroes…

15th February 2008

Raintree: Inferno by Linda Howard
With FREE story Loving Evangeline
A double dose of Linda Howard's heady mix of passion and adventure.

Don't miss out! From February you'll have the chance to enter our fabulous monthly prize draw. See special 100th Birthday Editions for details.

www.millsandboon.co.uk